LAST CURTAIN CALL

LAST CURTAIN CALL

DEMONIC MAGICIAN
BOOK THREE

Kleggt

Podium

Podium

LAST CURTAIN CALL

CHAPTER ONE

Scene Break

I yawned and kicked my feet up to place on a small summoned box. This was the life. A small break from performing and spates of violence, soaking in the sunshine. Leaning back in my favorite chair, I looked over toward Tanya as I brushed off my purple magician's suit. "Hey, what do these drop?"

She swept back her dark hair and looked up at her intangible screens. "Usual humanoid junk, plus occasionally fur or teeth."

The group had been grinding in my stead. After almost dying fighting against a demon, I was in the time-out chair. "Could I see one of the teeth?"

The Fateweaver shrugged and, after making sure Wolf and Quinn were fine in combat, stepped over to hand one to me.

Hyenids, the System had said. Essentially bipedal hyenas. Half were enraged melee combatants, then others were more placid casters. Knowing what I did about the animals back on Earth, it didn't take much to guess how they were divided up.

The tooth in question was rather sharp. A sizable canine. "If it's no trouble, could you collect and give them to me after?"

"Sure." She nodded and went back to the combat.

Ren gave me a glare as the woman passed—but the elf had nothing to really chastise me over. Nothing new anyway. I had been true to my word and sat out of the Quest grinding. Trauma still knocking around in the back of my head, I just sat and observed. Occasionally moved up so that I wouldn't be left behind. Ren kept in my proximity just in case something snuck up on me. Probably my own lax attitude, wanting to tip my fragile head onto the dry ground.

Still, the weather was lovely now that the clouds of the zombie attack had faded away. The Party was having no trouble getting through the Monsters, and we should hit the next level before dusk—if not sooner.

"Break request," Wolf growled from the front after tossing half a corpse across the dirt from his mouth. The bear shook his head out and yawned.

"Granted. Pull back when ready. We'll rest by Max." Tanya shepherded the troops in my stead. Well, that was her role now—something I was glad to be rid of.

The elf was already beside me, hat off to reveal her golden hair and chair out. She sat and removed her boots before putting her sock-covered feet up on my legs. Her bright-blue eyes didn't meet mine. Still somewhere between being annoyed at me but wanting me to know that she cared. I accepted the burden and appreciated that I wasn't left with the cold shoulder.

"Got a dozen so far, Max." Tanya held out a hand to provide me with the requested dental loot.

I withdrew a small hessian bag and allowed her to fill it before placing it back in my Inventory as one item. System made some poor choices on occasion.

Quinn stretched out his back and gave his eye patch a rub but didn't look too keen on sitting along with us. "Feel like I've been aging a year every day recently."

"How old are you?" I tilted my head.

"Thirty-two," he answered. "But soon to be double that judging by the grays in my beard."

"Beard does age you," Tanya said idly, picking at some food, before she looked up at him. "Not that it's a *bad* thing."

She wasn't wrong—at least in regard to her first sentence. Only four years older than me, yet he could pass as an . . . odd uncle? Not that I was keen to start designating familial titles to my companions. Although that ship had sailed once Ren and I had started calling Wolf our brother.

"I will take it as a compliment either way." Quinn gave her a bow. "I never turn down praise."

"Well, I also think you're pretty awesome," I added.

Wolf grunted. "A key member of our family."

"You . . . haven't died yet." Ren shrugged.

The deal had already been sealed, and the elf's attempt at playing nice didn't stop the fixer from pulling a face of absolute elation. Might even be blushing—and any words of thanks were stuck in his mouth.

My mind had already clicked past that, and I didn't want to dig further into him. The heavy thoughts must have been clearly visible on my face as Ren shifted her feet on me to get my attention.

"Spill it," she requested. Her arms were crossed, but she was having trouble giving me an earnest glare.

"In my fight against the demon . . . after my Domain ended, Roger was in his full form."

"Oh?" She tilted her head. "I wish I got to see. Can you summon him like that?"

I shook my head slowly. Not just because I was in my time-out chair, but his skill had sat inert since my recovery. The demonic rabbit hadn't died . . . so I wasn't sure what was happening there. "All in due time," I told her, much to her chagrin.

Tanya hummed as she went through her menus. "Almost paid off your token debt, Max. You should get some out of this—about four and a half more Quests to repeat."

The revelation was met with murmured groans. Easy enough fighting, but it got pretty drab—especially without me. We'd almost had some fun in the village before the undead had arrived, and now there was no stomach for it. I was also getting cabin fever from being pinned to my chair.

Wolf rolled over, his tongue lolling out of his mouth as he stretched. System was watching us . . . I could tell. Taking notes on what Abilities we should gain at the next level. I'd hate to try to guess at this stage. Would pale at being right. Would detest being wrong.

In this place of brief calm, I considered writing more in my diary—it had been a little while. As the others busied themselves with their own ways to relax, I penned some miserable words about Dungeons and how life was a struggle. It was all rather dour, and not what I had intended to put down. With a sigh, I snapped it shut and put it away.

"You know, you'll lose that one day and will feel much better for it." Ren pulled a face that was possibly an attempt at a sneer. Looked too cute to have an effect.

"What, you think I'll just dangle it over a ravine or something?" I raised an eyebrow. "It spends most of its existence within my Inventory."

"I can see why you two are fast friends, then." Her eyes narrowed.

I returned the gesture, unsure of whether we were flirting or about to brawl.

Quinn seemed eager to interject for either eventuality, literally diving across the gap between us. A flash bloomed in his hand as he caught an arrow out of the air.

Invisibility washed over me, denying them the target that they sought. Wolf knew I was sitting in place and rolled back to his feet, ready to step in front of me. Ren had spun from my lap, able to tell I had just vanished by her briefly floating feet. Bow out and entangling arrow blazing off in the direction of our unknown assailant.

"*Wait, wait!*" a male voice cried out. "Are you with the Crimson?"

I stepped up behind the man, leaving a hell bird in my chair. Dropped a sack over his head as my right hand came around holding a brick. I switched back, in the hopes that I wouldn't get caught fighting by the others—but Ren had clearly seen me. I shrugged, and she rolled her eyes.

Didn't take long for Wolf to drag the unconscious man out to the clearing we were trying to rest in.

"Who starts a conversation with an arrow?" I murmured. "Thanks for saving my life, Quinn."

He gave me a bow but was keen to find out what this new gentleman had been up to in trying to assassinate me *by accident.* He knelt down and bound his arms and ankles while I passed Ren the nullifying cuff.

She held the man's head up. Other than sporting a nice bruise now blooming on the side of his head, he was rather conventionally attractive. Short, tussled blond hair. Light stubble and a soft tan. Trim in an outfit of muted greens and leather. Human, as far as I could tell.

"No handprint," Ren said as she manhandled him. Perhaps getting a little of her anger against me out on the hapless foe. "Not a Crimson Shadow."

I clicked my tongue as my eyes went across his icons. "Hate to disagree with you, but I'm afraid you're wrong on that account."

"Really?" She glanced back at me but knew better than to assume I was making it up. "He has a way to conceal it?" After I returned a brief nod, she then looked over at Tanya. "Anyone you recognize?"

The Fateweaver stepped over and crouched beside him. "Hmm, no. But there's plenty I hadn't had the chance to meet." Her eyes went back up to the woodland area to the side. "Being alone isn't normal. Here, Ren, throw this out toward the bushes."

She handed the elf an idol, and the Oathwarden dropped our captive to the floor unceremoniously.

Hand back, she then lobbed it, and the item bounced into the shrubbery out of sight. She put her hands on her hips and stood for a moment, perhaps waiting for a compliment on her throw. I was too busy trying to put together the puzzle of this man. Although, that was clearly a lie, as I'd made note of her potential intentions.

"Dibs on bad cop," she turned around and got in there before I said anything.

"Oh. Go ahead. I was going to sit this one out." I leaned back in my chair and gave her a blank expression. "Due to my condition."

"Really?" Her jaw worked as she returned a blank glare.

"Perhaps it can be my turn?" Wolf ran his tongue across his lips.

Ren sighed. "We could just kill him right now. Have it over and done with?"

The group looked at me to gauge my plan. I closed my eyes and relaxed. "Whatever you feel is best. I trust your judgment wholeheartedly." She may have cursed me under her breath, or I could have just been hearing things. That was the trouble with the trauma status.

They were waiting to see if she would berate me for being a dick—but I was being true to my word. Still, I'd throw them a bone to give myself a little out from the growing tension. "I will be here if you need me to interject or request I do something, however."

"You're super sure he is Crimson though?"

I opened my eyes to glare at the man again and made sure it wasn't my mind making things up. No, three icons were still there. The one from taking her blood. One that was a buff to stealth, and the last for . . . I tilted my head to the side.

"While I am certain, there is also something else strange here." I stood from the chair and looked around. Of course, it wouldn't be something in plain sight. Did they already know their plan was foiled? Possibly only half of it. I caught Ren's look, desiring to be clued in to whatever mania had taken my reins.

Eventually, I gave them a shrug. "Keep it alive, but it might not give us anything worthwhile."

The elf raised an eyebrow. "*It?* Give us a little clue, asshole."

"Sorry." I plonked myself back down in the chair. "Brain is overheating a bit."

"It's fine. I shouldn't have snapped." She pulled a knife out from her belt. "But he isn't *human*, right?"

Not human. Well, that was a hard thing to quantify. He certainly looked it, and perhaps lived as one . . . but the icon gave the game away. They clearly didn't anticipate many people having the Skill that I did.

I exhaled through my nose.

"No, he isn't. He is a puppet or some kind of duplicate of the real Player tracking us down."

CHAPTER TWO

As Written

We sat in silence, watching the man as he slowly came to. Our plan already discussed, his fate somewhat decided. I even had a speaking part in the play—the group allowed it, seeing as just talking *shouldn't* melt my brain away.

"*Ow,*" he said, wincing as the nice bump I gave him throbbed in pain. I assumed anyway. "That was unexpected."

"You did just try to assassinate me," I replied and tilted my head.

His eyes went between each of us, taking us all in. "Ah, yeah. Sorry about that—I thought you might be Crimson Shadow."

I exchanged a glance with Ren, who took over the lead on this investigation. "Why would you think that of a group of strangers and attack first rather than find out or leave?"

"A brief moment of insanity. Where I hoped to gain notoriety by killing one of the bastards plaguing this land?"

My brow furrowed as I started to tune him out. The words weren't really important anyway. There were a few things I truly cared to know. If he was alone or had a group waiting in the wings. Tanya's idol would detect anyone else approaching from the same direction he had.

If he was alone, either he was sent here to try to kill me off or was scouting on us. First option had failed spectacularly, and the latter was more worrying. Then the question would be if he was planning to escape with information on us . . . , or was already relaying our position or worse as we sat here talking.

Strangely enough, I could feel some of the truth out already.

I tuned back in to the conversation and butted in. "Why don't you all go level again, and I'll sit and chat with our friend here?"

They all turned to me with apprehension on their faces, the newcomer included.

"Are you sure?" Ren raised an eyebrow.

"Always."

None of them seemed happy with my decision, but they reluctantly went along with it. I produced a chair near mine while the others packed away their things to prepare to go fight.

"Missed your name, pal." I gave the spare seat a pat.

"Dorian."

"That *is* a name," I said diplomatically, as he awkwardly got up and hopped over—we had not removed his bindings. "You'll have to forgive our caution, as we are on edge a lot."

"I can imagine. With the Crimson Shadow around . . . and random people firing off arrows at you."

"True." I gave him a smile before I looked over and watched Wolf power up before engaging the next group of enemies.

Dorian was silent for a moment as he also watched them fight. "Ah, I don't suppose you have anything for a headache. Not sure what even hit me."

"It was me," I replied idly. "And no, I don't."

"Ah."

What I did have, however, was a pain in my arm. Something gentle, in a way—more like a Tesla orb spreading purple lightning back and forth from my bone to the inside of my skin. Electric, but it didn't fill me with energy. Enough knowledge to start sketching out the rough picture . . . and see if it resembled a chalk outline.

"Where is your creator at, puppet?"

His brow furrowed. "What? I'm not sure what you mean."

I gave him a tired gesture with my head, and he craned his head back to behind us. Up against the back of his chair, the wide-bore muzzle of my demonic cannon. Already loaded and willing to play bad cop.

"You're pretty realistic," I continued. "That doesn't seem like something a normal Class would have. I'm going to guess . . . Guardian slayer?"

Dorian licked his lips and looked nervous. "You're talking nonsense. Let me converse with one of the more reasonable members of your Party."

Was I being a little crazy? *No*, surely not. I was calm and hadn't laid a hand on the man so far. *Nonsense* would be if I had started to cut parts of him off to see truly how detailed this puppet was.

"Request denied." I spun up a pair of mundane cards into my hand and placed them together, face-to-face. "Let's play a game. You try to guess if my card is higher or lower than yours. Winner gets to ask a question that must be answered truthfully."

"I don't want to play games—"

I held the covered cards up to him and slowly pushed one of them up, so that I could see one of the faces, and he got a peek at the other.

"Lower," he said.

The truth was, I knew what both of the cards were without even looking. Something innate to me now—some kind of parlor trick sixth sense. Not only that, but I could switch them at will. I turned them around to reveal he had the ten of clubs, but I had the king of hearts. Of course, he wasn't going to answer honestly anyway.

"What is your question?" He looked as though he had his improv skills burning a hole through his head, ready to repeat that he knew nothing.

"Who will mourn you when you die?"

He blinked. "Huh?"

I maintained an impassive glare while his brain tried to change tack. Should be an easy enough thing to answer—I had been the biggest loner in my previous lives, yet I had a handful of new friends that would definitely miss me. Even Fiona might shed a tear. For a Player to spend a few months here at least and not make any meaningful connections was suspicious. It was the nature of adventuring to gather around others.

He didn't seem to think so. "I don't understand your line of questioning . . . I'm not here to play games."

"Then why *are* you here?"

Dorian's mouth opened and closed. "Just adventuring, passing through."

"To go where? What level are you? What is your Class type? What was the last meal you ate?"

"I'm . . . I refuse to speak with you any further." He shuffled in the chair before remembering the cannon pressed up against his back. "You need to let me go."

"*Need* to? Explain why."

He didn't respond to this but continued to shift in his bindings. I'd worn out what little information he would give me willingly. I stood from my chair and approached him. Before he had the chance to do more than lean away from me, I had a gag around his mouth, swiftly followed by a sack over his head again.

The inability to speak, see, use Skills, and move was the best I could do. If his originator could use his senses or communicate through other means, then that should dampen the information he was able to transfer. That was a good thing to check actually . . .

I tried to add him as a friend and send my Chat details over.

The System wouldn't allow it.

His coffin had enough final nails in it already, but I had just added a few more. I stepped over to Tanya, and she shot a glance back at our captive.

"Not trustworthy, then?"

I shook my head and watched Ren fire off a couple of arrows in quick succession. "Couldn't add him as a friend or send him messages. Wouldn't answer basic questions and got flustered under the pressure of having to think after more abstract probing. He seems more of a scout than an assassin, but I'm unsure to what end."

She sucked at her teeth. "Undecided on killing him outright?"

Would be pragmatic, maybe. Put the chance of him communicating with anyone to almost zero. There was something though . . .

"No. I'll keep him alive." I looked back at the man and unsummoned my cannon. "My intuition is telling me something isn't right about this."

"Just your intuition?" She held out her hand and cast a spell at the fresh pair of Hyenids Wolf had gathered.

I nodded before giving up the truth. Would do me no benefit to hold secrets at this stage. "My arm is reacting to his presence. I believe he has been created by the one with the second Guardian's power."

"Oh." Her brow furrowed. "All the more reason to kill him?"

"All the more reason he put himself in a position where he could be killed." I shrugged and turned back to walk over to Dorian. It was a clever ploy that I'd almost fallen for. The trouble with the Crimson Shadow was that even when they were being devious for a change, their thoughts were still two-dimensional.

They knew by now how powerful and proficient we were. Sure, spying on us to learn our location would be helpful . . . but at this stage, they didn't have the option of chasing us down. That was the reason I chose a Quest location opposite the direction of Candlekeep. With no blood, they'd need to fall back to the Lady and be more conservative.

Sending a single figure with a bow wasn't likely to even scuff our armor. Capture or death was pretty much guaranteed. I was not a betting man, but I was willing to put down all this useless gold I'd earned on the fact that Dorian would do something once killed.

Especially if anyone had seen how we'd dealt with captives before. A quick knife while we were all gathered around—and he'd become a detonated bomb or bioweapon or transform into another eldritch horror. I stood before him and brought up my Map.

[Max: Any chance I could borrow Quinn?]

The group finished up the current pack and walked back over to me. We'd need to move our little base camp up soon. They were getting farther away, and respawns might be due in the near future.

"What manner of lunacy are you now proposing?" Ren crossed her arms and frowned at me.

"Just taking our guest for a stroll." I smiled and sent her across some coordinates.

She read them and turned sharply toward the fixer. "You're in charge of Max. If he gets hurt in *any* way, I *will* murder you."

"Ah?" Quinn physically recoiled, unsure what he was even signed up for.

"Grab his legs, bud." I rubbed my chin, unable to shake the manic smile. I'd need to steal something with wheels at some point.

A handful of grunts and slow minutes later, and we had arrived at our destination. We dropped the man to the rocky ground to his muffled complaints. I allowed Quinn to peer over the edge, lest I tempt fate a little too hard.

"If the drop doesn't do it, the water will take him out to sea." He stepped away from the precipice.

"Perfect." I rolled my neck out. "Say, Quinn. If we ever fix the world and can settle down here, what do you think you'd get up to?"

He raised an eyebrow and considered the question. "Honestly, I'd like to explore more. Without the pressure of constant conflict, I'd want to see every corner of this world. Assuming I haven't died in your stead anyway. How about you?"

Before I had the chance to answer, he held up his hand. "*Except* for being a magician."

"Ah, got me there." I grinned. "I'm not sure then . . . Maybe an artist?"

He tilted his head. "Really? I did not know you were much for drawing."

"Oh, I'm not." With a shrug, I opened up my Inventory. "Pretty terrible really. You should see the horse I drew in my diary. The one that almost killed me."

I withdrew it at an odd angle, my trauma-bound mind having it appear slightly too close to the fixer rather than into my own hand. It bounced from his forearm as he fumbled it, and then we both watched it tumble close to the edge of the ravine before plunging out of sight.

We continued staring in silence for a handful of seconds.

"Quinn." I turned a tired gaze toward him. "You are duty bound to never mention this to Ren, *ever.*"

"You have my word."

I honestly didn't know what to think. There was humor in there somewhere, I was sure of it. Probably a relief to have such a dour tome out of my possession. I'd just have to retain the good memories in my fragile skull and let the bad ones go.

"Alright, let's do the deed. I'll need to swipe the cuff at the last second. He heard me say that, so he might prepare to use a Skill immediately after." *Couldn't stop grinning.*

Quinn nodded but was slightly put off by my expression. "I assume you have a perfectly reasonable and safe way of doing that, then?"

My continuous grin didn't convince him, but what choice did he have? We propped Dorian up onto his feet, neither of which cared to keep him upright. His muffled pleas for mercy or something fell on deaf ears. Closer to the edge now and I saw the bottom for myself.

A split of the river had long eroded away at the rock to take it to the sea—I hadn't realized how high up from sea level we currently were. Nothing but a couple seconds of drop, but the degree of fatality was almost guaranteed.

With a nod to Quinn, I leaned forward. My skull, desperate to be opened up, fell down into the ravine as I didn't let up my grip on the puppet.

CHAPTER THREE

Chaos, in Parts

The air rushed past me. For a split second, I felt oddly at peace. Swiped the cuff from the falling captive and then appeared back up atop the ridge of the ravine, swapping positions with a hell dove. I wavered, and Quinn grabbed my arm.

"If you fall, I might as well jump too."

I opened my mouth to reply before being interrupted by the flash of dark energy. A burst of air rushed up from the ravine before lashing tendrils of black lightning pulsed and snapped out, charring the stone of the steep cliffs. After two long seconds of this eldritch violence, the power subsided, and the pair of us leaned a little closer to the edge.

"So, it *was* an explosive." I pulled a face at the destroyed foliage, some of it slightly aflame, as the remnants of Dorian washed away with the river.

[Ren: Everything okay??]
[Max: We are safe.]
[Max: Dorian disposed of.]
[Ren: Alright, hurry back.]

I was thankful to move farther away from the ravine. Although I had lost my prized journal, we had avoided a moderately clever assassination attempt. Quinn gave the destruction a brief glare before catching up to me.

"So we are potentially fighting against three who have defeated Guardians?"

"Possibly." I gave him a shrug. "I'm not sure it matters all that much, however."

In saying this, it wasn't like my newly gained powers were anything to shirk at—I just knew how to use them better. Burned away my Domain to deal with Tyler's army of zombies. Whoever created Dorian had been beaten out by a little patience and caution. If I hadn't knocked the puppet out, then he would surely have been killed by Ren in short order.

The explosion and reaching tendrils of foul energy looked to affect an area of at least sixty feet, so we would have taken some Damage, even from his poor hiding place.

"We shouldn't have to worry about any further Guardian slayers," I noted, as if that could cheer him up.

"You think so?"

I gave him a pat on the back as we walked over to the rest of the group. "*No.* Well . . . I imagine they were distributed throughout this continent. Which means two per area—unless there was one on the starter island. Or even two . . . So they might *not* be equally spread out."

He pulled a face and rubbed at his eye patch. "So the most likely options are the current four are all that we have to worry about—or there might be a fifth?"

"I'll see if Tanya will give me the contact's information. Maybe we can get some clarity where she isn't trusted by him."

Quinn murmured his acceptance, and we continued the rest of the way back to the Party in silence. While I was normally perceptive when it came to people, I wasn't too sure if he had something on his mind or not. Rather than prod him to open up, I allowed him to come to that point himself.

We emerged out onto the clearer plains of where the Quest was being repeated. We had missed out on the kills, but they had also gone slower in our absence, keeping themselves ready in case there was either someone else in the wings waiting to pounce . . . or in the event that I'd inevitably injured myself on something.

Wolf gestured for a break, and Ren immediately stomped up to meet us.

She gripped me by the chin and moved my head from side to side, inspecting me. "Seems like you're in one piece. Thank you, Quinn. He didn't do anything stupid, did he?"

The fixer gave her a blank stare that was almost too neutral. Like a deer caught in headlights. "No," he managed.

"Turns out I'm not entirely crazy, and the affable prisoner was, in fact, a living bomb intending to kill us off." I gave her a smile as she relinquished control of my face.

Wolf was lying on his side, tongue hanging out of his mouth, while Tanya leaned up against him with her arms crossed.

Ren gave me a brief nod. "Well, thank you as well." She hesitated as if she was about to walk away from me but instead just wavered in place before glaring off at the next pack of Monsters.

"Let's get back into it as soon as Wolf is ready. I don't want to linger here longer than necessary," I offered.

Expecting a grunt of agreement, or maybe just a curt nod, I was taken aback as the elf stepped closer and put her arms around me for a hug.

Briefly paralyzed, I watched Quinn walk off to talk with the others, a shrug of equal confusion his parting gift. I put my arms around her too, not wanting to waste a good thing.

Her face moved up to rest gently against mine, as her mouth neared my ear. "I know you did something stupid because my Oathwarden sense told me you were in danger," she whispered. She then squeezed me a little tighter than was comfortable.

"Is it telling you I'm in danger *now?*"

She pulled back so that she could look me in the eyes as she wrinkled up her face. "You're lucky that I love you, trickster. I don't like having to be mad at you."

"I'm just a magnet for bad times." I moved my hand up to hold the side of her face. "But next time you'll be right there, knee-deep in blood and shit with me."

"Promise?"

"Promise."

She smiled and gave me a brief kiss. "You're on thin ice, trickster. Peace treaty accepted, for now."

"Then let's kill and grow stronger together." I looked out at the System-created. "Oh, well—I guess *I* can't."

Ren sighed and released the hug to turn and look at the rest of the Party. "I can't in good conscience give you the go-ahead to join in."

While Tanya had said she'd break my leg if she caught me using <Shuffle> to remove my trauma status, she couldn't *actually* see my icons. It would be child's play to do the deed in secret and potentially heal myself with only minor repercussions. Of course, assuming I didn't instantly die from something, it would still be a hard sell to get them to agree to me fighting.

"Just think . . ." I began. "The amount of danger and pressure we are under. If I were allowed to burn from both ends, we could be safe and comfortable in a bed somewhere rather than grinding most of the evening."

She shot me a scowl. "*Don't.* Your health is not a negotiable commodity. If you make your condition worse, then it puts us all in danger."

I opened and closed my mouth. She was right in that respect. We'd set the ball in motion and would soon be reaping the consequences in the form of a final battle against the necromancer. For me to be anything less than peak performance could ruin our show. Bury us, literally.

Still, that just made me work my jaw in frustration. <Shuffle> danced in the back of my mind, and it knew all the right moves to get my attention. It was just a quick action, and then it'd be all over, one way or another. Part of me was clearly a gambler, and way too impulsive with what was literally a risk taken on my continued existence.

One look at the elf and I put that idea to rest. Even if I could accept the risk to myself, I couldn't put her through the struggle of me suffering worse than I already was.

"A compromise?" I asked. "Let me summon Roger only, nothing else."

Her tired expression told me I had more chance of that being accepted. "Group vote, okay? But I thought you said that Ability is inert?"

"It looks like it is, but I don't believe it."

She shrugged and led us over to the rest of the group, not wanting to argue over whether I should be distrusting of what the System presented me. We both knew I was a rule breaker.

"Max is requesting we allow him to summon Roger," she announced and stood with crossed arms.

Tanya pulled a face. "How exerting is it? Just the initial cast or continuous?"

"Just initial," I answered.

Quinn shrugged. "I'll defer to the expertise of the fair Ren."

Wolf didn't seem to care either way.

The women exchanged a glance. "Alright," the Fateweaver decided as she shook her head. "*Just* Roger and if you start bleeding or doing anything else unsavory, then you're in the time-out chair again."

I gave them a bow, and vertigo threatened to tip me over. "My thanks."

Of course, it wasn't that easy now, was it? The others prepared themselves to continue the grind as I brought out Roger's card and frowned at it. It was inert— as if it was a mundane card. He hadn't died . . . and even if that were the case, then he should be refreshed and ready by now.

As the combat began, I placed the card down on the grass and stepped a few feet back away from it. I scowled and missed having my hat. Today had *not* gone my way, and I wasn't about to let the System screw me out of having my security demon. I extended my palm out toward the dull card showing the white rabbit and glared.

A tether had been severed. Past the usual hand-waving of how magic worked in this world, I could see the threads of it. Or . . . not see, but *feel*. In the same way as I could attach lines of my power to objects to turn invisible, the cards themselves had some kind of intangible connection to my . . . core? Wherever the magic juice was stored.

Could I regrow it? Or find some way to connect it once more?

I made the first attempt gradually. Not wanting my hand to burst out with blood and be sent to the back to think about my actions, I'd have to be cautious with what I allowed myself to do. A wave of warmth ran down my right arm as I felt an invisible tendril move out and seek out the inert card.

In my peripheral, I could feel the icy glares that Ren and Tanya took turns in leveling my way. It was warranted. I couldn't deny that. Given my track record, it was just as likely I'd lose my hand or teleport to literal hell to . . .

Was that an option?

I held off on traveling with that thought any longer. Something told me I *could*—if I put in enough power and sacrificed enough. But what of the results? Just as likely I'd be trapped there, and it would be someplace hostile to me. The irony of teleporting myself into hell to avoid trouble here when one version of me had come here by teleporting away from danger in hell was amusing.

Still, that must be where my pact demon was . . .

My left hand raised, hoping that sharing the burden would hold off on self-damage as I increased the power pooling down into the card. Breaking some rules again. He was supposed to come here via a corpse—perhaps his exit from my Domain had confused the System and this was his punishment.

Well, I *needed* him.

Arcs of energy flickered around the card, scorching the loose sand of the dry area we were in. I calmed myself and tried not to force the change. Hands were clear—but I'd gotten the attention of Ren now. Performing under pressure was no big deal.

Expecting the card to bloom into purple light and become active, requiring a corpse to be struck to bring him back, I was instead surprised.

A magic circle of purple-and-black runes bloomed up around the small rectangle of the card. Much wider and more detailed than my usual summons. With the thrum of energy, a tall figure of white fur rose up.

Roger turned to me, purple eyes glowing. His ears were parted to the sides of his head, and what sat atop him made me grin widely.

He returned the big smile, taking down my magic top hat to pass back over to me.

CHAPTER FOUR

Hope Springs Eternal

After a few minutes of interest and confusion, the novelty of true-form Roger wore off enough to where the Party could get stuck into combat. It wasn't long before his pristine white fur was matted with blood and he looked even further from something that could be described as *cute*. Now untethered from using a corpse as a puppet, his combat efficiency was up—and he acted as a second tank to draw in more opponents while Wolf held the lion's share.

Indeed, everyone seemed pleased with the emergence of an odd sixth member for our show.

Everyone, except for me.

Certainly, he had returned my hat—and as my pact demon, having him do my bidding was the natural order of things . . . but everything else about this was not *natural*. We'd broken a rule. Twisted and come unmoored from the tethers of the System. He was designed to only arrive through a dead body. His time here was meant to be limited. Yet here he was . . .

Normally, I relished in existing through bullshit. Reveled in seeing what I could get away with. There was a point where I had slid past a line and could no longer stop. A slippery slope that I had cooked up myself.

It was only a matter of time before the System put me back in my place and probably punished me for my insolence.

In saying this . . . there was a good reason why part of me wasn't fearful of repercussions. Could just be the trauma, or the fact that I bounced from one near-death experience to another all the time already. More likely, it was my ego. Thinking the world needed me. Inadvertently, I had been cultivated to erase the Lady and how she was breaking the System.

Eggs and omelets, I was sure.

I watched as Roger dropped his large mace, the sharp weapon of one of the Hyenids piercing through his arm. His left hand went up and grabbed them around their lower jaw, his odd humanlike fingers filling their mouth even against the threat of being bitten. With a twist, he dislocated it, the crack causing me to wince. As he pushed the Monster away, it received an arrow through the throat from Ren.

Two more cycles of the repeatable, and we should be leveled up. Sun was gradually working its way toward the horizon. I craved the night and the promise of proper rest. Sitting idle was maddening, even if it was what was best for me. Of course, I did have the occasional hell bird circling around in the background . . . but that was par for the course.

The number of times I had summoned a demon out of sight and knowledge of the others and done nothing with them was . . . well, uncountable at this stage. Hitting that one-in-a-million trick was all the more impressive if it looked like you only made the single attempt. If there was one thing my upgraded <Sleight of Hand> was good at, it was allowing me to determine the perfect timing to cast and throw cards out of sight of everyone else.

If I had to sit and do nothing, the least I could contribute was keeping an eye on the surroundings. The fact that I was doing this while playing solitaire in mid-air with my mundane cards was neither here nor there. My brain needed the stimulation to feel active.

Tanya whistled me over, and I blew the game away to ashes. I could change the cards to whatever I wanted anyway, so at some point it stopped being about the game and started being something more performative. With a long glance behind me, I stepped over to the Fateweaver.

"Usually I'd leave loot distribution to the end, but I want you to have this now." She smiled, some odd excitement in her eyes.

"Oh?" I shrugged and openly accepted what she was offering. A legendary item.

[Gloves of Ego: +5 INT. When Mana is below 50%, spells heal you for 5% Health over 10 seconds. Does not stack.]

She nudged me with her elbow before turning her attention back to the combat. "Might keep you on your feet for a little longer."

"Thank you." I smiled and bowed, moving back out of their way to sit down on my summoned chair. Wasn't often we found legendary items, but the ones that suited me were always an interesting addition to my act. Headband of Woe increased my Damage for the Mana used, and now these Gloves of Ego healed me.

For the most part, that made my use of <Bloodletting+> less of a cost—or could get me out of a pickle if I caught an arrow through my soft parts. Plus, the Intelligence was an increase, and . . . as I put them on, I saw that they were white gloves. Not quite as silken as the typical magician ones, but they fit the look almost too perfectly.

Quinn stopped an arrow out of the air, protecting the bear from the next group they had gotten aggro from. Wolf burst forward and disemboweled the ranged Monster before engaging the better-armored one beside the first. Already, the fixer was in beside him to finish off the downed System-created with a jab of his sword.

Roger had recovered from his arm injury thanks to Ren's healing—which apparently worked on the demon rabbit. A wide swing of Jokkar's mace broke the arm of his opponent, their weapon falling to the floor as the elf pinned their other shoulder, rendering them defenseless. With a grunt, my pact demon put his strength into a heavy downward strike, which pulped the skull of the Hyenid and sprayed him with their brains.

Tanya was alternating between blessings and curses, improving the Stats of the Party while slowing and degrading the Health of the continuous stream of bad guys.

And Max, the most established magician and pinnacle of power in this realm . . . sat and pouted a little.

"Why don't you write in that sad journal you like so much?" Ren called from ahead of me, catching my dour expression.

I couldn't think of anything clever to respond with and didn't care to lie so brazenly to her, so I just shrugged. If anything, I should be sitting here thinking about our next steps. How we were supposed to assail the necromancer and his group—if they were still entrenched in their current position.

The camp we had upturned in the first area had a crate of spare blood—it would be wise to expect some of the groups here to have a similar stockpile. Especially Tyler's group, considering they were meant to be a roadblock for the whole area. A base of operations, really.

Thus, I felt confident that we would find them where we expected them to be.

Second point to note—what to expect when we got there. I watched as Roger headbutted a Monster and proceeded to stomp on them with his long feet as they dropped to the ground. The fort by the bridge was something clear and visible that we were able to destroy thanks to it being made shoddily and with flammable materials. I'd have to pick Tanya's brains on whether she knew how they were set up.

The ramshackle building had more Players and effects in place—going against only four sounded easy enough . . . but I had a feeling there was a good reason they were chosen to be the protectors of the area there. And if they had the power of a Guardian . . . Oh, that reminded me.

"May I have the contact details of the Eternal Wardens guy, Tanya?" I asked. "They might be more receptive to my questions."

She considered it for a second before agreeing. "Can't see the harm—it's you they are interested in, after all." Double-checking she wasn't required in the fight, she sent over his details.

Ren calmly put an arrow through the eye socket of one Hyenid before sticking a second with her entangling shot. She looked so focused when in battle—something I passively respected and appreciated, but perhaps she was right to browbeat me about not including her in the bullshit I often found myself soloing.

[Max: Hey, Dimitri? Max here, the magician that the Lady does not like.]

I pulled a face and looked back as the Party moved forward to the next group. Behind us, the respawns were still far away, so I didn't care to move just yet. It didn't look like he was keen to respond to me directly—and I wondered if perhaps that was a pretty weak entrance for someone so—

[Dimitri: Max. It is great to make your acquaintance.]
[Dimitri: I have heard plenty about you in passing.]
[Max: Super. Tanya told you I killed a Guardian, right?]
[Dimitri: She did but didn't elaborate past that.]
[Dimitri: I much prefer talking in person . . .]
[Dimitri: But I am eager to learn more about you.]

Already, I had a bit of an ick from the guy. A fan club was nice and all, but something best kept very far away and out of sight. Attention and adoration *were* the goal, but some of the people who fell down that path were . . . Well, they could be *a lot*.

[Max: You said you'd help after I got rid of the necromancer.]
[Dimitri: Very true—the desire to meet is something personal.]
[Dimitri: The leadership is keener for you to prove your worth first.]
[Max: I'm rolling my eyes. Anything I should know right now?]
[Max: Something that might keep me alive? I think there are two other Guardian killers.]
[Max: Three, including the Lady.]
[Dimitri: . . .]
[Dimitri: Please hold.]

I rolled my eyes again. By the time we cared or were able to see this supposed resistance group, we would have probably killed at least one of the Guardian users.

Tanya had been able to infer from what he drip fed her that each Guardian might be different and allow different strengths to their wielders.

The Siren had allowed me to reach my pinnacle, a true acceptance of my demonic power that led to my Domain granting me an actual stage to perform upon. It . . . didn't really clue me in to what that was actually *offering*, however. Perhaps my brain was too mushy to really consider it.

Idly, I got up and walked closer to the fray while my mind ticked over. Another Player could create a second self—or puppet that acted independently. The necromancer seemed to be able to summon a large horde of undead. The Lady enraptured people under a spell and grew in power the larger her cult was.

There was an underlying thread that was at the tip of my tongue, yet I couldn't quite grab a taste of the words. My eyes went up to my Chat, distracting me from salivating over the unknown truths.

[Dimitri: I cannot tell you all. I apologize.]
[Dimitri: If you have only recently defeated a Guardian, that narrows down which one.]
[Dimitri: We do not understand their powers yet.]
[Dimitri: So leadership is very keen to meet you.]
[Max: After the necromancer is dead.]
[Dimitri: Correct. Apologies. Although . . .]
[Dimitri: Whatever you are doing must be working.]
[Dimitri: Our morning reports tell a tale of the CS down here retreating.]
[Dimitri: You didn't hear that from me though.]
[Max: Understood. Take care.]

I sighed and clicked my tongue, unsure where my thoughts had left off before the barrage of messages. In the time I had spent reading his useless words, the Party had called for another break and was making their way over to me.

Roger was a sight of pure horror, completely drenched with blood and internal organs. Seemed happy enough, however. Wolf didn't have as much gore soaked through his fur but also had a contented expression. I was just glad he had found a more comfortable pace, and he wasn't burning out again.

"Any luck?" Tanya asked, her eyebrow raised. "Talks so fucking much, right?"

"Correct." I smiled. "And mostly a dead end—however, he did tell me that the Shadow near them have been moving back."

Ren wrinkled up her face and pulled her chair out right next to mine. "They're not in a stalemate down there like the campground was?"

The Fateweaver rubbed at her chin. "It is *something* like that."

"Useless bastards," Ren muttered, taking hold of my hand and briefly inspecting my glove before her fingers intertwined with mine.

"It's always just us," I said. Something of a more miserable statement than I was intending. Fiona's group was close to coming back to this area but would miss out on the fun. Wasn't sure where Leyla and hers were. Eternal Wardens were stuck with their thumbs up their asses. If the playing pieces could just align, then we'd have a small army that could push back.

Maybe that's what we'd need to go against the Lady and what forces she could consolidate as we closed in.

My eyes went up to my trauma status. I itched and squirmed.

I needed to be let out of this cage to be insufferable again.

CHAPTER FIVE

Room for Two

By far the strongest willpower I had ever exhibited, I had managed to not <Shuffle> away my restraints. The STAR on my left wrist illuminated in a soft golden color as the Party stretched out and groaned, making their way back to their audience of one.

Level thirteen.

I was almost apprehensive. Well, no—I was literally at the edge of the seat. The System loved me and would labor me with impressive Abilities that would have my allies rolling their eyes and our enemies quaking in their shallow graves. My first ascension since gaining my demonic strength, I wondered how ludicrous I could truly be.

[Level up—<13>]
[Stats increased]
[New Ability: <Last Act>]
[New Passive: <Summon Demon: Shade>]
[New Passive: <Befuddle>]

My eyes scanned over the three Abilities at great speed. The grin on my face caused my muscles to ache.

I looked up in joyous wonder to see the eyes of my whole Party watching me.

"Go on then, asshole." Ren nudged me. "Show us what the Magnificent Max can now do."

They were both eager and apprehensive to see it. I bit my lip before leaning over toward the elf to whisper in her ear what was about to happen. After all, I was on thin ice and didn't want to earn any more ire than I needed to. She returned a stoic nod, a poker face that was unshakable.

I stood and hopped atop my chair, chucking an apple out to Quinn, who caught it as deftly as expected. "Stand about twenty feet opposite," I asked.

He did as such, some confusion on his face.

Feeling calm, I outstretched my arms in readiness. "Now throw it at me, as hard as you can."

Quinn shrugged, while everyone else had moved slightly farther away from where we both stood. Tanya held a grimace, while Roger had his arms crossed and a smug expression on his face. As if he already knew. Wolf just wanted the apple after whatever this was had concluded.

The fixer wound it back and pitched it. A perfect throw, considering it was a humble fruit. Cratered through the air directly for me.

It struck the middle of my chest, collapsing my rib cage with an audible crunch. Blood sprayed from my mouth as my internal organs ruptured from the force, and with little ceremony, my body went limp. The gathered audience present for my death gasped as I thudded to the dry ground among a spattering of crimson, twisting and gurgling blood from my face as my last breath left my body. A final fanfare indeed.

"Nice throw," I complimented Quinn, now standing behind him.

He shifted and jumped. "By all that is holy, Max. *Why?*"

I'd earned scowls from Tanya and Wolf, while Ren was surprisingly hard to read. Not really annoyed but also not willing to be impressed by the fact I could now fake my own death.

"It has a long cooldown." I raised my hand to prevent the angry mob withdrawing any pitchforks. "However . . . other than causing you all some worry and giving me a brief out of a situation . . . it does something even *more* important."

Tanya now crossed her arms and glared at me. "Out with it then, or I'm withholding your token share."

Unfair and totally against the rules of the Party. Judging from how the rest—aside from Roger—were staring at me, I might be out of luck in that complaint. "To fully facilitate the process of my faux death, it also removes any and all buffs *and* debuffs."

I grinned widely. *Trauma was gone.*

The Fateweaver shook her head. "How is it you always get a free pass on all of this?"

"Well, I am a trickster, of course." I wagged my finger at her and turned to the elf before someone decided to stab me. "What about you, Ren? Anything awe-inspiring before I dig through the rest of what I received?"

She rolled her eyes and stood from her chair, drawing out her bow. Without saying anything, she turned and pointed a finger toward the closest group of Hyenids. Four figures standing and minding their own business as if we weren't currently in line of sight of them and nearly two dozen corpses of their brethren.

"Pick an element," she requested of me.

"Ice."

She whispered the word in Elfin, and a spark of white circled the arrow. Rather than aim straight for the pack of Monsters, she pointed it at a high angle. A pulse of air buffeted the ground, sending a wave of loose dust toward the rest of us as she released the attack.

At some point near the apex, Ren clicked her fingers and held her palm out toward the unaware Hyenids. Wolf readied himself to interject should she draw all the aggro. High in the air, the projectile burst into something resembling a cloud. Fluffy and white, with a shade of blue to the edges.

Then it rained.

Except, instead of droplets of water—or even hail—it was arrows made of sharp shards of ice. Dozens at a time, they pelted down upon the Monsters continuously. Most of them missed and just broke up on the ground, but those that hit pierced through the Hyenids, blood mixing and melting away at the gathering crushed ice.

When the last of them had dropped to the ground, she lowered her arm, and the cloud vanished. The last of the ice arrows struck the gathered debris alone.

"Drains Mana like a motherfucker though," she complained, shaking out her bloodied hand.

My heart did a little flip. A few steps behind me on the bullshit-o-meter, but she could catch up in no time. "Impressive," I said, if only because otherwise I was just staring at her with large hearts in my eyes. She gave me a bow, and I cursed <Last Act> for having such a long cooldown that I couldn't die right there.

I shook away the pink clouds threatening to pelt my own brain waves and settled in to go through my Abilities properly.

There was a new demon on my roster that I could summon. A Shade, which seemed to be a singular friend that would trail a target and instill them with debuffs and drain their life. Probably look really spooky while he did so as well.

<Befuddle> caused my <Pick a Card++> attacks to give the target one stack of Dazzle when struck. Not a great deal in and of itself considering how much Damage my cards could do. It was just another way of getting those icons on my enemies, however.

Another thing the System probably thought was reasonable. In my Domain, Dazzle icons just did Damage, so what would happen if I just sent cards out to strike the audience instead of performing? Strangely, I had a feeling for the answer already. My Domain would just fade away if I wasn't keeping the Power gauge up. Against Syther, it had been part fueled by my hatred for demons—but in a normal show, I'd receive terrible ratings for just assaulting the crowd.

I shook my head before realizing that Ren was standing right in front of me. Her blue eyes staring me down, she gave me another impromptu hug—if only to get close enough to whisper something in my ear.

"System gave me a really neat Passive, trickster. I don't want to say it out loud, however."

"Oh?" My eyebrows raised in anticipation.

"Promise to keep a secret? Just between you . . . and me?"

I nodded slowly, gradually becoming more concerned about what the System had given her that could require us to withhold such information from the others. Nothing . . . salacious, surely?

"You and I . . . are immune to becoming traumatized."

It took a couple of seconds to sink in, and I shivered. Leaned a little farther away to look her in the face. "Yeah?"

"On one very important condition." She pressed her nose up against mine. "Check your Status now."

Despite the fact that she was right up in my face, my eyes went to the side where my STAR menus tried to find a place to fit in my peripheral. There was something new there.

[<Eternal Vow>: If within 20 feet of your Oathwarden, you are immune to fear, trauma, delirium, and terror.]

I gasped. "*Never* leave my side."

Ren gave me a wide grin. "I won't. That's my *<Eternal Vow>*."

Tanya cleared her throat. "Not that I like being the wet blanket to your admittedly very cute romance, but your . . . Roger is currently eating a corpse."

I turned my eyes over to the side at the last pack they had slain, releasing my grip on the elf. The bloodied bipedal rabbit was hunched over one of the deceased Hyenids, currently scooping out their internal organs and chewing on them rather sloppily.

He paused, sensing our collective gaze upon him, and turned his head. "Ah. Sorry, is this a bit of a faux pas? One of you wanted to eat this tasty fucker first?"

"It's not very healthy," Wolf offered, not allowing my brain to decide whether we should be accepting of the demon eating the dead when the bear often did just that.

"It's not?" Roger scrunched up his face and stood, wiping his hands off on his thighs. "I'm supposed to be more careful about who I eat."

I assumed he meant what, but . . . No—who was I kidding?

"Max has me on a good diet now," Wolf continued. "Perhaps you could join me?"

At present, I wasn't too sure how I felt with Roger being a more permanent addition to reality. Watching the talking bear give the tall rabbit tips on dietary consumption had my mind looking for the back door. Escape with a little of my sanity. Shame Ren didn't protect against that. I gave her a glance, and she looked pretty content now. Either knowing that there were fewer things to worry about in regard to my safety, or . . . there was something else.

I had promised to drag her into the next high-stakes bullshit encounter I inevitably found myself in. She was not only looking forward to it but now had something to smooth our passage through such turmoil. Even if we emerged broken and bloody, we'd be stronger and rise above the odds together.

At that point, I had a moment of clarity. The selfish showman had always been eager to share the stage but could never truly commit. Our romance wasn't just built on the love and attraction to each other . . . but it preceded something even greater. A duo that could take the world by storm if I allowed her to live as close to the edge as I got. The others all had their parts to play, but it was between us two. Our grudge against the Lady and eagerness to save the System.

"You alright there, trickster?" She gave me a wry smile as Wolf and Roger continued their conversation.

"Hmm? Oh. I just realized that the greatest bullshit the System ever gave me was in allowing me to meet you."

She shook her head, but her smile widened. "You couldn't be more right, Max."

I put my arm around her and caught Quinn and Tanya talking in my peripheral. Six was a lot of yapping mouths for this once loner, but I had grown to feel comfort in their presence.

"Remember when I was sending you off to fight those goblins and put the arrow up against your neck?"

"How could I forget?"

She shuffled herself closer. "System also gave me a Passive that makes my arrows do full Damage no matter the range. So it would probably *actually* kill you if I tried that now."

"How comforting." I grinned as she snorted a brief laugh. "Just arrows or projectiles?"

"*Arrows* only." She sighed. "You're still the System's favorite."

"Well, you're *my* favorite." I removed her hat so I could give her a kiss on the head. Replacing it, I turned my gaze to the other two. "Let's head to safety. Sunlight is waning, and we will need the rest."

Tanya nodded, and they started to gather their things. I let the warmth of our odd group wash away all that had been troubling me. Things could be okay for now—I'd drink deep of all that we had fought hard to cultivate.

For tomorrow, we marched against the necromancer.

CHAPTER SIX

Stars in the Night

I stared out the window of the house we were due to sleep in. I had received my share of power tokens—four—after paying off my debt to the Party. Decided to wait until my brain was fresh to put them into something worthwhile. Darkness had now crossed the land, and the moon was full. Trees shook from the light breeze, their illuminated leaves dancing like—

"Come to bed, Max," Ren whined. "*You* said we needed the rest."

My eyebrow raised, and I turned my head back to her. "Sorry, I'm just antsy."

"Well, at least put some clothes on." She sighed and rubbed at her eyes. "I don't think I can sleep either if I have to stare at your bare ass all night."

"Want to do something instead of sleep, then?" I turned to her fully and put my hands on my hips.

She groaned and pulled a pillow over her eyes. "*Again*, Max? Have some mercy. I had to spend all afternoon leveling you up."

I rolled my eyes. "No, not that." *Although* . . . "Actually, I was thinking of something a lot more . . . dangerous."

Ren moved the pillow slightly so that she could glare at me. "Max . . ."

"Just you and me, a little bullshit underneath the moonlight. Burn off some energy and have some fun as the most powerful duo in the world."

She worked her jaw. "You can't . . . It's not . . . *Ah, fuck it.*" She rolled up onto her feet, covers clasped in one hand, barely covering her nude form. With a flourish that obscured her, the sheet then fell down to reveal the elf now in her full magician outfit. "I'm in."

While her vision was blocked by her trick, I had also switched into my clothing. Two peas in a pod, and well worth the bright smile on her face.

I lifted the window from the latch, hoisting it up so that we could escape. It was a foolish thing that could go wrong in so many ways . . . but while we were young, reckless, and alive . . . we'd grab out at some escapism. Palate cleanser for what lay ahead.

Switching positions with my hell dove on the ground, I held out my arms and caught the elf as she dropped. Exchanged a soft kiss, if only so that we could both hide the surprise that I'd managed to pull that off.

"Where to?" she whispered as I lowered her to the floor.

We had kept to the east after finishing off the Hyenids, as it seemed the best bet for staying away from any Crimson. Went a little farther south to give us a buffer. Reasonably close to the coast again. I sent across some coordinates.

Her brow furrowed and head tilted. "Hmm, alright. Lead the way."

"If this is stupid, we can head back and—" I was silenced as she placed a finger against my lips.

"I like our Party, but *us* . . . We never had the chance to properly court. Let's just have some selfish adventure. Live while we still draw breath."

I said nothing more, but with a brief bow, I then led us off into the night.

It didn't take us too long to reach the destination, only waylaid slightly as we stopped to kiss at certain landmarks that looked particularly romantic under the light of the moon. Our hands holding like we lived in normal times and this was a slice of soft reality completely separate from the hardships we usually lived in. Could almost believe that things could be like this forever.

But there it was: built into the side of the cliff. A nest of Smugglers, not too dissimilar from the Bandit cave that we had chewed our way through together in the first area. Not exactly a romantic haunt on the face of things, but the time we had spent alone was minuscule since meeting up with Wolf.

Ren squeezed my hand and let go to draw her bow. "Any plan of action?"

I shook my head and brought her in closer. "Maximum. Fucking. Bullshit." Each period punctuated with a brief kiss. Her eyes were ablaze with excitement, and I felt the same way. After my revelation yesterday, we needed this.

Rolling out my shoulder, I took the lead. She shadowed me, an arrow up to her bow, already prepared to begin the dance.

"I can hear it again," she whispered.

The musical tone of our introduction fanfare—I could too. I should have seen that as the sign I had to elevate her up beside me back then. Too proud to share the limelight despite knowing the necessity. But now it was *ours*.

"It's showtime," I whispered in return.

An alcove in the rock face, framed by wooden supports. Dark, but the promise of a lantern or torch on the inside held the briefest illumination and helped pick out the two shadowed figures standing guard.

Purple light painted the surroundings as three imbued cards burst and spun out from my hand toward the one on the right. Silvery white paired alongside our presence as Ren put a <Smite Shot> through the neck of the one on the left. Both slunk down to the floor, and we were bathed in naught but moonlight once more.

I strode forth, overconfidence humming within. Ten percent Power.

Into the cave proper, the roughly hewn tunnel curved to the side around the traditional outpost room where guards would be stationed. Seemed to be a hideout cliché, but we liked that sort of thing. The murmurs of System-created chatter, our audience sitting in warm lantern light around a table. I stepped through, cards already going off for the first.

An arrow to the temple of the second. The first not dead but severely maimed. The other two drew melee weapons. Oh no: That was some manner of horn or alarm. Purple card circled from the first opponent and lopped the fingers off my next target, causing the emergency instrument to drop from his hand just as he went to blow it. Ren then shot him through the neck.

Uninjured Smuggler was remarkably quick and darted to swing past me and strike the elf. I spun farther to the side and brought up <Card Fan+> in front of her to block their weapon. Through the air I had thrown her a dagger. She caught it as it spun and lashed into the man's stomach, managing to miss his ribs and bury into his organs. I turned to the maimed fighter, who was struggling to engage me directly.

A card went down into his foot, severing part of it and hobbling him. I lifted my hand up and caught the dagger that Ren had returned, not even needing to look. With one swift motion, I continued into throwing it straight at the Smuggler; however, the blade stopped around a foot away from him. Despite being System-created, he flinched from the attack as the dagger just hung in the air. My left hand raised to show the bright-red critical card in my grasp.

Ren finished her opponent off with a point-blank arrow shot to their heart, while my target dropped to the ground, part of his head now painting the back wall. I grabbed the hovering knife and spun it in my hand until it vanished, to be replaced by falling flower petals. I turned to the elf and grinned.

She returned a wide smile and gestured for us to continue.

And we did so. Three more rooms of Smugglers who fell from our constant assault. I'd spin my spear, and Ren would duck beneath it, letting off arrows and moving in perfect tune to my own antics with my tricks. Our dance had synced, but then again—we were both playing to the same tune now.

Both our suits now bore the signs of battle. We had taken a little Damage here and there, but other than the lasting signs of blood soaking our outfits, we'd been able to heal through everything so far. In fact, this was probably the most injury Ren had sustained since the fort . . . but I didn't allow it to sway my actions.

While she looked to me to be the leader and her protector, she also needed to be my equal. I wondered if standing at the back and hitting things with arrows without interruption had become as boring for her as I had felt in the beach Dungeon just using cards.

Even now, I watched her slide across the dusty ground to avoid the down-swing of a wide club. She turned along the way to fire an arrow through the lower leg of the Smuggler. As she spun back to her feet, her bow caught the edge of a wooden chair and swiped it toward the pinned man. The elf ran up and placed one foot on the seat to lash out with her boot and kick him in the face. He dropped to the floor, and the chair tipped slowly over while she drew back an arrow.

It was all very elegant and acrobatic. So enraptured with the performance was I that I didn't even clock the last opponent in the room diving for me, a sword en route to giving me a splitting headache. Instead of following through with his intent, the Smuggler stumbled and paused, his eyes turning back in horror to see the tall shadow looming over him. Eyes of deep red burned into him, the only features my Shade demon seemed to have.

It was enough of a distraction, and a trio of cards went through his skull, taking him away from the fright of seeing my new friend.

Ren stretched out her bow arm as she walked back over to me. "New guy is pretty creepy."

I nodded. "Might have to save my tokens and see if I can unlock two summonses at once."

"Two pups," she replied immediately as a statement of demand rather than question.

"All in good time, moonflower. Let's continue."

We did a brief amount of looting, not wanting to ruin the buzz we had going. Another two tokens each, but little in the way of useful equipment. A few bits and pieces to put aside for props, which was standard procedure at this point—

"Oh," I said as Ren stopped abruptly in front of me. There was an opening to our right, and another chamber with a . . .

[New Monster: Smuggler Elite <15E>]

"An elite," I repeated, as if we couldn't see the same message. "Oh, but look at what he is wearing."

More than a compliment over his fashion tastes, the almost comically large man sitting at a dining table had a brace of flintlock pistols across his wide chest.

"Quinn would *love* those," Ren murmured, trying not to get the attention of him and the four other Smugglers, for whom we were clearly in plain view at the doorway.

"Agreed." I ran my tongue across my lips and readied up a handful of cards.

She held her hand out and stopped me from stepping into the room. "Want to break some rules, trickster?"

I didn't even need to answer that—she could tell from the light blooming in my eyes. Could there be any other way?

A whispered word of Elfin and a small mote of flame circled the held arrow. Into my hands, I drew a couple of bottles of alcohol. Wasn't as good as oil, but it'd be better than a sack of flour.

Ren shot the arrow out at the right-side wall, a cloud of white and red flooding vertically across the stone. Her hand outstretched, arrows then fired horizontally across the chamber. Beams of burning light impaled the confused group or shattered on the far wall, leaving scorch marks wherever they landed. The two bottles left my hand to land atop the table, bursting and catching the furniture aflame.

The elf grunted as her Mana reserves dropped low, some amount of blood starting to run from her hand. I stepped forward toward the burgeoning inferno. As the lesser Smugglers dropped under the constant assault, the elite blocked some of them with a magical shield.

He raised a hand up, one of the pistols gripped tightly and aiming for me.

I grinned, wondering if my <Card Fan> could come up quick enough to block a bullet. All it would take was—

A flash and burst of smoke emerged from the end of the held weapon. The small metal projectile struck me in the throat, piercing straight through my windpipe and whatever the important artery in my neck was called. Didn't seem to matter right at this moment. I clutched at the wound as warm blood pulsed over my hands. Unable to breathe, I collapsed as Ren canceled the cast of her cloud Skill.

"My turn," I said, as I appeared beside the elite. A crossbow in each hand, I fired and struck him in the neck with both. As he turned to have one last-ditch attempt at my life, an arrow impaled his head. I looted the brace—as well as spare shot and gunpowder—from him before his body fell to the floor.

"I expected to be more annoyed at your new Skill, but given that my Oathwarden sense prickles anytime you're in actual danger, I know when you're just faking it." Ren wiped her bloodied hand off on her waistcoat and then grimaced at herself for such an action.

"That is a relief." I hopped over the burning furniture to get closer to her. "It has an hour cooldown, and it's very tempting to use it *constantly*."

"What happens when you upgrade it?" She raised as an eyebrow as we moved back into the corridor.

I shrugged. "Not sure if I'm saving my tokens or not. If it lowers the cooldown, then I'm sure the others would tire and become numb to me dying."

Ren shook her head. "True. I'd be the only one wailing when it happens for real, and they'd think you were pulling their leg."

"So many options for winding them up though."

"Right?" She gave me a wide grin. "The fact that it leaves your fake corpse around for ten minutes is super gross and cool."

I was humming with energy, and it wasn't just due to how well our date night was going. We'd performed enough tricks that . . .

We stopped at the next opening. End of the line. Before us was the widest chamber yet. A dozen or so Smugglers, another elite, and the boss of this whole place. A tough undertaking for just the two of us, even at our best.

But I was at 100 percent Power.

I held my hand out, which she took without question.

"Ren? Do you want to step onstage with me?"

There was some apprehension in her eyes, but her heart had lodged in her throat, preventing any words from coming out. Instead, she nodded eagerly.

I grinned and let the preshow nerves wash away. This one would be *special*.

Domain: <The Grand Stage>.

CHAPTER SEVEN

Twice as Nice

Buzzing but confused. I stood in an area of darkness, unsure of why I was not in front of a small crowd of Monsters ready to put on a show. The purple curtains to my side and radiant glow past them clued me in to where I actually was.

"Smugglers and scoundrels! Hold on tight to your seats as we welcome the one and only . . . Max the Magnificent!"

A wide grin pasted across my face—although such a thing was natural and expected with what was about to happen. Straightened up and made sure my hat was on properly. Took one deep breath in and then out before my feet took me into motion.

Out from the wings of the stage and into the illuminated area. There was the polished wooden floor of the stage and a glow that illuminated Ren, who had just given me the best introduction I could ask for.

Her suit, normally a soft pastel blue, was now sparkling and bright as if a haze of glitter followed it. Eyes brighter than those lights above us beaming down. Some nerves at the edges of her expression but completely overridden by the elation. She looked like a firework mid burst.

I strode forward to stand beside her, and we gave the crowd of gathered System-created a low bow in tandem. It took a lot of effort to keep my heart in my chest, as it was close to exploding. We rose and gave each other a look. This was new ground for us both, her especially. While our shared tricks were few and far between, we would just have to allow magic to dictate how well the show turned out.

My hand extended to put the spotlight on her, and I stepped off to the side by a dozen feet. Took my hat down and showed it to be empty to the vacant crowd. Red Dazzle icons hung patiently over their heads, waiting to be increased. From within, I reached and withdrew a hatchet.

Allowing my gambling nature to wash over and encompass my beautiful protégé, I tossed the weapon through the air, and she caught it. Still keeping eyes on me, I shook my hat back out and gave a look of animated confusion at the crowd.

Where was the second hatchet?

A figurative light bulb appeared over my head, and I returned my hat atop my head. Instead, I hopped onto one foot and made the show of struggling to remove my boot. A little more slapstick than I'd usually be able to stomach, but we were having more fun with this performance. As I shook the footwear in front of me, the second hatchet slid from where my foot had just been occupying. Perplexing, I was sure.

I grabbed it from the air and flung it over to Ren, who once again caught it with little issue. In fact, rather than just grasp at the small axes, the elf immediately followed the catch into juggling the weapons.

Slightly more advanced than the fruit that we had practiced with, I was proud of her and briefly enraptured as well. Doubly so as, with the faintest whisper that the crowd wouldn't hear, both of the hatchets burst into fire.

A quick side-eye to the crowd saw them squirm under the violence we were forcing them to endure. Physical pain for however insufferable we could be.

With a grin and flourish of my hands to the elf, I signaled the continuation of the show. She tossed one of the hatchets into the air toward me in an arc. Back in my hands, my hat was then thrown up to catch the object. The second came soon after, to which my held headwear easily received—flames extinguishing as they somehow fit in the small space.

My hand went in, and I withdrew a hell dove. Ren held her arm out, and I allowed it to fly over to her hand as I gave a bow before leaving the stage. From the shadowed wings, I watched her draw her cape around to obscure the bird. With an animated flourish, she then revealed that it had vanished, and instead, I was now there.

The lack of applause *was* concerning, but the collapse of two of the audience was music to my ears. Roger's absence was also odd—I'd have to bring that up at his quarterly review.

As Ren stepped to my side, I withdrew my card deck, shuffling the cards in several ways before offering her a spread.

She picked a card and flaunted it to the crowd, pacing the length of the stage back and forth to ensure they all remembered which she had picked. While I averted my eyes from the performance, she then returned it to the deck, which I gave several more shuffles to hide away her choice.

Stepping back toward the middle of the stage, I then worked up my shoulders. With one quick action, I threw the whole deck into the air. All fifty-two cards then fluttered to the floor. My arm extended, I held a finger out like a gun, closing one eye to focus.

There it was. Eight of clubs.

My spear burst up from the stage, impaling one of the cards.

As the last of the trick settled on the floor, Ren stepped over to remove the pierced cardboard. With her own faux surprise, she then showed it to the audience. It was indeed the card she had picked previously. Another two or three members of the crowd dropped from their seats.

I stepped up behind her, and my hand went along the outside of her ear, bringing out another eight of clubs. She turned to me, her eyes dancing with impassioned fire. Her hand went up to my ear, as she drew forth an eight of clubs as well.

Cannon dropped behind me and burst out three sets of Dazzle-inducing confetti, as I drew the elf in close to me. The remaining participants were shredded by the sudden forced violence, the show facade dropping as they died at the same time as I broke their suspension of disbelief.

The Domain faded to leave us in the wide chamber of the Smugglers.

"Holy fuck, that was amazing," she whispered before our locking lips put a stop to any further postshow opinion polls.

As we became inseparable and sank to the floor, I dispersed as many pillows and blankets beneath us as my Inventory would allow.

Greatest show in the System.

The chill breeze of the real world buffeted my overheated body.

"I'm still buzzing," Ren whispered, her bow up and ready as we stepped outside of the Smuggler's cove.

Darkness, still barely lit by the light of the moon, greeted us with the accompaniment of a world still half asleep. It was a familiar feeling: the juxtaposition of the dopamine and fanfare of the show before stepping out into the calm of reality. Of course, I didn't usually have to worry about being assaulted straight after a show.

"Same. It will last awhile." I smiled at her. "You were *amazing* . . . if I haven't said that enough."

"You definitely haven't." She stuck her tongue out at me before smiling out at the darkness.

Given that was something impromptu, playing it all by ear . . . she *was* fantastic. So far, my Domain shows were short affairs, which paired fine with our lack of experience in acting as a duo . . . but it wouldn't take much for us to work on something that could last and truly wreak havoc. Or delight, I supposed.

I chalked up this success to the fact that I had accepted she could be my equal for the entirety of the roller coaster. Up and down, not just the pleasant parts. Our strength as fighters always took a leap when we allowed the middle we met at to grow untethered.

"Looks clear," I noted. "Let's head back."

Her nod was the only acknowledgment. We had expected an ambush, as we had gotten greedy. Adventuring without our Party, in the middle of the night, and allowing our passions to leave us weak and assailable . . . but it seemed we had gotten away with it. Dangerous thoughts.

We snuck through the darkness, a quiet contentedness between us. Not only silent as we were being sneaky, but we wanted to ensure that we hadn't invited drama before giving each other a high five for our performance. For the magic show, I meant.

She paused and held on to my arm. "Max . . . Could we take a detour to do something?"

I nodded, wondering what energy she could honestly have left. The energy in her eyes said this was important, and I found it hard to disagree when they looked at me that way.

A quick glance at my Map as she led me away from our most efficient path said that she was taking us closer to the coast. I doubted that a swim was on her mind, but we weren't going quite that far—in fact, as we entered a small clearing, she slowed to a stop.

The peak of a small hill of grass, illuminated by the light of the moons. Surrounded by trees that fell away enough to where the endless sea could be seen along the wide horizon. A beautiful place. I turned my gaze to her to see what she had planned.

"This is . . . I'm sorry if this is awkward. I just feel like it's the right time now." From her Inventory, she pulled out her sword.

I gave her a gentle nod and took a few steps backward, allowing her the full breadth of the stage. The weapon had a glow of its own. Even though she had looted it from the cove all the way back on the starter island, it hadn't seen much use, but I knew she held it close for good reason.

She withdrew it from the scabbard and pressed the point into the soft soil, pushing down until it was stable. With a step back, she then knelt before it.

"You carried me as long as you could, but now I will be free of your weight. Find your peace among the stars, Flynn. Without worry or the shackles that always held you back. You are free."

I watched in silence as she ran her thumb down the edge of the blade. Once a bead of blood formed on the end of the digit, she drew a red X on the hilt of the blade. The elf exhaled and shrugged off the tension from her shoulders before standing and turning back to me. An awkwardness marred her expression, unsure of how to explain everything to me after the night we had just had.

"No need to say anything." I gave her a nod. "Sleep is calling out for us. Shall we?"

She smiled and as she held my hand; we departed the small shrine she had created.

Without stopping for romantic smooches, the way back seemed to take only a fraction of the time, and we soon found ourselves at the group of houses the Party were staying at. Half expecting them to be on fire or the bloodied bodies of our companions to be splayed about the area . . . I was cautiously optimistic in thinking everything looked normal. Still felt odd, however.

A switch with my dove and then I dropped a rope out of the window. Ren climbed up without issue, although the way she collapsed into my arms once through the opening signaled that she was more exhausted than she was letting on.

"Thank you," she said as she rose up. A brief kiss before she nuzzled into the side of my neck. "I'm not sure if that counts as a first date, but I had a great time."

"Me too." With one arm around her, my right hand came up to rub the back of her neck. "Just when I thought I couldn't love you any more than I already do, I am woefully incorrect."

"Life *is* surprising." She leaned back to look me in the face. "I was already committed to seeing this all through . . . but knowing what we could have in a more peaceful world . . . I would go to hell and back to have a place for our love to survive."

"Let's get some sleep." I kissed her forehead. "Tomorrow is a big step on that ladder."

Exhausted, with both our souls and hearts full, neither of us had an issue drifting off immediately. Well, at least I know I didn't. It was hard to tell if she had any issue when I was already asleep.

"Max?"

My brow furrowed and eyes burned at the glare of daylight streaming in through the window.

"Ren?"

That was new. The disembodied voice waking me up wasn't the elf for a change. I turned over in the bed to see her still in the deep throes of rest, mouth askew like she was dead to the world.

"I don't want to come in, in case you're indecent . . . Just let me know you're actually alive?"

My brain clicked around enough notches to clue me in to that being Tanya's voice on the other side of the door. Quite likely, the pair of us had overslept. Whatever dream I had been party to smudged the lines of our nighttime activities to the point where I had to question if they were real.

"We're alive. Be right there," I called out. "Start up breakfast?"

"Right you are." Her voice didn't sound too overjoyed that we were being lazy on *this* particular day.

My eyes went back down from the door to see that the bleary eyes of the elf were now glaring at me, her brow furrowed.

"I should kill you for waking me so early," she grumbled, not willing to move any more than the sentence required.

"If you do that, you'll never find someone who can rub your feet as well as I do."

She groaned and closed her eyes, although her face now relaxed. "Asshole. I *knew* falling in love with you was a mistake."

I smiled and brushed her messy hair behind her long ear. "Then I guess I'll just go and take these magic hands downstairs to eat breakfast without you."

"Max."

Her eyes were open once more, finally accepting that it was daytime. She squirmed around under the covers, fighting against the comfort she had settled into for the night.

"Yes, Ren?"

"We *could* die today . . . At least hold me close for another five minutes before we face the world."

I was already halfway to doing so before she could finish the line. It wasn't even a fear of losing each other or something ruining what we had. Death had always been on the plate . . . but we had taken a large bite of what could be our future. We loved the taste and craved more.

This time tomorrow, we'd either be lying together in a bed victorious or entwined and broken in a shallow grave.

The System wasn't prepared for what I would do to ensure it was the former.

CHAPTER EIGHT

No Nerves

Among aches and groans, Ren and I got dressed, finally leaving the warm comfort of the bed. Despite the conflict banging at the door today, I didn't feel apprehensive. Some manner of calm acceptance that we could die, or at least would earn ourselves a bloody nose or two, was all that filled my stomach. Which was probably why I felt hungry.

"You fall asleep immediately?" I asked while tying up the laces of my boots. Felt right to do things the proper, manual way. Added weight to our situation.

"No. Had some minor emotional turmoil I had to decompress. Yesterday was a lot of different feelings jumping up and down. Fine now though."

"As long as you're sure." No wonder she was back to her grumpy expression if she'd missed out on even more sleep than I had.

A couple of moments of silence, and then she was behind me. Her arms found their way into drawing me back into a hug from behind, her chin leaning against my shoulder. "*Dickbag.* Accept the trade request."

My eyes went up to view it. "No. Why are you giving me tokens *again*?"

"If you loved me, you'd accept."

"That's just manipulative."

"If you don't accept, I won't let go of you."

"You think you can threaten me with what I desire most?"

Warm air buffeted my face as she exhaled through her nose. "*Okay.* We both know the System loves kissing your ass, and for an important fight, we need that bullshit."

I hated that I partly agreed with her. Out of all of those in the Party, I had the potential to stand head and shoulders above the others. By now I had come to the conclusion that the System originally saw both of my souls as two individual Players. A Demon Summoner and a Combat Magician. Merged together, I had also doubled in effectiveness. Plus, with the Guardian boon . . .

"It's not entirely selfless," she continued, "as I have something I want you to get."

Her intention clear as day, I knew which ability was at the forefront of her mind. "Fine, but if we survive the day, then I will pay you them back, okay?"

"Acceptable." She gave the side of my head a brief kiss before moving away. Didn't even tell me her choice—that's how much she trusted that I knew her.

I received the six power tokens from last night, giving me a total of twelve to spend. First ten went to what she wanted. What we both deserved.

**[<Summon Demon> is now expert: You may now have
two active summoned demons]**

My eyes went over to Ren to see that she was waiting eagerly with more life now in her bright-blue eyes.

"You wanted me to upgrade my cannon, right?" I asked, unable to keep a poker face steady as her brow darkened her expression.

Before she had the chance to threaten violence upon me, two of my demonic canines yipped and jumped up at her from behind, wagging their tails, eager for her attention. The elf immediately melted, dropping to her knees to snuggle and rub their flaming fur. A bright smile illuminated her face, erasing whatever lingering weight she carried forward from our previous day.

"We'd best get downstairs before they decide to save the world without us." As much as it pained me to take her away from something that made her so clearly happy, we couldn't put too much of a heavy cart before the horses, lest we go nowhere.

With a pout, she agreed. Hellhounds++ went into their magic portals back to hell, and we left the room to find where the rest of the Party was. Roger had vanished at some point in the early evening, but with his card now back to normal, the most likely explanation was that the System had corrected the error we had enacted. Seemingly without punishment—which was nice.

Out of the quaint house, the others were grouped around a grill on a patch of gravel. Unsurprisingly, they leveled some valid glares toward the pair of us. Half of me wanted to use my fake-death Ability to trip down the short steps and burst into pieces for the humor of it . . . but accidentally giving them trauma right before our battle would probably earn me more than some pointed ire.

"I was half expecting you to use your fake-death Ability to break the ice," Tanya said, lifting a plate with my cooked breakfast piled upon it.

"I'd *never* do that," I managed to say with a straight face. With a sweep of my arm, I dropped my chair out. A wry grin went up at the side of my mouth as I watched Ren mirror the action, adding her own flare to the process.

Quinn had all but forgotten why he was mad at us, but Wolf was statuesque in his admonishment. I knew why, and it wasn't because we had slept in. Back before we'd fought Hadrian, I had made the bear a promise that I'd never leave him behind. He hadn't been party to our late-night adventure, and out of all of them, he was most likely to know that we had run off.

Something to make up to him when I could without letting the other two know what I had been doing instead of sleeping.

"Glazing over whatever reason you look like shit this morning," Tanya began, her fork pointed toward us in silent accusation. "We're definitely doing this in the daytime, right?"

I wrinkled my face and looked up at the sky. It was becoming overcast, with the threat of gloomier clouds that were . . . Yes, the wind was bringing them our way. Couldn't argue with narrative ambience. "Likelihood of leveling up today?"

Attacking at night had its pros and cons. Trouble was, I figured that the undead could probably see well enough in the darkness. No point jumping into the cauldron.

"Getting to fourteen . . ." She sighed and rubbed at the bridge of her nose, as if she hadn't already thought about the answer a dozen times. "Thing is, most of the decent Quests are in Crimson territory now. We're talking . . . two days at a brisk pace, a week to get to fifteen."

I shook my head. No time then. We might be able to spare a day or two before going for the Lady, but we had to strike while the iron was hot and her groups were retreating or without blood. Fourteen might only grant me something marginally useful, and the time wasted would be a detriment to our efforts. It had to be *now*. I could feel it in my bones.

Mostly my right forearm bone, which was slightly concerning.

We fell into a silence as we ate our scrambled eggs and ham. Drank coffee, which seemed to work wonders on both my and Ren's spirits. I still had two power tokens burning a hole in my pocket. Too many options to choose from— even saving them might be sensible . . . but no, I would spend them and claw at any possible bonus for what lay ahead.

First one went into <Shuffle>. Now, instead of it being a simple cast, I could affix it like a curse to a single target. Every five seconds, it would change one random debuff to another random one. This made it much more useful in combat, I felt. The previous downside was the per-target cooldown; now I could at least labor one enemy with potential death on a consistent basis.

Next went into . . . <Last Act>. Not just because of how amusing the Ability was—although, that *did* play a part in my decision. Instead of having an hour's cooldown per use, it now regenerated a charge every time I lost 20 percent of my max Health. My *Max Health.* Not that I was keen to inflict injury on myself just to feign my death, but with <Bloodletting> and the other bullshit I got up to, it made it a handy defensive skill.

My eyes left my menus to see that Tanya was watching me. I wondered if I had perhaps missed a conversation, as Tanya's expression sank, and she revealed the reason for the look.

"I keep expecting you to use the Skill."

"Oh." I tilted my head to the side. "We've just eaten, so it would be unfair. Plus, I'm sure you'll get the chance to see me beaten up against the Crimson Shadow." I caught the glare of Ren in my peripheral—not appreciating my pessimism. "Ren will get beaten up too." Oddly, this seemed to calm the elf.

Less so for our Fateweaver, who rolled her eyes. "I'd prefer it if this wasn't a proverbial bookend on the bloodied shelf of our exploits."

"You'll have to give us more incentive than poetic grumblings," Ren complained, sinking into her chair as the coffee seemed to be wearing off already.

"If you all live, then I know of a vendor that sells sweet cakes."

We both sat up to the edge of our chairs, a Pavlovian response. "You've been holding out on us?" Ren questioned.

The Fateweaver shrugged, a smile on her face. "It's nowhere safe, and you're not the only ones with cards up your sleeves."

As the elf stood—as if she was about to go wring the information from the woman—a waterfall of cards dropped from both of her sleeves onto the loose gravel.

My eyebrows raised as I saw the Dazzle icons pop up on the rest of the Party. Perhaps the best part of the trick was that I had absolutely no hand in it. They weren't my mundane cards fastened to my belt, and I did not place inside or summon them from her sleeves. Entirely her own efforts.

"*Shit*," she said. "Can you pick those up for me, Max? I clearly didn't think that through."

With a nod, I smiled and leaned forward to get them within my reach. Before I could start to vacuum them up, she leaned her face down beside my ear—her wide smile visible only to me.

"I can see Dazzle icons," she whispered before turning and sitting back down.

I raised an eyebrow at her now stoic poker face. Well, as best as she was able to put on—probably good enough to give none of the others a second glance. I knew her better, however. Her eyes were practically on fire with excitement. She *could* see the Dazzle icons. Was that just because she had performed the trick, or would she be able to see mine too?

While my brain ticked around, my eyes met Wolf again, who had still maintained his death stare.

He had a point.

I stood with a sigh, the cards already now sucked up into my Inventory. "Before we proceed with the plan, there is something I need to tell you all. Last night, Ren and—"

"We know." Tanya rolled her eyes. "My proximity idol."

Quinn shook his head. "Your outfits stand out under the moonlight almost as much as in the day."

"*Oh*," I replied.

"The assumption was that you both just went off to screw somewhere romantic," the Fateweaver continued. "Given we might die today, that made sense. I fell asleep before you got back, but I'm hoping it wasn't actually something dangerous?"

My eyes went back to Ren, who looked like she didn't want to weigh in on this conversation at all. *Dangerous* was a rather subjective label to apply to any of what we got up to.

"I'm afraid it was something even more selfish," I eventually said. Mostly because Wolf wasn't convinced in the slightest. "We went to kill a bunch of Smugglers."

The fixer rubbed at his eye patch. "Doesn't sound especially romantic . . ."

Ren exhaled through her nose. "I'm sorry we didn't involve you all. With how much pressure we've been under lately, we needed a break to blow off some steam and catch up with some ghosts." She looked over at Quinn, who was readying up a question. "Not *literally*." He settled back down.

Tanya shrugged. "You're both adults. It's reckless and goes against what we're trying to keep together . . . but things are kinda fucked, and I don't hold a grudge against you for going up for air. Next time, *tell us* though."

"You did a show without us, didn't you?" The pointed question from Wolf made us both tense. "Familiar smells on you both."

The less I thought about that, the better. A quick bath before we went and died sounded all the more needed now. "Correct. I used my Domain, and Ren took part in the show."

"It was amazing," the elf blurted out before standing. "You'll love it when you all get to join in as well. Now I'm going to go wash."

I watched her leave and sat back down. Best keep a cool head and not share the event with her. Instead, I turned my thoughts to the day ahead and what it would be like when the full Party became entwined in my demonic Domain. Seemed inevitable but unthinkable. My musings were jostled away as the bear had come around to my chair.

"Forgiven, brother, but I am still sad about it. Do you not think I am worthy?"

"*Wolf.*" I gave him an exasperated grin. "It's nothing like that. After the teleport-scroll thing . . . I needed to show Ren that there was room for her on the stage, that I could accept her sharing the danger that I put myself through."

The bear grunted but gave a slow nod. "And the result?"

I removed my hat to rub at my hair in thought. Getting messy, still needed that cut. Even though Ren had agreed to be my protégé previously, she'd still mostly stuck to the script of her actual Class. The occasional bit of trickery here and there to whet my appetite but nothing too wild. Last night she not only partook in the show, but her fighting style was a lot more involved.

"It went well." I smiled. "Some new strength for the hardships ahead."

"Speaking of," Tanya interjected. "I had a question for you."

I gestured for her to continue as the bear gave up on being annoyed at me and laid down beside my chair.

"Can you summon Roger into the body left behind when you fake your death?"

An interesting question. In some ways, it was a corpse as far as the System saw it, albeit only a temporary one. Having a Roger that looked like me would be . . . exceptionally creepy, yet I couldn't deny there might be practical applications of such deception.

With a wide grin, I stood from my chair and rolled out my shoulders.

"Think of an amusing way to kill me and let's try it out."

CHAPTER NINE

Building Suspense

Dear Lady,

I appreciate your previous correspondence in relation to my Guardian powers. At this juncture, I will have to decline your mentorship—as I have had a better offer from the Eternal Wardens. Down here in the south, I am even farther from your desperate stench! Break? I'll allow you one if you need, but I have yet to even reach my peak. I do not gamble. I just win.

Yours insincerely,
Max the Magnificent

Tanya had a courier item, so we had sent off a polite message to Lady in Red before leaving our place of rest. I wasn't entirely sure she would take the bait, but trying to place us in the southwest might give us the element of surprise when we suddenly turned up at the necromancer's place in the center of the area.

We could use any help that we could get.

The gloom of our impending fight covered the sky from one side of the horizon to the other. Pensive and full of potential rain—yet staying dry at this juncture. Dark enough to dim the usual daylight that would illuminate our trail through a patch of woodland. Now shaded greens and muted browns lined our silent procession.

It turned out that *yes*—Roger could inhabit my fake corpse. Seeing my own body being used in this way was a lot more awkward than I had first imagined. Doubly so when Ren came out of the house and pulled a face.

Not to mention the act of dying hadn't hit the notes of amusement we were aiming for. Quinn still looked a little queasy, and I think Tanya regretted asking the question in the first place.

Still, another note taken. Something else I could use in my acts. The time taken for us all to get cleaned and prepared seemed to blur past, my mind rearranging thoughts and preparing tricks or possible scenarios taking up the majority of my brain power. Roger went away before my corpse expired, as I didn't want to find out what happened after the ten minutes just in case it was something the System didn't like.

Ren was calm as she walked beside me. More relaxed than I'd seen her possibly ever but focused solely on the task at hand. Which was—getting us to the site of the necromancer without issue.

I'd sent a quick message to Fiona to let her know what we were up to. Received some well-wishes from their group—they had faith in us. If anyone, it had to be us . . .

And it *would* be. The plan? Go and kill them all. Couldn't put it any more simply than that. Even with Tanya's previous knowledge, we didn't know exactly who would be there, how things were arranged, or what we'd have to face. Sometimes improv was just pushing the right dominoes into position, and I had a whole handful waiting to be placed.

We knew it to be a small trading post with a handful of buildings. What the Crimson had done to it in the absence of normal proceedings was anyone's guess. Another fortress seemed unlikely. Tanya had raised the point that a large undead army like we had seen would take up a lot of room. Any ramshackle structures built would more than likely be pens or ways in which to store and corral the raised zombies until they were needed. Probably a watchtower or similar, if they were smart.

They weren't. But we'd give them the benefit of the doubt so that we were prepared.

Ren had several throwing knives on her belt, alongside as many glass bottles of water as we could affix to her. I had plenty in my Inventory that I could hand over too—the power of her <Smite Shot> turning the liquid into something holy being a huge boon against the walking corpses. Despite her usual role being at the back of the group, she had made the decision to keep up with me and my bullshit.

There were still nerves within me about that prospect, but I gave her my blessing. We had proved we could work well together against the Smugglers—it was time we cut our teeth on something with higher stakes.

Wolf had the zombie-curse immunity idol and his show outfit on. He didn't really need more than that—and was content enough to know his role in proceedings. Getting stuck in and dismantling anything in his way. Any defensive Skill or potion we had available would be going toward his performance. After Tanya ran some numbers with him, she had called his defensive capabilities beyond her understanding. That meant *good*.

The Fateweaver and Quinn knew the supporting roles they had to play and would actually be staying as far away from the main stage as their Skills would allow. They weren't built to be the same kind of powerhouses as we the original trio were. While the magicians took the main stage, they'd give their support from the shadows, keeping safe behind the curtain as much as activities allowed.

As for me? Other than spending the last hour or so arranging my Inventory over and over, I also had three wands and scrolls loaded in the holders we seldom used. Ren was equally equipped, the majority of any such magical Equipment shared across between the two of us. Other than that, what else did I need? I'd practiced everything that I could have. My demons were primed. Every mote of strength I had available was spent and ready.

Ren nudged me. "What shall we do after we crush this, trickster?"

I raised an eyebrow at her and smiled. Amusingly enough, the cliché thought of celebrating at a tavern didn't fit exactly well with this adventuring Party. None of us drank alcohol, which made sense for most of us—although Quinn was a surprise. He said a misspent youth vomiting up the stuff had all but washed any desire to imbibe it further. Ren had never said why she avoided it, but I filled in the gaps with whatever I felt was acceptable.

"A day or two back at the cottage sounds like bliss," I replied.

"That was *my* pick as well." She stuck her tongue out at me before focusing back on our surroundings.

One day, that might be our continual state. No conflict or struggles. Just peace and the soft comfort of love and friendship between us. Shame that nugget of our future was buried beneath so much muck and bloodied corpses. Still, my shovel had been sharpened, and I was prepared to put in a good day's work to reach what we craved.

A quick glance at the Map, and we were getting closer. Several hours of trekking had gone by like nothing, our nerves and apprehension too shaky to have a firm grip on the passage of time. The sky had darkened further, yet no rain had fallen so far. Something else adding to the tension.

Wolf stopped ahead of us and waved his nose in the air. "Stench of death is strong."

"Already?" I brought up the Map again. We weren't even downwind.

"Stay alert," Tanya said, as if we hadn't already been. "With the Guardian's powers, it could mean Tyler has been able to raise another army already."

Something we'd planned for. Not that we wanted to—after last time. Without a demon there to goad my Power bar to its peak, I doubt I could woo the undead enough to get my Domain the traditional way. Knowing what we were getting into—and being on the attacking side—we had more confidence in going against a horde.

"Full disclosure," I mentioned. "My right arm has been feeling restless."

"Any pain?" Ren asked, concern across her brow.

I shook my head. "Just means we are getting closer." A little bit of stating the obvious that didn't quite hit on the dramatic level.

She pulled a face at the statement but then pointed a finger out at the scenery. "It's not just the smell of potential zombies."

The group stopped to look at what she was signaling. Just slightly ahead of us, some of the vegetation was withered and dried. No, it wasn't just that patch—but several areas in my vision seemed to be in some stage of decay.

"Rotting away at the very land," Quinn grumbled, his hand on the pouch holding his Class Keystone weapon.

"Disgusting," Wolf agreed.

Our hearts hardened to cutting the cancer of necromancy from the world, we pressed on.

"Scouts?" Ren whispered.

I narrowed my eyes through the foliage we were hidden behind. A small group of zombies, maybe half a dozen. Generally too simpleminded to provide early warnings in the traditional sense, that just prompted more questions. Did the necromancer have some sort of tie to them, like Tanya's proximity idol? Was this just to dissuade Players or Monsters from getting any closer?

They looked to me to make a decision—I could see it in their faces as I turned back to face them. A glance at the Map said we were pretty close. We had the time to spend circling around and avoiding this group . . . but if there were similar groups all the way around, then we'd have to bite the bullet eventually. Didn't matter how quickly we killed them if Tyler knew either way.

"I'll distract them over to the right. The rest of you go to the left and we'll leave them in the dust."

Some hesitation in their acceptance, but they did agree. I was gambling on the undead sending notification to the necromancer if they died—so if we kept them alive, then we might pass without a trace. Naturally, if I was wrong, then we'd just have to fight a little harder if we were expected. I had a feeling it was going to be a rough day either way.

On my lead, I emerged from the bushes and ran toward the group. Five pairs of yellow eyes turned toward me, and I flanked more to the right to draw their attention away.

The Party escaped to the left, scurrying past while I kept all eyes on me. It was only natural, of course. Walking backward, I tried to look past the undead to see when the others had gotten far enough out of range. Looked about—

Right foot caught on an errant tree root, causing me to stumble. Cliché, perhaps, and it didn't take the zombies long to capitalize on my error. It was only natural *for them*, of course. A hand grabbed at my arm, preventing me from falling over backward. Before I had a chance to thank the kind gentleman, a second zombie slammed into me.

I hit the ground, the air immediately knocked from my lungs as the decaying corpse landed atop me. Sharp teeth bit into my neck with unexpected strength, a burst of my warm blood soaking through my suit as I squirmed ineffectually against their weight.

From a dozen or so feet away, I used my invisibility to watch the undead eat my fake body for a couple of seconds before shivering and moving to catch the Party up. They weren't too far ahead, and I watched Wolf's eyes follow me before I dropped my invisibility.

"Should be okay," I murmured. "Unless it's *not.*"

As much as they disliked that statement, they were too focused on the bigger threat to be annoyed at me. Even as we continued, more of the land looked desiccated—dried, as if all life had been drained from it. I wasn't a gambling man, but . . . I should probably stop saying that.

I wasn't a *betting* man, but my assumption would be that the necromancer needed to draw on life power from his surroundings to summon his zombies. Made some more sense than having to find corpses the traditional way—especially with the amount he had first sent our way.

We headed slightly more to the west, hoping to find some higher ground that the Map seemed to promise. Getting eyes on the trading outpost without being spotted would be a boon. Even using my hell dove to switch into the air invisibly might draw attention since I couldn't also hide the demon.

It turned out that such thought was unnecessary.

At an outcropping of dead trees, we stopped and hid ourselves against the browned bushes. I could feel the tension as the group tried to take in our environment.

Finding the high ground was easy enough, as the area before us had become sunken into the terrain. It was as if we were at the edge of a very large dish or, rather, a pond. Gray, murky water swirled slowly around a central area.

Oh, it was not water—but milling zombies.

The central trading outpost had been reinforced with a circular wall of stone to keep the undead at bay. At least twice as many that had attacked us the other day.

Ren narrowed her glare, putting her hand over her eyes slowly to block out what little daylight came from the dark clouds above.

"More than one Party," she murmured. "Can't tell much, but more than five for certain."

Crowds of our hungry audience lay in wait, blocking the entrance to the main stage. There was no red carpet to allow us access to the venue where we could spar with our contemporaries.

We'd have to slog it though, elbow to elbow against the unwashed masses. It wouldn't take long before we were noticed and a plan against us would be raised. Still, we couldn't let a group of hecklers ruin the performance for everyone else.

I grinned and gave the group a nod.

Our biggest and most elaborate show started now.

CHAPTER TEN

Wave After Wave

The way my right arm was humming, I would be surprised if Tyler did not know I was getting close. Perhaps he hadn't received his boon with as much bodily trauma as I had and was none the wiser.

We would hope.

A clinical calmness had spread across me—and Ren too. Several hundred undead in the way of our true target might put off most Parties. There was no bowing out early now. Nonrefundable deposit—we had expected this to be the case.

Still, the elf and I did more than mush our hearts together. After our grand performance in front of the Smugglers, we had been buzzing with ideas and new things to try. *On the battlefield*. Bending the rules of what the System had allowed, we had a secret up our collective sleeves.

The best opener to any show yet put on.

Tanya handed me the spell-critical idol. Not directly useful for this first trick, but not everything was about me anymore. In front of me, I summoned my cannon and angled it out to the zombies ahead. Into my hand, my whole card deck, passed over to my protégé, waiting by my side.

The whisper of a word in Elfin and the whole pack bloomed with radiant light. Back to me and then I loaded it into the cannon. Things that shouldn't be possible but *were* . . . because I had been untethered from the strict rules of what was allowed. Ego let me consider myself the System's favored tool for fixing up the Lady's blight—and until I died, or it proved me wrong, I'd allow it to boost me to the stratosphere.

Bag of ball bearings loaded next, and then a sack of every nail and screw I had been able to ply and steal throughout my journey. I dropped my Health using <Bloodletting+> by 20 percent to gain back <Last Act> and hold two lightning-Imp++ cards in my hand without needing to jostle the loaded deck within my siege weapon.

Ren healed me back to full, and I gave Wolf a nod. As soon as the first blast went out, we'd be in trouble. Getting to the stone wall to assail the outpost was priority. Wolf would clear us a wide berth to our destination, and should it be unassailable through conventional means, then Quinn would blow a hole through it.

"We've been through a lot together," I said quietly, the hum of energy in my arm keeping me calm and collected. "Today is our darkest day, but through our strength, it can become our brightest. Have no mercy and stay alive. Kill. Protect one another. But most importantly . . ." I gave them a last glance as a smile crossed my lips. "Make a good show of it."

The cannon fired.

My deck of mundane cards split and sent the contents out in an ineffective arc, barely making it halfway to the milling horde. But . . . they weren't mundane at present—they had held the radiant charge just as we had hoped.

I held my left hand up, my eyes glowing bright purple.

"Be at peace once more."

The mundane cards bloomed into life as I took control of them. Boots drew me forward, and I was joined by the others. Cannon aimed higher in the air so as not to blast us in the back. Wolf thundered up beside my right, keeping pace, while Ren was close by my left.

As the first wave of cards struck the zombies, my cannon threw the two other payloads high into the air. Congealed blood and decaying flesh burst from the gathered dead as my cards swung through necks and skulls, destroying as many brains as I could. Once a card had dealt damage, it turned to ash. A dent in their forces but we had to get to the outpost as soon as possible.

The two cards I had been holding hit the ground as we met the first wave of the foes before us. With my two lightning Imps rising from the ground, I switched three of the mundane cards still in motion into my imbued magic versions. Purple light flickered in arcs through the zombies, who were only now starting to turn and see that a threat had arrived.

A swath of the enemy was then pelted by the metal shrapnel that had flown in a high arc. Scoring weak flesh and felling a couple but not doing a lot of damage. That was . . . until my two Imps brought to bear their critical spells—my first roll of the day and I had hit all sixes. I commanded it, and the wide arcs of crackling energy burst out, striking between the figures, occasionally twisting and bouncing off the small pieces of debris I had just peppered the area with.

I wasn't opposed to breaking the laws of physics, if the System didn't complain.

Another large group of the undead fell, their foul meat burned off or heads exploded from the powerful attack. My cards had gotten us 20 percent of the way in, and the Imps had just about worked another 20 percent.

Still far from the outpost, an army blocking our way. Figures could now be seen peering over the stone walls. We had only a short time before we'd be under ranged assault.

Now it was Ren's turn.

The elf grabbed her hat and spiraled it up high into the air. A moment later, she spun on her feet, sliding across the dry gravel now supping at the spent bodily fluids of the dead. Arrow drawn and out at her headwear. Struck it at an angle— around forty-five degrees, and a cloud tinged with golden light started to billow into shape. With her hand out, the first radiant beams sprung forth over our heads to land among the throng we were soon to chew through.

Scores fell as we continued our approach until she couldn't hold the spell any longer. Sixty percent toward the outpost.

A red beam illuminated me. The air rippling before I even heard the sound of the attack leveled my way. I was jostled to the side suddenly as Quinn pushed me out of the way. From the air, he plucked the projectile and was knocked back a dozen feet from the force. I could be mistaken, given that I was trying to do ten things at once . . . but it looked like a bullet.

The brace of pistols he wore didn't have that kind of range, so we must be dealing with something more modernized.

"Sniper fire," Tanya called out, helping the fixer back to his feet.

Not exactly *great*. We didn't really have the luxury of cover, or even the ability to zigzag. My Imps had been doing their best keeping the sides of the zombie corridor from closing in on us, but any attempt at slowing down to be safer would soon see us enveloped and drowned in zombies.

"Quinn, arm me." My feet slid to a stop so he could catch me up. This would be a risk, but if I could kill a couple of birds with one stone . . . I'd do so.

As soon as my hands were full, I looked back toward the battlements where four figures were standing. The red dot on one in dark clothing in the middle signaled the possible sniper—and I wasn't about to wait around to find out for sure.

"Distraction upward," I requested. My right eye twitched, and my forearm burned.

After plugging a zombie in the head with an arrow, Ren then twisted upward, firing off her ice arrow, burning light blue into the gloomy sky. That'd do.

A rush of air and I was atop the battlements. Finger pressed on the flintlock pistol blew straight through the female sniper's head. The skintight leather suit was a little impractical and cliché, but any further thoughts were drowned out by the flashes of light as different Skills and shields bloomed around me.

Something very sharp struck me through the chest before a giant mace came down and cracked my head open like an egg. I didn't have much chance to watch the proceedings, as <Demonic Transposition+> took me back to my Party—although I was a little behind now.

Too dangerous to stick around and solo the whole outpost. I *was* full to the brim with hubris, but . . . I started running as the walking corpses were cutting the path behind us off. Quinn turned, and I gave him the nod. This wasn't a solo show anymore.

His boomerang, now lying in the limp hand of my fake corpse, exploded. A wave of hot air washed through the area as the light briefly stunned all of those not expecting the fireworks. The figures were no longer on the battlements, and the dozen-foot-tall wall was now around four or five in a rounded section. Not quite perfect but something we could work with.

Wolf burst into a flickering red light—his turn at last. He collided with the zombies ahead of us like a bulldozer, the corpses burning and shredding away from his mere presence even before his wide paws turned them into broken messes.

I caught the group up. "Mage and a warrior with a large hammer. Didn't see the necromancer."

Tanya nodded. "They'll definitely be prepared now, probably bunkering up."

Although I agreed . . . something was telling me that wasn't right. What would I do in this situation? Well, my crowd work needed some finessing, but . . . Oh—that was it. My teeth clenched together. "Prepare for contact," I growled, bringing my magic cards up around us to slash through the press of bodies.

"What?" The Fateweaver scanned her eyes around the horde before looking back toward the outpost. "*Oh*, the assholes."

Simple really. Just as my demons were our allies, the undead were theirs. In theory, that meant they didn't need to worry about being attacked by the horde. Which could only lead to . . .

I watched as a mountain of a man with a long white beard hopped down from the battlements. A giant hammer in his hands, the head of which was about as large as Quinn. Part of his white-and-blue-striped shirt was burned and charred, but any damage from the explosion looked to have been healed up.

Ren immediately fired an <Entangling Shot> off at him. A flare of a gray shield and the attack deflected away into a group of zombies. From the battlements, two other figures. The mage in red robes that I had noticed, now without one of their arms, and another who was possibly a caster—in similar battle garb as Tanya was. Either I had killed another that I hadn't seen, or . . .

Much more likely was there was a rogue Class somewhere. Imps away, I brought out two Hellhounds. Told one to protect Ren, while the other would follow me.

With a growl, I gripped at my right wrist and pooled all my Mana and then my Health into a single card. With a flash, it was away. Darting past the bear, it then switched around at awkward angles on the way to the Party ahead. Burning straight through any zombie that was in the way, it eventually reached its target. I smiled as the gray shield went up again, and my card was weakened but darted to the mage. Another shield—this one in a shade of purple. My card ran out of energy, and I relinquished my grip, a heal from Ren washing through me.

The two figures dropped down from the battlements to follow the large man.

And then a third joined them. Purple eyes glowed with fury as the body of the sniper suddenly tried to choke their healer out using the length of the rifle.

A simple trick where I hid Roger's card alongside the brighter attack one. From this distance, I could see the crimson handprints on their heads. Wolf was about ten seconds from being in melee range of the hammer guy.

The clouds finally gave up, and rain fell from the sky. Obscuring our vision and beating the smell of rotten flesh into the air. But as I watched the mage move over to help the struggling healer out, I couldn't help but smile.

And as four further figures stepped up atop the broken battlements, I almost burst out laughing.

There he was. Green energy whipped around him as his cloak billowed from the power circling the long staff he held.

My right arm clenched, and purple electricity started to spark around me, small bursts of energy blowing dust away from where I stood.

"Showtime," I whispered.

CHAPTER ELEVEN

Churn

Wind whipped around us as the rain pelted down. Any more of a storm and I would have admired the horror movie the world was trying to push us toward. No such joy for either of us, as I wasn't about to let a little inclement weather ruin the greatest show.

Tyler raised a hand up, and we tensed, ready, still following behind Wolf as he closed in on their hammer fighter. For a brief second, everything went quiet, as if the sound had been drained from the area. My ears popped, and the low vibration of his cast Skill thundered through the ground.

The dried dirt eagerly soaking up the provided downfall started to shift and squirm beneath my footing. We slid to a halt as fingers and arms burst out from the ground, soon followed by the rotting heads of the undead. Wolf reared up and stomped down on a handful. My cards spun around on our left, dismembering limbs. Ren and Quinn took down more on the right.

"Stay near Wolf," Tanya called. He had the protection idol that would allow us to be immune to zombification. As we gathered closer, she waved away the spell-critical one I had held to replace it with a similar one to what the bear had.

<Card Fan> went up to deflect the swipe of two sneaking up on me, right before my cards severed their necks. I bowed, and Ren rolled over my back to lob a glowing bottle of water at the gathering horde. It burst and melted where it struck them. My cannon dropped and landed on a couple more. Two shots of confetti to wash through the throng like a tidal wave of Dazzle icons. So many.

They were making this too easy—as soon as the fighter got in range, I would just pop <Finale+> and stun him for Wolf. All of these zombies around us would also—

A wave of energy washed through us, and a blue light blinded me as I was sent tumbling back. I collided with the press of decaying bodies, my magic cards darting around me wildly to prevent any hungry mouths from picking me off in my disoriented state.

I made it back to my feet with little issue, barely removing a pair of outreaching hands before turning back to my group. Although, now I couldn't see them. Thunder struck ahead where the hammer-wielding fighter was engaged with Wolf, but between them, the other three of my Party, and my current position . . . The horde had filled that space in no time at all.

Finger outstretched, I put the upgraded <Shuffle> on the large man, hoping to assist the bear with some random luck.

Before I could start cutting my way toward Ren and the others, there was a sharp movement behind me. Too quick to be a zombie.

The pain of something long and pointed pierced through my suit fabric, breaking skin, scratching at the back of my ribs as it went past and into my lungs. Burning sensation. Blood where there should be air. Some manner of poison. My body felt slack, and I slumped down into the rain-slick mud.

"I know you've got a fake-corpse Skill, asshole," the roguish character sneered as his cold eyes darted around the roving throng to find me.

He realized too late that I hadn't used it. From my place on the ground, a burst of three empowered cards launched toward him. Whatever dodge or Damage reduction he had had only done half the job, and the purple lines sliced through his jaw, opening up his cheek and one eye and removing an ear. Stumbling, he stayed upright as his flesh began to regenerate.

An arrow then struck him through the other eye, a second through his throat.

Beside me, Ren rolled through a pair of zombies, a burst of holy water melting them as she gave me a heal.

"No sleeping on the job," she said, too focused to pair it with a smile.

I nodded and stood, hitting the corpse with Roger's card now that he was outnumbered back at the outpost.

"What, no smart comment to make? You'll have me worried." She turned to place a <Smite Shot> through the skull of a zombie.

Something about hitting the ground had knocked some of the bravado from me. Plus, it got my suit all muddy. With a sigh, and as a trio of cards encircled us, I took my jacket off and dropped it to the dirt. Roger stood to our side, and I held his mace in the air with my mind as I rolled my sleeves up.

There it was.

My right arm was . . . aflame. Purple energy lapped and swirled around it in a way that reminded me of my Hellhounds.

No time for further ruminating over it. We needed to make sure Quinn and Tanya were doing fine. Incorrect, Max. I shook my head out—the stage needed me. I couldn't hide in the back. They were depending on us to blow minds.

"Roger, go protect Quinn and Tanya as you would me."

"Yes, boss!" He gave me a nod, his purple ears flopping over his face as he ran.

"Sure they'll be okay?"

I turned my eyes back to Ren. The rain had dampened her suit but not her spirit. She was fired up and ready for this. Too many zombies though. We'd tire soon enough, no matter how much anger or justice we felt in our hearts.

"No. I'm not sure if I'll be okay yet." I gave her a soft smile, my cards illuminating the area as I protected us from the crush of the unending horde. "But now is our time to shine."

"Twice as bright, even if we burn out." She nodded.

Wolf had done us the favor of being my opener, but it wasn't fair for him to be under the limelight alone. My feet dug into the softening ground as I gathered my cards up. Purple energy illuminated my eyes as I burst forth, cards flickering like an omnidirectional saw. Breaking down the undead into piecemeal sections as I thundered to our companion.

Over my shoulder, Ren fired an arrow. The one that increased the chances of debuffs. Surprisingly, it struck the fighter in the side. From what I could see at this distance, he already had a slow on him, Dazzle icons, and a bleed. Oh, the bleed vanished. He was being supported and having the debuffs removed—annoying.

Two of my cards switched to my summoned demons, bringing up two of my new Shades behind him. I snapped my fingers and hit him with <Shatter>, turning his handful of Dazzle icons into a slew of different debuffs. Ren's arrow seemed to have the effect of doubling the amount of stacks he had—and now there were almost ten different maladies attached to him with the addition of the Shade attacks. Too many for his healer to remove in good time.

A bloom briefly blinded me as a white spherical shield illuminated him, the debuffs now ticking down and falling away without affecting him. I slid to a stop, now only fifteen feet away, and gritted my teeth together.

Hand gripped my wrist, and I burned everything away into a single card. The air screamed as it moved through the short distance, the shield flaring even brighter as I struggled to push through it.

"Not happening, little man," he boomed, a circle of energy in the shape of shields hovered around him, knocking the bear back as he tried to attack.

"*Wrong*," I seethed.

A wide blanket of dark fabric swirled around me, obscuring his sight. Something provided by Ren, who had been clearing zombies away from behind me. Standing still was a bad idea. When the cloth fell down, I was no longer there—yet my card persisted, trying to burn its way through his defenses.

It was just a game where I couldn't really lose. While they advanced under the cover of the horde of zombies, it also left them blinded.

He turned his head to try to spot me, perhaps noticing that neither of my Shades were behind him any longer. Relief probably would have washed over him had panic not taken center stage as his shield dropped down.

Over in the background, my two doves had swooped low through the disinterested army of corpses to rise up into the face of the healer holding the spell up. A little bit of a tired trick at this point, but what worked worked.

My empowered card entered his side at a low angle, and I twisted it up at a slant, cutting through his arm on the other side. His own defenses faltered, allowing Wolf to jump forward and bite through his arm. All the way through too—I was as surprised as I was dissociating. Which was a modest amount.

Card through his throat, and arrow in his head. Before I had even considered switching Roger over to him, a crackle of green energy flickered across the battlefield and struck the falling corpse.

Only, he was falling no more.

I gave Wolf a quick once-over. Not too unhealthy, the idol protecting him from the diseases the zombies held leaving them just weak attackers that barely made a dent in his powerful hide.

"Too easy," Ren murmured, bringing up a glowing <Smite Shot>.

The zombified fighter raised his hammer, only to receive her shot in the shoulder. Skin and muscle melted away, the arm dropped from the rest of the body. My cards made mincemeat of what remained of his head, spraying remnants of brain and skull around the area.

A heal washed through me, but my eyes were focused ahead. It looked as though the rest of the enemy Players had started to retreat?

Mania tried to take hold of my senses—I wanted to laugh. Running so soon? Couldn't stomach the show they had signed up for. Instead, my glowing eyes clocked Wolf as he swiped through a handful of corpses.

"We need to get to the outpost."

He turned and nodded. There was a dullness to his eyes, but he didn't seem to be slowing down. "Get behind me. I will clear the path."

Ren renewed her shield on him, and I stood and wavered. My right arm was pulsing with . . . power? It was like a heartbeat, or a marching tune, readying to meet an equal. I knew now the curse of killing a Guardian.

I had to destroy anyone else that had one. Needed to be the strongest. The best performer.

A shock wave of energy as Wolf powered up, and then he was off. I switched demons, two stone Imps, just to see what they did. Although . . . my attention was soon drawn away.

As the bear pulped through the zombies with ease, the necromancer paused at the precipice of the outpost wall. His companions now moving out of sight, he held up a hand.

Probably not just to wave goodbye . . . Although . . .

Green light flickered around him, and a corridor of zombies started to glow. Almost as if they were lit from within, like a lava lamp or a—

Naturally, the three of us were in the middle of this corridor.

As Wolf slid to a stop and our defensive abilities flared up, I was blinded and deafened.

The long row of zombies exploded, catching us off guard.

CHAPTER TWELVE

Blown Away

The ringing in my ears signaled that I probably hadn't died. As my blurred vision vibrated back into taking in the world, it was hard to tell how much of me had made it through the attack. Blood, rotten flesh, and thick mud covered my suit. Some of it was tattered now, my legs looking a little rougher than normal, but they took me to a stooped standing position.

Ahead of me was the elf, whom I could almost mistake for being dead if it weren't for her piercing blue eyes glaring at me. Just beside her was Wolf, who had tried to weather as much damage to protect her as he could. His head hung low and his breathing was haggard. They were both covered in gore.

None of us had found the capacity to talk yet. The explosion having knocked the air from our lungs just as it had rung about our senses in our heads. I turned on complaining legs to see the rest of our Party.

Roger had attempted the same self-sacrifice as the bear and for his efforts had completely died. Back to hell, with the empty corpse of the rogue lying inert and in several parts on the mushy ground. Tanya looked shell-shocked, a dent in her breastplate assisting the lack of breath we all felt.

Quinn was clutching at where his eye patch used to be, fresh blood seeping between his fingers.

"Good thing I'd already lost that eye," he murmured, his other arm hanging a little more limply than usual.

"Potion up," I told them. "Speed is of the essence." Their half-vacant nods were good enough for me.

So, I turned and stumbled over to the prone elf, who didn't appear keen to move from the layers of filth and rain soaking through her suit.

"Ren," I hissed. "*Ren.*"

"What is it?" She held a hand up, requesting my assistance.

With a grunt and a feeling like my arm was about to tear from the rest of my body, I lifted her up to shaky feet and put my arm around her. "Look." I gestured with a shaking arm toward the outpost. "Our red carpet is finally here."

The explosion had done a disservice to the horde of undead. Blood, bone, and decaying flesh now lined the corridor of the attack. A carpet of mulched corpses that the constant rain turned into a slurry of deep red and muted green.

"I'm too mad at them to be mad at you." She sighed and coughed up a bloody chunk. Might even belong to her. She put a heal through herself and then shuffled toward the bear as I drew a pair of health potions into my hands.

Still trembling, but it was not fear. Not even elation actually—my rocked brain unable to even be a bad narrator and paint my maladies as boons for the show. One potion. Two potions. All was right with . . . Well, I was mostly okay now.

"They still retreating? Would have been better to capitalize on our disarray." Tanya stepped up to us, stowing away a couple of empty bottles of her own.

I looked around at our group. If the necromancer had just led with that and then told his goons to pulp us, we'd probably be as good as dead. There were still zombies standing outside of the attack he had hit us with . . . but we'd clearly put a greater dent in them than he would have liked.

Possibly part of his Ability made it seem as though there were more than there truly were. Now just sparse groups wandered aimlessly, as if their connection to his will had been severed.

"Thinking they might have teleported, Max?" Quinn stretched out as Tanya wrapped a clean cloth over the side of his face where his eye was missing.

I held my right arm out. A fresh flicker of purple spiraled around it as a thrum of energy helped me focus. "No. He is still here. Probably feels as though we would win out at range."

Not that we were too shabby in melee either, with Wolf and my bullshit. For them to have such confidence though . . .

"Traps," I said. My eyes darted through the mashed bodies of the exploded zombies. "They were here to defend the area, so traps are likely."

"Magical then," Tanya said with a nod. "Anything physical would have been ruined by the explosion."

"Start preparing for that." I moved past her to walk over to the elf.

Wolf looked glum, but there was still energy in his eyes. Ren was more miserable than anything, standing against the bear with her arms folded against her chest. Outfit totally muddied, bloodied, and worse.

"Cheer up." I smiled. "We still live."

"No smiles until I get a hot bath." Her brow furrowed further as if to nail home the point.

"Not even if I got you a present?"

Her eyes were too tired to roll, so she just shuffled awkwardly. "Only if it was something to kill these assholes quicker so that I can get a hot bath. Or . . . sweet cakes."

I shrugged. We had been out of those for too long, unfortunately. "Let's say it's the first one." With my hand extended, my two hell birds hovered out from behind the bear, a long metal object barely carried between them.

Ren pulled a face and retrieved it. "This is the rifle that they were using. Oh, it's *legendary*!"

Almost a smile. "Do you have firearms in your world?"

She returned a half shrug. "Very rare and a lot more basic than this. I've seen a flintlock pistol before, and some kind of hunting rifle . . . but this is . . ."

"Allow me." Tanya stepped up and smiled. "Bolt-action sniper rifle. Unfamiliar with the make . . . but it functions the same as things I've used. Like your bow, you have to draw this bolt back, but then it goes back forward to chamber the bullet. Which . . . Small-capacity magazine. Looks like it replenishes like your quiver though—so no need to worry about reloading." The Fateweaver held the weapon up higher. "Got a scope up here with four, eight, and twelve times magnification. I'd keep it low since you're used to eyeballing ranges. Then click the trigger when you want to erase something."

Ren's mouth opened and closed a few times as the weapon was returned. "I don't know . . . Aren't I supposed to be more of a cliché?"

"Give it a go, elfin ranger princess." I smiled. "No pressure—save it for later if it's not something you like."

She shrugged and pushed away from the bear. While the idea of her using the weapon was amusing—and strangely attractive—she did also look rather awkward with it. Perhaps I shouldn't be pushing her to learn new things while we were between career-ending performances.

Pouting, she then worked the bolt, dropping to one knee and shouldering the stock. One eye narrowed, she glared down the scope toward a group of zombies farther off. A swirl of radiant light rotated along the barrel before she pulled the trigger.

A crack and blaze of golden light and the imbued bullet pierced through the head of the nearest zombie, followed by three more farther away.

Ren clicked her tongue and stood back up, racking the bolt to eject the spent casing. "Will take some getting used to."

I shook away the hearts from my eyes to see that the rest of the Party were equally impressed and apprehensive. My gaze focused back on the outpost. They were waiting for us, and it was burning me up that there wasn't an easy solution to getting rid of them. No higher ground anywhere for Ren to prop her new Skill up, or for me to spy from.

Decay had spread from this location and needed to be cut out so that the rest of the world could survive.

"Defenders have the advantage in a siege," I murmured. What use was a cannon other than to destroy the walls? Most of the building seemed like it was stone when I'd visited briefly, so pelting it with fire wouldn't do much. With a necromancer, flinging in something dead or decaying wouldn't move the needle. Time was . . .

We didn't *have* time. They might be hoping for reinforcements.

"They'll be expecting us to come through the hole we opened up." Ren tilted her head as she rested the sniper rifle across her shoulder.

I sighed and shivered slightly. Definitely the rain and not the sight of her with the high-powered weapon. She was right, of course. "I feel silly for saying it, but I almost prefer being ambushed."

"It is easier if the fish jump right into your boat." Her eyes narrowed at the outpost in case there was any movement.

"We had the advantage of stealth at the fort as well. Being inside the outpost would probably work in our favor, but there's no way of doing that undetected."

Ren clicked her tongue. "Really, trickster? Got no extra bullshit for us?"

The cogs whirred around in my head, and I smiled.

Two things surprised me. First, was my genius. Second was how high my hell doves could fly.

Assuming that the groups we were against had some form of invisibility detection and could pluck my birds from the air—the only other option was to out-range them. And indeed, as I switched places with the small demon, the wind sucked the air from my lungs in surprise.

The outpost sat below me, like a child's toy I could almost scoop up and crush with my hands. At least, if they weren't already full of something. With gravity willing me toward the hard earth below, I let go of my radiant payload and switched back to the safety of the mulched ground. The rain had lightened but not ceased, which should assist in our little ploy.

Our Party stood and watched as the bound sacks of flour tumbled down through the sky.

"Saw three, maybe four, in the courtyard. Defensive positions. Some kind of large hatch or underground area has been built."

Quinn shook his head. "A rat's nest that we will soon burn out."

Ren was propped up against the bear, using the sniper rifle's bipod to aim up at the falling object. I heard her exhale, and then she fired.

All three bags burst, dispensing the fine powder down above the outpost. One of them retained the radiant glow, intending to sprinkle as much of the area with holy energy as possible.

Bolt back and forth and she whispered a word in Elfin. Dark-green spots speckled along the black weapon before she fired again. I thought a brief apology to my flying demon. A burst of feathers and then a cloud grew from the struck bird. Green edges to the fluffy white.

We moved. A rain of caustic acid pattered down from the summoned magic as Ren held her hand out. I took the rifle from her so that she could draw mana potions and down them. Between the five of us, we had an overabundance of them, so she could cast the Skill for as long as she could stomach the magical liquid.

Tanya led beside Wolf, one of her idols able to prompt us if we came close to any set traps if they were created via spells. Quinn lagged behind with me, looking the roughest out of the five of us.

Blood ran from the elf's outstretched hand, soaking through her shredded sleeve. Well, she learned from the best—I couldn't fault her on that.

The enemy lying in wait would need to seek shelter from the constant barrage of acid that would scour away at every surface it could reach. The holy flour sanctified the ground, our hopes being that no undead could be raised from it.

A simple trick that easily turned the tables on who had the advantage. Now they wouldn't be able to accost us as we entered the outpost. We'd be ambushing *them*, and not even from the expected hole we had created.

For when I had been in the sky, I saw the lay of the place. It was important to know the stage well, and I now had an entrance planned that would be unparalleled.

My arm tingled, knowing that one of the Guardian's chosen would die very soon.

CHAPTER THIRTEEN

Without Flame

I wasn't sure why I was so happy. Despite the exhaustion knocking on the door, I felt electric. Perhaps it was the fact that I'd be stepping up onstage with a full Party soon enough, and after all we'd been through, this was our reward.

Below me, Ren ceased the cast of her acid cloud. I reached down, and our bloody hands slapped into each other so that I could help pull her up onto the makeshift ramp of the various furniture I had acquired over the journey. It wobbled under our combined weight, and the elf shuffled her body into mine.

Was enough of a distraction to have me forget about the hygiene issues of us mashing our self-inflicted wounds together.

"I can read that face, trickster." She smiled, leaning slightly away so that she could look up into my eyes. "There's a Passive that grants me proficiency in all ranged weaponry."

That explained that then. It had been an oddity that she had taken to using the firearm like it was no different to her bow. Appreciated and something I had yearned for an explanation for—now I had it.

"What *I* want to know though," she continued, pressing herself closer to me again. "Is why you find it so attractive? You like me handling this *long* object? Is it the power that I have to erase your enemies with a quick *flick* of my nimble finger?"

My tongue caught in my mouth briefly. "*Fucking hells*, Ren. After the show, okay?"

She pulled away and bit her lip, the smile on my face enough to let her know I wasn't deflecting her advances . . . but we did have a show to put on.

"Crowd is waiting then, trickster. I'll follow your lead."

My bravado knew no bounds, and I had chosen the most overt way to enter the outpost now that the suppressive fire from above had ceased. With a hop across a chair—and then a second—I was atop the stone wall, leaping immediately onto a wooden beam that I clambered up.

I had seen it from the sky. Wooden scaffolding for a house currently under construction.

A quick push and then I was at the flat roof. Basic wooden boards were my stage. Now I could see the damage that Ren had wreaked. Stone and wood throughout the area had scoured lines through them. A couple of small stalls had collapsed from the damage. If any vegetation had survived the decaying power of the necromancer, it had now been melted to mush.

Three figures remained in the outdoors, but there was a broken hatch leading into a dark tunnel in the center of the outpost, giving a hint to where the rest of the audience were hiding.

On stage left was another fighter type. Shield held with lines running down it—he had managed to escape most of the Damage. Stage right had the dying body of who knows what. They had not managed to get into any worthwhile cover, and their body was a mess of exposed muscle and bone. Center was a spellcaster, who was looking rather annoyed at me.

"Greetings and—" I paused as my feet burst into ice, pinning me to the thin wood. If I had a gold coin for every time this happened . . . but instead, I raised my hand up, two fingers aimed toward the mage like a gun.

He was charging up a spell in his hands. Looked like an ice bolt or similar.

"*Bang*," I said.

His head flung back, brains splattering against the drab building behind him. I blew my fingers as Ren faded out of invisibility, crouched down not too far from me.

"Didn't know you could do that," she murmured, working the bolt to eject the empty casing.

I held my left hand out, cracks in my skin oozing fresh blood. "I'm not supposed to." Purple eyes, aglow with the elation of the show, looked down at her. "But I do what I damn well please."

She shuddered. "Fucking hells, Max. After the show, okay?"

Any grin that graced my face was soon shaken away as the structure we were perched upon trembled and groaned. With expert dramatic timing, it became untethered from the wall behind us and slowly tipped toward the outpost center. The fighter had cut through some supports, clearly unimpressed with Ren's acquired weaponry.

The elf stood, taking my hand, and she twirled into my grasp as if we were in dance.

"Is it concerning that violence has become our love language?" she asked.

I shrugged and ran a finger down the side of her face to push some errant hair out of the way. "It doesn't matter, as long as we live."

The building tipped farther, obscuring us both in a cloud of wood and disturbed flour from the soaked ground. To the side, the fighter stood ready with his shield up and a spear pointing toward our landing place—waiting for the debris to settle to take a jab at us both.

Quite a large shield as well—clearly a defense-focused Player. A pair of growling hounds behind him caused him to turn to address the new threat. Rookie mistake.

The dust around us blew away with the rush of Ren's rifle firing. Into the back of his shoulder, piercing through the metal plate. His shield went lax in his grip, and I was already beside him. He lashed out with his spear, a billowing cloth appearing in front of me, taking the brunt as it skimmed my side. Jar of treacle smashed into his face, briefly blinding him.

<Shuffle> had him slowed. I stepped back away to mirror his movements—but while I did so without issue, he bumped up against the cold metal of my cannon with a clang. First blast buried a dagger into his lower back. He stepped forward, and Ren shot him again, the burst through his chest causing his hand to go up and clutch at the wound. Dropped to his knees. Cannon fired again, putting my Spear of Luck straight through the back of his head.

As he slumped over dead, confetti burst through the air, and I took a bow. In the background, my hounds were finishing off the Player on death's door.

"Fuck bows," Ren snorted. "This thing is *obscene.*"

The three other members of our Party clambered through the part of the wall previously destroyed. Wolf struggled a little but managed. Looked tired. We all did.

"Beats me how you both fell from a building and are okay." Quinn frowned at all the debris across the ground.

"I sprained my ankle actually," I stated. "Same one as back at those steps. It's agony . . . but in a way, *I like it.*"

He exchanged a glance with Tanya, the latter of which brought out a painkilling idol for me to sequester away.

"Actually, it's also the ground here. Can feel that the holy energy has seeped through." I shot a glance over toward my hounds and realized they were pacing uncomfortably now that they had finished the other Player off. I sent them back to hell with a quick apology.

"Nice when bullshit actually works, huh?" Ren looked around the outpost to ensure we weren't missing anything.

Ren may have consecrated the ground from further zombies rising up around us, but that didn't stop people hiding away in the buildings or those lurking below the earth.

Wolf sniffed at the air, and I joined him walking around to the hole that had been dug in the middle of the ground. An ugly blight to what must have been a very pleasant outpost at some point. Now everything was drab, as if Tyler had been erasing the very vibrancy and color from the area. The dark sky certainly didn't help, but at least the rain had all but stopped.

A shadowed pit a good fifteen feet wide that vanished into the unknown once the dim light of day failed to pierce through more than a dozen or so feet. More rounded at the peak and flatter on the bottom—which made sense for walking down it.

"Many smells. More death," the bear huffed and sat down to glare at the pit of definite danger.

"No way of knowing how extensive or deep the tunnel is," Tanya said as she came to join us. "Could try flushing them out, however."

Part of me just wanted to reach in to the necromancer and split his head in half like an orange. The other part wanted to do the same but on a grand stage, surrounded by my group. Still, the less of me that got maimed the better—it would certainly make the celebrations with Ren a lot less awkward if I remained in one piece.

I gestured for the Fateweaver to continue.

"I could make some gas idols, and you could use the cannon to fire a torch in after them." She tilted her head in thought. "That means taking away both your current idol and the anti-zombie one on Wolf."

Currently, I quite liked the amount my ankle didn't hurt—even if it still ached a little. If we went down there as a group, then there would probably be traps. I wasn't keen on being stuck underground. Didn't really have any bullshit for that unless every collapsed rock was small enough for my Inventory.

"They obviously have something important down there," I eventually said. "To avoid direct confrontation with us and allow most of their groups to be killed off . . . It can't be good. Likewise, he isn't likely to be hiding away in a corner, hoping we leave him alone."

"Entering the hole would be playing into his hands," Ren agreed, nodding as she ran a hand slowly up the sniper barrel.

For some reason, I lost my train of thought for a second, before I looked between the rest of the Party. All eyes on me. Waiting to see what I would determine the best course of action. The leader of the group—if only because my bullshit kept me alive despite all odds.

I held my right arm out. Still aflame with purple energy—the necromancer was still here. "Seems pretty simple actually." I smiled.

A few moments of silence passed between us before Quinn sighed. "Fill us in then, Max."

"Oh? Oh, yes." I shook away my roving thoughts and centered myself. "Simply put, we will do exactly what we came here to do—put on a great show."

Tanya nodded. "Pragmatic." She filled Quinn in on the exposition, as he still looked a little lost. "Either they have a way out of the hole, or they don't. We might as well wait them out and keep our advantage of being able to ambush."

"Precisely." I clicked my fingers. "Out here, we have the time to set up a stage. Prepare our performance on our own terms."

"And if it drags out and gets boring," Ren added, "we'll just collapse the tunnel and see what they do."

Wolf huffed. "Hopefully just die. I detest the undead."

We could only hope. I shared his current feeling on the walking corpses. Despite blunting the main force of the necromancer, I didn't feel like we had accomplished much. Our strikes had been powerful and decisive, the Crimson Shadow getting caught up in underestimating how overpowered our little group was.

They could have sent the sniper woman out to assassinate us, surely—but perhaps her stealth wasn't that great, or they thought she was more important standing around this cesspit. If there was one thing our enemies excelled at, it was making terrible decisions.

I started ordering everyone around. A little more assertive and controlling than usual—but this was the big piece, a bookend to our latest struggles. Victory wasn't just for our survival; it also painted all our turmoil with validity. It would be hard-won, I was sure. No one-tapping Tyler in the head with the rifle or watching him become pulp beneath Wolf's paws.

Something had been itching at the inside of my skull ever since we'd fought the living stagecoach. Our enemies had their own cards up their sleeves—bullshit of their own that only a few held tight to their chest. Tyler was one such individual, and all the roving corpses had been just distraction. Grass to hide the snake in.

Just as we all got into position, things hastily arranged and plans set—the hiss of said snake rolled through the area.

Yet instead of being a sharp tinny noise, it was a low grumbling. A thunder that shook the very cobblestone we stood upon.

The ground started to vibrate and shift as long cracks ran across the outpost.

As a wave of putrid death washed through the area, any cocky grin I tried to maintain faded away to cold disdain.

The necromancer sought to bring giants against me, not understanding that I was a titan that stood above all.

CHAPTER FOURTEEN

Big Brain

The human mind was a fascinating thing. Even now, standing atop a house and watching an impossibly giant zombie rise from the ground, I didn't feel any less sane. Maybe it was the gradual changes. A world that was similar to mine but with a video game slant. An elfin princess akin to classic pop culture. Talking bear. Demonic powers. Eldritch beings. War against a cult fighting for control over this world. Love.

Taken at face value, this was as horrifying as it got.

Even the head of this corpse was thirty or so feet tall. I could sense the rest of my Party was frozen in indecision. The sheer size. It was unbelievable in a way I thought was amusing. My disbelief had been suspended long ago, to a degree that I'd accept *anything*. Unflappable to a detrimental degree.

A smile across my lips as the face of the undead rose up to my level. Two large orbs of yellow bore down on me like twin moons. The stench of decay washed over me as a wide mouth opened—large enough to take a chunk from this house, let alone consume me.

As more of its body displaced cracked stone and thick dirt, steam ran from the gray-green skin of its torso. The sanctified ground burning at it but the Damage paling in total compared to the whole.

The reason for my grin was twofold.

I *knew* where the necromancer was. A simple matter of allowing the power surging my arm a place to want to be, like a divining rod. Inside the skull of the giant zombie. Piloting it like a macabre robotic suit, only made from a corpse way too large to be anything natural.

The second reason was another truth I somehow knew, as if being in close proximity to another Guardian enabled shared knowledge to be wedged into my mental bookshelf.

Whoever kills a Guardian receives their powers.

Not really here or there. I *was* killing him, whatever happened. If one of the Party got the powers, then it *might* be more efficient to divide up the powers—but if I lucked into them, then so be it.

[Max: Necro inside the skull.]

No sooner as I had sent the message than there was a burst of power as Ren shot the zombie with a radiant bullet. A handful of decaying flesh dropped down to splatter on the ruined outpost, and the eyes of the Monster turned to where she had shot from.

It wouldn't find her. An odd role for the pair—the elf had been sent to the outside walls of the outpost, riding atop Wolf. A last-minute change of plans once we saw what our audience would be. Given her shots had more downtime than when using a bow, she could fire and then they'd arc around the outpost, keeping to the blind spot of our biggest fan.

The large undead instead turned focus back to me, a giant hand swinging through the air intending to knock me into next week. I clapped my hands.

From a different rooftop, I watched the building I had been standing on burst into loose tiles and collapsing wooden supports. From within the wreckage, my demonic cannon fired, the angle now slightly off—but my Spear of Luck imbued with radiant energy slammed into the corpse.

Rather than take a disliking to the damage wreaked, the zombie instead burst into translucent black flame. An effect that gave it . . . incredible agility. Rather than the obscenely large corpse being lethargic, it had now become spritely—a fist now swinging down toward me as it twisted in place.

A trio of cards flung from me, twisting and gouging marks down the arm as it cratered down onto me. Cooldowns were *rather* unfair sometimes. My body was pulverized, shattering as it became sandwiched between giant fist and collection of obliterated wood.

My real body exited a nearby alleyway. Couldn't dazzle the Monster, which was unreasonable. Lucky for me, the presence had the same effect on my Power meter as demons seemed to—although at a slower rate; it was only a matter of time. No Dazzles, but there was a debuff from an idol Tanya had left among the rubble.

Hand out, I put the extended version of <Shuffle> on the zombie. A sniper shot blew another chunk of flesh from the head that was turning down to see me—Ren's debuff skill adding an icon.

A long leg extended out of the crater now opened up in the center of the outpost, the arm still within the smashed building helped push the Monster all the way to be standing up outside of the confines of the underground place it had . . . grown?

Easily two hundred feet tall now. My circling cards hacking away at a lower leg did nothing to move the needle. As his hand raised, he took a handful of loose tiles from the debris up with him.

My right eye twitched as the giant lashed around, sending the shards in a spray to clatter in an arc just beyond the walls. No doubt at my Party. I trusted that they were safe and had dealt with it in a suitable fashion. The crack of Ren's rifle told me that I was correct.

Atop one of the houses, two Imps began casting their fireballs. I drew the attention of the zombie by flickering my cards in front of his face. A large foot lashed out at me, drawing up loosed rocks from the ground. I spun away, my <Card Fan> preventing my bones from breaking but the force still sending me into a wall. Air knocked out of my lungs, I watched as a large fist drew back into the sky.

He froze in a figurative sense as my <Shuffle> switched to a literal stun. A brief thing that he recovered from in barely two seconds—but it gave me time to move. I darted down the alleyway, circling in between buildings to be out of sight. My mundane deck followed me around like a cloud, obscuring some of my movements.

The building I had just passed exploded, the massive foot of the zombie kicking the top floor and roof clear out of the outpost. I slid across slick cobblestone in time to see the twin fireballs strike the zombie, the twitch of pain followed up by a wide swing of his fist. I'd already sent them back to hell. Instead of Imp, the zombie caught a handful of lanterns next to a campfire Quinn had set up in the loft of the building.

As he drew back a hand now alight, a radiant sheen flooded over his body. Cannon fired, pelting the zombie with a sackful of pebbles I had gathered. Pulses of pain ran through the giant as chunks of rotten flesh burst away from the skeleton beneath. My cloud of cards zipped toward him, one of them burning bright red as I had hit the lucky critical.

Dipped my Health into it before it struck, regaining my charge of <Last Act+>. It exploded just as the rest of my basic cards turned to ash against the Monster. Ren's ability faded away to reveal we had shredded that leg almost completely. A rifle shot struck it, chipping the bone.

Any small celebration was short-lived, as the necromancer had clearly had enough of us. Hand slammed down into the ground, crushing the stables, and then he dragged it in an arc—the flaming fist destroying building after building in an attempt to completely level the place.

Health potion to my lips, I had maybe eight seconds before I'd be smashed on the warpath. I looked at my hands to see that they were now in white gloves. We were getting closer.

And speaking of . . .

A rush of air and I was standing on the head of the zombie. Footing was uncomfortably squishy beneath my boots. With narrowed eyes, I could see that Ren and Wolf were bloodied but still moving. If only we had Quinn's boomerang again, I could get through this thick skull. There didn't seem to be a handy hatch.

Some irony not missed in the fact that I had to break a skull to win. Should be a cinch.

Left arm out, I used the scroll of fire wall, followed by the scroll of air gust. The shimmering green waves of air fanned the flames to spread across the head, as I jettisoned anything flammable from my Inventory. Clothing, straw and hay, parts of wood—and a couple of lanterns.

Missed my chance to switch back with my hell bird, and I wasn't keen on finding out if <Last Act+> worked on fall Damage.

Actually, *yes I was.*

Just like much of my debris, I slid off the front of the raising zombie's head. A smile on my face as I dropped past his view. Scroll of water spray covering his dry eyes in fresh dampness—how kind of me.

With a whistle that rushed by my ear, a rifle shot struck the zombie in the eye—this one empowered with ice damage. Wet from my attack, they both froze solid. I fell and ran my mundane deck around me, a fool's errand—but it softened my fall enough to land on something soft.

"Back onstage, Max." Quinn placed me down on the ground, and with a nod, he left. Quite the catch, I'd have to admit.

"Imbecile," a loud voice rang out. "How are you this relentless?"

I grinned as purple arcs of electricity ran around my body. "Time is running out. Why don't you leave your toy and . . ." My mouth opened and closed, but few words came out.

Black dots flickered in my vision as I looked down and pulled the arrow from my neck. In the blurry distance, a group of figures. Reinforcements maybe? Or people who were in the hole? How rude.

I looked up to see the fist above me, increasing in size.

"Now perish!"

My body became pulp, and the real me walked away with another potion already halfway down my throat. Pretty sure that was one of *my* one-liners. Was I cliché? Well, more than usual? The added Players were a complication to the plan . . . yet also a boon. I tilted my head from side to side and then was gone.

Appeared outside the outer wall to find all four of my Party there.

"Tough crowd," Ren said, hopping down from the bear. Her shirt on the right side was split, and residual blood from a wound that had healed covered the area. Bruising on her head too.

"I've had worse." I shrugged and smiled. "Things are going to get dicey. More Players and the big guy isn't dropping."

"Plan?" Tanya asked.

"Why, we're going to put on a good show, of course." I looked up at the zombie, who was trying to use what remained of the fire to thaw out his eyes. "I *have* a plan, but I don't know if it's a good one."

Ren frowned. "It's not going off on your own and getting nearly killed, is it?"

"Oh, no." I shook my head. "I'll be taking you along with me."

Not really used to fighting titans of necromancy, they were all willing to give my plan a try. Worst that could happen is that we'd all die.

And so, as Tyler regained sight in his giant, and <Shuffle> gave him 5 percent less Intelligence for a bit, he turned to see us running across the open field where he had blown up all his corpses.

The bear with two figures atop and two flanking either side of him. He fancied his chances of catching us up—what with those long legs of his.

So, as Ren and I sat huddled up against a shadowed portion of the outside wall, we watched the corpse stomp past us. Our hastily constructed faux selves seemed to do the job, and Wolf did well not to jostle them off of his back.

Not long after we were well behind the giant, we heard the murmurs of talking and thuds of boots against stone. The interloping members of the audience who did not have tickets to the opening.

I grinned and gave Ren a nod.

"Let's dazzle the shit out of these motherfuckers," she whispered.

CHAPTER FIFTEEN

Breaking Rules

I could see why Crimson Shadow had tried to ambush us at every possibility now. There was a certain . . . excitement to it. Having the advantage while your target was unaware. Not exactly a trick—but something almost adjacent. While the giant zombie chased after Wolf et al., Ren and I were practically exploding to make ourselves known to the others.

It didn't take long before we got what we wanted.

Eager to catch up to the necromancer and have their share of the glory, seven figures dropped down from the wall in rough groups. Before they had a chance to set off, their focus was immediately grasped by the most attention-hungry of us all. *Moi.*

Standing proud and tall, I held my cape out to the side as if I were about to tussle with a raging bull. I drew the horned ire of their realization but acted before they had the chance. Amateurs, compared to yours truly.

"Abracadabra, assholes!" I said with a manic grin, swishing my cape away to reveal the most dazzling protégé a magician could ask for.

Her first trick bloomed from the end of a high-caliber sniper rifle. A solitary clap that blew the mind of one of the gathered audience. Their healer, no doubt. An efficient trick was the one that had the highest impact, and there could be no greater opener than hobbling their survivability.

Cape went over in a swirl to obscure Ren. <Card Fan+> up to deflect a leveled ranged attack from the one who had almost killed me not a few minutes earlier. Couldn't rush a finisher like that—you had to earn it. As I completed the motion, I revealed that my cannon had replaced the elf.

A jet of flame washed over the hell bird that I switched with, as I arrived behind the group within arm's reach. One of them had vanished. The second of my doves fluttered around the face of the caster, and I couldn't wash the grin from my sorry face.

I bathed myself in the turmoil. Supped at every increasing Dazzle icon as if each were a five-star review. I was a paragon. Unmatched. Destined to rise above all.

Yet, I wanted *more*.

Spear twirled in my hand as they clocked I was now in among them. Cannon fired off confetti. <Shuffle+> hit the man with the crossbow. He immediately dropped his weapon and clutched at his face, clawing at his eyes.

Or at the gray shapes these mannequins all had in lieu of detailed faces anyway. Sketchbook time. A wave of calm swirled through me as my demonic energy started following the script. Only a few lines to remember but plenty of choreography we had to get right. At least, unless I wanted to lose my head.

Ducked the swing of a large axe while my spear blocked the lunge of a sword. *Clang.* Chair out, I stepped upon it to level a head-height kick at one gray face. *Crunch.* Dropped back to the ground and rolled to avoid the axe kicking up sticky mud. Twirled the spear to create room, switching to a dagger that I threw before going back to the spear.

Mundane cards burst out from my belt and circled this little group of rough sketches that were trying to get the better of me. *Bang.*

I turned my head to see Ren atop the wall, currently fighting the rogue who had vanished. Blood on her side but she was now holding her own. Using the rifle to block the quick jabs of their daggers. Although I allowed her to be in danger, I would snap back at any heckler that dared interrupt her work.

Curtain flashed up around me as my cannon fired empty again, and I was gone. Invisibly, I ran over to the wall. Ren dropped to her stomach and rolled away from the rogue, holding her rifle flat between both hands. With the boost from a handy chair, I grabbed onto it, and she assisted me in coming up to meet her assailant. Couldn't see me but could sense my presence. Bound in blood and love.

Invisibility dropped as I spun up three magical cards in front of me. His lunge stopped so that he didn't lose the arm in my meat grinder. Still, he fancied his chances.

"Got the attention of the big guy again," Ren notified me.

We'd have to wrap this up then. Power meter was almost full. We had some bullshit to do and a day to win.

Cards spun out in front of each other, hovering in the air in a vertical column. I gripped at the empty air below them as if they were a sword and made to swipe at the fuzzy shape of the rogue. No surprise that Ren was still in full sparkling definition while my enemies had been reduced to drab props.

Sparks rang out as my faux weapon clashed with his. Off in the distance, my two ice Imps started to pelt the giant zombie with their slowing ice attacks. And what of the spellcaster I had been harassing with my bird? The crack of glass, whispered Elfin word, then blast of the rifle behind me was a tale that I didn't need to view to understand.

The second crack of a whip circling around my midsection was something of an unknown. I gave the rogue a brief shrug before I was yanked from the top of the wall. Ren followed me down, landing into an expert roll across the mulched earth, while I just landed on my back and lost the air from my lungs.

She continued her acrobatics by standing and following through into striking my assailant with the butt of her rifle. Ha, *butt*. In trying to regain my composure, I found that there was a familiar warmth running down the side of my head. Old habits died hard, but my skull was—

Thoughts vanished as the cloaked mannequin representing the rogue jumped down from the wall, intending to land on me with both daggers entering my soft and ever-tiring form. I blinked once, and every spear or pointed weapon appeared around me, standing proud and pointing to the sky.

Normally something that would slide away or be knocked from position by any weight put upon it. The damp mud did him a disservice. Impaled, sprays of gray zigzagged down upon me.

A blast then knocked everything over, like we were bowling but chose the wrong end of the alley to stand at. It loosened up the lasso to the point I could roll away free and gather up some air into my body. *Loved* that stuff. Ren was slightly bloodied but had used the confusion to roll atop my restrainer, pushing the rifle against their throat like a bar.

<Card Fan+> went up in front of her to deflect a thrown attack. Jaw clenched together at the attempted interruption, I brought up my own crossbow. Fired, turned, dropped. Another raised and fired. Flipped it into the air and it switched to a loaded one. Caught it and fired.

Thud and a groan. I turned my eyes to the side to see that Ren's mannequin had turned the tables. Given her a bloody nose with a headbutt and was trying to choke her out with her own weapon.

I was there before I had the chance to think, as if I had turned into a streak of purple lightning. Empowered card circled him, cutting through his throat before he had the chance to even address me. Strength left him as shock overrode his bloodlust. Ren headbutted him back, and I pushed him off with a kick.

She seemed lightheaded. One hand to help her up, the other with a health potion in hand.

"Keep it. You'll need it more." Her unfocused eyes went past me. "Shit, dodge—"

No, I was too slow. We both received the wide swing of the great axe. Something empowered—probably one of the Player's key Skills. Thankfully, I took the brunt of the damage—unintentionally, of course, but I'd fool myself into thinking I saved her on purpose.

Right leg severed straight from my body. The deep gouge split through muscle and broke through most of the ribs on my back—almost severing my spine. Due to Ren's positioning, she took a deep cut to one thigh and a second over the shoulder. Mostly force damage from the aftereffects of the Skill as she was flung across the ground.

The cannon fired its final blast of confetti, covering my failing body with as much fanfare as it deserved.

I played a quick game of hide the knife as he looked between my faux corpse and the elf loading up a bullet in her rifle. Turned out it *was* in his eye socket. <Shuffle> on the chap who had gouged his own eyes out. Sleep. I withdrew the Blade of Shadow, stepped over, and pushed it through the parts he needed to survive. A pool of gray soaked into the welcoming mud. A new home.

The shadow of our pursuer drew closer. Eyes ablaze, he had started summoning groups of zombies—too far out to be a threat but the intention was to catch us out eventually while he was literally punching down.

That just meant I needed to be on his level.

Back over at Ren, I helped her to her feet. Still unsteady. I brought her in for a brief kiss, soft despite the pain and viscera that painted this picture. "I need you to go somewhere safe."

"Leaving me *again*, trickster?"

I smiled, my eyes glowing bright purple. "I need you alive for the finale, but I have to be the biggest asshole for a hot minute."

"All eyes on you." She smiled and gave me a nod.

I'd just have to trust that she could do that. My place was ready for me and would take only a moment to set up. A rush of air and it was done. Sent two cards out to the distance to refresh the Imps. Roger had come off cooldown, and now one of the recently slain enemies was running off to enjoy himself. Now I was up high—although not quite face level to my opponent.

Closed my eyes. Full power but this time it had to be different.

Activated my Domain and I was flooded by a warm feeling. Elation. There was no real audience, much to the chagrin of all involved. A Guardian, however . . . That was something worth impressing.

My hand raised, and I pinched my fingers together. One obnoxious over-the-top trick coming up. All I needed was the chance.

Sometimes magic broke the rules.

As the necromancer lumbered forward . . . I stood there, shaking, hand extended. Blood completely soaked through my white gloves. Arm running with the stuff actually—a pool had been steadily forming on the roof below me. We had intended for this to be a group show where we could all be on the stage . . . but I had stolen the limelight once more.

Couldn't have done it without them, of course. Even now, they slowed the advance of the titan zombie while fighting off the groups of summoned zombies. I could pick them out even from here. Seemed tired but they fought on. Each second they bought got me that much closer to my goal. Left hand brought another health potion up to my mouth as more blood dripped from my right hand. If anything, I'd like to thank Ren for the inspiration.

And I would, later, if I survived this.

My Domain was expanding, I could feel it. While not the usual purpose, I liked to think a true showman could turn any precipice into a stage. My position atop one of the few houses still standing was illuminated by lights in the sky. Two rows slowly alternating between purple and white light. Some of the broken parts of the building were now repaired by waxed wooden planks.

The outpost below even had a few dozen haphazardly placed chairs, as if any audience could stomach either the giant zombie or what I was about to do.

Glass clattered down to the ground as the fifth potion hit my lips. Or was it sixth? Tyler had just about reached the outpost now, despite the protestations of my security team. I'd hoped for a little longer, but you worked with what you had.

Every part of me ached. Blood started to run from my ears. My nose. Elbows and knees started to stiffen up. It was as if I was funneling my very soul away. Perhaps I was. I shuddered and downed another health potion. Considering how much I hated the taste, this was altogether a rather unpleasant experience.

Ren was safe, in prime position. I could feel it.

First foot over the outpost wall. Tyler had taken a modest amount of Damage. Would love to <Shuffle> that motherfucker but couldn't right now. Wouldn't need to after my first attack, as one of us would be dead.

Shadow washed over me as he blocked out what little light the overcast sky provided. My spotlight kept me illuminated, however. Another potion in my shaking hand and I dropped to my knees. Not enough strength to hold me up anymore.

I blinked away the blood from my eyes to see the cracks running down my arm. Crimson and purple intertwined. The harsh zaps of my arcing electricity actually hurting for the first time, as if my skin was now hypersensitive. Maybe it was, as what I thought was sweat running down my torso was just more blood. How much of the stuff did I have?

Yellow eyes bore down on me as two giant fists raised up in the air. "Valiant effort but otherwise useless. Do you have any last words for the Lady?"

I looked up at him and grinned widely, my whole body prickling and shaking.

"Yeah . . ." I chuckled, convulsing with pain. "Is this your card?"

CHAPTER SIXTEEN

Don't Stop Me Now

I was learning not to be as selfish as the nature of my vocation pushed me toward. Or at least, that was my excuse.

Kneeling atop a house alone in the midst of a ruined outpost, covered in my own blood and holding out my hand as if I could stop the literal titan standing in front of me . . . Well, it certainly looked as though I was hogging the limelight. A good trick always drew your attention away from where the real magic was happening.

Is this your card?

The words were so cliché and fitting but filled me to the brim with joy. Perhaps that was just the blood loss and mania. Above me, the necromancer in the skyscraper-sized zombie with fists raised high didn't seem to find it as amusing.

Before his attack came in, I went for the reveal. Blood-slick hand twisted and I raised it up to the dark sky. *Ta-da.*

From the ground of the outpost, a card of bright magical energy emerged. My Domain *allowed* the impossible. Required it. The amount of Health I had drawn away while repeatedly downing potions furthered the stretching of what I was granted by the System.

It was . . . beautiful.

Vertically, it rose. Splitting the rock and stone of the outpost. Perpendicular to me, it stretched out a good thirty feet along the top edge.

Tyler paused and tried to look down, but by then it was too late. The muscles in my right arm tensed and burned as I clenched my fist. Sent it to the sky.

The whole area became illuminated in purple light. My body shuddered, unable to control such unimaginable energy. Edge of the card hit the groin of the giant zombie as it tried to right itself to move.

A spray of gore and other bodily fluids rained down from the point of impact. My card increased in pace before shooting into the sky like a firework.

Rather than burst, it vanished with a thrum of energy that vibrated the air surrounding the whole outpost. My arm hung limp to my side, and I fought the urge to pass out.

Silence briefly and then a hideous ripping sound. The line of purple drawn straight up the center of the large undead started to separate the two halves. Muscle and sinew tearing from each other as it could no longer hold the weight of its ridiculous form. Like the grinding of two large stones, the skull split as well, immediately ejecting a slurry of decaying brains to join the near-liquified internal organs that were splashing across the outpost, filling the hole the zombie had emerged from. The stench was overwhelming, a hideous main course to follow the gut-wrenching starter the audible tones had served up.

Purple electricity swirled around my arm as a figure came into view. Although my vision was fading, I knew it to be Tyler.

Robes soaked through from the brain matter of his piloted corpse, all I could see was the anger on his face and desire to destroy me. But what could I do?

Two Imp cards beside me, as much as the cast pained my tired arm. Classic fire. Maybe because I couldn't stop shivering.

The necromancer was hovering in the air, some spell keeping him afloat. He shouted something at me, but it just sounded like murmuring. To prevent my Imps from doing any damage, an arc of green energy went across his front, almost like a curtain—briefly amusing. In his own hand, some foul bolt of eldritch energy or something started to power up.

He didn't know that I was still a distraction.

And *then* he did, when it was too late.

The crack of Ren's rifle met my ears, and a beam of radiant energy pulsed up from down below to core the necromancer in just the same way as his zombie suit had died. Brains burst from the top of his skull as his summoned titan still crashed down to the outpost gradually. His magic effects vanished into nothing, and his own inert body followed suit.

I had shared.

Tried to move myself nearer to the edge of the roof to try to spot the elf. Vertigo, as my struggling limbs instead took me overboard. The brief rush of air almost comforting on my pained body but also grated against my nerves. Of course, then I fulfilled destiny by introducing my skull to the cobblestone street.

I rolled away from the sight of my burst head and took a deep breath of air thick with the stench of death. Turns out that fall Damage did count for <Last Act+>. I broke the healing charm that I saved for a rainy day. It had rained today, so seemed like a good idea. At first it just made me feel worse, as my nerves kicked into overdrive and feeling returned via sharp prickles across my whole body.

It was enough to stand, although my head almost went for a round two against the ground. Instead, my throbbing eyes looked around for Ren.

Most of the outpost that wasn't dust and debris was cluttered with the spent body of the giant zombie. I had expected it to have faded away, but no such luck. In my peripheral, however, was something odd. Narrowed my eyes but was soon distracted by the radiant hair of the elf nearby instead.

Not *quite* so radiant as it was soaked through with zombie juice. She lay prone on the ground in a puddle of the stuff, scowling up at the sky while her rifle lay next to her injured leg. Collateral from the lateral clattering of the shattered aspirant. Oh, that was a weird one. Might be losing some marbles.

In agony, my feet shuffled across the dirtied stone ground until I was close enough to—very carefully—lean my head down. "Arise and shine, moonflower."

"Leave me be." She continued to glare past me, angered at the sky. "I heard a *whisper* in my head."

"Welcome to the shit show." I wavered and managed to drool blood onto the ground beside her. "Did say I'd share, didn't I? Got some danger and bullshit of your own."

"Guardian powers."

"Yeah."

Her eyes went to me, still a healthy amount of ire in them. "I'm not mad at you for it, but I'm also not *not* mad at you."

"I can live with that." Still wavering, I held a crimson-marred arm down to her. "How about this? I have something that will turn that frown upside down. Promise."

While at first she didn't seem swayed in the slightest, the addition of the promise broke through any defenses. A hand came up, and I struggled to right her. Almost ended up on the dirtied ground myself, but through miracle alone I stayed upright. She put one arm over my shoulders and used the butt of her rifle as a crutch.

"Same leg again," I noted.

She grumbled something, but I didn't catch it. Might have dried blood in my ears.

The pair of us shuffled away from the large corpse taking up most of the outpost, and I directed her toward one of the few buildings still standing and not awash with rotten bile. Trying not to tip us both to the ground, my muscles shook as I softly kicked the door open.

Ren's ire turned to a raised eyebrow as we moved ourselves over the threshold and up to the System-created woman standing there.

"She must have respawned already," I said. "Caught a glimpse of her through the window."

The elf groaned. "Fascinating, trickster. Thank you for dragging me here to tell me."

"No." I smiled. "Go a little closer."

A difficult task when we were the only things keeping each other up, but with a renewed scowl at me—she did as such. Eyes moved about randomly as she interfaced with the options presented to her.

I watched her face. Wanting to know what kind of power she had gained from killing the necromancer. Still worried for her safety, of course—I doubted anything could really erase that persistent emotion when we had the love and care for each other that we did . . . but I was confident this was better than me hogging both abilities. I was already too full of my own ego.

The annoyance washed away from her face to be replaced by neutral surprise. She turned away from the modestly dressed woman, and her eyes sparkled—almost unable to get her words out.

"*Trickster,*" she whispered, as though she had just pulled a fast one and didn't want anyone to know. "I just bought *four hundred* sweet cakes."

I leaned closer to her, attempting to push some of the grime-slick hair away from her face with my bloody hand. "*So did I.*"

She gasped, and we hugged, not wanting to get a taste of anything unsavory by being any more intimate.

But this was . . . This was *enough.*

We stared at the flickering flame of the campfire, as far from the outpost as our tired legs had been able to take us. Not far enough to avoid the smell. Wrapped in blankets, the five of us had been rather silent. Any elation from winning over the undead and setting the outpost free struggled to get through our damp and bloodied clothes. The trio who had run the necessary distraction looked rough around the edges, having fought through the emerging zombies after their jog. I had no idea where Roger had gotten to with all that had happened.

Despite our Health being topped up to full, Ren and I still looked at death's door. Color drained from our faces, clothing torn and matted to our bloodied and gore-drenched skin. We both needed baths . . . and possibly exorcisms. Still, existing and decompressing had taken precedence.

My right arm was still twitching and shivering, even with the warmth of the fire and blankets around me. Still had my skin attached, which was nice, but the muscle throughout my arm felt like I had chewed it up just like against the Siren.

I looked over at the elf and brought my menus up. No doubt about it, her name was now the same golden tone as my own. She hadn't mentioned any new bars or Abilities—but that could wait for later. She currently had a handful of sweet cakes at the ready, chewing on one slowly as her unfocused eyes glared at the campfire.

There was the feeling that the power gained from a Guardian depended on which Guardian it was and what kind of Class you were. A Siren in the mythological sense was a monster who lured you in with an attractive song—offering you something you desired.

Like fanfare bringing me out onto the grand stage.

To be the greatest magician up in the limelight to wow people to death—that's exactly what I had wanted since landing my soft skull in this world. Now I could bring that into reality, facilitated by my demonic power.

Without knowing *what* Tyler had killed, it was hard to pair his power to something that made sense. The ability to generate a crowd, along with the biggest fan possible. As a necromancer, creating zombies was his thing before the boost, so I didn't expect Ren to start summoning anything. Would it be something related to drawing a crowd together? Or was it about safety or proficiency?

My knack for painting everything in a showmanship shade did me a disservice. Not everything revolved around me and my predilection for being a show-off.

Ren caught my idle stare and moved her hands away as if I had been eyeing up her handful of baked goods. The indignant glare told me *I had my own*.

Trouble was, I didn't have the appetite right now.

Victorious, and without any losses on our side. Almost seemed too good to be true. Saved the outpost and got rid of one of the Lady's most important Players in the area. Now she'd have the decision to either bunker down to assail Candlekeep with the retreating groups hungry for her blood, or she would need to march away from the city to deal with us herself.

A cornered animal was often the most dangerous, but I also wasn't keen on having an army after me.

Tanya roused, blinking her eyes and shaking the fog from her mind. "What's next then?"

They turned to me for guidance, as if I wasn't just a simple man slowly losing his mind while craving both attention and violence. My tongue lagged in my mouth as I struggled to put into words the epilogue to round off the last hour of absolute horror.

"We'll go to the cottage again," I managed eventually. "Recover. Then we'll gather what allies we can and head to Candlekeep ourselves."

The trouble with wishing to put on the greatest ever show was that such a thing could only live in the future. Past performances were done and dusted, decaying away as soon as the curtain fell. There were always shinier accolades and larger crowds to be wooed, and it was what took me ever forward.

My career had yet to peak.

After it did? It was hard to imagine I'd retire, just as much as I doubted I could ever be content running smaller shows. Some part of me yearned to be stronger. More powerful. Completely full to the gills with bullshit. But what then?

I shook the thoughts away. "Let's get moving. Unfortunately, I promised Ren the first bath, but I'm happy to go last in return."

The elf nodded eagerly, flakes of pastry bouncing down her blanket like an avalanche, but she said nothing. Any worries I had about letting her join the cursed-by-higher-powers club were once again washed away at seeing the energy in her eyes.

With both of us acting in tandem, our enemies had no chance. A duet for the ages, she was no longer my protégé, but a true equal. A double act beyond compare.

The world was ours to dazzle.

CHAPTER SEVENTEEN

Show's Over, Folks

The travel back to the cottage was . . . tiring and drab. It would perhaps be amusing in hindsight because it mirrored our return to the fallen fort . . . but right now, I didn't have the heart for that. I'd assumed Ren and I had borne the brunt of the combat, but seeing how withdrawn and beaten the rest were, the zombie hordes had done a number on them that I was too stage blind to clock.

Not that they held any grudge about it. We knew diving in headfirst was a risky plan. If the Crimson had been *smarter* or *better*, then we'd be undead chow. But then . . . that was always the crux of it. We always played a better hand than our opponents. I shouldn't will them to be more competent when they were the aggressors.

And so, after defeating an almost unimaginable horror, we walked in near silence under dark skies. Not only the necromancer and his group but others as well. A large dent in the Lady's forces, I hoped.

Our travel back to our temporary home was uneventful, the System itself traumatized over what had happened. Each of us bore a little of that burden as well.

Even now, as we had settled in at the cottage, conversations were brief and muted. Content with a little safety and time to decompress. Needed it so that we didn't crack like thin pottery.

It was dark now, dusk arriving with a continued cover of gray clouds. No rain but it mirrored our moods in a narratively satisfying way. Campfire flickered with the slight breeze. Bright and warm.

Tanya had used all her idols to set up alarms around the entrance so we'd know in good time if we were followed. Was a shame I hadn't screwed things up over at the first zombie fight, otherwise we'd still have that teleportation scroll to return here after our outpost victory. The Fateweaver was now sitting on the floor up against Wolf, knitting.

The bear himself was fast asleep. We had cooked the heartiest stew imaginable, which he had thoroughly enjoyed—and was content enough to hit the rest button as soon as allowed. As much as he had been improving lately, I was slightly nervous about him getting worn out like this again anytime soon.

Quinn was also asleep. Somewhat unlike him, he'd retired early to the cottage. At first I'd tried to *casually* accuse him of getting bitten by a zombie and trying to hide it—but as we each proved that we were safe, that cliché had died. I would have been able to see the debuff icon anyway. Originally, he had only signed up for showing us around for a short period, but now he was knee-deep in the blood and filth. He'd come into his own though and cooled his temperament to fit in well. Especially with Tanya.

And Ren?

The elf was beside me on the swinging chair among the flowers. Not such a dreamy scene during the night but there was comfort in it. On her side with an arm around me. Awake but silent. Lips had been sealed; no information about her Guardian powers had come out just yet.

At first I wasn't sure if she was mad at me for getting her that without warning her first—or maybe just the day endured was enough to be grumpy about. After her bath, she seemed relaxed and content, so I didn't think any grudge was held. I went last, as promised, which was only brief torture. Once I hit that hot water though . . . I could have died. In a good way, for a change.

"I can hear your brain working overtime, trickster," she said softly.

"Lots of things to process."

Her hand ran up to feel around my jaw. "Huh. There *is* a little stubble growing. Miracles do happen."

I smiled and closed my eyes. Something about this place always made the horrors of the world seem like a bad dream. Things had been getting progressively weirder and more dire, and we had become more extreme and dangerous to combat it. Untethered from reality.

If I didn't know any better, my head injury at the start of all of this was just me going into a coma. A fevered dream where I saved the princess and fought impossibly ridiculous enemies to . . . save the world. Perhaps I shouldn't give that too much thought. System already slipped me enough untapped power under the table without it nodding along with my every manic thought.

"You doing okay though?" I eventually asked.

"Hmm. I'm slightly . . . Well, I feel awkward."

"Oh?" I opened an eye and turned to look at her.

She nodded. "I've always had a strong Class, but stumbling into all this unearned bullshit power is off-putting. Is this how you feel all the time?"

"It's what gives me an ego, at least." I smiled and put my fingers through her hair.

We were actually relaxing in casual clothes. After our outfits went away for repair, they stayed there. Comfortable and plain clothing that kept us warm enough out in the evening air. It felt right—like our performance had an actual *end* and we'd gone home to recuperate.

"I can't be like that." She pouted. "If I flaunt the fact that I have a *rifle* and Guardian powers, the System will come and kick my ass."

"No. I mean, I survive it. You did want to share the same fate."

"I still do." She smiled. "Thank you, by the way."

"For burdening you with greater powers?"

"Yeah. I mean, if you had taken it for yourself, I wouldn't have minded . . . You are still the strongest of us all, so it *would* have made sense. But . . . the fact that you shared the power with me means more than any ring or tangible gift could."

"Oh. I guess there's no point giving you this then." Into my hand I produced the ring I had stowed away since the campground.

"Max . . . Are you . . . ?"

I wrinkled up my face, realizing I'd perhaps stuck my feet in my mouth while my brain was still recovering. "It's not . . . a proposal, as such. Just something to say I love you and that my soul is bound to you."

"*Handsome dickbag,*" she cursed me. She extended her hand and allowed me to push it onto her ring finger. "Well, I'm going to wear it like an engagement ring and flaunt it at all the jealous bitches."

"Which ones are they?" I smiled as she admired the blue stone in the gift. It *was* her color.

"*All* of them." She smiled and leaned closer to give me a kiss as her freshly bedazzled hand cupped at the side of my head. "Oh." She moved away. "What's this behind your ear?"

The sparkle in her eyes told me it probably wasn't a dagger or a remote explosive device—although at this point, I was expecting anything. As her hand moved in front of my face, I saw that she held a similar ring that had a brief spiral of purple gemstone inlaid.

"My color." I grinned. "You've been holding on to this?"

She nodded. "Since the campground. Just a little symbol to say that I love you too."

I allowed her to push it onto my finger. Not only was I unsure if the System had anything like a marriage ceremony, but I doubted her elven traditions were anything like what I knew. Still, I was pretty sure our intentions were clear. Admiring the swirl of the purple, I couldn't wait to accidentally deglove my finger with it in battle.

"Now all that's left is for us to become King and Queen of this world." She grinned to herself and lay back down, nuzzling her face on my chest.

"Don't tempt me," I murmured. Once the Lady had been dealt with and the world presumably returned to normal, there'd be some questions they'd need to answer. Assuming I kept my uncontested power, perhaps I could be voted in. Or however they were chosen. I turned my head to the future Queen, who looked as though the warmth of our shared gifts was enough to set her off to sleep.

"Before we snooze," I prompted, "how about cluing me in to what you know about your Guardian powers?"

She hummed before propping herself up. "I'm still . . . learning to understand it. But I think you've earned a *little* something."

"I certainly have." I grinned, but apprehension danced around behind my eyes just in case she summoned a giant . . . Dire Boar? Or sprouted dozens of sniper rifles from her arms. Not sure where I got that one from.

"Hat, please."

From my Inventory I brought out my top hat and handed it to her. She placed it on my stomach and sat up properly beside it. Pushing the hair away from her face first, she cleared her throat and then turned to face me.

Her hands went together in front of her and then moved apart. In between them an object appeared as if she was summoning it from her Inventory as slowly as I could. A short black rod that had . . . white tips at the ends.

My heart skipped a beat as my tongue stuck in my mouth.

With a short twirl of her magic wand, she then tapped on the rim of my hat. Raised an eyebrow toward me. Her other hand then went in and withdrew . . . a white rabbit.

"What . . ." My mouth opened and closed in shock and awe. "*What?*"

Ren put the rabbit on her lap and gave it a stroke before shooting me a wink. "Looks like someone just graduated, huh?"

I stood at the window, staring out at the fresh dawn greeting the world. It was early—way too early to be up given what we were recovering from. Still, I found myself unable to rest and had woken before anyone else. Ren looked like a pointy eared angel, drooling on her pillow amid a mess of radiant hair.

With the events of the previous day, I had expected . . . something. Retaliation? Messages from the Lady or her ilk threatening us and pretending we didn't just dismember an important part of her forces?

We'd stolen a Guardian's power from her. Now we were even. The Lady herself and whoever could make the puppet clones. I was thankful they hadn't objected to us attacking the outpost again, but perhaps they knew when to cut their losses.

As for Ren's powers? It was hard to pin down the explanation without know-ing who the Guardian was. But she now met me in the middle in another way. Able to borrow some of my Skills, or at least something like that. It wasn't overtly described—just as mine hadn't been—so we were trying to make sense of it ourselves.

Mine was wish fulfillment, giving me what I desired. What I craved and hungered for. Hers was similar but had a different nuance to it. Without patting myself on the back too hard, I reckoned her Guardian was about boosting your growth to something closer to the end goal. Grabbing her inevitable power from the future to use now.

Tyler had been a necromancer and had become unparalleled in the act—able to summon armies and a titan. Ren's determination to be my equal and protégé in the field of magic gave her a taste of how much bullshit she'd also have one day. It was both humbling and exciting to see what she would truly be capable of.

A ping in my Chats diverted my attention away from pretending to look at the scenery. Eyes read over the text, my brow furrowing. I sighed deeply and closed my eyes. *Now* I felt tired.

"Everything okay, Max?"

I turned my eyes back to Sleeping Beauty and gave her a glum shrug. Would have been a blessing if I told her everything was fine and let her get back to sleep for a few hours. But no, we were ring bound now, and she had to suffer alongside me for eternity. I was pretty sure how that was how it worked.

"That was our friend down in the Eternal Wardens."

"Oh." She closed her eyes and tried to bury her face in the pillow. "They heard the news."

"It's not that." I turned back to the window, my fingers stretching and clasping in turn. Practiced motions for summoning my cards.

Couldn't have been something that simple.

"They are under attack from something they say is worse than the Lady and request our help."

CHAPTER EIGHTEEN

Next Leg

Magic came in many forms.

It wasn't always a fanciful illusion, an unexpected sleight of hand, nor even a mysterious power that defied expectation.

Sometimes it could just be *life*. A state of mind, really.

I stood outside the small cottage surrounded by steep rocky slopes and looked out to the woodland beyond the pathway out of this safe haven. Dew still clung to the verdant grass. Birdsong graced the shadowed canopy of the tree line ahead, where muted browns and a variety of greens painted the landscape. Rising above it was a deep-blue sky, clear of any clouds.

Such peace was a harsh juxtaposition to how our previous day was spent. In this way, it *was* magical.

But that wasn't the only thing . . .

"What are you thinking about, trickster?"

I turned my head and smiled at the elf. She had her radiant blonde hair tied up, the only piece of her pastel-blue magician's outfit missing being the hat that usually covered it. While fighting the titan zombie had been exhausting for us all, there was a renewed energy behind her piercing blue eyes.

"Mostly just glad to be alive, I suppose." I put my arm around her, and she leaned her head on my shoulder. "Didn't even break my head open this time. No trauma status for a change."

"Dickbag. I saw you fall from the roof and crack your head open. If it weren't for your feign-death skill, you'd have made me a widow already."

I snorted and adjusted my top hat, something near glued to me—it matched the sparkling purple suit perfectly, so it was only natural. Ren and I were neither married nor properly engaged, but a post-zombie-apocalypse exchange of rings had further officiated the next step in our relationship.

From behind us, the lumbering form of a giant grizzly bear squeezed his way out of the cottage and into the open.

"Morning, Wolf." I gestured over to the remnants of last night's campfire. "Want me to get breakfast started?"

He grinned and ran his tongue around his lips. "I could certainly eat. Some fruit would be nice, not just meat."

I gave him a bow and released my grasp of our ranger *slash* healer. Was difficult to stow her away into a normal Class designation now that we had procured a sniper rifle from one of our enemies. It helped that I—of all people—was an expert in suspending my disbelief, plus we knew for a fact that one of the worlds the System drew people from had higher tech than this baseline fantasy malarkey, but even so . . .

For some reason, a talking bear made more sense than a firearm. But, then again, that wasn't even the most interesting thing about her recent power spike either. She'd gained the ability to copy some of my Skills after killing the necromancer and absorbing his Guardian power. I was itching to see her in action since she was being coy about showing it off.

Hadn't even been a whole day and I was chewing at reality for a taste of another dire situation to fight our way through.

"Quinn wasn't on the couch . . ." Ren stepped over to help start the fire up again. *"Do you think . . . ?"*

"No." I furrowed my brow and looked back at the quiet cottage. "I mean, *maybe*. But . . ." Wouldn't judge it, if there was anything going on between them. I wanted them to both be happy.

Tanya had still been coming to terms with possibly being lost to her family on Earth forever, with no way to escape this world. Quinn had cooled his apparent need to woo anything with a heartbeat, and the pair had come to get along rather well.

"I think it would be good for them both, if true." Ren stood back up straight to look through her Inventory as the fire bloomed into life. "They kind of ground each other."

"Like we do?"

Wolf huffed an interjection. "More like the opposite." With a big stretch, he lay down beside the growing campfire. "Since meeting you both, you've become equally overt and dangerous."

I smiled and raised an eyebrow at the elf. "Is that so?"

The bear closed his eyes. "Not that it's a bad thing. Now that you have both sorted through your various dysfunctions, it should make the rest of our doomed adventure more bearable."

Ren rolled her eyes. "Enough with the gloom, Wolf. You don't want your stage outfit to become *mandatory*, do you?"

". . . No."

The cottage door opened up once more to reveal Quinn. In his usual garish yellow shirt with leather chest piece, his shoulder-length black hair had been tied up for a change. He covered his bearded mouth as he yawned and then took to rubbing at his eye patch as he made his way over to us.

I let Ren take over the breakfast preparations and stood to greet our fixer. "Morning, Quinn. How are you?"

"Not terrible, Max." He grimaced. "Some minor nightmares of grasping hands and baleful yellow eyes in the shadows . . . but I believe I am starting to get used to the constant terrors you drag us through."

"Perfect. I'll have to think up some worse things then." I smiled, but he didn't seem to appreciate the humor. "Tanya on the way?"

He shrugged, and his eye went up to his Inventory to find his chair. "Might still be sleeping. She was pretty exhausted last night after all the activities of the day."

I tried to ignore Ren giving me eyes in my peripheral. Clearly he just meant the whole killing a zombie horde and taking down a key member of Lady in Red's followers.

"Why do you ask? Keen to get us into the fray once more?"

"Not . . . exactly." I exhaled through my nose, but before I could give a vague answer, I was relieved to see the Fateweaver exit the cottage.

Tanya's hair was dark and loose, so it was worth assuming that she had just had a quick bath, which is why her exit was delayed. Why Quinn wouldn't have known that wasn't something I cared to question right now. In her somber clothing and metal breastplate, it seemed as though she knew that the day was unlikely to be one of rest.

With the Lady up near Candlekeep now on the back foot, there was a temptation to go full speed ahead and try to crush her once and for all . . . but ultimately it was too dangerous with how little we knew about her current capabilities. With all her gang—the Crimson Shadow—falling back to bolster her attempts to take over the city, we could be walking into an army.

So we'd have to start building our own. We'd made some oddball allies along the way . . . Not quite enough to call it a traveling circus, but soon we were to make more.

"Morning," she said, giving us all a nod. "Looks like you're raring to go get some experience and power tokens."

"Almost," I said and gestured for her to come sit. "I received a message earlier this morning."

"Oh?"

I let the suspense hang for a bit as we all got situated. Wolf kept one eye open while the rest of us sat in a rough circle by the low fire. Apprehension on their faces, which was warranted. After a day like yesterday, it would be nice to have a whole week off—but reality didn't often play by the narrative you desired.

"The lovely chap from the Eternal Wardens sent me a message," I began.

Tanya nodded. "Great. They heard we killed Tyler, so now we are 'allowed' to go meet with them and discuss this"—she waved a hand between Ren and me—"Guardian bullshit."

"*Not quite.*" I gave them a reassuring smile that was maybe 20 percent effective. "They're being attacked by something and would like us to come help."

"Something other than the Crimson Shadow?" Quinn put his hand up to his chin. "Surely it cannot be anywhere as vital or dangerous as them?"

All I could offer in response was a shrug. Normally I would have been more likely to tell the Wardens to kick rocks, and it served them right for snubbing us for so long. But we needed allies.

"They wouldn't even say what," Ren added. "Which makes me not want to care."

"Worries me a little." I looked out to the quiet woodlands and exhaled through my nose. "Something that isn't tied to the Lady or a Guardian but is enough trouble for one of the few Guilds in the area . . ."

I wasn't too keen on having to add a third Party to our drab, conflict-laden lives. After killing our way through the starter island and first area of Othea, we had allowed the System to bring in new Players that weren't troubled lunatics. Knocking through the ramshackle fort of the Crimson Shadow, we had found the second area just as steeped with those aligned to the Lady's cause.

Somehow survived ambushes, a kidnapping, attacks from Monsters and strange Players . . . and now were apparently heroes to some degree. An unlikely romance and a few newly settled friends, and this was us. Two magicians and a supporting cast, ready to take a grand show on the road to dazzle and destroy all that opposed us.

Ren must have clocked that my mind had started to wander, as she circled the wagons back around the crux of the matter—her personal thoughts aside. "We could use a few more fans though. The Wardens might not be the best audience, but it sounds like they're desperate for our show in particular."

"It's a detour," Tanya added. "You're making a name for yourselves, so it's really up to you where you choose to blaze a trail. The southwest does have a decent Dungeon, so we can get you up to fifteen, but I haven't completed it before. Have you, Quinn?"

He shook his head. "I've heard it's quite the challenge, but the rewards are worth the effort spent. Should we be successful, of course."

"And we *will* be." I gave them a grin. How could we not? Ren and I were now a pair of the most powerful people—certainly for the quarantined section of the world we were forced to live in. It was hard to imagine we'd be undone by a *Dungeon*, when you considered the list of our past achievements.

"Don't count your chickens just yet." Ren kicked off her boots—which vanished rather than dropping to the grass—and swung around to put her feet up on my legs. "Just because we believe the Lady and what remains of her followers are all northwest doesn't mean we will have it easy."

She was right. Days where we had no conflict were few and far between. After knocking down the fort, we had earned a few days' break from it all, but with our destiny starting to circle the drain, I saw no opportunity for us to sit idle without regretting it.

"Assuming we don't run into anything interesting or injurious," Tanya began. "We'll reach the Eternal Wardens before dusk. Hopefully, whatever ails them likes to attack in the morning and not night—so we'll have a chance to settle."

"Better not be vampires," Ren murmured. A random and concerning hope to speak out loud and tempt fate.

"Let's get some coffee and we'll make a move then," I decided, to their nods of acknowledgment. Still so much to do and learn in this world.

But the show must go on.

CHAPTER NINETEEN

Where Wolf

Despite what we had endured, the world didn't seem to be that different this morning. If it weren't for the muscle aches and occasional slideshow of horror in my head, I would be easily convinced that the fight against the undead had been a bad dream.

It had been a shame to leave the cottage once more. Our existence had been bouncing from one conflict to the next, so the idyllic and oddly peaceful area had become something of a home for our weary souls.

But time marches on, and so did we.

"There's a Quest over here," Tanya noted from the front.

As we stepped up closer to join her, a notification popped up in my vision. "Kill a rampaging wolf." Simple enough, all things told. It was on the way, so I gave the nod that we should complete it.

While the Eternal Wardens were desperate for our assistance, we weren't about to drop everything and rush over as quickly as possible. Could be a trap, after all. Plus, they hadn't scratched our backs first—and our power dictated that we should be the itchiest.

My brow furrowed, and I looked over at the elf. I'd managed to extract out of her the fact that she had five of my Skills to replace some of her own, thanks to the Guardian's power. *Which* five was something she was keeping secret—which I found remarkably unfair. That said, I'd had my share of annoying bullshit over the course of our journey, so I allowed her to keep it to herself.

Definitely <Sleight of Hand> though, based on the tricks she had performed for me. The summoned rabbit could be <Summon Demon>, although she had no demonic power—so perhaps it gave her a more mundane thing to summon. Clearly not dogs or we'd be drowning in them.

We moved off of the stone road and into the wilderness, pushing through some bushes until we were in more of a clearing. A field of wild grasses and patches of flowers stretched out ahead—an abandoned farmhouse sitting a few hundred feet away. From here, I could see a few packs of wolves roving in patrols through the area.

One of them happened to be a much darker shade of gray. Black almost. The glowing red eyes did little to deny the allegations that he was probably the rampaging wolf—although it didn't look like he was doing any rampaging at present. Just . . . standing there, looking menacing.

"Dibs?" Ren asked, her arms crossed.

The way the Monsters were arranged, it looked as though attacking our target would draw the ire of all the other packs moving around. I raised an eyebrow at Tanya for final approval.

Our Fateweaver nodded. "Get Wolf over to the right . . ."

"Which wolf?" Quinn asked.

"*Our* Wolf," she replied, energy draining from her face by the second. "Then any bad wolf can go off to the side so . . ."

"I'm not *bad*," Wolf grumbled.

Tanya sighed. "Fine, just do *whatever* then."

With a smile, Ren flipped her hat from her head to have it land on the ground. Hand extended, her sniper rifle then rose up from within her headpiece slowly.

A mixture of different emotions ran through me. Pride, envy, attraction, and then envy again, as I wasn't used to sharing the stage with someone who could be as insufferable as me. I threw two cards to the ground before drawing two more into my hand. Purple light bloomed from them as I powered them with magic.

From the pair dropped, two Imps stood from circles of arcane runes. Gray skin tone, the miniature humanoids with thin facial hair and small horns gave me nods of greeting. These were the lightning variant.

Wolf stood off to the side of us, on our right as requested, so that he could draw in the aggro from any pack that Ren drew toward us. Quinn and Tanya remained near the back to offer any required support . . . but I had a feeling we had this covered.

Ren twirled the rifle in her hand before gripping it and going down on one knee. Eye up to the scope, a bead of radiant energy swirled down the barrel before she clicked the trigger. A crack and the skull of the evil-looking wolf burst open.

"Well, that makes this sort of thing easy," Quinn murmured before clocking all the eyes now turning to glare our way.

Close to twenty wolves—each of them larger than your standard fantasy fare . . . although not quite *dire*. Whatever that really meant. There was still an odd separation in my mind between the aggressive and almost unbelievable amount of brutal Player-on-Player violence, as well as the almost cardboard box full of cliché and flat video game tropes we had to grind through on the side.

I flicked the two cards from my hand and had them zipping through the long grass while the elf was still working the bolt to load her next shot in. Some quick napkin math had her around 30 percent slower than her bow, for maybe twice the Damage potential. A reasonable trade-off for a legendary weapon. In saying that, any brain-puncturing Damage killed a target *whatever* you used to do the deed.

A point made with streaks of purple and red, as my cards arced into the first pair of wolves coming for us. Slit throats or gouged faces. I carried on the attack, weaving through the field to the next pair, embedding the cards into the skulls of our foes.

Another shot and Ren blew the foreleg off one attempting to dodge. They were fast.

Just before the gathering pack reached the jaws of Wolf, my Imps finished charging their attack. Like lightning itself, two prongs of bright white arced from their hands with a sharp crackle. It struck the nearest wolves and then danced between the others back and forth—briefly stunning a swath of them and allowing the rest of us an unhindered volley from our ranged weaponry. The smell of burned fur and charred skin washed across from the group.

Ren and I took down four of them before they had a chance to recover, her shot causing roots to grow up from the ground and restrain most of the force. I dismissed the Imps as Wolf powered forward and slammed into the group. His wide paws slashing through or crushing bones with each strike.

"Not a great experience," I complained, holding off on attacking further as it seemed that the bear was capable enough to pulp everything that remained. "At least it was simple."

"The day is young, trickster." Ren stood and rested her rifle across the back of her shoulder. "Shouldn't push too hard after yesterday."

I wanted to ask, "Why not?" but that might earn me some valid glares. I'd managed to escape her bad books and had no intention of annoying her. *Especially* after yesterday. Instead, I gave her a nod to show I agreed. "Mostly I'm just eager for a few more power tokens to increase some of my Skills—or all of them, if we get lucky."

"That will be our priority," Tanya interjected, "once you both get to level fifteen and we've helped out the Wardens."

"Any chance we can find power spheres in this area?" I asked, not really hoping for much. We had been pinned here, unable to travel to the third area—which had kept the Lady from taking the world by storm . . . but I felt like I was missing out. I craved that extra increase in strength for a few of my most-used skills.

The Fateweaver sucked at her teeth. "Ah. It's not *likely*—I'll put it that way. It would be like finding a legendary item. I've found one before, but that's it."

"I've never seen one," Quinn added.

I pulled a face and turned to see Wolf walk over, licking his chops. Job done.

Our fixer had once said he didn't like how we were tied to the System. Having to level with arbitrary numbers and thresholds to get Skills or do things. I would have to agree. Despite being someone who regularly broke the alleged rules, part of me still squirmed to be free of the structure. Maybe there was something greater out there we could strive toward.

"Coming, Max?"

So distracted by my ambitions, I hadn't noticed the others were making their way back to the road. I smiled at the elf and nodded. Used <Demonic Transposition> to switch with a hell dove and landed on the cobbled stone before they had clamored through the last of the bushes.

"Wish I had chosen that one," she grumbled.

"Do I get to make any guesses? It will kill me to not know until you use them."

Ren shrugged but had a sly grin on her face. "I'm not sure. I quite like having this hidden bullshit that you don't know."

Earned that. Segments of our history together had been building a karmic cannon that now finally hit. Would be hypocritical to start pouting about it . . . but I *did* want to know.

"Fine." I waved my hand and let her have the victory. Five was a decent amount of Skills, but there were several I didn't think she'd take. Useless to speculate but unless she started summoning cannons or going invisible, there wasn't an easy way to know.

My surrender seemed to perk her mood up further, and she grinned. How strange that not so long ago she had nothing but a sour expression to show the world, no matter her mood. I wasn't egotistical enough—which was saying something—to assume I was the cause of her change. But I was here for it and adored it.

"Given our power level," Tanya began, blowing away the love hearts floating between us two magicians, "we should have no issue with taking down the area boss a little southwest of here."

"Something else Big Sister could kill in one hit?" Wolf asked.

"Unlikely." The Fateweaver adjusted her collar to let some warmth out. "Although most things aren't designed with high-caliber modern weaponry in mind, there's a few mechanics that block Damage or prevent certain Damage thresholds. Rare but an area boss is likely to have such things." She looked between Quinn and Ren. "Modern weaponry, as per *my* world, at least."

During our time of rest I had explained some of what I knew about guns to the elf, and she had gone on to prod Tanya for more information since the latter had military experience. At first she was shocked to know that firearms were reasonably common on Earth. I suppose in the same way that orcs or magic would seem bizarre to me.

Or at least, they would if one half of me wasn't a demon hunter who'd done just that in literal hell . . . on one version of Earth. Given that I was also a magician, the things that I saw as normal didn't pair well with most of society, nor reality. One of our Party was a *talking bear*. The elf and fixer were from different versions of a *fantasy* world. I could summon a demonic cannon.

It all just washed out eventually. Would go insane questioning everything. Suspension of disbelief was key, and I couldn't even see my disbelief anymore. It was down a bottomless pit in constant free fall.

"Will miss the woodlands when we ultimately leave them," Ren said, interrupting my thoughts.

"Maybe the whole world is like this? Would be nice to find, like . . . a small cottage by a lake."

"Oh, that would be amazing." She closed her eyes as she walked—imagining it as the scant sunlight that managed to pierce the verdant canopy passed over her face in small handfuls.

With a smile, I looked up ahead. Scenery *was* nice, I couldn't deny that. Seemed as though we were coming up parallel to the rest of the abandoned town. Must be some Quests or points of interest in there.

My footsteps slowed before I paused in place.

I turned my head to the side and furrowed my brow. The rest of the Party came to a stop to see what had caught my attention.

Resting against part of a broken wall was a man who wasn't there just a second ago.

Mid-thirties, maybe. Rough beard and shaved head. Leather armor that looked to be more sheaths and pouches than anything. Dark cloak that was a decent backdrop for the overt display of what type of Class he might be.

"Can we help you?" I asked, my fingers slowly curling into a fist.

No icon over his head to say he had taken the blood of the Lady.

"My name is Leon," he said, a smile growing on his face. "I'm an assassin hired to kill you all."

CHAPTER TWENTY

A Moment of Our Time

My hands went to my hips as I stood and pulled a face at the assassin. Despite the weather being pleasant, there was now a singular dark cloud hanging over the appearance of this man standing casually in front of us and promising death.

"Well," I said, "I appreciate you being forthright. Are you planning on doing it right now . . . or is there some sort of foreboding quota you need to meet?"

A glance over to Ren and she didn't look too pleased either. Hadn't drawn her weapon but I knew it was only a short second that she'd need to try to put a bullet through him.

"You'll be happy to know I'm declining the contract." Leon smiled and leaned back against the stone wall.

I nodded slowly, unsure if this was still a bit. "So you came here to tell us because . . . ?"

"Oh, you misunderstand." He smiled. "Up until this very moment when I greeted you, I had the full intention of assassinating you. However, now that I see you all, I have changed my mind."

"Sudden burst of empathy?"

"Self-preservation actually." He rubbed at his nose and gave each of us a once-over. "Two of you I could take easily. The bear . . . Maybe if I could keep him at range. But you two . . ." He pointed between Ren and me. "Not a chance—especially if all of you are working as one."

I exchanged a glance with Ren. She mirrored my current disbelief that our potential killer would be so forward—the alarm signaling caution in the back of my head was loud enough to drown out my ego bristling at his silver words. Might be pragmatic to kill him, but that seemed like paranoia trying to shuffle in front of the controls.

"Was it Lady in Red who gave you the contract?" Quinn asked, not looking too pleased to be one of the easy marks.

"Not something I can answer, friend. You seem like intelligent folk, however." His eyes went back to me. "Quick with your hands too. Two magical spells out while my attention wasn't on you. A bird above me and an attack that is powering up behind you."

"I like to be well prepared," I replied. Impressive that he had caught them both, despite me being certain he wasn't paying attention.

"Indeed. Max, isn't it? This just goes to further drive home that my decision was a smart one." He put his hands on his hips and grinned. "I *do* enjoy it when I am correct."

Ren crossed her arms. "Can *we* hire you? To kill the Lady?"

"*Yes* and no." He raised an eyebrow. "She is just as dangerous as you and surrounded by twice as many competent people. I will decline that outright."

If not to kill us and not to trick us or use a sneaky way to get rid of one or two of us . . . what was his game here? Maybe he was fishing for work and figured we might have something worth his time.

"How about this then?" I allowed the card held behind my back to vanish away. "A bounty on anyone who has joined with the Crimson Shadow?"

He nodded slowly, his eyes going back and forth. "What are you offering?"

I shrugged. "As many dead bodies as all the gold I own can buy?"

Leon rolled his eyes. "Gold is pretty worthless. Power tokens are preferable."

With a tut, Ren shook her head. "*Ah.* So that you can get more powerful and take on the Lady's contract afterward? She probably wouldn't mind you killing off her minions if we died at the end."

What social graces and faux friendliness the man had thrown in front of us from the outset seemed to be waning. Perhaps we were a little too smart . . . or this was some manner of test. Part of me didn't trust anyone who had the slightest notion of killing us. I looked behind the curtain to see what this performance was really about.

A solo Player not aligned with the Lady, who had been making a living as a contracted assassin? The metal pole groaned under the weight of all those red flags. There couldn't have been that many clients before the Crimson Shadow started to gather in the world, and traveling alone was a recipe for danger.

I could thread plenty of assumptions together, but as of yet, there wasn't much to show for my efforts. An empty tapestry. While Ren haggled on pricing, I allowed the world to dull around me as I tried to look for . . . the sparks.

Some sign of the other game afoot. Movements or the hint of magic. Eyes from odd angles. Something worse hidden away or gathering intel on us. Being static was a mistake—our time being wasted at the least.

Nothing particularly odd about our location. Cobbled road had no raised parts or discoloration. The wall behind Leon was too short and decrepit to be hiding a full Party—unless they were all exceptionally small. Even then, Wolf would be able to smell them. I glanced over at the bear to read his current expression.

He seemed on edge. Not particularly aggressive toward the man standing in front of us . . . but he could sense something wasn't right.

"Why don't we walk and talk?" I suggested, gesturing down the path and interrupting whatever the group had been talking about.

Leon shrugged. "The day is nice, friend. I'm in no rush while it's peaceful here in the shade."

"You won't negotiate while we're on the move?"

His tongue ran across his teeth. "I'm sure we can come to an agreement shortly. Then you are free to do as you please."

There was his mistake. Subtle but something changed in his eyes—if only briefly. His mind was cycling through an inner monologue that was telling him to keep us here. *But be subtle about it.* He was being affable enough, for certain.

"Perhaps you're right." I smiled. "We've had a rough week, and I get testy when tired."

I watched the story play out before me, even as my ears put the next bullshit from his mouth on mute. Two icons appeared over his head, plain as day for me—again, I had been underestimated.

Physical Damage resist. Explosive Damage negation.

[Max: Showtime imminent.]
[Ren: Understood.]

Her reply came back almost as instantly as mine was sent out—more fuel for the assumption she had taken my Inventory-manipulation Skill. I thought it might be fair that I'd take some of hers too—although I didn't know what I'd really make use of from her Abilities.

"Sorry, one question, Leon," I interrupted again. "Was it worth it?"

His mouth opened and closed, a frown across his eyes. "What?"

"Dying for a cause you're not even part of."

An explosion rocked the area—high up in the sky. My cannon spun away from the object it had intercepted; a stream of dark smoke hissing from its damaged shell as it careened off into the tree line.

"*Shit,*" Leon said and went to move.

Ren already had her rifle out, her shot cracking out toward him. A spray of blood painted the gray stone wall as he blurred away—not quite fast enough to dodge a bullet. His Skill had him moving quickly, but before he could get out of the area, he tripped on some stone debris I had made invisible, hitting his head on a reappearing tree that had the same treatment.

I shook the pain from my hand in extending the size limitations further than I should, as Wolf stomped down on the man's head.

"Came from the north," I said, stretching my neck from side to side. "He planned to keep us in place and bomb us from afar. Resistances so that he'd survive."

Ren kept her eyes on that direction, her foot up on part of the wall as she stared down the scope. "And the cannon?"

"The card behind me was actually a mundane one. When I sent the dove up, I gave it the cannon card to hold with its feet. He could sense the energy but not the right location. Activated it when I had . . . a feeling. Actually blocking the projectile was just luck."

Tanya swore under her breath. "Good to know our continued existence runs off of random acts of chance . . . but then, what's new?"

With a tearing noise, Wolf removed the would-be assassin's head from the rest of his body but spat it out. He'd been a lot better about his dietary choices lately, and his health had improved in bounds. Back to the energy levels when we had first met him.

Quinn had his eye narrowed out to the sun-kissed woods, hand resting against his Class weapon—the once-a-day explosive boomerang. "Should we chase them down?"

"No point." I shook my head. "They'd be running if they were smart and setting up a trap if they weren't."

"Allow me." Ren stepped away from the wall. "Been wanting to try this . . . If I fuck it up and die, then I love you, Max."

I raised an eyebrow and watched her remove her hat. Hand went in and she withdrew a pure-white dove, setting it free immediately. The realization of what she was about to do hit me a little too slowly as I was busy patting myself on the back, knowing that she most likely *did* take my summon Skill.

Ren vanished, and the dove appeared in her place. My heart dropped straight through my stomach and onto the ground. Eyes went up to the sky to see her floating there, rifle up. A blast rang out from the long gun before a deep rumbling shook the earth farther away.

As she started to fall, she switched back onto ground level, spinning in place out of balance before falling into my arms.

"Bet you thought I didn't have the upgrade that allows me to switch back, huh?" Her bright-blue eyes were burning with excitement, a shit-eating grin across her face.

"Caught me," I said, too flustered to put up a lie. I stood her back up to her feet, and she gestured at the woods with her thumb.

"No chance I'd hit one of the idiots even with my accuracy, so I just shot their explosives stockpile instead."

I peered back into the sky, where dust clouds of dark gray had started to rise in the distance. Looks like it might have even set a fire off.

"Can't just have one normal day," Tanya said as she shook her head. "Let's get moving then. This area makes me antsy."

"Lead the way, Wolf." I nodded to the bear, and he turned back to the road. Sure—the rest of Leon's Party might be an issue for us in the future, but we weren't about to chase down everyone that hated us. We'd given them a second chance to live a better life . . . and stay out of our way.

Assuming they hadn't just exploded or been burned to death, at least.

I put my arm around Ren as she put her rifle away. "So. Summoning, transposition and return, <Sleight of Hand> . . . And?"

"<Mana Manipulation>." She pouted. "It allows me to dump Mana into my heals and shields to make them stronger, which is pretty overpowered."

"But you were hoping to be able to take some of the cooler things?"

"You have *so* much bullshit," she said and sighed. "But I'm happy with my choices."

I was about to ask what she had given up to copy over those Abilities when Tanya called me over. She was kneeling down by the headless body—checking to see if there was anything worth looting.

"You'll want to see this." She held up an envelope.

"From the Lady?" Had to be. I stepped over and took it from her with a brief nod. Just as I was about to pop the seal, Quinn stepped to my side and placed his hand on it.

"There is a curse on it. *Do not move*," he said, sweat starting to form on his brow.

CHAPTER TWENTY-ONE

Ten Minutes

The five of us stood frozen, the quiet woods around us waiting with bated breath to see what was about to happen. I looked Quinn up and down to see if he was about to educate me more on the supposed curse or if I was now doomed to stand in this place forever. He didn't seem to get the hint that I wanted him to weigh in.

Ren broke the silence. "Can you get rid of the curse?"

A brilliant question, and one I should have asked.

He raised his eyebrow but didn't move his single-eyed stare from the envelope that we were both now holding. "I'm *trying*. You might not assume it, but having one eye makes the process more difficult."

I ran my tongue across dry lips. "Do you know what it does?"

A bead of sweat rolled down the side of his face, eventually getting lost in his goatee. "Nothing good."

"I guess that's why they call it a *curse*." My expression dulled.

Ren crossed her arms and scowled at the pair of us. "If we have to spend ten minutes just standing around after almost getting blown up for doing *just that* . . . well, I might grab the curse myself. Perhaps I should have taken <Shuffle>."

"*You dare*." I narrowed my eyes at her, despite feeling the pressure of the situation. Maybe it *would* take us ten minutes—it would be a *thing*. We'd look back at it and laugh.

"Alright." Ren turned and stepped over to lean against Wolf. "You have ten minutes."

My eyes went over to Tanya for some backup, but she just gave a tired shrug. Instead, I leveled a cool gaze at the fixer still melting. "Maybe we're going about this all wrong—I could just zip it into my Inventory for a time it is safer to open?"

"You can't," he replied, still staring at it. "I'm also holding it. You can't loot it from my hands."

"Then . . . let go?"

"It might set off the curse."

Part of me assumed it must be something overwhelmingly dire for him to be so hardheaded and awkward about it. I wasn't even sure it *was* cursed . . . There was nothing I could sense at least—and I had a basic attunement to everything magical. Or I thought I did anyway.

Which was just as good at this stage.

"*Eight minutes.*"

I exhaled. "Quinn. I will not be undone by an envelope. One of us will need to let go."

"I agree—but will the curse go onto the one who releases or remains?"

My teeth clenched together. He had a point, despite being the one who was supposedly going to fix the situation and knew what was going on.

Wolf yawned. "Would it help if I touched it too?"

"No!" Quinn and I said in unison.

"*Seven.*"

There were a number of things I could do in this situation, but since the fixer had decided to invite himself into the problem, I didn't want to leave him with the potential curse. Knowing how bad some of them could be, I'd never live down the guilt of trying to do some bullshit that got him killed.

"I . . . think I might have it." He pulled a face and narrowed his eye—and I was pretty sure he hadn't blinked this whole time. "Just allow me to . . ."

We all waited patiently as he remained unmoving.

" . . . *Five.*"

"No, no—I've done it . . . Yes!" He nodded eagerly, joy in his eye as he looked up at me. Without waiting, he lifted his hand and stepped back.

I hit <Shuffle> on him, and he stumbled on shaking legs before hunching over and expelling his breakfast. Tanya rushed over to put a hand on his back.

"Food poisoning essentially," I said. "Rather a weak curse, all things considered."

The Fateweaver gave a sigh of relief. "I have something for that, I think. Wow, this must be how Ren feels with you." Her face went a little flush as she realized what she'd said, so I turned away to allow her to avoid further embarrassment.

I rotated instead to face said elf, who was always worried over me breaking myself—and was only partially surprised to see she still had crossed arms and a scowl leveled at me. I could read the reason behind those bright-blue eyes. She knew I'd used <Shuffle>.

Didn't know *how* she knew, of course, but I watched as she became briefly unfocused.

[Ren: He would have died?]
[Max: In less than three seconds.]
[Ren: . . .]
[Ren: I'll keep it between us.]

I tilted my head to Wolf, who appeared disinterested with the current proceedings. He looked up at me with his amber eyes before the letter still in my hand caught his attention.

Must be time to read it, I supposed. Surely the curse was a one-time thing? I'd already opened it before I considered the alternatives—just in case Ren started counting me down again. Didn't need that kind of pressure.

Magician. If you are reading this, you must have killed Leon—which, while unlikely, is something I have accounted for. Soon the necromancer will chase you down with powers you do not understand. That is, if this curse does not kill you first.

—Lady in Red

I rolled my eyes and screwed the letter up. "It was written before the Guardian and necromancer shit."

"Useless then." Ren shook her head. "Let's get moving. I'm sick of the day already."

"Not as much as Quinn," Wolf countered.

The fixer himself did look rather green—even sweatier than before and now exhausted from throwing up. It didn't please me to gamble with his life, but only in the direst circumstances was it reasonable to use <Shuffle> on my ally. I'd nearly killed myself before with the debuff randomizer, but for him, it had been an easy decision to make. A risk but better than guaranteed death.

"We need to get someone who can put curses on things," I thought out loud. "Then getting someone to pick a card from my deck would be potentially deadly."

The elf shrugged, but her ire had withered away to neutral annoyance. "How often do you get to do that?"

"Only one perfect time is necessary."

She wrinkled up her nose and gave me a side eye, as if she had some smart remark to make, but kept it to herself. Now a magician, she had started to *believe*. In *what*, I wasn't sure. *The bullshit*. Watching her switch places with a white dove and explode a munitions stack from midair was . . . frightening for a few reasons, but I also *loved* it.

"You did great back there. Can't remember if I said." We walked together, with Wolf in front.

"Flattery, trickster?" She turned her face to me, and a smile illuminated what was once prime grumpiness. "I very much appreciate that. Now I can see why you have so much fun putting yourself in dangerous positions."

I was sure to regret allowing her to take the Guardian's power. For some reason, I felt the sour Ren of our earlier journey would be a lot more pragmatic with the new Skills. After dazzling our way through the bloodied aisles, she had come out of the ordeals with a streak of glamour of her own. Like glitter you couldn't get rid of.

A natural extension of her being happy and comfortable in our group, so I wasn't complaining . . . just unused to the taste of the humble pie now that I had to do my share of back seat worrying about her pulling off death-defying stunts.

"What was next on the horizon, Tanya?"

"I'd suggest we detour to a small outpost a little southwest. Let Quinn recover for a little. It will delay our arrival to the Wardens . . . but fuck them."

"Hear, hear," Ren agreed, while Wolf grunted his agreement.

"Make it so," I confirmed. The man did look unwell still, even with the debuff now gone. No use turning up to our destination with one of us on death's door—unfortunately for them, our Party's well-being was paramount.

Progress was slower with the fixer being slightly broken, but we took it easy and allowed the good weather to soothe our moods once more. The random appearance of the assassin felt like a bad dream after another hour of walking. Most things in this world had been. I tried to keep the worst at the back of my mind and focus on cultivating what good I had around me.

A sharp pain stabbed in my brain, and I winced.

"Okay, Max?" Ren managed to spot my discomfort like a hawk.

"Maybe a looming headache? Just a little pulse of pain, nothing terrible."

She brought out her gun and became more alert, not really taking my word at face value. While I had exhibited some precognition on occasion, this wasn't it. Just an ache because I was a living being who continued to function. At least, I hoped I was living.

"You ever wonder if our *actual* bodies came here?" I asked the surroundings.

Ren pulled a face. "What are you asking?"

"I'm two people, sort of—right? But they couldn't mash two bodies together, otherwise I'd look even more of a mess. So . . . what if it's just our souls that are put into re-created bodies in this world?"

"Did a fine job of it if that's the case," Tanya offered. "Not a mark or blemish out of place on me."

Ren narrowed her eyes at the far woods. "Seems . . . I don't know. I guess it's possible—a transfer of consciousness then? I think I've read a story about that before."

I nodded. "Essentially, sure. I guess the question then is . . . are our old selves dead, or did they continue and we are just the split?"

Quinn gagged and coughed out an unhealthy amount of saliva. "Ugh. I am not a fan of thinking over . . . the ramifications . . . Getting my head around it is . . ." He held his hand up to his mouth to prevent anything—words or otherwise—from falling out.

"From our point of view . . ." Ren began. "It doesn't really matter either way, right? I certainly feel real and alive, even if Othea still has the dumbass version of me there."

"Agreed." I smiled but gave a glance back to Tanya. She looked deep in thought, barely focusing on tending to the queasy Quinn. If a version of her had survived her car crash, she would technically still be with her family there . . . even if wasn't the better her that she had been striving for in this world.

I daren't prod her for her thoughts. She had a lot riding on being able to go back on an emotional level. Less so these days—I figured she had come around to focusing on being the best Tanya this world needed. All I could do was sit back and be there to support her when needed.

"We'll be there shortly, trickster." Ren took me out of my thoughts, but it was clear she could tell what I had been thinking about. "How about I rub those shoulders out when we're settled?"

"I could have sworn I saw you hovering on white wings. You truly must be an angel." My wide grin disarmed her completely. Her hand came down to intertwine with mine. Amusing given how clueless and alone I had arrived in this world . . . Now I had . . .

Well, all of *this*. I looked around at the rest of my Party. Almost enough to warm my heart. Well . . . my insides did feel warm actually. The pain in my head stabbed through my brain once more.

"Max? Something's . . . wrong." Ren let go of me to move to the tree line.

Amber, red, and gray danced among the horizon.

I turned an eyebrow up at Tanya. "I'm guessing that's the outpost?"

While she nodded, apprehension in her eyes, I raised up my right hand.

It was shaking. Restless.

Demons were nearby.

CHAPTER TWENTY-TWO

Favored Foe

I stood, slightly bewildered by the scene in front of me. The outpost that had promised us safety was lit by a raging fire. Smoke billowed into the sky. Figures danced and laughed among themselves.

"Max? Max?"

My head turned to the side to see Ren there. "Yeah?"

"You're dissociating again, and your hands are already bleeding."

I frowned and lifted them up. Hadn't even been casting any spells and yet she was right. Was sweating too—but that might be the residual heat of the inferno before us. As we stood there, white gloves began to form over my extended hands.

Power: 52 percent.

"This is *potentially* bad." I ran my tongue across dry lips and looked back into her bright-blue eyes. Some worry in there. Valid.

Other than making myself a spectacle and wowing audiences, there was one other thing that caused my Guardian-granted Power meter to rocket. It had done so against Syther, the one-eyed demon that I had killed when I'd abandoned the Party.

But the sheer number of demons here was . . . staggering, in comparison. They must be System-created, but how and where from? Was this some kind of invasion event? Did someone put them here? Why wasn't I currently tearing the miserable fucks limb from limb?

I gasped for air as if I had been holding my breath. Everything was dull to me except for the horned figures illuminated by the fires and the throbbing adrenaline giving my brain a heavy-handed prompt to get the violence started.

It was only natural. Half of me had been a demon hunter—my very vocation was destroying these abominations in hell itself. Despite my affinity for them and being affable with my own demonic summonses, any outside my control just disgusted me and prompted me to act.

Power: 76 percent.

"We *have* to kill the demons," I said.

Ren squeezed my arm, taking me out of my focus slightly. "I know there's no holding you back. Just be safe. We fight together."

I looked her in the face and smiled. Glad that they wouldn't try to talk me out of this compulsion—as I'd only go and do it without them anyway. My greatest weakness, in a way, aside from the self-styled need to break my skull open on every new bit of terrain I came across.

"Tanya, Quinn." I flexed my fingers, the power dying to escape and be brought into reality. "Keep an eye on our backs. This could be a trap."

They probably acknowledged, but I was already stepping toward the outpost. In my hand, two cards. Two ice Imps summoned on my right. Roger's card at the ready, but two purple cards twirled around my hand as I walked down the cobbled road.

The outpost itself either hadn't been burning long or wasn't being allowed to collapse from the constant fire. Gave more weight to this being a scripted event, or it could be . . . *demonic* flames.

The Monsters themselves were nothing like my summonable companions. Around the same height as me but with androgenous toned bodies. Tough red skin, black horns, and piercing yellow eyes. Certainly more of a cliché look than a giant rabbit, but that just made them all the more detestable.

As soon as the first one turned and locked eyes with me, my adrenaline spiked and it was go time. Two cards of purple light, among five other mundane ones, shot out like a shrapnel blast. The demon's sword came up to deflect one, while the second carved through his shoulder. Behind him, a second demon went to move in, but his head exploded with radiant light as Ren placed a bullet between his eyes.

Now *that* certainly shook the hornet's nest. As two more cards bloomed into life, I took stock of the outpost. The buildings formed a rough circle. The center of the space between them housed a large fountain that was full of burning wood. Five more groups of three to five demons, no sign of any normal System-created living or dead.

With a mental gesture, my Imps fired off their magic. Two groups nearer the back received a gleaming bolt of ice each, impaling one but slowing the rest in an area. Would give us more breathing space while we—

The air crackled as something flashed its way toward me.

Wolf slid out to the forefront and took the attack, a sheen of light amber running across him.

I snarled at the grinning demon a little farther back. "Ren, focus on the casters."

"On it." She crouched down, and the sound of the bolt moving told me one demon was about to have their smile wiped away.

Onto my shoulder a white dove landed. What an interesting idea. I sent one of my Imps away to replace with a hell dove and had it perch on the elf's shoulder. Wolf had decent magic resist, but I didn't want him to be a punching bag while he dealt with all the melee demons.

Especially as they were *my* kills.

While the bear roared and powered into combat on the right, I swerved to the left. Magic cards circling me, a duo of purple arcs as I spun a spear into my hands. Ren blew a caster away. Two ran at me with their dark-metal swords. Things became fluid as lightning arced around my body. Blocked the first strike, the second dulled, but sent me stumbling back. Flourished the spear to delay them as my cards continually darted around them, cutting and moving away.

Enough to make the first one lag. My spear found his face. Other demon went to swing for me, but then I had vanished. Invisible. Pulled my cards down into the top of his skull and reappeared. I stepped back, narrowly avoiding the downward strike of a large war hammer wielded by a larger demon. It struck the cobbled road, breaking apart stone.

I put my foot on the head of the weapon and gave him a wink. Switched places with Ren and she shot straight through his neck before we switched back again and I rammed the spear up through his lower jaw.

Dropped Roger's card on the demon as I turned to see who was next. <Card Fan> came up and blocked the arrow of an opponent in the back left. I jumped up into the air, landing on top of my summoned cannon, spear now loaded into it—and I fired.

From this peak, I surveyed the show. We had chewed through half of them already. Wolf and my Imp taking the bulk of the demons down piece by piece while Ren eradicated high profile targets. Quinn and Tanya offering support from the back—the fixer had even started to douse the flames of the first structures with one of his Skills.

All in all, this was rather *pleasant*. If you ignored the pressure in my head that felt like my own horns wanted to sprout and the figurative warning light blinking away as my Power bar neared filling to the brim . . .

I dropped down in front of my cannon as it blasted me with confetti. Part of me wanted to hit <Finale> right there and start mopping up anyone who was stunned . . . but that was letting them off easy.

Second confetti shot and energy surged through me like I had suddenly become drunk. Power: 100 percent. No Domain though. These demons didn't deserve to see me at my best. Waves of anger rippled through me as I moved but couldn't focus. A slideshow of picturesque scenes. I moved from one death blow to the next, as if my brain only cared about seeing the last pained look in their eyes before I destroyed them.

Which was . . . *true*, in all honesty.

My feet took me to a wavering standstill, and I felt somewhat more sober. Brain took a while to settle down while I stared at the last corpse I had created.

"You alright, boss?"

I turned my head back to see Roger inhabiting the larger foe, his purple eyes raised in questioning. I realized that I was soaked through with blood. Some of it my own but mostly not. "I think so."

Turning fully, I regarded the carnage I had left in my wake. Lifted up my hands to see that the white gloves had now left me. As Quinn continued to extinguish the burning properties, the rest of my unfortunate companions came over.

"First off," Ren began, "that switching thing was amazing. We really need to workshop that more."

"Agreed." I nodded along.

"Secondly, are you *actually* okay? You went a little feral there, but you seem lucid enough now."

I checked my mind for any defects—any *unexpected* ones. Mostly likely the Power had gotten frustrated I hadn't brought my Domain into being, and the resulting tantrum was the energy being dissipated in turning me into an unrelenting demon-murdering machine. None remained, so my purpose was fulfilled.

"Well, either my brain's about to rocket out of my nose, or I'm just fine."

The grimace on her face told me that she wasn't too sure either option was palatable.

"How's Quinn, Tanya? Anything else to report?" I would have stepped closer to the elf, but given the state of my outfit, I didn't want to get her covered in demon blood. *It was all for me.*

"Still under the weather but I think giving him the task of putting the fires out has kept his mind busy enough." She smiled and looked back at the man doing just that, her gaze lingering on him for a few seconds before she turned back to me. "Didn't spot anything suspicious behind us."

"Likelihood of finding a house with a bath that doesn't smell like charcoal and sin?"

Wolf cleared his throat and spoke up. "This one doesn't look harmed."

We looked over at the one he was gesturing to. He was right—but rather than relief, it just made me furrow my brow. I turned in a slow circle, eyeing up all the structures in the outpost.

It was the only one unblemished. Pristine, in fact, even though its neighbors were scorched and smoldering. I raised an eye to Ren, and she lifted her rifle to her shoulder.

"Could just be a Quest thing," Tanya offered.

"*Could* be," I responded, but my mind was elsewhere. So were my feet, as I found myself creeping toward the unmarked building as if it could sprout legs and attack us . . .

Shouldn't put that out into the world.

It even felt mundane as I stood before the closed entrance. No magic auras or weird feelings my arcane knowledge might prickle at. No sense of foreboding doom—but just the same, there wasn't a good feeling either. A true neutral house.

The muzzle of Ren's rifle rested gently on my shoulder so she could shoot past me if something hostile appeared when I flung open the door.

"You realize I'll be deaf for a week if you fire that there?" My eye twitched in anticipation.

"Just don't listen to it."

I exhaled through my nose. "I'm not sure my selective hearing is that profound."

"Could have fooled me," she murmured.

Didn't hear what she said as cogs were clicking around in my mind. More rules needed breaking, I was sure. My hand went inside my jacket, and I brought out another hell dove.

Eyes went over to Roger, as he was prodding at one of the dead demons. He caught my gaze and smiled sheepishly—odd in the figure he was puppeteering. "Thought I might know some of these assholes, but nope!"

"No matter. Come over here. We're going to try something *new*."

CHAPTER TWENTY-THREE

Demonic Transposition

With the last of the flaming houses now put to rest, the terrible smell of smoke still lingered in the air. Unfair, since damage to the surroundings was minimal, but the constant pressure of it had me feeling tired.

Or it could just be the blackout-like rage that had caused me to pulp the remaining demons to death in ways that I could not recall. Definitely the *smoke*.

"What makes you think this will work?" Ren had removed the rifle from my shoulder after Tanya had confirmed that hearing damage was a likely side effect of using me as a stand.

"It most likely won't." I turned an eye to her before looking back at the pristine house before us. "More a case of . . . does the System *know* that? I've come to understand it is less a static set of rules than it should be."

There was a very specific use case that I was relying on to make this work. <Demonic Transposition> swapped me with a targeted demon I had summoned. Simple on the surface. Technically, Roger *was* a demon that I had summoned. All good so far.

However, the difference between him and my dove was that while I was borrowing the latter from hell, the large rabbit was my pact demon. He was bound to me and, in some ways, me to him.

Would this bond allow me to shift some of the targeting across? I was willing to find out.

Roger stood patiently as I sent the hell dove up into the top-floor window. It didn't immediately combust or fall foul of anything offensive, so I raised an eyebrow at my pact demon.

While I was a magician in the basic sense—someone who did tricks and illusionary forms of "magic"—the System gave me the fantasy flair that paired with an innate understanding of the moving pieces. A mix of both worlds that allowed me to do the unthinkable on occasion.

My eyes narrowed as I tried to find the invisible strands that determined targeting for my spells. Hand raised and there was the string leading from me to the hell bird in the house. Was easy enough to sever and reattach it . . . but I couldn't move it. Frustrated, I stepped over to the rabbit inhabiting the demon corpse and placed my hand on him.

Severed the connection from my hand and felt the end of the tendril of energy twirl around, resisting being attached to Roger instead as if they were repelling magnets. Useless. Just needed more power.

Drained my reserves as if I had pulled the plug from the sink. A swirl of Mana that thickened the line and caused it to be brighter in my mind's eye. Slowly, I was gaining more control of it. Teeth clenched together, and then there was a snap.

I stumbled forward into the flapping wings of my dove. Eyes went up to the window, and a demon head poked out, his purple eyes glowing down at us.

"Whoa, boss. That felt weird."

"Secure the building and open the door," I requested of him, and he vanished back inside.

"That didn't look too easy," Ren said. Stepping over and placing an arm on me as I wobbled.

"Never is," I replied. Hadn't bled for it but it was mentally exhausting. What a bad day we'd had so far—and this was before we'd seen what was troubling the Eternal Wardens.

"Probably nothing wrong with the building either." She clicked her tongue and pulled a face at the rest of the outpost. "Still have a bad feeling though."

"Same. Be nice to not have constant combat encounters on the way to our destination." I shrugged, even knowing I may have doomed us to just that.

The door swung open to reveal Roger standing there with his arms crossed. "Seems okay, boss."

"Hmm, thanks, Roger. Make sure you drop the body outdoors when you leave."

He nodded and walked out, two steps away from us before he faded away to mist, the empty body of the demon puppet now flopping to the ground.

Quinn looked to be improving but was just about as exhausted as I felt. Pushing ourselves too hard, just after the hell we'd gone through.

"I'm going to say you go bathe first, Max," Ren offered, seeing what others felt about the notion. "Just because you are literally caked with demon gore."

Reluctant acceptance had me stepping forth into the odd building before the others—perhaps her intention all along. It looked . . . normal, as if it had just chosen to sit out of the event that was happening around it.

"Keep your eyes peeled, just in case," I warned them as I was already halfway up the stairs. Would have been nice to share a bath with Ren, but we didn't really have the time to be distracted by romantic notions. Maybe at our next stop.

Bathroom door closed, and I was over to the tub. Taps turned on. Normal water. One of these days I was sure it would be poison gas, or spiders . . . The System liked to keep me on my toes. Set my outfit to repair and removed my underwear.

Into the water before it was even half full. Eager to get some comfort and energy back in my body. As I sighed and leaned against the side of the wooden bath, I figured it was a good time to get caught up on some admin work.

[Max: Hey, Fiona.]
[Fiona: Max. Not dead yet then?]
[Max: Sorry to disappoint.]
[Max: Have an update for you.]
[Max: Necromancer is dead, along with a couple of other groups.]
[Fiona: Impressive—so the east and center are relatively clear?]
[Max: Correct.]
[Fiona: We're moving to the second area with another group.]
[Fiona: Priority will be leveling, but we can assist you.]
[Max: At some point we will need to march on Candlekeep.]
[Max: Your help would be greatly appreciated.]
[Fiona: When the time comes, you'll not find us absent.]
[Fiona: I'm . . . glad you're okay and still kicking ass.]
[Max: I know. Stay safe, Fiona.]

Normally, I'd talk to Ruby, as the goblin healer was a lot more affable. With Fiona being the leader of her Party, I wanted to approach the request for assistance in a more . . . official capacity.

Taps off, the water was nice and warm—and the bath as full as my head.

[Max: Anything you can tell us?]
[Dimitri: Unfortunately not.]
[Dimitri: I realize how unconventional that is . . .]
[Dimitri: But you will understand once you arrive.]
[Max: If it's some kind of trap I will be really pissed.]
[Dimitri: It's nothing of the sort.]
[Dimitri: I have to go now.]

I grumbled to myself. This stunk to high heaven. The Eternal Wardens had been keen for me to show up and meet them for a while, but I wasn't sure why. Promising answers on the Guardians had been less of a draw now that we had a rough idea—or at least since we knew how to work them, then the details didn't mean much.

Other than if there was an easy way to get rid of the Lady. I daydreamed about Ren taking her out from half a mile away. Things were never that easy.

So I cleaned off the blood and grime from the rest of me. Would have been nice to have a proper soak—but having to share the extravagance with the rest of the Party had me feeling guilty if I took too long.

Out. Dry. Clothed once more. I sighed and floated some mundane cards around my hands. Drew four different kings into my hand. Flicked them away and then drew five of the same king into my hand. Lifted the hat from my head and a waterfall of cards fell out onto the wooden floorboards. All jokers.

A point to this exercise? I wasn't sure. Sometimes motions took me, and I followed the feeling until a result was shown. A bit like . . . a tarot reading or something. Despite being relaxed and clean, it felt as though something uncomfortable remained, a splinter in my mind. Knew it was there but fingers were too clumsy to grip at it.

Shook myself and went out of the bathroom, immediately almost striding straight into someone waiting.

My mind skipped a beat as I thought it was Quinn, but it wasn't.

Older man with a gray mustache and a blank look in his eyes. Heart skipped a beat from the jump scare. "Sir?"

"Terrible weather today." His mouth moved, but the rest of him didn't.

"*Max!*"

I skirted past him and hit the stairs, racing down to meet with the rest of the Party. They weren't alone, as two other System-created had appeared in the living room area, equally as inert.

Ren had a sour scowl on her face, unimpressed at their appearance. "I guess the outpost is bringing back all the NPCs."

"I suppose." I continued from the stairs and over to the window at the front of the house. Wolf was lying by the front door to ensure we didn't have any surprise guests. My eyes went slowly from left to right. "*Oh.*"

The elf leveled her glare at me. "What is it now? Something to stop me from having a bath?"

I ran my tongue across my dry lips. "I mean . . . potentially *not*, but . . ."

Not taking my limp sentence as an answer, she came over and jostled me to the side to look—rather than going to the other window.

"The *fuck* is this?" She sighed and pressed her forehead against the window.

That was enough to get the other two over and looking out on the other side of the room. Made sense why Roger had thought there was nothing wrong, in retrospect.

I placed a hand against the glass, warm already. "I'm hoping this isn't real."

Quinn moved away from the sight and put a hand over his face. "I think I may just throw up again."

Tanya was silent, her brow furrowed, trying to make sense of it. Amber light illuminated her clenched jaw, as if the lighting took a few minutes to catch up with the change in location.

Ren seemed fed up with everything. Couldn't blame her.

I just wavered, my legs energized but weak. A grumbling in my stomach that almost rivaled Quinn's, but I was led to a different solution to rub away at the terrible feeling flashing through my body.

Wolf shuffled away from the door, not clued in to the picture just yet. But I . . . I stumbled to the door, smiling despite the emotional turmoil gripping at me.

I pushed the door open, allowing a warmth to wash through us. Now there could be no denying we weren't imagining this.

Turning my head away from the jutting spikes of rock, the ruddy hues, and the perpetual bursts of flame, I looked at the dark sky and closed my eyes.

"Welcome to hell," I announced.

CHAPTER TWENTY-FOUR

Into a Pocket

Hell.

You would think, given half of my past, that the sight of our current location would bring about strong feelings in my core. But of what? Hatred? Fear?

Instead, I felt nothing. This was a construct of such place, not the real thing—for however you liked to use the word *real*. The flaming pillars of molten rock, the jagged edges of the terrain, and the amber-to-brown rainbow that decorated the entirety of the sky were all so . . . pedestrian.

"I'll take the blame for this one."

I turned my head to look at the elf, who had a tired expression across her face. "How so?"

She stepped up beside me and crossed her arms. "Well, I *had* said I'd go to hell and back for our love and *now* look what happened."

"As much as I love some decent foreshadowing, I don't think you are at fault." I wrinkled up my nose and took in the smell of the place. Burning superheated stone, and . . . no idea. Something else about it was off.

"This is a home away from home for you?" Some of the grump eased away from her face as she tried to read my expression.

"No. It's too . . . *fake*. Too System-created. The hell I knew was a place of unrelenting violence that slowly eroded away at both your soul and sanity. I just feel a little extra warm here. So far."

"Hmm." She nodded slowly but didn't seem convinced. "Given how you react around demons, I am expecting the rest of us to suffer while you carve through everything . . . until we find a way out?"

I turned around to view the house we had arrived here in. It was decaying already, the wood not really burning but just turning to ash. Would be a handful of minutes before only debris remained. My eyes went from the building and over to Quinn and Tanya, the latter of the pair not looking too great.

"You okay, Tanya?" I stepped over, Ren following.

The Fateweaver turned her tired eyes to me. "Never better."

"Wolf, take Ren and Quinn, see what the local threats are—any potential path forward."

They each gave me a nod and set off—the bear looking rather unsettled by our new environs too. Ren caught my eye and started to talk to Wolf about how he was feeling. I turned back to Tanya and gave her a soft smile.

"You don't *have* to talk to me, but I'm here."

"It's just that . . ." She sighed and rubbed at her eyes. "I *thought* that the world might be purgatory . . . and then when I came to terms with not going back and tried to live for *now* . . . to move on with the group." Her eyes went over to the trio. "And *with* Quinn. Now that I'm in actual hell, it feels like a real punishment for not staying true to my family."

I nodded. "So if we escape this hell, then you will see that as validation for your life choices instead?"

"Well . . . that's the crux of it, isn't it? The sensible part of me knows this is no different from the forest or a Dungeon . . . but guilt often doesn't care about that." She gave me a glum smile. "I'll survive, Max. Thank you. I'll just be constantly perturbed."

"Noted. Check in if you feel any worse." I gestured to the others, and we went to catch up. "*Quinn* though? Sly dog."

Tanya smiled, and some life came back into her eyes. "We tried to downplay it. Nothing serious, but it's nice to have . . . someone who cares and understands, you know?"

"You deserve happiness." I smiled but raised an eyebrow. "If that is in the shape of Quinn, then more power to the both of you."

She rolled her eyes. "Can you keep it between us?"

"Of course."

As much as it pained me, I'd even keep it from reaching Ren's long ears for now. A struggle to hold something from her but it wasn't my place to spread secrets that were not mine to tell. We arrived at where the others had stopped to look over an apparent ledge or decline lower than us.

"What do you think, Max?" Ren gestured down to the plateaus of parched stone and rough spines.

There were demons. Plenty of them . . . In fact, far too many. All milling around doing who knew what.

"They make me angry," I said. "Not in a good way."

Quinn rubbed at his eye patch. "Well, before you go off and have a terrific time murdering through every demon you meet, we might want an actual plan of action for how to get out of here."

A valid point. Although all demons needed to die, it wasn't likely that erasing all of them would be the key for us to portal back home. No point asking Tanya if she had another scroll either, as she would have brought it up immediately.

"I'm not an expert on these things . . . but it seems as though there are pocket areas that don't show up on the main Map. This just so happens to be the place where demons are generated and stored until they are needed in the actual world . . . unless there is a Quest down here or something?"

My postulations were met with resigned shrugs and grunts that held no information.

I, however, was already chewing on a thought based on this hypothesis. What if our return didn't have to be the same location that we had arrived here from?

It stood to reason that there would be other areas that received demons from down here. Some of those might accept some extra passengers . . . so what if we could appear nearer Candlekeep—or the Eternal Wardens . . . or even past the area-three barrier?

We just needed to find a way.

The air shifted just to the right of us. A solid rock wavered beneath some demonic power, and Ren raised her rifle up.

Out of the air, a large figure emerged. White fur, long ears, and bright-purple eyes. Roger looked us over with a scowl on his face.

"What the *fuck* are you assholes doing down *here*?"

"Sightseeing tour." I crossed my arms. "Want to be our guide?"

He groaned in response and rubbed at his eyes. "This isn't *good*, boss. Once the Demon King hears there are humans and human-adjacent species . . . and a bear . . . down here, he'll flip his fucking nut."

"Sounds like we'll have to kill him then," Wolf suggested.

I nodded. "Will you be our tour guide for *that*, Roger?"

"Boss. I have a family here. I can't shit where I eat. Or . . . fuck where I eat? I forget which way it goes—which is *bad* because it's part of my probation."

"If we kill the king, will we be able to renegotiate the terms of that?" I raised an eyebrow, trying to coerce my demon into risking it all because I said so

"Yeah . . . I suppose so." His fuzzy hand went up to rub at his chin. "Would do wonders for my sex appeal. I'd be a fuckin' *icon*. Alright, I'm in—murder train full steam ahead."

Ignoring for the moment that the System must be translating what a steam train was, I was content enough that it hadn't taken that much persuasion to get him on board with . . . Oh, I guess we were marching on a king now?

"Not that I don't like a bit of bravado," Ren began, one step ahead of my mental process, "but we don't know whether that is a good idea, possible, or something that would take us back home."

Quinn nodded along. "The first thing you should have asked our dear demon friend is if he knew a way for us to get home."

"Nah." Roger shook his head. "I only get out of here when summoned. Plus, even if I did know, I might not tell you now because usurping the king sounds fun as fuck."

Not quite the level head I wanted us to go into this with, but about what I had expected from my pact demon. By my estimation, this should be somewhat like farming out a repeatable Quest, just with a boss at the end of it. Would be nice to assume we'd get some manner of reward out of the effort— but . . . Hmm.

"Say, Roger. Do you know what levels the demons are here? Are there many much stronger than you?"

"Oh yeah, I'm like . . . middle of the road here, excluding the Higher Court and the big nob himself. Can't see numbers or shit though."

I nodded and took my hat from my head to rub at my hair. Caught the gaze of Ren, as it seemed she had a similar line of thought as I had. One of the things that I adored about her.

"That's a dangerous game," she said before I'd even spoken the words. "It will have to be a Party vote."

Quinn looked apprehensive and remarkably sweaty. Tanya still seemed to be being eaten up by her guilt. Wolf was fed up with the oppressive smells and keen to get things rolling. Despite how odd the situation was, Ren was calm. Roger had already stated his opinion.

"Right then. Party-vote time." I returned my top hat to my head and gave them a wide smile. "There is a slight chance that we are currently in an advantageous position. If the System doesn't see us as being in the second area anymore, that could mean we are no longer level locked . . ."

Tanya hummed. "So you are suggesting we purge hell, hoping that we get experience and then go higher than level fifteen?"

"Precisely. Assuming all of that is possible. It would give us an edge up over the competition, with the downside of potentially being here longer, without being able to influence the outside world." I crossed my arms.

Given that we were still looking for an exit, our actual time here was variable. Even saying that—Roger seemed to travel through time differently when he was down here . . . Maybe there was some time dilation we'd be wary of. As much as it would be dire to return to Othea to find the whole world was under control of Lady in Red, I was reasonably sure things moved quicker here than there—to our advantage.

I took a deep breath. "Hands up if you are okay with trying to power level and kill the Demon King on the way to finding our way out of here."

Naturally, I raised my hand up.

Roger was in as soon as I mentioned regicide again. Ren was second to raise her hand, still looking rather done with the day and how our lives seemingly just spiraled into worse situations every few days.

Wolf was next. He had been quiet, and I'd have to check with the elf to see how he was doing. I had banked on the power trio being down for the constant violence. Quinn hesitated but his hand went up gradually, his eye looking more toward the Fateweaver than anywhere else—his thought process clearly visible.

Tanya remained with hands down but leaned her face forward so that she could cover it with her abstaining palms. "I'm sorry. I don't want to be here—even though I know this is the best option for us."

"Escape is always our first priority. As soon as the option presents itself, we will go—I promise you this."

She sighed. "*Fine*. Let's go fuck up some demons."

"Woo!" Roger yelled.

I rolled out my neck. While the idea was mostly my creation, I wasn't as eager as I had made out. The outpost full of demons had caused me to black out with violence. Now in literal hell, I wondered exactly what a danger I'd become.

Roger led us toward a pathway, the time to find out soon upon us.

CHAPTER TWENTY-FIVE

Just Visiting

For as much as the dull palette of hell started to grate on my nerves, the fact that the System had created this place was a point of interest. I had long wondered if there was indeed a hell for this System world, and now I had my answer. Was I happy about that? Perhaps I would have been more content to gain this knowledge while being as far away from the actual place as possible.

As it stood, we'd just have to make the best of a bad situation. Interestingly, while the area had the Party mood at a low point, Ren didn't seem to be too bothered with the predicament. Annoyed, sure, but not oppressed by the heated gloom or violent scenery. Perhaps in her world, hell was viewed differently, or she could distance herself from the imagery and superstition of the place better than the rest of us.

Well, aside from the literal rabbit demon accompanying us and yours truly, of course.

I wouldn't go as far as to say I had a spring in my step, but the possibility of outleveling our opponents had strengthened my positivity enough to the point I was no longer worried about leaving. I wanted out, just like the others—but I'd eke out whatever advantages I could wherever we went.

Now that we were fully armed and ready for inevitable battle, Roger had taken us down a winding path that led to the lower levels of hell. Emerging from the cliff-like rock face, we found ourselves in something that could almost be described as civilization.

A small town of dark, ruined wooden buildings, arranged on either side of a central road that ran from the cliff and beyond. It didn't take me long to clock the reference here, and Tanya seemed to be on the same page.

"Looks like a Wild West town," she murmured.

Ren pulled a face and glared at the darkened windows of the nearest buildings. "Looks like misery to me."

"Ah." Roger paused and scratched at the side of his head. "Probably some assholes hiding around here. It's the only way through though."

I tilted my head and looked at each of the buildings ahead of us. "Well, let's be smart about it and not do the cliché thing and walk straight down the middle. Let's circle the back left here and keep out of sight."

"Remarkably levelheaded for you," Ren said but nudged me with her elbow.

"Murdering my way through the day is one thing, but walking into an obvious ambush . . . I'd like to think we have learned by now." I gave her a smile as she half-heartedly rolled her eyes.

And so, we made for the route I had devised. Some of the buildings didn't even have back doors—as we passed them by, I couldn't help but feel a little clever at the simple plan. Even if we were spotted and attacked, it would only be from the one direction. Roger was flexing his paws back and forth but didn't seem to be nervous about anything specific.

Halfway through the town and I felt the tension rise up within me. Demons were near; part of me could sense it. A sharp pain throbbed at the back of my head. I could feel eyes watching me, so I stopped.

Quinn slowly drew one of his remaining flintlocks. "Trouble, Max?"

"Almost guaranteed." I withdrew Jokkar's mace to hand to the rabbit, while a trio of cards swirled around beside me.

The space behind us was mostly open rocky plains. Occasional spurts of fire perhaps, but otherwise nothing immediately looming to jump out at us.

"How is it you don't know this area well, Roger?" Ren asked, sweeping the end of her barrel between the windows and alleys behind the wooden houses.

"Why would I? Usually have better things to do than fuck around every inch of this place. This area is what's known as the Outer Circle, and I spend most of my days—"

"Shh!" I held up a finger and furrowed my brow. There was a creaking noise, faint but just about audible over the rolling ambience. My gaze went to the designated hearer of the group—Ren having paused her roving muzzle to settle on one of the bigger buildings.

Wasn't easy to guess what it was from the back here but I was willing to assume it was a saloon.

My Power bar was slowly filling.

The snap of breaking planks put the nail in the coffin that it wasn't just our imaginations. A second, louder creak and the building began to shift as if it was collapsing.

"Shoot it," I commanded, flicking my cards out immediately.

Ren's rifle blew a hole through the aged wood, punching through to the street beyond, no doubt. My cards splintered shards from the building as I curved them to slice rather than stab.

The reason for my lack of patience was soon clear as a spray of dark blood emerged from the hole the bullet had punched. Equally, the marks I had scored started to run with the stuff as well.

"Demon buildings?" Ren asked, working the bolt on her rifle.

"Worse," Roger said, shaking his head. "Demon buildings."

Her eyes narrowed, but she knew better than to get into it with the rabbit. Either he hadn't heard or was intentionally ignoring her. I'd remind him about his manners once we got out of this predicament.

"Are we really going to fight a literal town?" Tanya asked.

"I can't think of a good enough pun right now." I grinned. "But yes."

Two cards in my hand, I went to throw down two frost Imps—which now seemed like odd things to live in hell. They struck the ground just behind me near our backliners . . . but didn't summon.

Instead, the normal arcane circles bloomed into life—only they widened and moved toward the two behind us. Mouth open, I turned but didn't have time to act. Confusion flashed across their faces before both Tanya and Quinn vanished in a puff of magical energy.

"Max?" Ren growled.

[Max: Report in?]

Nothing for a few seconds, as the building ahead of us groaned and pulled itself from the foundations, trying to turn just as its neighbors started to shift into life.

[Tanya: We're okay.]
[Quinn: Other than the shock!^]
**[Tanya: Back in the normal world . . . a little farther than
the outpost we left.]**
[Tanya: Can you get out the same way?]

I furrowed my brow and brought out another demon-summoning card, only for it to immediately crumble to dust. Second one, the same.

"I've somehow reverse summoned our Party members. Either they will be in Othea with a time limit, or I've locked my Abilities out until either they die or we go back." I stood there pulling a face at the complete gall of the System.

"Wow," Ren said. I couldn't tell whether that singular word was labored with exasperation, disbelief, or annoyance. Perhaps a little of all three.

[Max: No. Go somewhere safe until we can talk.]

Wasn't planning on hanging around to see how the Chat function liked the time dilation here with a host of Wild West–looking structures wanting to chew on me.

"Looks like the only demon here to help is whatever resides in me," I said, grinning and blooming my magic cards with a mix of mundane ones to orbit around me.

Roger coughed.

"Oh, you too."

Ren fired again, this time with an <Entangling Shot>. Vines cracked through the ruddy stone around the saloon and grabbed onto the lower planks.

"Wolf, move to the far-left corner and start breaking things. Roger, support him. I'll be going to the middle to get the real party started."

"And me?" Ren asked.

I held out my hand, which she took, and twirled her into a close hug. "Why, you're coming with me, my dear."

With a few awkward seconds standing still and nothing happening, she then wrinkled up her nose. "You forgot you can't summon birds for <Demonic Transposition> already, didn't you?"

"Feels like I have been robbed of one of my senses." I gently allowed her to stand.

"Would have been awkward if I went to the middle and you remained here, huh?"

I pulled a face and looked over at the saloon, struggling against the restraints. "I'd never live it down."

Ren smiled and jostled me with her elbow. "Let's kill some demons, Max the Magnificent."

Didn't need any more prompting than that. Once again, we were supping from the cup of boons that had come from my acceptance of her being equal in all things. She knew me inside and out and had developed a knack for the show quicker than expected.

Such a far cry from the grumpy Oathwarden on the beach, her defiant scowl requesting I teach her to ply the same amount of bullshit into our combat—and now she did. High-powered sniper rifle aside, she not only looked the part but had been working on her own tricks with the Guardian-granted Abilities and was more receptive to my desire to tangle with fate and see how chewed up I could get.

A pair of cards into my hand as she fired a radiant shot through the building. It screamed in pain—which was unusual, but I'd believe anything at this stage of my life. Third card I had then drawn was critical and crackled with a crimson light compared to the purple of its contemporaries.

I let the first go so that I could put all my strength into this singular one. It grew brighter as my Mana sank away before I started dipping into my actual

Health. My legendary gear boosting Damage with all the power used to cast a spell, and as soon as I cast it, some of that lost Health started to regenerate.

Card twisted into the air as I sent it vertically to arc around and crash down into the tile roof of the saloon. Punctured through and exploded, blowing loose fragments to the ground as a wash of thick dust billowed from the open holes where there was no glass. Shortly followed by streams of blood.

By now, the two adjacent buildings had shuffled almost all the way around to face us. They had no eyes or mouth, so I wasn't too sure how threatening they were. Probably not a good idea to just walk through their open doorways . . . but intrusive thoughts had me wondering.

Off to our left, Wolf crashed his way through the farthest building, the whole thing collapsing in a way that was far too moist considering. The next in line was currently being beaten by Roger, his mace taking huge chunks out of the outer woodwork.

I dropped the demonic cannon next to Ren, just in case it decided to take her back home. She must have read the intention, as she gave me a scowl. A faux pas but better than accidentally taking me back home. If anyone was equipped to deal with hell, it was me. That said, I seemed to have no problem with the siege weapon, and I went to grab some lit lanterns from my Inventory.

"Here, Max." Ren whispered a word in Elfin before throwing over a now-glowing radiant lantern before repeating the process with two more. Each one vanished as it reached me, immediately going into the cannon.

First blast struck the house to the right of the saloon, oil and metal shrapnel bursting against buckling wooden planks. Radiant flame erupted and flickered around the body of the building in no time at all, a shriek emerging from the decaying structure.

I grinned and spun more cards up. Down two Party members but we had a hold on things so far.

"We are getting experience from them. Decent too." Ren fired another shot, a wry smile at the edge of her mouth.

Power meter humming as it continually grew. I turned my attention to the empty plains behind us.

Only, they weren't so spent anymore.

An empty bullet casing bounced across the ground as Ren turned to see what I was looking at.

Her face wrinkled up, and the rifle lowered.

"What the fuck?"

CHAPTER TWENTY-SIX

Walkies

While we stood in the wavering heat of hell, with several living buildings turning to approach and probably eat us up, a mixture of different emotions went over Ren's face in seeing the approaching horde.

I wasn't too sure whether to feel confused or elated . . . but leaned toward the latter.

An estimated fifty Hellhounds were bounding across the desolate rocky expanse toward us. Most of them were the smaller and slimmer build, but some were the larger upgraded kind I could now summon.

"Perhaps we actually went to *heaven*," the elf murmured, a sheen of awe now in her bright-blue eyes.

"Depends on their intent." Despite saying this, I could feel it—see it in their happy little flaming dog faces. I relaxed.

The tidal wave of demonic hounds washed over us, and we were surrounded by wagging tails, happy yips, and requests for pets.

Ren lifted one out of the pile, clasping it to her body as she wielded it awkwardly toward me. "*Look*, trickster!"

I raised my eyebrows and smiled. The positioning of the scars across the body of the wriggling beast couldn't hide the identity of who they were. He had fallen in battle against the Dire Boar, all the way back on the starter island. "I was right; all demon dogs go to hell."

"These must be all the little pups you've summoned before. There's . . . a lot more than I remember."

I gave her a shrug, but she was too distracted by the friendly hounds to dig into my nonanswer any more. It wasn't the biggest secret that I often summoned demons just out of sight and knowledge of my Party, even skirting the expert perception of the elf. It always paid to have options and contingencies in place. Of course, I had noted that she had started doing the same with her own summonses—so she was bound to make the connection eventually.

Ren sank down to the floor, melting among the affection rendered. "Just leave me. I can die happy here," she announced between several of the hounds trying to lick her face.

"Tempting." I looked over at the buildings to see that most of them were . . . running away? Maybe not running, but they were turning away from us. Over to the side, Wolf thrashed through wooden walls before seeing what we were doing.

He and Roger paused their onslaught as the living buildings retreated and moved back over to us.

The rabbit had a bemused look on his face and plenty of wooden shards in his fur. "Turn my back on you for one minute and you've already raised a fucking army, boss."

"Yeah." My brow furrowed, and I looked at my hands. Pretty normal, considering. Yet . . . Hmm.

Ren was completely prone on the ground now, drowning under the affection of our Hellhounds. Well, not really ours but . . . close enough. If there was a horde of dogs that I had summoned previously, then there was likely to be Imps somewhere too. A couple of Shades and . . . a whole lot of hell doves that might have a grudge against me.

Cannons too? No, unlikely, as I had been able to summon one here just fine. It was inanimate so was probably just the same one every time. I should mark it to find out.

"You okay, Wolf?" I stepped past some of the dogs as they went to join the cyclone of flaming fur, burying the elf.

"Normally I am accepting of the situations you drag us into, but I'm having trouble understanding this." His amber eyes looked out at the barren scenery.

It *was* a bit much. We'd spent the majority of our adventures in forest or woodland-adjacent terrain. Even the towns or small villages had been as close to nature as you could get. For a former average grizzly bear, this hellscape would be a stark difference to what he'd known all his long life.

"It is equally as strange for me," I admitted, partially truthful. "We will have to persist but escape as soon as we can."

"As always, you can rely on me." His glance was one of earnest loyalty—in this for the long ride after what we'd been through already.

I smiled. "Well, let me get this show in order then."

Snapped my fingers and the Hellhounds paused the suffocation of the elf and turned to face me. They each took a few steps over and then sat down, at full attention for my next order.

No longer accosted, Ren sat up and gave me a scowl before getting her outfit back in order. She stood and crossed her arms, almost able to hide the excitement of seeing me command authority over the demons.

"Roger?" I asked and gestured him over. "Demons come back here after they die topside, but what happens if they die in hell?"

He rubbed at his chin and narrowed his purple eyes. "I guess we just vanish for good, boss."

Just as I thought. I put my hands on my hips and looked over the sea of patient faces awaiting my order, some of them tilting their heads to the side. They *were* System-created, but I had some attachment to them.

Ren walked around to stand beside me, so she could pretend the dogs were all looking at her—I was certain. "You're deciding if you want to send our children off to war, aren't you?"

I raised an eyebrow. "Not that I would have used all of those specific words in that manner but yes."

"Conflicting." She pulled a face. "Do they have an option to deny such a request?"

"Does anyone?"

Ren turned to me and narrowed her eyes. "Your ego is already inflated enough. If this is leading up to you turning into a Demon Prince and ruling over all the denizens in hell, then count me out."

"You wouldn't want to be my queen?"

"Not of *hell*." She rolled her eyes.

"We could make it a vassal state and be rulers of the main world?" I attempted a convincing grin.

"Ugh, *fine*." With a sigh, she brought a hand up to rub at her eyes. "If only so I can visit the pups every so often."

A done deal, pretty much. I'd leave her to regret meeting in the middle later on and turned my attention to the large rabbit instead.

"Roger, do you know where I'd find my Imps? Or any clue as to where we should head to next?"

His nose twitched in thought. "There's . . . a route. Would be too dangerous normally but with all these rat things we could get through closer to the inner circle of hell."

"You expect violence then?"

"Crave it, boss." He licked at his lips. "But it'll be better than wandering around the wastes here, where there will also be other assholes to fight."

I sighed and looked to my equal for her view of the proposition, but she was already crouched down and petting two of the hounds that were doing their best to ignore her advances and focus on me. A little guaranteed violence and shorter walk, compared to the unknown on a longer trip.

"Very well, Roger. Make the necessary preparations . . . or however this works?"

"On it, boss."

While he placed his mace down and stretched out, I tried to decide if I was a fan of this new development in our adventure. Part of me was worried about Quinn and Tanya. They were capable, of course, but being only a duo made them an easier target for any potential trouble topside. If they were smart, they'd be hiding out until we could join back up.

There was the option that they could go to the Wardens ahead of us . . . but I didn't like that. While our time in hell had no obvious end at present, it would be even worse knowing the pair got into something terrible and we couldn't assist. After her recent revelation, I'm sure they could find something to busy themselves with—and hopefully Tanya's mind would be at peace no longer being in this dreadful place.

I didn't mind the change of scenery personally, although I can see why it might not be to the tastes of the rest of the Party. A distraction from our goals, certainly, one where we had to gather what advantages we could from the situation . . . but ensure it didn't cause problems for our true target. We needed to reach the Eternal Wardens and then prepare to march on Candlekeep and the Lady.

Simple on the surface. Not so easy while we resided in hell.

Roger gripped at the air in front of him and tore through reality, opening up a passageway as if it had been paper obscuring a secret entrance. In this split, I could see a village or town of dark hues beyond but little else.

"I'll hold it open so you and all the little turds can scurry through, boss." He grinned as his hands held the top corners of the hole through the air.

Neither Wolf nor Ren looked particularly pleased about being the first to pass through this unknown portal to somewhere else—we hadn't exactly been having good luck with that sort of thing so far. So, as the most Demon Prince adjacent among us, I took the mantle and the first steps toward our new destination.

Expecting some kind of energy or vertigo to pass over me as I stepped through, I was almost underwhelmed, as the process was no different from passing through a normal doorway.

A slight change in atmospheric temperature and some darker tones to the scenery but otherwise relatively the same. We were among a small gathering of rocks just beside a road that led through the small town ahead. There were figures moving around, but I couldn't pick out much detail among the faux gloom. I stepped aside so that Ren, Wolf, and the multitude of Hellhounds could join me—before finally Roger stepped in.

"Just have to pass through this town, boss, and we shouldn't be too far from where your Imps could be."

I nodded but wasn't too convinced. "We *have* to go through. Can't go around?"

"No, there's, like . . ." He waved a fluffy paw at the inert backdrop of our current locale. "Gas clouds and fire shit."

Ren crossed her arms. "I don't see anything."

"That's how it gets you." He shrugged. "I've lived here my whole existence, so if you want to—"

"*Okay*, Roger." I held up my hand. "I'm more worried about us gathering undue attention from powerful demons now that we have a squadron of pups loyal to me."

"I'm more worried about dining opportunities," Wolf murmured.

The rabbit shrugged again and hoisted the mace up over his shoulder. "We'll burn those bridges when we cross them."

After exchanging a glance with the elf, I decided to lead us onward. Day wasn't getting any younger, although there wasn't really much chance of guessing what stage of the day we were actually at—even ignoring the time dilation that may be between here and the world that at least had a sun.

I flexed my fingers as the horde of hounds fell into step behind the four of us, striding abreast of each other. A terrible and odd sight for anyone, even in the hells. Stone road took us right up to the town's edge, where the first inhabitant sitting on the porch of their abode turned a yellow eye toward us.

A crocodile demon, if I had to dissolve them into basic descriptions. Something that itched the back of my mind and put me on edge. Still, other than the long-snouted row of sharp teeth and dirtied dungarees he was wearing, there was nothing overtly threatening about the demon.

At least, until he clocked our guide.

"You ain't welcome here, Roger," he hissed, standing himself up from the wooden chair. Other eyes in the vicinity turned to meet us. "Thought you'd learned the last time, but seems we have to teach you a more *permanent* lesson."

The sounds of metal weapons being drawn drowned out the long sigh escaping me.

CHAPTER TWENTY-SEVEN

Beneath the Crust

It was difficult to stay mad at Roger.

Actually, no—I was still rather disgruntled that he had led us into a spat with a town of crocodile demons just so that he could get his revenge for whatever slight had come before now. I may have given him the benefit of the doubt, but he was constantly stating that intent almost verbatim—while in the midst of beating the demons into pulp—so our role here was rather transparent.

Even less enthused was Ren. After battling a few crocs side by side with me, she had tired of the forced battle she had been dragged into and instead went for the boring option of perching on an overturned wagon and sniping as many assailants as she could. No flare at all.

Wolf had taken her place, and we stood shoulder to shoulder against the onslaught of foes. With little skin in the game, he too was cool on the idea of surging off into battle and was allowing the rabbit to take more of the brunt of frontline combat. With each of us having a retinue of a dozen or so Hellhounds, the croco-demons had a difficult task of engaging us from the outset.

Those hardy enough to wade through the chomping maws of the dogs were quickly mushed to the ground beneath the bear—while any joining the fight from afar had their brains excavated by one of Ren's high-powered shots. I played the middle, assisting them both by debilitating and wounding all that dared oppose us.

No real flare from me either.

Although part of it was being hand led into this current nightmare, I was also feeling a little out of sorts with not having access to my summonses. Well, technically I had *a lot* of summonses—so that was a rather strange complaint. Perhaps it was more of the restraint rather than the effect that had me grouchy.

Certainly, having a small army of demons made combat a lot easier. There was a whole town's worth of crocs to chew through, but the dogs made it seem like nothing at all. If any received a wound, it would slink back past its brethren and the elf would heal it.

I chose to ignore the fact that she could do that, and the hellish pups didn't seem to mind her divine energy running through them. Either something else our bond had muddied or the System had stopped caring at some point. It must be getting desperate.

Cards flashed through the thick neck of the next demon as the Hellhounds brought it to the ground. Chest exploded in the one behind them from Ren's divine-infused shot. Whatever enemies remained wavered and then started to turn tail.

An odd thing, which I put a pin in for now. Weapons lowered as we watched the last handful run off into the gloom farther ahead.

"*Yeah*, run, assholes!" Roger twisted the head of the croc he had been bludgeoning, their vertebrae grinding in his grasp. "This is *my* fuckin' town now!"

He dropped the inert demon to the ground and licked his bloodied lips before turning his gaze back to us.

"I'm not entirely convinced this was anything more than you using us to settle a petty squabble," I said, stretching out my right wrist.

"*No*, boss. A convenience for me, sure—but this *is* the way we need to go." His grimaced grin told me he might be bending the truth a little.

"I don't want to use my control over you to get you back in line, Roger." My tone cooled, and I flexed out my hands. "Best remember where you stand."

"In hell, boss." He raised his mace up over his shoulder. "And I think you'll find, down here, your control doesn't mean shit."

I maintained eye contact with him, the two pits of purple energy staring back at me. Was it my fault that he had become so wayward? He *was* acting like a demon would. It was only natural for him to be deceitful and bloodthirsty. Although we were bound, control was a one-way street—I was sure of it.

My eyebrow raised. "Say that again."

"I'm just saying, your power in hell doesn't hold so much sway . . . boss."

"How far are you willing to go to test that, knowing your death here would be *absolute*?" I stood stoic as purple electricity started to arc around my body.

He remained statuesque, second-guessing his attempts to undermine my leadership. In truth, I didn't know what would happen if he died down here— whether the System would allow me to bring him back as part of my Abilities, whether I'd need to form a new pact with a different demon, or my Skill might just be broken for good.

I was willing to find out if he didn't stand down.

Even if what he was saying was true, a click of my fingers and Ren would put a radiant bullet through his forehead. Not that I wouldn't relish the opportunity to get my own hands dirty.

"In saying that . . . I appreciate your help with this personal matter, boss." His impassive expression finally broke, and he gave me a brief bow.

"No problem. Forewarning is appreciated next time."

Roger nodded eagerly and then looked around rather than uphold the eye contact.

I turned as I felt the press of the elf beside me, some hint of excitement in her eyes. "I was hoping for a little show there." Her hand came out to gesture toward the mutilated bodies. "These guys gave experience, and they dropped loot though. Dig in."

Where was Tanya when I needed her?

In saying that, I considered how feasible it would be to purge more towns like this of their demons. Actually . . . considering they were System-created, it was interesting how they had enough personality to talk animatedly with us and had the brains to retreat and survive. Much like Roger, in a way, who also didn't come from another world like Players did.

Any further thoughts along this odd route were set aside as I caught the elf glaring at me—with even Wolf taking part in the looting, I couldn't avoid lending a hand.

Which turned out to be a miserable process, with the hounds constantly getting in the way—and the demons seemingly only having gear that was suitable for the bear. A couple of Intelligence gems I'd need to socket sometime and some . . . gold coin, for whatever narrative sense that made, but otherwise I was underwhelmed.

[Max: Defeated the town, and then another town.]
[Tanya: Quick work! We're on our way to a safe place.]
[Tanya: Will hunker down and await updates.]
[Max: Perfect, will keep you in the loop.]

I looked back over to Roger, who had defaulted into a more awkward state of avoiding me while we finished up with the corpses he'd caused us to make. I'd rather he be a comfortable ally than force him to prostrate himself before me—which is why I went with the unsaid threat rather than trying to control him. He was a demon, after all. Couldn't blame him for forgetting his place.

"Did we lose any hounds?" Ren appeared back beside me, squinting to look over the mass of flaming demons.

"I can't count higher than twelve, so . . ." I winced away from her scowl.

Wolf huffed, trying to push his way through them all. "There were two that fell. They turned into dark mist."

"Aw." The elf pouted. "At least they don't leave mangled bodies for me to sob over."

"I suppose since they don't drop loot, and they're even less . . . *real*, even compared to System-created, they just cease to be once dead."

"*Real*," she murmured, rolling her eyes.

She was enamored by them, but she understood my point of view well enough—despite the grump she was putting on. Perhaps even saw things the same way as I did. The dogs were conjured tools for me to use. It was only by a quirk in the System that they came back here after I had created them.

At least, that was my best guess. It couldn't be that I was plucking the Hellhounds from a large natural pool, otherwise there would be a lot more of them here. More likely, the only ones that existed were ones I had drawn into being. And . . . *sure*, that made them all special in a way. I respected and cared for them even if they were even more temporary than normal System-created.

"Where to next, Roger?"

I pushed those thoughts away. Otherwise, Ren and I would start to sink under the weight of the undue affection from our horde of hounds once again.

"Just over this way, boss." He lifted an arm to point to the left side of the town where the road split. "There's a little way to go, but I reckon your Imps would be that way."

Not entirely a selfish ploy to have us get revenge on the township then. I wondered if we had to be wary of the ones who had escaped. "Have you noticed, Ren, that Monsters down here seem to be a little . . . smarter?"

Her nose wrinkled up. "I suppose so, yeah. Normally System-created are pretty two-dimensional and easy to wrangle. Both the crocs and the buildings had enough sense to flee—which could be something simple, but . . . I'm not sure."

"Strange feeling?"

"*Always*, trickster." She raised an eyebrow at me before checking behind us.

The group of hounds parted so that the three of us could walk behind the large rabbit as he led us to the left road. I'd gotten some knack of expecting dire events to jump out at us on a regular basis. Now that we were kicking up dust in hell, it was only a matter of time before someone with a big stick came to find out what we were doing.

But then . . . that was the crux of it once more. All our troubles previously had been Players. There were none down here—or at least, I hoped not.

Was the demonic royalty we had agreed to usurp just a Dungeon or a set of static figures we could go punch with our usual aplomb? I had the odd feeling in my stomach that they weren't—that things were different down here in this space for some reason.

"You look like you're chewing something distasteful there, Max." Ren gave me a brief smile before she resumed scowling at the darkened houses along our route.

"There's a feeling like . . . we've stepped into something worse than it appears."

Wolf groaned. "Don't say that."

A struggle more than just pulping demons until we could go back to the normal world. But what exactly?

"Don't think too hard," Ren continued. "We haven't seen enough to really know much. Whatever it is though, we'll bullshit through it together."

"Of course." I smiled, and some of my inner turmoil cooled. The three of us were more than capable of surviving this—out of anyone. I shouldn't be so dour and hard on myself.

I raised my hand toward the back of Roger, and he flinched, despite not being able to see me. There were the wiggling worms of connective magical power I was getting used to. No need for me to be sad about not having my summonses when I realized that not only could I use <Demonic Transposition> with my pact demon, but also my cannon and any one of these hounds.

Not as convenient as a sudden bird, perhaps—but I could still work tricks without a full deck. Just had to lean into the *improvisation* a little more. I hadn't even gone a little crazy in fighting the crocs. Next combat, I would add some flair back into the mix and have fun.

Ren vanished from beside me, replaced by a white dove that looked rather surprised to be in hell. The elf was now on one of the rooftops, a crouched position atop dark tiling. Rifle up, she put her eye to the scope—looking out at the distance ahead of us.

"Good news and bad news," she said rather flatly.

CHAPTER TWENTY-EIGHT

Tightened Production

As it turned out, both the good *and* bad news were that we had some demons to kill. More struggle for this odd life in another . . . plane of existence? But also potential rewards. I could almost taste the next level, even over the ash trying to pet its way into my lungs.

"Do you know this type of demon well, Roger?" I asked, trying to fan some cool air on my face. It wasn't working.

"Not like . . . first-name basis, boss." He gave me a shrug and turned his purple eyes back to our potential prey.

I stared at him for a few seconds before giving up. While the heat of hell hadn't been that bad at the start, the longer we were spending down here, the more I had started to feel it. Ren hadn't been complaining, but her signature scowl had settled back in to be a permanent fixture once more. Wolf had been as irritated as I'd ever seen him.

We needed to find a way to acclimatize—or at least find somewhere in the hells that wasn't so heated.

I gave up and yawned. Allowed the world to know that I was tired already. My urge to put on a show waned even if my desire to pulp demons into mush in the name of gaining experience still drove me forward.

"Let's just play this straight then? Ren up on a roof. Wolf, I will assist you." I was pretty sure that one of my Passives gave me heat resistance, but maybe this was something different.

The bear grunted and moved forward, but the elf just turned a tired glare toward me.

"I feel like a sack of sweaty ham cutlets, trickster. I'm worried about our long-term prospects here." She removed her hat to fan at her face.

"You look as radiant as ever, but I understand. I'm losing my edge too."

"Flattery gets you nowhere. Until I get a bath." Ren swept the top hat across her body and vanished, to be replaced by a white dove.

I turned my attention to the roof a little ahead where she now stood. "Roger. This place is rather hot for us. Is there a cooler area we can move to along the way?"

He shrugged again before catching the look in my eyes. "Sure, boss. After we find your Imps, we can circle around the more central areas to somewhere it isn't so oppressive."

Although I smiled at him, there was no humor or goodwill in it. I knew that it wasn't just the heat that was getting to me. It was how the area was steeped in demonic power. Thick with the bastards. I hadn't lost control over the crocs, but it seemed to be wearing me down again. The current opponents had me feeling . . .

"Boss?"

I blinked away the haze of thoughts to see that they were waiting for me. Rolled out my shoulders and I followed on behind Wolf. Down the end of the road out of the croco-demon town and there was a field—or rather an expansive plain of pure overheated rock. Spined dinosaur-looking demons roved around in packs of three. There were scores of them, stretching out to what appeared to be a dried-out forest. No doubt our intended destination.

The creatures themselves were made of dense bone, their bodies tight bands of the gray-white material. Tusked maws and jutting spikes along their back. Bright-yellow eyes in the skulls and wide feet that looked just as deadly as Wolf's.

"I'll move closer once you've made a dent," Ren called from the building, now slightly behind us.

I raised a hand to confirm her statement. Wasn't much in terms of cover or vantage points within the expanse of rock. With her radiant powers, it turned her already lethal sniper rifle into a precision scalpel that tore demons from this existence. Being a demon myself, I . . . No, I wasn't a *demon*. Had to remind myself. I was a *magician*.

At my signal, both Wolf and Roger ran side by side toward the first pack. I approached at a slower pace, cards twirling around my hand. Before they got the attention of the first Monster, Ren struck one of the three in the head, exploding their skull with golden light.

The remaining two turned to our assault, immediately casting something that washed over Wolf and Roger—dazing and rooting them both. The bear activated a Skill to wash away the debilitation and powered into them. Roger remained in place, not reacting to the other large demon coming toward him.

My cards were out, circling around the rabbit and biting into the Monster. Chipping away at their bone armor before I had to release the power. Drew a critical card and launched it in a blaze of crimson to strike and burst at a foreleg, crippling the demon. Roger recovered and brought his mace up.

Wolf tore through his demon, spitting shards of bone to the ground as the rabbit finished his off with a heavy blow to their head. Ren's next shot cracked through the air to strike the next pack, piercing through the chest and bringing up entangling roots to pin the others in place.

I hummed to myself as I stepped forward to continue to support the other two. Shot a glance back at the pack of Hellhounds whom I had left back near where Ren was perched. If she was going to be out almost solo, then I wanted to leave her a backup in case something tried to sneak up on her. Plus, I didn't want to see any more of our little flock getting turned to mist underneath the sharp feet of whatever these demons were called.

Usually the System provided a handy pop-up when I encountered something new, but it had been relatively quiet since we'd landed down here in hell.

Surely nothing to read into there.

While one hand idly slashed cards through the enemies, I brought up my Chat.

[Max: Hey, Ruby, how are things?]
[Ruby: Peachy <{n>n}>]
[Ruby: Although we were attacked . . .]
[Max: Crimson Shadow?]
[Ruby: Oddly, no. A couple of assholes who worked
for the marketeers, we think.]
[Ruby: We killed them—sorry if you wanted answers.]
[Max: No stress. Good to tick something off the grudge list.]
[Max: We are currently in literal hell. Let me know how you guys get on.]
[Ruby: Seriously? I can't believe you half the time <{?>?}>]

I *did* want answers, in fairness. Knowing more about the group that had been stalking Players for their gear might have added a few more bad actors that needed erasing. Who did they sell to? It must have been the couriers that Ruby and Fiona had just gotten rid of, so hopefully that was at least a chapter ended, even if further corruption still lingered out there.

What most impressed me is that they had done the deed. The group had been struck with ineffective indecision when we met them, hunkered down in place with the fighter, who was unable to lead the gathered Parties toward any sort of goal. Now that they were returning to the second area, it sounded like Fiona had gotten a confidence boost and knew how to deal with the stakes. Sparing the Paladin looked to have worked out in their favor as well.

Good. We'd need them to step up soon enough.

My focus returned to the battlefield, and in my peripheral I noticed three of the demons bearing down on me. Perhaps I should have been paying more attention.

Cannon went out in front of me just before they arrived, my Spear of Luck splitting the head of the first in half. Ren shot the second, blowing out the shoulder joint, causing it to crash into the dried ground and slide my way. Third circled around my siege weapon and chose to dance with me.

Cards out and I whipped them around like flashing blades. Damage wreaked but not enough to fell it. It attempted to gore me, but I turned and dulled the attack, so instead just tumbled to the ground from the force. Dusted up my sweaty suit.

Hand was shaking as I stood, but it wasn't from fear or damage.

Power meter was rising.

I had come too close to the demons, and now my hunter past was disgusted and angered. The dinosaur attempted a second goring attack, but this time I blocked it with <Card Fan> and grabbed hold of one of the many tusked prongs emerging from its head. Magic card bloomed in my other hand and I sank as much energy as I could into it before I plunged it down like a knife. Through the skull and into the brains.

Ren's shot finished off the wounded one, and I looked over at the other pair of our Party as the one I'd killed slumped to the ground. We had been drawing too much aggro. Wolf had three on him, while Roger had two of his own. Even as I stepped toward them, another trio was coming up on my left again.

Well, two could play that game.

I turned back to my new assailants and gripped at my right wrist. Single card that I sank all my power into, draining some of my life. Behind me, the padding of my hound horde approaching. It would take a bit of micromanagement, but as I blinked away the amber hue of hell, I started to see the underlying threads of everything.

White glove was now wrapped around my outstretched hand, even as warm blood started to soak through it.

They were slightly more unwieldy than my cards, but I'd always had a mental connection to direct the demon dogs . . . With some focus, I could . . .

And there it was. Card released just as the large demons collided with me. I closed my eyes and planned the show out from the safe darkness of my own mind.

All movements in wire frame, my mental notebook planning out the choreography of it all. As the first went to gore me, I'd step to the side so that a hound could take a bite—but before the creature could retaliate, my pup would move away. Like a conductor, I moved the little shapes of my summonses in my mind. Avoiding the slower and deliberate attacks of my enemies—the Hellhounds would fall back into safety on one side while others darted in uncontested.

While this was happening, my illuminated card scored through the scene in my mind. Sometimes just to damage and others to waylay or block an attack going toward my little helpers.

Despite being doused with sweat, I felt cooler. More at peace.

Even as the show got more complicated, the flow of it was just . . . perfect, in a way. A practiced precision that felt natural. Could feel my hands burning but otherwise this was relaxing. A meditative state almost.

Stage directions to the most accurate degree, playing out in real time even though I was well away from the situation.

But then it was over—a gap in production as my hounds had nothing to weave within, no more targets for my card to interact with. I let go of all the threads I had been controlling, and my eyes blinked open.

"Max! Max, you asshole!"

I turned my head and pulled a face. Seems as though I had become an over-achiever once more. Caught red-handed, soaked with my own blood. A river of broken gray demons lay between my throng of hounds and the perturbed elf as we had fought our way far beyond the original trio attacking us. *Far* beyond.

That was a lot of corpses I had to go back to loot.

CHAPTER TWENTY-NINE

Residual Warmth

The oppressive heat of the hells turned minutes into hours. Soon enough, hours became days. We fought and killed, always just slightly more powerful than whatever demonic presence Roger dragged us along to. Eventually, we acclimatized. To . . . some degree.

With the System playing favorites, Wolf also received a Skill that gave us heat resistance. Even in this odd place, we found the helping hand of the world itself guiding our purpose.

The Imps hadn't been too hard to track down. The Shades were a little more difficult, but there were only a handful of those. Having a small army of demons made the process of carving our way through hell relatively painless. I'd hardly had a chance to even crack my head open on any of the jutting rocks that littered the place.

Truly a hellish existence.

Ren had calmed, and we had become used to this battleground. Every day, her scowl lessened until we now had a neutral expression as the default. We'd even found the time and privacy for some acts of passion, an accolade few could claim given our surroundings. No baths or cold water had crossed our path, but we became used to the sweat and stink of each other. Blind to it.

At a basic guess, I determined that every three to five days spent in hell was equal to one on the surface. In keeping touch with Tanya, we knew that three whole days had now passed for them. So for us—despite there being no sun to truly gauge—we must be getting close to two weeks. Of sweating, of murdering demons, and of growing as fighters.

No news from the Eternal Wardens or Candlekeep so far. Neither was a good sign. We hadn't come across an exit . . . so there was little we could do. The rest of our Party had held out in place for a day before I sent them to go meet with Fiona and her lot. They'd be safer as a seven than trying to get by as a duo.

For us down here? We had . . . changed.

Could see it in our eyes. The way we held ourselves in places of safety. The ruthless efficiency that we made with our kills. Even Roger had now taken a back seat to our battles, not wanting to get in our way. Our outfits had been stripped down to something more commando-esque. Potion bottles lined our belts, scrolls and other useful consumables across makeshift bandoliers.

Survived almost two dozen ambushes. Almost lost my arm. Ren almost lost her eyes. Wolf sank through part of the ground and almost vanished from existence entirely. But every cut or bruise just honed us further.

We had looted enough gold to buy a palace. Our Equipment had been replaced entirely with better things—my Intelligence alone increasing by almost twenty points, not including the straight-up Mana- and magic-Damage percentage additions. But it wasn't just the System-defined gear that had seen an upgrade.

Ren now had jagged blades at the back of her boots and a longer one at the front of her rifle, like a bayonet. We both had scaled-armor shoulder and knee plates. Wolf was a veritable tank of tough bone armor with several long tusks extending from his shoulders. We were molded to our surroundings and took every advantage we could muster.

And the experience? Not quite the waterfall we had hoped, but I *had* been right—we could surpass the level-fifteen restriction from the second area. We were now a couple of battles away from level sixteen.

Fourteen had granted me another defensive Skill. A Party buff called <Shared Hand>. It worked in a similar way to <Card Fan> but had three uses per Party member and less Damage absorption per card. Much longer cooldown too—but had helped us in our engagements so far.

Fifteen had been the upgrade for my Class Keystone, <Demonic Magician>. Now my opponents would gain additional Dazzle stacks depending on how high my Power bar was. Not too engrossing at low levels, but with all the other Passives I had under my belt, things could cascade at a terrible rate even when I wasn't trying to put on quite the performance.

Only downside of being in hell that I personally disliked was the lack of power tokens. With the hundreds of Monsters we slaughtered every day, we would have a fortress full of the upgrade stones if they could actually drop. Still, couldn't ask for everything.

Ren gave me a long kiss, savoring my lips as she buttoned her shirt up. My hands held her face as she tried to move away. The ash and sweat had caused streaks like war paint over us both, but her eyes were as piercing as ever. Pools of bright blue that were as calming as their much-desired watery equivalents.

"Get suited up, trickster. I can feel the doom calling to us."

The elf being holy adjacent and me being demonic adjacent had allowed us both to grasp at signals down here in hell. After the eighth ambush, we started to get a feel for when and how we would be attacked. Enough to sleep without one eye open—we'd just awake right before, as if an alarm had been set.

"Hitting sixteen will be great. I feel hell will soon run out of demons, and twenty is a pipe dream."

"The only pipe dreams I have," she said, pointing the bandolier she had in her hand at me, "all involve clean running water."

"What we need is, like, a . . . bathhouse? With a sauna, a big pool of clear water, a soft breeze . . . and some privacy."

Ren groaned. "I would *literally* die. Fuck this stupid world and that Lady bitch. The first thing I'm doing as soon as the bullshit is all over is whatever you just said with your filthy mouth."

"Crass, but sure—it's a date then."

"I've seen what you do with that thing, trickster. You *deserve* to be in hell." She grinned as she turned her head away to adjust her gear.

"As long as you're with me." I raised an eyebrow.

"Naturally. I have my own mouth crimes to atone for."

I rolled my eyes and my shirt sleeves up. Had ditched the jacket and top hat for most of the fighting lately. Only kept me warmer than necessary—I hated to admit that we had hardly been putting much flair into our fighting. Didn't seem necessary, especially after my Class upgrade. Just by the nature of my normal combat ability and the occasional cannon, we'd rack up enough stacks of Dazzle for a <Finale> stun when needed. Past that . . . we just killed the demons.

And I *loved* it.

Stopped having the rage outs from being too close to the demons, as eventually I just got used to them. Despite their higher intelligence than the usual System-created we were used to, we'd become accustomed to their mannerisms and ways of fighting.

Stood from the uncomfortable bed and stretched out. Ren gave me a pat on the back as she passed, and I followed her out through the door and down the stairs. Demon homes were few and far between, and the majority were unfit for our purposes—but the occasional settlement would have a structure with four walls, a roof, and a bed. If we were lucky, some didn't smell like demonic bodily fluids and we could turn any corpses away from us to stare at the walls rather than our sleeping habits.

I would be the first to admit we had become slightly unhinged.

Two worms wriggling in the filth together, bloodied and sweaty—but in love and happy for it. Closer emotionally and as fighters. Our drop into hell had been something of a trial by fire, but we had emerged as better people—or, rather, were working our way to emerging. Still no exit door in sight, but it would be nice to go back to the normal world.

If it could even accept us as we were now.

Down the stairs and into the lower room. Wolf was already in his battle gear, the dark wooden furniture that had been in the space the evening before now trashed into parts in one corner where he had nested up to sleep. All except for one chair near the glassless windows, where Roger sat with his large feet up on the windowsill.

"Next village has *tall* fuckin' demons with long legs, boss. Was just telling Wolf that he could probably snap through them like twigs."

I nodded before giving the bear a pat on the flank. He had been holding up alright. Some days slightly more tired than others, but he hadn't faltered. One of his new Abilities was giving him an energy boost on the regular, so we only watched for other signs of exhaustion.

We double-checked we hadn't left anything behind before I pushed through the door and stepped out into the street. A horde of Hellhounds on my left and a squadron of different Imps on my right. The Shades were off in a loose circle at a distance as an early-warning system for if we were going to have trouble.

And we *were*. We could all feel it.

Not just an ordinary ambush . . . Something worse, I was sure. Ten or so days maiming our way through the hells had been a nice holiday, but we were bound to get the attention of someone who cared eventually. Roger had tried to fill me in on the various titles and structure of those in charge here, but it had slipped right off my brain.

With few words spoken, we traveled until we reached the next killing field. Just as he said, the demons were on tall legs—almost like stilts. They reminded me of giraffes, if only instead of the neck it was all the other limbs that were way too long.

We had been lucky that many of the demons dropped rations in some way or another. The agreement had been not to eat demonic meat, but we had been saved from that opportunity by a type of random crate that provided food—and drinks. Otherwise, we would have dehydrated by now.

Critical card bloomed into my hand.

We were fast friends with the destiny the System forced upon us, but as each new day passed, all I cared for was returning and putting an end to the Crimson Shadow.

Magic card flew out and struck a leg, bursting and severing the limb. Demon cried out and dropped, as Ren put a radiant bullet in the head of the next. Wolf burst forward with incredible speed surrounded by hounds as a throng of Imps started to power up their ranged attacks.

I'd *miss* this when we eventually got to return—I couldn't deny that.

Already on to the third pack as my next card illuminated my face. I held it there as a shadow washed over the battlefield toward us, and my eyes went to the ruddy sky.

A dark figure, wide wings slowing his descent, dropped down and slammed into the dry ground, cracking the rock and causing a wave of disturbed dust to filter out around his landing spot.

I narrowed my eyes as the crown of bright silver upon his head caught the light, flickering the promise of death just as his grin widened.

"Looks like I'll be dining well tonight," he growled, a sword of flaming red appearing in his clawed hand.

CHAPTER THIRTY

Numb to It

The demon standing before us stretched out, readying his blade to attack. Seemed a bit shortsighted to me when we hadn't even become well acquainted. My hounds and Imps tensed in anticipation, as Ren and I exchanged a glance.

Would be the first higher demon we had encountered, if you could call it that. An assumption on my part due to the fact that he had a little silver crown upon his head. Clashed with the dark coloration of his horns—and drove my desire to know *more*.

"Are you a Demon Prince?" I asked, the taste of regicide on my lips.

"I am Gil-p'tak, eleventh in the line for the throne. Worms like you should be kneeling before me."

"Pass." I ran a hand through my messy hair. Still hadn't had that cut. "I'm getting to that age where I have to be careful how rough on my joints I am."

"*Bullshit.*" Ren rolled her eyes. "Would be the first time you ever cared about your own safety."

"I'm getting better." I crossed my arms and hoped that she would believe the lie. Her scowl determined that she did not.

The demon with the name I wasn't going to try to remember wasn't a fan of our playful bickering and held out his sword toward us. "Silence, worms. Mortals thinking they could just brainwash these demons into following your control. You should be flayed alive for your insolence."

"Don't threaten him with a good time." Ren sighed. "He might take you up on that just to earn some suffering points for his character progression."

"I don't know." My head tilted slightly. "I think I'm all progressed out. What I *could* use, however, is a fancy silver crown."

She nodded. "It would suit you."

I held my hand out to the ever-angering demon. "What say you . . . uh, *Gilpak?* Care to join the side of the future Demon King willingly?"

"Bastards! I'll kill you where you stand!"

"Thought as much. Shame." I clicked my fingers. "Moonflower, erase this stain from my future kingdom."

Her rifle went up, a swirl of radiant energy circling down the body of the weapon as she aimed it at the demon. In response, he raised a hand, some form of magical shield blooming into life in front of him.

Ren vanished, replaced by a bird, and the prince couldn't turn quick enough. Radiant blast blew his shield-creating arm off at the shoulder joint, and she returned to beside me. The white dove puffed into feathers as the fiery sword of the demon struck it.

"Apologies, my king," the elf said, rolling her eyes. "I seem to have just made a bigger stain on your kingdom instead."

"It'll wash out," I murmured. "I'll be sure to discipline you later."

Wolf sighed and turned his gaze toward us. "Have I not suffered enough?"

"This *is* hell, bud. Alright, gang—let's wrap this up before things get too heated." I narrowed my gaze and gave the Imps the signal.

Ren fired another shot—the demon managing to deflect it with his blade, but he still succumbed to the entangling vines. As one, my group of Imps charged up their magical strikes—a volley that few things had been able to weather in our time down here.

"Nice try," the prince growled. "But you are out of your depths."

Energy washed over us all as he activated his Domain.

Ren, Wolf, and I now stood alone in a . . . wooden cabin? Although it was large—more like a warehouse in size. Attached to the walls, stacked three high, were hooks where bodies were hanging.

Mutilated and damaged in a variety of ways, and . . . Oh, they were all *Ren*.

The elf snorted and pointed a finger at one. "That one looks just like that time the horse kicked your head in."

I rolled my eyes. "Not entirely a shared delusion then. All of these look like you for me."

She wrinkled up her face and stepped up to the closest one for inspection. "Ah, look. I can see your actual heart here—that's kind of cute."

For me, her corpse was missing her jaw and lower legs, maybe eaten by something. "Despite your eyes being rolled back, they are still vibrant and beautiful, even in death."

"Aw." She turned and wrapped herself around me, and we shared a soft kiss.

Wolf exhaled through his nose and sat down on his backside.

After prying the elf away from me—a difficult task—I stepped over and placed my hand on his shoulder. "Who is it you see, brother? One of us two? Quinn?"

"No." His amber eyes glanced at me. "They are all bears."

"Oh." My mood cooled off. While Ren and I had become unhinged enough that blood and death didn't shift the needle, Wolf had retained his dour and grounded view on things. "Is it like . . . your old-world siblings?"

He shifted but shook his head from side to side. "Perhaps that is the intention, but I no longer recognize or relate to them as such. Although I am glad this does not traumatize me, it is humbling to consider how far I've come from being an animal to being a family with the both of you."

"Sometimes blood we share on the outside is a stronger bond than the blood that is on the inside."

The bear pulled a face. "No need for such concerning platitudes. My only desire is to get out of this place to have some time away from your incessant rutting."

"It is getting a bit much, huh?" I looked over at the elf, who was inspecting more of the Max corpses.

She had asked me a day or two ago if I thought the hells had been changing our personalities. Whether we were becoming corrupted or influenced by sin. Certainly, we had been mercilessly wrathful, even more than before. Lustful? Shamelessly so. Greed or gluttony? Not exactly. We coveted more experience and ate well enough from the rations looted but nothing out of the ordinary.

Other than being envious of the rest of our Party being in the real world, there was no additional jealousy either.

Pride? I'd always been prideful of our capabilities—it was part of putting on a show, of course. Then again, we had been doing a lot less of that, as our time was almost wholly devoted to the first two aforementioned sins. And sloth? Not at all. We'd been almost constantly on the move and killing, only stopping for sleep and acts of passion.

So, my diagnosis? Things were just pretty fucked. Constant oppression from the atmosphere in hell and the need to keep killing day in and out had worn us down. Sure, we were a little less sane—but our physical closeness was more due to our love and doomed situation rather than our actual morals slipping away.

At least, this was what I believed.

"Oh, I wish I could show you this, trickster!" She waved her hand at a body. "Remember that dream I had the other night?"

"The one where a demon crawled out of my body like it was a skin suit?"

"Yeah! For this dead version of you, someone has stuck the wrists of your severed hands into your eye sockets, so it's like you're trying to escape your own head." She turned back to me and beamed.

Okay, so things weren't entirely as normal as before. A Max from just a week or two ago would have been panicked and disgusted—heartbroken, even—at seeing so many mangled corpses of the one I loved. Did it no longer bother me because I knew it wasn't real? Just a figment of demonic power within this Domain? Had I just become so numb to death?

"You're very sweet, Ren, and I do love to see you energized . . . but let's deal with this macabre illusion and get back on track."

Her wide grin softened to a calm smile, and she nodded. "You're right. It's just not every day some limp-dick demon thinks showing you a warehouse full of your dead soulmate is an effective fighting strategy."

"Right? Our first Domain here in hell and it's this? How are we even supposed to die from this?"

Wolf righted himself onto his paws. "Can you break this one, Max?"

I puckered my lips and looked around. From where we stood, it seemed to be arranged like a supermarket or library, perhaps. We were close to one wall, and there were aisles between more stacks of dead us on hooks. Beyond the distance we could see was a thick, fogged darkness. It was unlikely the Domain was infinite, even for a prince, but it gave that appearance.

"Unfortunately, this isn't really moving my Power bar for some reason." I gave him a shrug. "So I don't think I could override it."

"Maybe these bodies will come alive and attack us?" Ren offered, considering prodding one with her rifle muzzle to check.

My demons and Roger hadn't been drawn into the Domain, so that was something to keep in mind. Whether they were now gone or just standing outside this pocket bubble waiting for us remained to be seen. Their summoning cards were still inert and gray in my deck, so I couldn't invite them—or inadvertently escape.

"Let's walk and see what comes out to bite us?"

They agreed, and we did just that, heading . . . southward, perhaps. Toward the looming darkness in the distance to see if anything turned up. Occasionally I'd check behind us to see if anything stalked us or changed at all . . . but no, it remained mundane.

Even the different corpses didn't really register after a while. Missing limbs, shredded flesh, and pale skin. All blurring into something boring. One caught my eye, however. "This one has half your shirt ripped off, showing your stomach. It's quite the fashion statement."

"Oh, yeah?" Ren raised her eyebrows and put her rifle away. She grabbed the bottom of her frayed shirt and rolled it up to mimic the body I had seen. "What do you think?" She gave a brief twirl.

"Fetching, although I may be biased."

She wrinkled up her nose and let the fabric fall back down and withdrew her weapon again. "Don't think I'd ever leave the house like that. Not my style."

"I'll put in a complaint with the dead-body fashion department. Oh, maybe these are all split versions of us that died along the road we've taken?"

Wolf grunted. "I doubt you would have died thousands of times, even if you ran headfirst into everything. Which you almost always do."

A true enough point. I was actually trying to get a feel for the Domain and ascertain what it actually did. Often they were just battlegrounds that gave the demons a better advantage or different Abilities. We hadn't seen the prince so far, and it didn't make sense for there to be no threat against us—we couldn't be contained indefinitely.

"My assumption is this is like a . . . Venus flytrap, if you're familiar?"

They both gave me a nod, the System at least translating that into something they did understand, even if they were used to it by a different name.

"The idea is that we arrive, get spooked, and panic. Lose all hope and become disgusted by the corpses and then *wham*. Something comes and gobbles us up."

Ren nodded slowly. "So, because we don't really give a shit, the demon is hiding away?"

"Essentially."

"Can I just start shooting stuff and see what happens?"

I took another look around as we paused. Didn't seem like we had moved at all really.

"That seems to be your thing now, so go ahead."

She spun her sniper rifle around in her hand, a blazing trail of radiant energy following it, before she snapped it into place and aimed off into the darkness ahead of us.

As her finger pressed against the trigger, something large shifted behind us, displacing the air.

CHAPTER THIRTY-ONE

Cracked Crown

We rolled to the wooden floor as a dark shape swept over us, the rush of air that was following the demon actually quite cooling.

Both of us back up to our feet, we turned to see what looked like a giant bat—or vulture—swoop off toward the darkness.

Ren's radiant shot was quicker than my magical card, but both projectiles blew toward it. A shrill scream pierced the infinite warehouse displaying our corpses, and then there was silence again.

"You alright, Wolf?" I turned to the bear, who had been a bigger target.

"Yeah." He shook himself off. "It was going for you two, so I went ignored."

Ren stood and rotated her rifle to face behind us, ready in case it repeated the same attack. "He needs to do that again. Did you feel that breeze? *Wow.*"

"One hundred percent," I agreed while the bear nodded along.

Although, the chances of this becoming an enjoyable experience in the long term weren't too great. Even if the stacked rows of our mutilated bodies didn't budge us, there was only so much Domain time we could endure.

The elf glanced at me while I was busy in thought. "Got any demonic bullshit for this, Max?"

I rubbed at my head. "Without being able to activate my own, I don't think so. Half of my summoning cards are inert, and I have no Power or Dazzle anywhere to draw on. However, if any of us can do something, it would be you?"

"Yeah?" She scowled at the darkness behind us. "Something with my holy energy?"

"Possibly." Two ways out of a Domain were either to weaken the demon enough or break through with a higher density of your own power. Usually via another Domain but I saw no reason why other elements couldn't work. "The question is how to do this in the most shark-jumping way."

Ren pulled a face. "The System translates that phrase, but it doesn't have any relative meaning in my language."

"Oh. Jumping the shark is where you go beyond the point of absurdity or believability."

She raised an eyebrow. "Isn't that what we *constantly* do?"

I tried to cast my mind back through the last . . . month? Arriving in this world, meeting a beautiful elf who fell for me and a talking bear, fighting increasingly dire odds against a group of criminals and Monsters, destroying a titanic corpse before being plunging into hell . . . not to mention all the magic.

"We're a little out there," I eventually agreed.

Wolf huffed. "Well, I'd like to be a little out of *here*."

"A fair point, brother." I gave him a short bow. "I think I have a plan, if you are ready, my love."

"Constantly." The elf shot me a grin.

My arm came out, and the scrolls affixed into my wrist mount shuffled about as I replaced them with a thought. Although we had been in a power token drought down here in hell, plenty of the Monsters dropped a variety of scrolls.

Mundane card left my belt and zipped into the air ahead of us slightly. I cast weaken-state scroll on the floorboards, a circle of energy appearing and increasing all elemental Damage within.

Ren shot my card with her rifle and then held her hand out. A cloud began to form, golden edges around the gloom before bolts of radiant lightning rained down. To accompany this, I then used reduce-area scroll to shrink the cloud down, increasing the pressure the attacks had on a smaller area of the Domain.

Each bolt struck the wood with a burst—and didn't appear to do any Damage. I knew a little different, however, as something in my core could feel the vibrations of pain the attack was causing. Like a needle poking at the inside of a balloon.

"Anything I can help with?" Wolf asked.

"Watch behind Ren, if you please." I turned my gaze to the elf. Pale arm extended, fresh blood ran down her hand, creating little rivers to her elbow. Her expression was rather dull and neutral.

We had started by wanting to meet in the middle. At some point we had, and then . . . things just blurred together. More like each other than ever. Our love had settled into a solid foundation of unspoken companionship. We pushed ourselves to the limit and beyond, and our time in hell had totally sanded down any apprehension or remaining awkwardness that our romance held.

I repeatedly threw out magic cards, hoping to cycle for—*Ah*, there it was. The bright crimson of a critical attack.

On the whole, I felt sorry for those in the real world. We were already ruthless and overpowered compared to most. Our filter had now been further ground down between constant violence and impassioned embraces under the dull atmosphere of a land seeped with evil.

We'd emerge from our scarlet cocoon as demons, one way or another.

Held my own arm out, mostly for the visual of it. Poured all my Mana into this one card and then started on my Health. Blood started to run down my arm, and I caught the look of the elf as she caught me mimicking her. Gave me some come-hither eyes. Would kill for those eyes. *Had* killed for those eyes.

Didn't release the card yet. Dangerous because I had no limit on how much Health I could degrade away. Health potion in my left hand, just as Ren pulled out a mana one. We stood and maintained eye contact as we downed them, dropping the empty glass bottles to the floor after. Only, they didn't hit the floor as I stole hers from the air, and she stole mine.

Wolf grunted. "I feel something."

"*Me too*," the elf murmured before turning her head back.

So did I, and it wasn't just the desire to find a demonic hotel to get an early night. The presence of the large bat from back behind us, intending on swooping back down for a second attempt.

I turned and slashed out with the card, releasing it to scour the thick air like a beam of crimson light. The bat loomed into view and immediately aborted the dive to instead gain altitude abruptly in an attempt to dodge my card.

Left hand grabbed my right wrist, as I controlled my projectile and curved it around to follow the demon. The weight of how much power I had filled it with made it difficult to control, doubly so with the distance it was now traveling. "Don't stop," I commanded the elf.

"Oh, I can go all day." She grinned and furrowed her brow, trying to force extra strength into her cloud attack that was beating down at the floor of the Domain.

My feet slipped apart and gripped into the ground as if gravity had just been increased on me. He was trying to attack, to dissuade me from slicing at the creature gaining higher toward a ceiling that didn't really exist.

Ah, but that was it, wasn't it?

Larger Domains were weaker by nature. Much like a balloon, I just had to help stretch it out. Card swerved in the distance as I brought another potion out with a shaking hand. Instead of trying to slice him though, I forced him to keep flying away from us.

Muscles tensed and twitched. I started to feel lightheaded from the range that I was grasping at.

"Corpses look different," Wolf noted, keeping an eye on our surroundings.

I couldn't risk taking my aching eyes away from my projectile but saw Ren glance around in my peripheral.

"You're right. They're . . . less detailed? Smudged or blurred almost."

We were nearing the popping point. I could feel it now. Critical card was a small blob of red light at an impossible distance in the darkness above. Could no longer see the bat now . . .

I exhaled, and a wave of energy burst around us; a flash of vertigo pulled at our stomachs with an acrid pop. Feet shuffled on dried rock, and I looked up to see the surprised Demon Prince, his eyes wide and looking at us.

"Just what are you motherfu—"

A dozen fireballs, a handful of ice bolts, a couple of lightning strikes, and one very pointy rock struck him before he could finish his sentence. As he stumbled and dropped to his knees from the assault, a wave of Hellhounds leaped upon him, tearing through his ruddy skin.

"Boss!" Roger hopped over to the three of us. "I was trying to get into the Domain, but it was too strong for me. You got out?"

"Oh, yeah." I wiped the blood from my hand across my grubby shirt. "Simple really."

Ren stepped up to me and grabbed my face, hand still slick with blood as we shared a couple of long kisses. She pulled away and wiped the rest of the crimson to mar my shirt as well. "Wonder what my Domain would be if I had one."

"You want to be a demon?"

The elf tilted her head from side to side. "I'm probably not in the right mind-set to make a sensible decision on that. It's *probably* not a good idea, right?"

"Even if possible," I agreed diplomatically. "That's a big change in your core being. Not advisable."

"If you become Demon King though, you'll not stop me from becoming your Demon Queen?" She bit her lip, which made it very difficult to dissuade her.

Before I could throw cold water on the idea, one of the Hellhounds whined beside me. I turned and knelt down next to him to see that he had the silver crown the demon had been wearing in his mouth. A little demon blood on it, but that seemed thematically appropriate.

"Oh, that's a good boy." I smiled and gave him a pat on the head as I took the crown for myself.

"Ah, boss—that's not a good . . ."

Too late. I had placed it on my head. Back up straight, I raised an eyebrow at the elf. "Opinion?"

"Top hat is much more fitting, but you might as well keep it. We could use more . . . costumes." Her eyebrows moved up and down, as if I couldn't read her intention like it was on a billboard already.

"A fair point." I reached up and grabbed at it.

Only now it wouldn't move.

I pulled a face and looked at my pact demon, the rabbit already grimacing and trying to melt away from my glare. "What have I done, Roger? You could have been a *bit* more prompt with any warning."

"You're . . . a Demon Prince now, your highness."

Ren whistled, but Wolf didn't look impressed. No doubt it was due to the part of me that was a demon. Now I had glued an object of monarchy to my fragile skull, I had invited myself into the most dangerous game of all.

"So . . . now, I'm eleventh in line for the throne?" I crossed my arms, an act only slightly painful for the recovering right limb.

"Pretty much, yeah." He shuffled awkwardly. "That means you're even more of a target, your highness."

I clicked my tongue. When it didn't rain ash, it poured.

Ren placed her hand on my arm, a finger dancing circles on my tattered clothing. "So, what are your first orders as demonic royalty, my prince?"

I grinned and pulled her in closer.

"First off, *eleventh* is much too high a number. Let's go lower that."

CHAPTER THIRTY-TWO

Bleeding Hell

The nicest thing about wearing a crown was the sense of self-importance it gave me. That and the lust for greater power . . . Although, in part, I had held both these things already throughout most of my journey. Now it was just more visceral and overt.

Even currently, as the air ruffled through my hair, I couldn't shake the manic grin across my face. We were losing ourselves to sin and needed a way out before we became nothing more than those we despised and killed.

Still, until then, I'd enjoy it.

Ceiling burst downward as I cratered through it, wooden shards and pale dust clattering to the large room below.

Dozens of pairs of eyes looked up to me in shock as I used a withdrawn sheet to hook onto a beam so as to not break my legs—as amusing as that would be. I swung and dropped down to the wooden floor that was long soaked through with demonic ale and discarded food.

A banquet hall. Going through the full motions. Guest of honor at the head of the table wasn't me—but I was about to clear a few chairs for my Party to enjoy the proceedings.

"Number ten!" I growled, standing up tall and pointing a finger at the larger demon halfway eating what looked like a whole demonic lamb. "Fuckin' die!" A card bloomed into my hand. Not the best one-liner, but I'd certainly said worse. Luckily, two weeks down here in hell had all but erased any shame or embarrassment Ren and I had previously held.

And speak of the lovely lady.

Enter stage right—as a white dove vanished to be replaced by the elf on the other side of the room. A radiant bullet shredded through a handful of smaller demons, who were unsure what was going on.

"Kill them!" the tenth in line to the throne yelled, tossing his snack onto the long table.

My card left my hand and spiraled through the air—not aiming for the head demon but instead into the middle of the room. It cut the chain holding up the ramshackle chandelier. It fell, and the candles bounced over spilled alcohol, lighting up the banquet table with unusual green flames.

I spun in place as the nearest but not dearest group of demons tried to stumble from their chairs and draw weapons. Into my hands another cloth—this one a deep black. Held it out to the side, obscuring part of the wall. Swooshed it away just as the wooden planks burst inward—Wolf powering into the gathering and slashing through three of the demons immediately.

Roger and the Hellhounds followed in behind him like a broken dam. A tide of gnashing jaws and white fur to cut a bloody swath through the unprepared merrymakers. I was already atop the table now, striding toward my target while twin cards zipped around to cut down those around me.

"Upstart rat droppings, you think you can stand against me?" The demon stood and held out a hand toward me. A wave of energy washed over us.

A jungle.

"If we're going to go through *this* another ten times . . ." Ren grumbled, not willing to finish the threat.

"You could have shot him first."

She scowled at me. "I thought this was *your* ego thing. Didn't want you to hold it against me."

"My dear, you could tear my still-beating heart from my chest and I wouldn't hold it against you."

"Aw." Her grump faded away. "I'd hold it against *me* though. Cradle that cute little heart."

I smiled before catching the glare of the bear from my left. He had gotten taller . . . Oh *no*. "Ren, we are sinking."

We both looked down to see our ankles enveloped by the thick mud around us. I had been too busy looking at those blue eyes to really take in the Domain itself. Somewhat lazy of me, in truth. The demon might be waiting to strike right now . . . although it didn't seem likely. I had a knack for this kind of thing.

Left leg sank a couple more inches into the mud as I pulled my right out. Dropped a plank of wood and stood on it—repeating the same action to remove my left from the filth. Surface area just about held me up. I looked at the elf, who had her arms crossed and was accepting her fate.

"Waiting for me to be your knight in shining armor?" I asked, eyebrow raised.

"No. Quicksand is a myth. It won't be deep enough to keep drawing me down."

I watched as she slowly sank another inch into the mud, and her eye twitched. With a quick slurping noise, she vanished to appear over at the side, away from the dangerous pit. The white dove was immediately enveloped by the muck. Took me a couple of seconds longer, but by moving the planks ahead of me, I was able to escape. Wolf just . . . wasn't sinking.

"Dare I ask, brother?" I tilted my head as he wandered out.

"One of my Skills prevents restraints, slows, disabling attacks, and difficult terrain." He looked up at me and shrugged. "I get bullshit too, you know."

That was certainly fair—I couldn't hog all the special Abilities—although Ren was getting her fair share these days. I held my hand out to rotate a few different scrolls through my holster before my eyes went through the surroundings.

Strangely, despite what little real-world experience I had with jungles, I had expected more . . . humidity. And life. There were tall trees and vines, plants with large waxy leaves, and a constant mulch of composting vegetation wherever I looked . . . but no bugs or animals.

No demon either, which was somewhat dull.

"You know, out of everything . . . I miss being able to teleport the most," I complained.

"Yeah?" Ren had her rifle out now and was scanning behind us. "Even more than the normal Othea?"

"Part of me is sad we'll return. Our time here in hell has been something of a fever dream, despite the nightmare situation."

She nodded. "We've certainly had lots of ups and downs . . . and more *ups and downs.*"

Wolf grunted and turned his nose to the air. Anything to avoid our loose innuendos. "Hmm." He rotated a little farther, sniffed a couple more times. "This place is unusual."

"No life?"

He looked back at me with his amber eyes and nodded. "Not just that, brother. Even for a Domain it has a secondary . . . ick to it."

Ren lowered her rifle. "An illusion within an illusion?"

I frowned. That didn't seem right. Went to rub my aching head and saw that my hand was already bloody. Was it blood? I held it out to show them. "Can you both see this?"

The elf exchanged a glance with the bear. "Have you been overdoing your magic already, trickster?"

Hmm, they *could* see it—so it was less likely to be an illusion. I rubbed at my head anyway, getting streaks of scarlet across my forehead. It ran down my face in cool rivulets . . . which was odd. Blood was normally warm.

"Health check," I ordered them.

As I twisted my body about to make sure I wasn't falling apart, they did the same.

"All clear," Ren announced.

"I cannot see anything wrong with me," the bear confirmed.

"Always me, isn't it?" I shook my head and held my hand out. It continued to drip, as if something was forcing the blood out through pressure.

Ren wrinkled up her nose and looked closer at it. "Perhaps we'll just slowly bleed to death one by one and that's the Domain. Dibs on being last."

She gave me a shrug and moved away, no apparent obvious cause for my blood-letting. My Status screens didn't give any information, and my Health bar was still moderately full considering our quick banquet bout.

So why didn't I feel happy just ignoring it?

Moved my hand up to my face and sniffed it. Not . . . unlike my unusual blood, as far as I could tell.

"Need me to taste it?" Ren offered.

I shook my head. "Too dangerous in case it's something bad." The fact that she had put such an act on the table that neither of us seemed bothered by was perhaps concerning in the long run, but . . . she *did* know what it tasted like. *Mostly* by accident.

"We'll just continue," I eventually decided. "It's not something that has a clear answer to just yet, and I'd rather find the demon to put a hole in him as soon as possible."

They nodded, and we set off . . . whichever direction felt most right to me. We'll call it east. Left hand came up as we walked, and that one seemed fine.

"You know why that is?" Ren nudged the air beside me as she fell into step. "That's your *sinning* hand."

I pulled a face. "How would they know what I get up to with my hands?" I had committed plenty of atrocities with both, so it seemed rather arbitrary. "So why are your hands fine then?"

"What, *you dare*, Max Dickbag? I am clearly an innocent soul."

"Bullshit." I held up my dripping right hand. "You, of all people, know why they call it a *dominant* hand."

She bit her lip—and then we both walked into the stationary bear as he stopped to glare at us.

"If we must fall into horrors beyond my understanding and almost perish on the regular, I'd rather our last moments together aren't your dribbling howls, like mewing animals in heat."

Perhaps he had a point. We were just here to assassinate a Demon Prince, but Ren and I had gotten so detached from reality we were casual and loose with our approach to fighting. Just enjoying the change of scenery, if I were to be honest.

"I apologize, Wolf. We'll try to keep it together so you're not such a third wheel." I placed my hand on his shoulder to assert the authenticity of my statement.

"Yes, well—*Ow*." He shuffled away from me and scowled at where my hand had been.

"You . . . okay?" I furrowed my brow and stepped away, allowing Ren to move in and have a look.

The elf tilted her head, moving in closer to him, before away. "Oh dear. Where you touched Wolf, he now has a wound that is running with blood." She turned to me and eyed up my hand. "Glad you didn't let me lick it."

"If I had a gold coin for every . . ." I let the sentence fade away as I pointed a finger out and deliberately moved it around to touch the back of my left hand.

"*Max*." Ren shot me a scowl.

Sure enough, the small dot where I had prodded now looked like I had taken some nasty damage, and a trickle of blood ran down to my wrist.

I flared out my nostrils and looked up at the elf. "C'mon, Ren. You don't want in this sinking ship as well?"

"I swear if you dare touch me with your cursed hand, you will *not* like where I grab in retaliation."

It made some sense now why my head was still dripping with blood even long after I had rubbed it. My gaze swept around the area, trying to see if there was an overt cause or solution to our problem. No, not really.

"Got some terrible news, Ren." I looked back at her and smiled, streams of crimson marring my face.

"What is it?" She grimaced.

"I have a *really* itchy nose."

CHAPTER THIRTY-THREE

Undue Power

Despite my affinity for the demonic, I was starting to share Ren's chagrin for potentially being subject to another nine or ten Domains. Mostly because, at present, I had managed to touch myself in three further places accidentally, all of which now also continuously bled.

Both Ren and Wolf traveled well out of my reach. Perhaps for the best, as I seemed to catch myself on a protruding branch or thick amount of foliage every so often. Wouldn't do for me to grab out at them for stability.

"I'd be more impressed if we were actually just attacked," Ren said, perhaps for the third time.

Another point in which she was correct, however. These higher-level Domains that were meant to just torment us to death were rather boring given that we weren't exactly pushovers. Blood and gore had been completely normalized to us. We'd almost frolicked in the stuff at this point.

I stopped and looked around us again. Didn't seem like we were making much progress or had come across any different terrain in our travels. A landmark or some manner of guide toward what we were meant to do would be swell. I'd even accept . . . a giant snake to fight? Or a gargantuan tarantula?

"Can we not just do the piercing-attack thing again?" Ren stopped and crossed her arms, scowling off at the unchanging scenery.

"Hmm. The answer isn't no, but it might not work here without a way to stretch the power of the Domain." I sighed and rubbed at my head, causing further blood to run down my face. "*Shit.*"

"Huh, I was worried I might have to eat your corpse after you bled yourself to death, but I don't want to catch whatever dumbassery disease you clearly have."

I shrugged and resisted the urge to put my hands on my hips. "We both know you'd have caught it by now, no matter the manner in which it was transmitted."

"I'd still eat you," Wolf offered.

There was perhaps some reflection to be done on the fact that I found that statement reassuring. I would still be palatable, even in my current state. Perhaps the bear had something going there though—my current act was rather tasteless.

I drew out my deck from my belt and had the mundane cards flutter out to orbit around me. Closed my eyes and relaxed. There was always more than one way to pull a rabbit from a hat. No point sitting around waiting for the opportunity to dazzle when I was more than capable of creating my own show.

A Domain was a pocket dimension created by a demon's power. To be a part of this System, there must be some manner of underlying magic to them. I was a master of manipulating magic—to some degree. I just needed to find the tethers or whatever.

In my mind, I sank away from current proceedings. Cold blood ignored. Cards rotating around me, barely an inconvenience. My two partners in demon crime silent mannequins on a dark-gray workspace.

I took a deep breath, and white outlines came into view. The power of the Domain . . . looked like an onion. Spirals of System tethers ran around us in a large sphere. More powerful than I had imagined, it would be nigh impossible for me to stick a hand in and just switch off the power of the Domain. Shame, but perhaps doing so would have been anticlimactic anyway.

There were thinner threads that ran from me and to outside this sphere, but they were faint. The connection to my own demons. No ability to pull them through or us out, unfortunately. As my mind tried to focus, the wispy lines faded and shifted away like trails of smoke.

Unacceptable.

It did lead me to a realization, however. This spiraling line that had constructed this faux sphere representing the Domain . . . It was all one line leading to one entity. The demon himself.

I opened my eyes as the swirling cards turned to ash.

"Ignoring us is rather rude, dickbag." Ren scowled at me, as they had probably been speaking to me while I was away in my mind.

"I do apologize, my dear." A wide grin went across my face as I raised my arm. Purple electricity started to arc around it. "Let me get the manager for you."

<Domain Escalation>

A whisper of Demonic went through my ears as I clawed the new Ability from the fabric of the System itself. I *deserved* it, after all—I was going to be the Demon King.

Ahead of where my bloody hand pointed, a tear in reality cracked and hissed before the Domain's progenitor appeared before us.

His eyes were at first filled with surprise, then pure contempt, as he growled in my direction. "Festering shit, who are you to summon me in my own—"

Then one of his eyes was filled with a high-caliber sniper bullet, glowing with holy light.

With a pop, the Domain washed away, putting us back in the banquet room. Only a new kind of feast was in progress as Roger led the hounds and Imps in devouring the killed demons.

"Changed your mind on if shooting the demon with little ceremony is a knock on your ego yet?" Ren asked, stepping down from the table we were on.

"That *was* like a kick in the balls," I complained. "Clichés and tropes are there for a reason."

"I *did* warn you." She rolled her eyes. "Next time I'll let you monologue a bit and get injured? Oh, you've stopped bleeding at least?"

Hands went out, and it seemed as though the injuries remained, but the persistent blood loss had ended. I touched my hands together, and no further wounds bloomed into existence. Splendid. My eyes went over to the larger demon missing part of his head. Another crown for the taking.

"Dibs!" Ren called out.

"Ah!" Roger stepped out in front of her. "Not a good idea, Mrs. Boss. Wearing the crown would make you in line for the throne above boss, so you'd have to kill him. Or he you."

The elf stopped and pouted at me. "Seriously? That's like the *one* thing I wouldn't do to him. Not for a drab accessory like that anyway."

With a shit-eating grin, I stepped over and picked the crown up and placed it on my head. There was a flash of demonic energy, and the two merged.

"Ah, I was going to say not to do that either, boss." The large rabbit crossed his arms.

I gave him a blank expression. "You had *plenty* of time to warn me."

"Did I though?" He tilted his head.

Ren narrowed her eyes and walked toward the demon slowly. "I've been wondering, Max . . . If I killed Roger, would his body vanish, or could we use it for *stuff*?"

The rabbit twitched. "What kind of stuff?"

I nodded my head slowly. "Oh, like feeding to Wolf?"

The bear shook his head. "I'd prefer to eat him while he was still living, if that's an option."

"No," Ren continued, "like if we could carve out his insides so only the fluffy skin part was left."

"You're thinking we could build a giant prop top hat and dress me up in the skin of Roger so that you could pull me out of the hat like a trick?" I furrowed my brow and rubbed at my chin.

"Sure . . . We'll go with that."

Roger stepped back away from the persistent elf, knocking over a couple of chairs. "Alright, I'll come clean!" He tried waving her away, and she paused. "With one crown, you're free to move about as you please. Once you bind two or more . . . Well, it puts a beacon on your head."

"Demons will start hunting me down?" I smiled despite myself. The demon hunter became the hunted demon. *Absolute shivers* down my spine.

"Yeah . . . And I want that, 'cause maybe if you die, boss . . . then I can be free."

"What if Max becomes king?" Ren asked, finally racking the bolt on her rifle to eject the empty bullet casing.

"Yeah, that sounds better." The rabbit ran his tongue around the bloodied fur on his upper lip. "I meant *I want you* to become king sooner, so you can free me."

My right eye twitched. With my sensible self long eroded down to a nub, there was a temptation to pop the demon through the skull for being so brazenly indignant. How could he act like that toward a prince? Regardless of whether it made me a threat or a target, I could feel my demonic power growing.

I had cobbled together my own Ability to make a demon show themselves in their Domain. Checking my System menus, it wasn't there—in the same way as my Domain itself wasn't.

Our little side quest in taking over this hell dimension had turned into a way for us to gather more undue power—once we returned to the surface we'd be beyond compare. The Lady wouldn't know what hit her.

Of course, I ran the risk of overshooting. Raining down hellfire on her troops as the very loud and proud Demon King of hell would just as soon get a throng of willing adventurers hunting *me* down. There would be some steep irony in ending the constant violence by sinking us into further violence, just from the other side.

"Leave him be," I decided.

Not particularly because I cared for mercy, but I felt his continued existence was part of my demonic puzzle. He was partly created as a stand-in for the patron I used to have back in my previous life. Would be foolish to end his life and then find out that the System considered him my tether to any demonic power I wielded and I was cut off from it.

"Dropped a legendary item," Wolf muffled, the arm of the previously princely demon in his mouth.

Ren scoffed. "Bet it's some bullshit for Max the Main Character over there."

"Unfair! You have a *literal* sniper rifle."

"We're in demon hell fighting demon princes so Mr. Demonic Magician can become Demon King. It couldn't be any clearer unless you wrote it yourself."

I took a second to consider whether I had penned any such drivel in any of my journals. No, nothing so grandstanding. "Perhaps I should write someone else in as my Demon Queen then?"

"You fucking dare, Max." Her hands gripped at the rifle tighter. "I will tear this reality to shreds and kill whoever it is before killing you."

Wolf huffed and settled down, rolling his eyes at the charade we were about to pull off. Scene was playing out like the performance it had to be.

"Ren, my love. You have neither the guts nor the ability to kill me."

She bared her teeth and swung the rifle up to point at me. "Take that back, you shit."

I opened my arms wide. "Prove me wrong then."

"Last warning, trickster. Make me your Demon Queen or else."

"Nah." My smile widened. "I don't feel like it now, *peasant*."

Her finger clicked the trigger, striking me straight in the forehead. Back of my skull blew open and painted the back wall with my brain matter. Arms still extended for a slow two seconds before the rest of my body got the message and I dropped over backward.

The real me appeared next to the elf, twirling her around as she wrapped the gun around me. Lips locked, we slunk down against one of the tables—until Wolf cleared his throat.

"Again, legendary item. Looks like it would be useful for Ren."

"Ha!" The elf grabbed my chin to give my face a little shake. "Get fucked, magic man."

"If we had less company," I murmured, turning to look at the sea of Imps and hounds waiting for further instruction. As the elf hopped over to the bear, I gestured for Roger to follow me.

I took him a little farther away, mostly because it seemed to cause him increased tension. We stopped at the corner of the banquet hall, and I leaned against the wooden wall to look back across the gathered summonses. At the other end, Ren was explaining how useful her new trinket was to a very uninterested-looking Wolf.

"Roger. What's with the wavering loyalty as of late?"

"I'm a demon, boss. It's kind of my nature to be a shit." He shuffled awkwardly. "Being at war for so long . . . I haven't seen my family. It was fine when it was like a short vacation . . ."

My right eye twitched again. "You think this is fun for *me*, Roger? Every waking moment is filled with violence and the dry heat of hell sapping my sanity away. Every night I have to scrape the gore from Ren's hair and pretend that being baked in sweat and grime is normal. Wolf has been so corrupted that he has turned into a bear."

"Erm, pretty sure he always was one, boss."

"Shh, shut it. *Shut up.*" I placed a bloodied finger up to his fuzzy lips. "Silence."

My brow furrowed as a chill worked its way down my spine. I looked at the rabbit with a little more calm focus in my vision before turning my head to the others.

"Look lively," I announced. "There's a powerful demon landing at our location in . . ."

The building vibrated, sending clouds of dust raining down from the rafters.

CHAPTER THIRTY-FOUR

Hellborne Magician

I hummed a little tune to myself. Not even really a show tune at this stage, just my failing mind skipping along the lake of sanity like a thrown rock. It spun and hopped about, but the distance between each bouncing point was dwindling. The rock, which I was sure was *me* in the metaphor, threatened to sink below the surface, never to return.

"Move your fingers, Max." Ren held my arm, a bandage at the ready in the other hand.

I wiggled them as requested.

"I can see your tendons move about. He-he." She smiled up at me before her brow furrowed. "I think . . . I'm starting to really *lose* it, trickster."

I nodded slowly. We had killed another three Demon Princes in short order. Or long order. It was hard to gauge the time as we seemed to no longer feel tired—or were just in a constant state of exhaustion. Since the ball had started rolling on the whole demonic-king business, we hadn't stopped and slept.

We'd hit level sixteen, but our STARs had remained gray and inert, as if the System didn't consider us existing any longer. Like we were lost to it and doomed to sink into this quagmire of death and sweat forever.

Crown number five sat on the bloodied floor just ahead of me.

This fight had been a little rougher than most. Even now, the barbed tentacles that hung from the dead prince's mouth still squirmed across the stone tiles as if they could escape or take another bite from me. He could see through invisibility, much to my chagrin. I'd learned that lesson by way of a broken leg and patches of flayed skin. System had fixed my leg up but was being slow on the rest of the damage. Unusual.

Ren was right though. The longer we spent seeped down here, the more unhinged we were getting. Although the rampant lewd acts and acceptance of violence had started off as something we could ignore, we'd trudged past the benefits of insanity and struck the rough ground of the reality that we were becoming unraveled. Insane.

"I'm not even sad," she continued, tears running from her eyes as she bandaged over my wounds. "Or . . . *anything* really."

"Exhausted." I smiled. "We're hitting the limits, I know. I promise you we will get out of here soon."

Her once-radiant golden hair was no longer a beacon in this place. Matted and stuck together from weeks of sweat, grime, and blood. It was now in the roughest- and saddest-looking ponytail we had been able to manage. Pretty sure my hands were soaked with something unpleasant when I did her the disservice. Our duty of care had . . . slipped.

Wolf had just become more sour over time. Still had all the patience in the world for us two—especially considering what we got up to—but he had long given up on pretending to be fine with our current situation. Roger had toed the line a little better but had become more avoidant the more crowns I had accumulated. As if he was scared of what I was turning into.

I hadn't changed *that* much. The slight amount of extra muscle was a nice addition for someone so usually lean but made sense considering we had been fighting nonstop for weeks.

"Chin up, moonflower." I ran my hand along the side of her face.

She held it there softly and kissed at my wrist. "Let's wrap this up and get moving."

I nodded, and we stood up. She wiped the unintended tears from her face, smearing the briefly clean tracks with the residual dirt that existed around the rest of her.

"Hey." I placed my hand on her shoulder. "If it's the last thing I do, I will get you a warm bath once this is all done."

She tilted her head and gave me a glum smile. "I believe you, trickster. It'd be a dream come true. I *would* say I'd do anything for you if you made that a reality, but I already do, and we're basically soulmates, so . . . you'll just have my eternal gratitude *plus one*."

"Don't say that." With a smile, I let her go to step over to the discarded crown. "I'll end up finding a way we can live forever so I can cash in on that."

"Imagine the shows we could put on with hundreds of years of practice."

I shivered. An odd feeling down here in hell, but the elf always knew how to press my buttons. Hand went down to the circlet of silver, but my eyes turned to Roger.

The demon was leaning up against the wall, and while he normally avoided looking my direction the last few . . . hours? Days? Currently, he was staring at my hand reaching for the ornamental symbol of power.

"Something to say, Roger?"

He jolted, realizing I had been watching him. "No . . . boss. I mean, you sure you want to do that?"

"I have no idea what the fuck I'm doing, Roger. If you know a reason why I *shouldn't* be doing this, then speak up."

The rabbit twitched and looked over across the reduced group of my summoned demons. "A crown grants you a claim to the throne. Two or three means you've taken over a swath of hell itself, like a political thing, right?" His furred hands came together. "With your demonic side, five crowns would be empowering that side of you . . . That amount of political power is a direct threat to the king himself, and you'll—"

"Boring!" I placed the crown on my head, the object absorbing into the others that had formed the singular one decorating me.

It had been quite a while since I'd had a taste of humble pie. A necessity sometimes when we lived with so much natural bravado and false confidence.

Immediately after the deed was done, I felt a pang of pain shoot through me. A sickening, sour stream of bile that ran from my core up through my chest and neck. It wasn't vomit, however, and rather than make itself known through my mouth hole, the feeling continued up to my head. I held my hands up over my eyes. Let the darkness calm my senses.

Heartbeat throbbed through my skin, rolling around the outside my brain before my thoughts could neutralize the imagined toxin that had slunk its way through my insides. I took a deep breath as two points of sharp pain vibrated on the top of my head.

Inevitable, really.

I growled as two horns grew out of my skull, bursting through the skin and parting my hair. It was *unpleasant.* I took another couple of deep lungfuls of stale air as the puncture wounds healed up, leaving me feeling . . . fine.

Removed my hands from my face and stood up tall, turning around to Ren.

Her eyes ran me up and down, the bright-blue pools the only thing about her not torn down by the wear and tear of this existence. "First thought—*yum.* Second thought . . . You okay? Not possessed or even crazier now?"

I brought a finger up to prod at one of the horns. Only four or five inches in length, not too sharp at the end but still pointed. Slight pressure on my skull when I pushed them, but I would hope they'd break off like antlers if they caught an attack rather than rip my skull apart.

"No . . . I feel *okay.*" Furrowed my brow and looked at my hands, as if they would be a good signal of my well-being. "System says I'm part demon now." That wasn't all—it now clearly displayed my demonic powers.

Domain: <The Grand Stage>, <Demonic Regeneration>, <Domain Escalation>, <Corruption Resistance>, <Demon Form>.

My Domain and the regeneration were straightforward. Both from my prior life topside and tied to my Power bar.

<Domain Escalation> allowed me to summon the creator of a Domain, which had been useful against the last few corpses we had made. Probably useless when we escaped from hell, but it was likely we would have died without it. These princes didn't like to show face when in their little pockets of control.

<Corruption Resistance> was a Party-wide aura that stopped us from getting too hot or insane from being in hell for a long time. Wasn't sure when I had picked that up, but it explained how we had survived in such a hostile place. Still, it was only resistance and not immunity.

If only I had . . .

I rubbed at my chin. System seemed to favor me today, *finally*. Inside this interface, where my demonic Skills were laid bare, was a little icon showing how many spare crowns I had. Four, at present. And it didn't take a genius to realize that I could use these spare artifacts the same as power tokens for these Abilities.

"Terrible news," I said, grinning. "I have become yet more ironclad with bullshit."

"You realize you have fangs, Max?" Ren tilted her head to the side, any concern now washed away and replaced with . . . intrigue?

Ran my tongue across my teeth—ah, my canines were extended a little. "All the better to eat you with, my dear."

She nodded slowly, her mind clearly busy imagining things I didn't want to be privy to. Not if we wanted to be productive for the next hour anyway.

My eyes went back to the menus while she daydreamed. Couldn't upgrade my actual Domain, which seemed unfair—but then it was similar to my Class Keystone.

[<Corruption Resistance> is now advanced: Resistance is now doubled]
[<Demonic Regeneration> is now advanced: Regeneration is now doubled, and 15% healing rate is applied to nearby allies]

I turned to watch Ren blink her eyes and take a breath. "Huh. Either I have a new kink that has grounded my sanity, or something just changed."

"As much as the former sounds delightful, it's actually because I have upgraded our resistance to hell."

She pulled a face. "You can do that?"

"What *can't* I do?" I gestured to some of my wounds, which were now healing up at a much faster rate.

"Oh!" She ignored the obvious bait and held up her arm. Her STAR was glowing golden, as was mine on inspection.

Lost no longer.

I switched through the screens quickly, not wanting to distract myself from the demonic information. New Ability was called <Spotlight>. Another taunt where ranged allies would have reduced threat and increased Damage, while I would take increased Damage from those watching me. Seemed fair. Passives reduced my fall Damage, and something else that doubled the chance of a critical card after casting a critical card—but it didn't stack.

Abstract, in some ways, I thought unironically as I tried to turn more into an actual demon.

Didn't want to waste one of the last two crowns on <Domain Escalation> since it wouldn't be useful long term. <Demon Form> was . . . Yeah, fuck it. I was in for the ride.

[<Demon Form> is now advanced: You can now toggle the form on cooldown. Increased demonic Power gain when form is active.]

I swirled a summoned sheet around myself to obscure my body, letting it fall back to the ground to reveal me as a normal human with no horns or sharp teeth.

"Aw." Ren crossed her arms. "Cured already? I want a refund."

"Do you have a smoke-cloud scroll? Let me show you something." While she nodded and handed it over, I looked around the room.

Roger looked . . . scared. His nose twitched as he sat on a table, his eyes completely glued to me. Wolf was asleep—a rarity but something I'd allow considering how tired out he could get. Hopefully my resistances and regeneration would have him feeling more himself soon enough. The handful of my small demons left watched me intently, no change in their loyalty despite my change of being.

I took a stroll away from the elf, across the stone square, away from the outdoor eatery area of this tall bridge over the lava river. An interesting place to fight and certainly made a change from woodlands and small villages . . . but I did miss that simpler life.

Around twenty-five feet away from the curious Oathwarden, I stopped and turned back to face her.

Aimed the scroll out and started running as I cast it.

Cloud of white smoke bloomed into being, and I passed through it, hitting <Demon Form> just before jumping out of the other side.

A more numbed pain this time as horns emerged from my skull. However, there was also a larger pressure and brief agony from my back this time. No time to panic as I landed on the smooth stone in front of the elf.

My purple wings buffeted the air, swirling the smoke away and assisting my landing. Her matted hair briefly shuffling from the breeze.

"*Motherfucker . . .*" she whispered, eyes wide. "Let's go get you some more crowns."

CHAPTER THIRTY-FIVE

Clash

Sweat ran down my brow. Soaked me, really. Tired eyes went over to my group.

Ren had dark circles around her eyes, which probably paled in comparison to my own but was a first for her. The elf's face was covered with soot, smeared in places where she'd tried to wipe away the constant sweat or the sprays of blood and bile from our opponents. Part of her neck was bandaged up where she'd insisted I bite her with my fangs. We'd learned there was indeed a line where things went a little too far.

Mostly post-act, where I'd thrown up her blood across the bed and floor of the shack we had requisitioned. She had just rolled her eyes and reminded me I was a *demon*, not a vampire.

Wolf looked like fresh hell, which . . . was a terrible metaphor given our situation. He had been insistent that we gave him more armor, despite it causing him to sweat further. His water rations had doubled, but now he looked like a macabre porcupine. Jagged bone spikes ran from the plates we had fashioned across most of his back. He'd even insisted I pop a couple of decapitated demon heads on a jagged point or two.

How far from grace we had fallen. No longer in our magician outfits at all but covered in dirt and bodily fluids in whatever armor was thematically useful.

Roger had lost one of his ears in the last fight, the other one now wrapped around his head like a strange hat or turban. He had bulked out a little now as well, and since I ascended to having a demonic form, he had a renewed fealty that settled into an acceptance of the route we were careening toward. I had never imagined going against the Demon King would be like . . . this.

My other summonses had been reduced to four Hellhounds and three Imps. One fire, one ice, and one stone. Both Ren and I had been saddened to see them diminish, even with how numb to everything we had become. With no way to replenish my forces, we just had to make do—but every fight slowly whittled down their numbers. A shame because the full horde of casters had been certainly powerful.

We'd almost hit level seventeen already in chewing our way through a large town. Three weeks of constant turmoil was good for the experience bar, it seemed.

Our efforts had been interrupted, however, by the trio that now stood before us.

Three princes had put aside their differences and decided that they wouldn't be picked off one by one. They had landed on the other side of the wide town square, crushing the town hall with their arrival.

Left one was a sickly yellow color, his face more of a sunken hole full of jagged teeth. Long arms ending with sharp claws. Spine-laden dual wings like a butterfly. A good thirteen feet tall, even hunched over as he was. No weaponry but I was sure he could tear us apart with his hands alone.

Middle was a bright red and wearing a smart suit—odd in contrast to the more barbaric outfit of Yellow. Not that much taller than me, his sword was taller still and hung in the air beside him. With the arrogant look on his humanoid face, it looked more likely that he'd prefer to kill us with smarm and his superiority complex if possible.

Right was a giant and held a large crossbow, which I was starting to believe was just a ballista. Deep-gray skin speckled with darker shades around his shoulders and neck. Wide backpack filled with the long spear-like ammunition. Several tiny demons similar to my Imps crawled over him and looked to be the ones who dealt with the actual operation of the weapon. They had pointed faces and ears, reminding me of goblins, but they were a bright off-white in color.

Each had the silver crown denoting them as a prince of hell. In line for the throne and in danger of finding themselves nothing more than lootable corpses for yours truly. Of course, several weeks of grinding away at Monsters had us outfitted with greater power than just the levels earned.

Best gear for our level gemmed with our main stats. Countless consumables and spell scrolls. Weapons aplenty. The whole System experience totally ruined as we had broken into the bank and stolen more than a Player should usually have. Given to two characters who could manipulate their Inventories with just a thought . . . Ren and I were poised to change the world.

"Did you three want to monologue before we get this over with?" I grinned and tilted my head, hands already running with blood from our massacre through this town.

"I'm surprised that *you* are the usurpers," Red said, sneering down his nose. "A wretched human, his elfin whore, and a dumb beast."

<Spotlight> illuminated me, their attentions drawn as I was bathed in bright white. "Now, that's a nasty fucking mouth you have," I replied.

He turned barely in time, the radiant bullet still striking him. Head flung back and then he reset to glare toward us, his lower jaw now missing, destroyed. One of his hands went up to cast his Domain while the other grasped at the bloody hole rent through his face.

Wolf roared, and Red's attempt to expand his demonic power faltered. Confusion spread across his brow, not knowing that the System loved to fill us with what we needed to be as insufferable as possible.

Cards whirled around me as the battle got into full swing. Three each to my Party to give them some extra Damage reduction. I ran toward the one with the crossbow. The bear illuminated with pulses of energy as he burst toward Yellow. I could almost hear Ren's breathing calm as she went down to one knee and racked a new bullet.

Nice of them to deliver me three crowns at once—I could barely wait to upgrade my Skills and see if I would grow more powerful.

Crossbow turned toward me, the gremlins readying up to fire. I went invisible. Confused shouting rose between the small demons as they weren't sure what to do. I dropped my <Demon Cannon> to their right side as <Demon Form> burst wings from my back, and I leaped up into the air with a rush of energy.

Gray himself turned to point his weapon up at me while his handlers screamed and tried to warn him about the siege weapon right beside his leg. I held out my hand, and a critical card bloomed into my grip, right when I needed it. Without his helpers doing the necessary maintenance, he would be a sitting—

The ballista-sized weapon clunked with a sharp snap, the jagged bolt slicing through the air and impaling straight through my chest. Broken bones and shredded organs. Card fluttered and faded out of existence. Wings went slack, and my body careened back to the ground.

With simple joy in his dark eyes, he turned to deal with the cannon, mostly continuing to ignore the gremlins bossing him around.

I loved <Last Act>. Never got tired of using it. My real body appeared a dozen feet away from where I had been slain, hovering slightly in the air as red lightning crackled around the still-held critical card. It left my hand as I dropped from the air at a more measured pace and the magic attack exploded on his head.

As I descended, I took this brief window to gaze out at my troupe. Red lashed out at Ren with the psychically controlled sword. The elf vanished in a puff of white feathers to appear off to the side, a second blast from her gun blowing the raised left hand of the demon off. Wolf had the wrist of one of Yellow's arms in his mouth, his spiked armor a lot more bloody than usual, as the body of the demon seemed to be bleeding in multiple places. Imps and hounds were assisting Ren, while Roger was attempting to help the bear.

Gliding was pretty neat. I'd have to include it in our shows somehow. I turned my gaze back to the demon I had slain and . . .

Eyebrows raised, and <Card Fan> went up before bursting immediately—the jagged spear lodging itself in my collarbone area, almost severing my arm clean off. Despite losing half of his head, the prince had one of the white gremlins mashing their hands in his remaining brains to control the rest of his body. Rather genius, if unrealistic.

My cannon blew a spear through his thick leg. I landed on the ground as a second bolt was being loaded in, the winch winding up with a creak. With a grunt, I pulled the offending weapon from my body. Should be able to regenerate from the damage in no time. Clearly, I was going about this wrong.

Twin cards bloomed in my hand and went out, purple beams darting around the demon before swirling like a tornado. Lashed out at the smaller demons. Severed hands and the winch started to unwind. Split torso and one fell from the shoulder of Gray. Pulsed both cards into the gremlin working the brains, shredding both of them and bursting from the other side of the demon's head.

Inert crown rolled across the floor as my cannon fired off some confetti.

"How lucky you are to meet your next Demon King," Ren called out, gesturing toward me.

The two princes turned to me as a second wave of confetti blasted through me.

<Finale+>

Weren't a lot of Dazzle stacks in play—although the weird mix of Passives we had now granted a decent amount even when the performance was rather dry. It was enough for a modest applause, and the demons paused in place. Yellow was quite resistant to stun, but Red stood in a state of surprise.

In fact, his skull *burst*—as the elf put a radiant shot straight through the back of his head. I felt her heal run through me as I looked over at the last of the trio.

Recovered from the stun already, they slammed the ground and pushed Wolf away, a wave of dry stone emerging and causing the bear to have to slide back.

Of course, this was just so they could activate their Domain.

Energy washed over us. A woodland, something oddly pleasant. Springtime, beams of light piercing the canopy overhead, soft grass by our feet. Immensely relaxing.

I looked over at Ren, who had fresh tears running tracks down her face.

My right eye twitched. How *dare* he do this to us? My white-gloved hands balled into fists. A false promise of something we desired. I could see the will to fight tangibly leave the elf's body, and Wolf looked practically starstruck. But I was *furious*.

I dropped <Demon Form> and closed my eyes. They would pay for this.

<Domain Escalation> ripped through the air, bringing the prince out to land among a group of trees. Confusion on his face as he shook his wide maw.

"Of course," I said quietly, "a demon only respects and understands power."

The monster roared in response, my Party members both lagging with their readiness from feeling so close to home. This wasn't *my* home though . . . but I could bring it.

Purple electricity snapped and arced around my body as the demon prepared to run toward me.

Domain: <The Grand Stage>

Yellow paused. Two Domains couldn't occupy the same space at the same time. In activating mine, I had challenged him to a duel of power. The strongest demon would win.

"Here," I continued, "let me help you . . . understand."

Hands went out, and I gripped at the air. Could feel my power trying to escape and win. Like it was squished down inside me and waiting to pop and expand like a giant popcorn kernel.

The prince could see my attempts and sought to stop me physically. A shot that blew out a chunk of his shoulder had entangling vines circling both his lowered hands as well as his feet. A groaning crunch from my left and a tree collapsed down in front of the angered Monster—courtesy of Wolf.

That was all the time I needed.

Pooled my Mana and Health into my hands rather than a card. It was agony, but breaking the rules often came with consequences. Fingers dug into the imagined bubble in front of me and pierced through.

Dark circles appeared in the sky, cratering through tree trunks, leaves, and the blue beyond alike. With a growl, I pushed with all my might, tearing a wide hole through the Domain. The sky split, trying to resist my attempts at pulling it away.

But it was too late for his power to retain control. We reached the threshold, and my Domain took over. Woodland foliage and the soft light of day replaced by the stage illuminated by bright overhead lights, the Demon Prince now restrained in the audience, the tree still lying across him.

I gave him a bow and turned to my equal, dressed in her sparkling pastel suit, hair and face once again unblemished.

Bright eyes sparkled as she smiled at me. "Performing for royalty, trickster."

"Get used to it." I gave her a wink and turned to our captive.

Wouldn't be long before we were dazzling the throne itself.

CHAPTER THIRTY-SIX

Exhale, Adjust

Darkness. A rare comfort but only given by my own effort in keeping my eyes closed.

We had decided to take a rest after killing the three Demon Princes. While my shoulder wound had some odd ache that persisted within it, we had all healed up in no time at all. Something about the crate load of health potions and similar consumables we had farmed out made the process simple enough—even if detestable to my tongue and stomach.

Despite the taste of much worse as of late, the near-alcoholic tang of the bottled relief still didn't sit well with me.

I opened my eyes. Sleep was trying to draw me into its clutches, but we didn't have the time or safety for something like that. Somehow, we had been able to persist without a proper nap for . . . possibly days now. Our very beings stretched thin, making do with what we had as the corpse of our intent slid near to the finish line. How foolish we were to think destroying hell with our own hands would be an easy task.

Not to say that it was *difficult* . . . taken in the small chunks that we had been delivered. The fighting had been tough but not too deadly. We excelled in combat—had done so for quite a while once the System had fed us too much power and didn't have the heart to walk anything back. The severity came from the near-constant stress of constantly being in hostile land, the very atmosphere itself trying to grate away at our senses of self.

Now I sat here on the warm ground, cross-legged. Three silver crowns arranged just in front of me. A golden glow to the STAR on my left wrist, eager to give me a new nugget of power. It barely registered these days. Was I more of a magician or a demon now? I had mostly been the former up until the last two or three days. Now I . . . didn't feel like *Max* anymore.

I felt . . . untethered.

[Max: Checking in.]
[Tanya: Day four out here.]
[Tanya: We've now met up with Leyla's group as well.]
[Tanya: Set up a temporary base awaiting your return.]
[Tanya: No word from Eternal Wardens at all.]
[Tanya: Trying to get information from Candlekeep.]
[Tanya: How are you all holding up?]

I turned my gaze away from the windows to look at my Party. Wolf was a bloodied ball of sharp bone needles, now having a deserved nap. The only one of us capable of briefly falling in and out of sleep at the drop of a hat. He hadn't eaten a single demon since we'd arrived, which I assumed was the only reason he still had his stoic wit.

Ren was crouched down just off to the side of him, doing some maintenance on her rifle. Given that it was a magical item, I didn't think it was actually necessary—but since Tanya had shown her how, it had become an action of comfort. Something normal among all this insanity. Although her eyes were as bright as usual, they were becoming more deep set and tired. We were starting to run on fumes.

I, of all of us, knew this. Didn't even need to mention it to the others but I was occasionally plagued by the feeling like my internal organs wanted to liquefy. Usually a handful of seconds of panicked pain that I was able to hide away. We already had enough worries.

And the cause? Nothing remotely demonic or worth a Status icon. I was just pushing myself too far. Without sleep or rest, my body ached every time I sank too much Health into <Bloodletting> or shifted in and out of <Demon Form>. It was survivable, but the body required rest to get over the trauma of the constant conflict we put ourselves through.

I just wanted to get out of here. Would push myself to the limit to be free of this overheated prison. Any amusement or delight once found in *killing all demons* or grasping at strength we weren't previously allowed had gone.

[Max: Things are just peachy.]
[Tanya: Bullshit. Don't push us away, Max.]

I allowed myself a long sigh of stale, hellish air. It was odd. Technically, we'd now spent more time without Tanya and Quinn than with them. Given that for them it was four days since we parted and for us it must be nearly three weeks—there was a difference in mentality where they probably still worried for us, yet we had become numb to their existence.

[Max: It's been almost three weeks here.]
[Max: We are alive and in good health.]
[Max: Changed in some ways. The mental toll of the violence.]
[Max: Residual corruption from hell itself.]
[Max: But . . . we are getting close to coming home. I promise.]
[Tanya: Don't make a promise you don't know you can keep, asshole.]
[Max: It is a promise I will keep.]
[Tanya: Good. When you get here, you do what you need to rest, okay?]
[Tanya: Your safety and health are the most important thing.]
[Max: Thanks, Tanya. Give my regards to the others.]

I wiped away the silent tears from my face. It was interesting how any sort of human connection would just open the floodgates now. Wasn't even sad or didn't have any guiding emotion to have them fall so freely—it was just like I had something untoward in them and they were watering as a response to eject the foreign object. Clearly I was repressing a lot.

Turned my head to see Ren walk over and she sat herself down beside me.

"Hoping something will happen if you keep staring at these crowns, trickster?" She leaned over so her head could rest on my shoulder.

"No. I'm pretty tired of things happening actually." I leaned my head against hers. "I wish for a life after this where nothing really happens at all. Just rest and maybe a show here or there."

She sighed. "We both know that's never going to happen. We're *death forged*, remember? Destined to fight against the odds and get dirty solving the issues plaguing existence."

"I hate that I know you're right." Still, something a little less traumatic than spending time in hell would be appreciated.

And we weren't killing our way through *all* of this miserable place. Roger had rightfully been a little worried that we might roll up to his own village and chew through his family—but I assured him I wouldn't. I'd seen enough demons to not want to meet his many wives and children. That kind of familiarity might break my dissociation in ways I could never recover from.

We only went through the bad guys as needed, now on our way to the palace or castle. Wherever the Demon King resided, probably sitting on a throne of spikes and skulls. Everything a shade of red or black. I was tired of that palette.

"What did the System grant you now?" I asked the elf, more to get out of my own head than anything.

"I can empower one of my shots to have a chain effect every so often."

"Like a chain lightning?"

She nodded, grinding her matted hair between my shoulder and face. "Yeah but can be any element that I can cast with my other Skills."

"So . . . radiant would be pretty nice, huh?"

"Wouldn't it?" She moved away to look me in the face, her soft smile something that tugged at my heartstrings in seeing how completely spent she was.

Despite Tanya's offer of all the rest we needed, I doubted that Lady in Red and whatever had silenced the Eternal Wardens cared to give us a month or two to decompress and get back to our normal state of being.

"I'll check mine in a second." I put my arm around her. "Still working up the courage to inhale these three crowns."

"You think you'll get another demonic power or something? It's hard to imagine you can get any more destructive than you already are."

I shrugged for lack of a more concise response. In truth, I wasn't too sure how the System even decided to give me more demonic Skills. While some of them were something I took myself by exerting my control over Domains and the like, others had just been freely given—perhaps at crown thresholds? Then again, I doubted that a Player was meant to do any of the bullshit that we were currently doing.

System had to run a little improv to keep me from tearing it in half.

"If anything . . . I'm worried that I will become too powerful to really exist."

Despite not looking directly at her, I could almost hear Ren's eyes roll. "We're not even level twenty yet, right? There are actual people beyond the exclusion zone that have full Stats and the best gear and shit. You're worried because you can grow horns and have some very niche Skills."

"Well . . . when you put it like that."

"You've always been a few steps ahead of everyone else, trickster. You can go invisible, summon cannons, and pretend to die. Not to mention your area stun, potential insta-kill debuff swap, and insane power boosting with that legendary item . . . If it wasn't for the Guardian skills, I'd just shoot things really good."

It was my turn to roll my eyes. "You're being a little modest there too. But in saying that . . . I wonder if the Demon King is a Guardian."

Her fingers stretched out and relaxed a few times. "Hmm. We'll know if we get closer, right?"

I nodded slowly. While we knew very little about these entities given power over the System, if *I'd* created this world, then the leader of hell would be a prime position to fill with one of these near gods. But, like Ren said, we wouldn't really know for sure until we got close enough.

"Hey, boss?"

We turned to glance over at my rabbit demon. Almost looking as beat-up and worn down as the rest of us now, he gave me a brief bow as he stepped closer.

"Got some intel for you, about the remaining princes."

"If they're on their way, then just wave these corpses at them and tell them to give us an hour or something." I gestured to the bodies of the three we had just slain.

"Nah. They're actually standing with the king. They intend to help rebuff your attack and get a huge amount of the land you've taken as a reward."

I pulled a face. "And how do you know this, Roger?"

"Demonic bird told me." He maintained a neutral expression.

Ren stretched her legs out and exhaled. "Won't be any land to divide up because Max isn't going to lose."

"After checking my calendar, it looks like I don't have the time for anything *but* winning." I smiled at them both.

"Not to piss on your parade, boss, but the king is quite powerful." He crossed his furred arms and looked over at the dead princes. "Like, I've seen you deal with these chumps no problem, but the head honcho himself is . . . a shit too big to flush."

Demonic plumbing aside, I wondered what that actually meant System wise. Was he a level-twenty boss? An elite or other designation we hadn't come across yet? Somewhere along the way, we'd become unclipped from the usual cardboard cutouts the world generally presented us with. While the demons here in hell weren't *smart* by any stretch of the word, they felt more real and natural than anything on the surface.

And that wasn't just me having an affinity for the bastards.

"*Regardless.*" I waved the giant rabbit away. "It doesn't change our trajectory. We march on the capital and kick whomever is on the throne off of it. So simple it can't go wrong."

"Assuming that after we do this a way out of here comes available to us," Ren said.

I looked at Roger, but all he could offer was a shrug.

To come this far and not have a way to escape . . . I wasn't sure what we'd do. Surely, with enough power, we could tear a hole through reality. We had found a couple of teleportation scrolls, but they hadn't worked. Something about the demonic nature of this place, perhaps. Agonizing.

"Well, pick your Abilities already." Ren pressed on my shoulder as she pushed herself up to her feet. "I'm hungry for a conclusion to all this."

With a long sigh, I reached forward and plucked the first crown from the ground.

CHAPTER THIRTY-SEVEN

Ace in Hand

A warm breeze rolled through hell, making me feel . . . sticky. Not an uncommon feeling down here for a variety of reasons—but something I was growing ever more tired of. Even the brief splash of water from our stores did little to help. Didn't want to waste our emergency hydration on getting clean when grime and gore were only around the next corner.

I picked the third crown up from the ground and placed it on my head, the silver headwear absorbing into the main one that was permanently affixed atop me. My bones ached all the way up from my feet to my fragile skull. As if my skeleton was eager to burst from my skin suit and leave this wretched place without me.

Simple fact was I was dying.

Drank too deep from the cup of demonic power and started drowning myself.

If the others could see it, they made no indication. Ren could read me like a book, the text printed twice the size, but hadn't twisted my arm about all this danger. If they didn't know, I wasn't about to tell them either.

I would go to any lengths to get us out of here.

Trying to ground myself, I ran my tongue across my teeth. *Normal*, as I was in my human form. A weird sentence that hardly touched the sides of what a bizarre existence I now lived. I was half sure I'd wake up soon, my body between fresh linens with the soft elf beside me—and this would have been a nightmare.

For now, I relented to the System menus telling me I had four crowns to spend on upgrading my demon abilities. I did not wish to—I wanted to rebel. Mashed around the options on the intangible screen until it gave me something else that I wanted. A new Skill, perhaps—as my current ones only had one upgrade level left, and I was avoiding touching <Domain Escalation>.

There we go—if I chose to discard them permanently, I could gain some Stats . . . or three of them granted me a new Skill. With two more crowns awaiting my claim, I could wait and get two Skills or get a new one now and upgrade it—possibly snatch a Skill or two just by forcing the System to give me things.

I blinked away the screens and shook my head. With such a limited resource, I'd be pragmatic and wait till I had all six awaiting my attention before making a decision. Would be kicking myself if I spent them all now and then missed out on something really broken.

As I was *clearly* lacking that kind of thing.

Speaking of which, I hit my golden STAR to get my level-seventeen upgrades. Ignored the usual stat distribution . . . Eyes ran through my Passives quickly.

First gave me a 10 percent Damage boost when below 50 percent Health—very nice, very dangerous. Second gave me a boost to Dazzle chance for five seconds after I landed a critical hit. While most things died after my cards exploded on them, I was quite a big fan of the System pushing the whole critical-card thing.

Most important, however, was the new active Ability.

<Demon's Ace>

Brow furrowed, I drew it from my deck to hover in front of me. The symbol on it was a heart, but it had twisted horns. It shimmered between red and black, while the card itself seemed to be bathed in flickering shadow rather than the typical arcane purple.

"New card, trickster? What does this one do?" Ren stepped over now that I had finished deliberating over my power increases.

"Hmm. I'm not entirely sure."

"Oh?"

I held my hand out and allowed the card to move through the air, slowly at first, and then I sped up. Sliced around just the same as any of my normal cards would. Then I let it fade away.

"There's some bullshit you're not telling me about." The elf crossed her arms. Her shredded and dirtied outfit was sobering. We all looked like we'd been put through a literal meat grinder.

"It acts like a proxy for my Skill casting, and it also counts as a demon."

She nodded slowly. "Aren't most of your Skills cards you throw already?"

I shrugged. That was why I wasn't super energetic about the reveal. Maybe my mind was just lagging, but the ideas were coming through like old sludge.

"Here, hold your arm out for me like you're casting a spell." I raised my eyebrow, and she did as I asked with no hesitation. Hand outstretched to the open space ahead of us.

I vanished and appeared twenty feet ahead of her, then held my hands up as if she was about to rob me. Twin magic cards blooming with purple light shot from her hand, spinning toward me. They severed my hands from my wrists before gouging through most of my neck.

Fake body gurgled and slumped to the floor, handless, as the real me appeared back beside her with my hands in my pockets.

"You can use transposition again, at least—and could turn the demonic card invisible?"

"Correct on both counts." I gave her a glum smile. "Even more than that, he even has a little Inventory of his own. Or her own, I suppose. It's unclear."

"Really?" Ren raised an eyebrow at the card now hovering beside me.

"Just three items. I assume so that I can load the cannon from afar . . . but . . ." I sent the card over to one of the corpses belonging to a slain prince. With a small gesture, a glass bottle ejected from the card, full of radiantly blessed water. It broke on the body—which started to melt away.

"That's some fucking bullshit in the making." She shook the disbelief from her head. "I'm surprised you're not giddy over it. All the remote tricks you could do now."

"I'm *tired*, Ren."

Her brow furrowed before she stepped forward and pulled me into a tight hug. Although we'd had no shortage of shameless physical contact in our time down here, this simple act threatened to tear my heart in two. Or that might just be the demonic power.

"I can fill those ears with mushy reassurance if you like," she offered. "Or bitch you out. Maybe even find somewhere private . . . Tell me what you *need*, Max."

A heartfelt promise to do literally anything to make me feel better. While our physical and mental health had taken the abandoned mine cart down through the barbed wire factory, our love had endured. Pristine and unwavering.

"You are my strength, Ren." I kissed her gently on her dirty forehead. "With you by my side, I am invincible."

"Honeyed words, trickster, but I need you to promise me three things." Her hands ran through what clumps of my hair were just thick with sweat and not near solid with dried gore.

"Anything."

"Kill the king. Live. Make me your queen."

I smiled. Two of the three sounded pretty doable. *Living*, however . . . I could only do my best. Perhaps she could see the darkness swirling me down the drain as she leaned a little closer to my ear.

"Let me tell you what we're going to do on that throne if you succeed."

My eyebrows continued to raise as she whispered to me. Once her lewd fan fiction ran out, she leaned back away, her blue eyes sparkling.

"You had me at . . . Well, all of it really." I tilted my head. "Are we going to struggle to adjust to the normal world when we escape?"

With a shrug, the elf let me go and stepped away. "I imagine we'll settle back down closer to how things used to be, but we *have* changed. We won't know until we get there, so let's get moving and find out."

I gave her a bow and then turned to the bear. "Ready to make a move, brother?"

He groaned and righted himself up to his feet. "I *dislike* hell and demons." His eyes went between me and Roger. "Aside from you, brother."

The rabbit rolled his eyes but didn't contest that. He seemed just as eager to get this all over with as the rest of us were. I looked up at the swirling nothing that classed as the sky down here. Odd that we hadn't come across a flock of my hell birds after all this time. They often had short lives acting as defensive shields for me—so I could understand if they held a grudge.

We started to move.

I spun the new demonic ace out and around my hand before letting it float beside me. It felt different from the others. Not quite like it had a will of its own . . . but there was a power to it. Probably whatever latent energy that allowed it to be classed as a demon. Didn't move of its own accord or have anything to say, but if I told it to maintain a set distance with me . . . it did.

So it continued to hover just over my shoulder as we walked, slowly turning. Two purple cards swirled around my extended left hand while I shuffled my mundane deck in the air just over my right—cutting the deck every so often. I frowned and thought.

Loading up my ace with bottles or weaponry might be helpful . . . but what if it could activate spell scrolls? A bending of the rules . . . but what was new?

I filled up the three slots in it with some of the magic scrolls we had accumulated in our time down here and sent it zipping out thirty feet ahead of us.

With a grin, I made the gesture with my hand, tugging at the invisible strings of the magic that joined everything together. Partly sure the scroll would just be ejected out onto the ground, yet knowing the System would play by *my* tune anyway.

Fireball ejected from my demon card in a high arc. I switched places with it, sending out a large sphere of electricity from a jolt-orb scroll. Switched back and immediately had the ace blow a smoke-cloud scroll to obscure the fact that I had vanished. The two spells sent out into the air collided, exploding and crackling like a large firework.

Ren's hand pressed against my lower back. "*That's* the trickster that I love."

I smiled and gave her a wink. Some amount of faux bravado holding that confidence up but a genuine streak of happiness wormed its way through. I was only a few steps away from outclassing everything in this world. A way to reset my transposition or increase my invisibility and it would be hard for anyone to contest my power.

Especially with the rest of the Party backing me up. Supporting the show.

"Almost a shame that we'll have to leave soon . . ." I winced away as both of them shot me glares that near killed me on the spot. "For one single reason."

Ren rolled her eyes. "Level cap."

"Once we return, we won't be able to get any higher than seventeen with the area cap being fifteen."

She shrugged. Any energy used to maintain the ire toward me evaporating. "You know it would take weeks to get to twenty though. Maybe even months."

"Of course. I wasn't suggesting we stayed." Okay, I was partly fishing for a reaction to that idea. "Only that being max level when going against our other problems would have been another layer of safety."

"Boss, there is a chance that taking the throne would get you to eighteen." Roger caught up to us. "Not that I know how all of that fucking stuff works, but it's likely there will be more than the two princes assisting the king."

"An army then. A last stand." I gave him a nod.

Normally something I'd wince at. Large groups usually were our weakness due to our damaging Abilities not being multiple target. With the spell scrolls we had accumulated, we could give most mid-tier mages a run for their money. Especially with Ren having the Inventory manipulation now too. I had watched her switch scrolls through her wrist-mounted holder once, and it was . . . well, very attractive.

A version of me from the past might have rolled my eyes at the System just giving her a way to use sleight of hand in a literal sense, but I didn't really care at this point. Easily given or not, I wasn't going to gatekeep Ren's progress as my partner in illusion.

While my eyes were tired and dry, my bones threatening to erupt from my skin, and my organs a few shakes away from disconnecting from each other, I . . . forgot where I was going with that train of thought.

There was some calm settling within me, knowing this stage of our adventure was soon to end, one way or another.

Next stop on our tour: the demonic palace itself.

THIRTY-EIGHT

Army of Three

Towers of deep purple twisted up toward the amber sky like jagged needles. There was something remarkably Gothic and arcane about the architecture of the demonic palace that felt as though it was physically assaulting me, even from this distance.

The remainder of our journey to this place had gone mostly uncontested. Several small villages near emptied already, as if hell itself was running dry. I knew that couldn't be the case. Most likely, the king had drawn all those nearby demons in to build an army to stand against us.

Even more probable, as we gazed down from our high ground at the roving throngs of Monsters in loose regiments. A few hundred maybe—I didn't even care to try to count them.

"I'm exhausted just looking at them," Ren said, pulling a face and leaning against her rifle.

Wolf grunted to signal that he agreed but said nothing further.

For me . . . I was mostly glad that Ren had received that Skill that made us immune to a few mental debilitations, including trauma. No doubt it was the only reason we were still sane and functional at this point; otherwise the slew of violence would have had us crack from the pressure weeks ago.

[Max: We're making our final stand.]
[Max: I'm not sure how the time translates . . . but shouldn't be long.]
[Tanya: We're all rooting for you, Max.]
[Quinn: You can do this^]
[Quinn: Don't die without me there to avenge you!^]
[Ren: I won't let him die.]
[Tanya: See you all soon then. Godspeed.]

I gave the elf a smile as we both closed the Chat messages. After she had taken my <Mana Manipulation> Skill, her protective Abilities had become as broken as my offensive ones. Barely even registered the heals and shields she provided, but they allowed me and Wolf to go all out to an even greater degree than before.

It was one of the reasons I looked down at the hordes of demons in the valley and felt completely neutral at the prospect of carving our way through them to get to the palace.

"Tougher bastards will be inside," Roger mentioned, sniffing at the air. "The two other princes, elite guards, and anything else capable of being more than fodder."

"And the king himself, of course." I stretched out my arms and sighed.

The end was so close and yet still a rough battle ahead to get there. My hope was that we could go home after usurping the throne, but who knew at this point? Too tired to make a second plan if the first fell through.

"Alright, troops." I put my hands together and drew their attention. "This is the fight we've been stockpiling for. All those buffing potions and scrolls, we want to use every boost and advantage we can. Save anything rare or in short supply for when we get to the palace, but otherwise, let's roll through the chaff as quickly as possible."

"A speech without reference to showmanship." Ren gave me a wry grin.

"Hell has . . . ruined me," I said and shook my head. Would be nice to get back to the point where the normal me had more control than the demonic side. "Although that was partially you as well, no doubt."

"Don't pretend you didn't have an equal share in the debauchery, trickster." She rolled her shoulders out and lifted her rifle. "Almost a shame that we'll go back to something more grounded soon enough."

While I gave her a nod, I wasn't so sure it *was* a shame. There was only so much punishment I could take. Our more normal love life from before was . . . Well, thinking back to the tower—we'd always leaned on the side of slightly unhinged.

"We'll run through this nice and simple." I let the thoughts over our relationship dwindle away so that I could focus on the battle plan. "Chew through and clog up the front using the valley, while my ace and Ren batter the ones near the back. Idea is to break them and cut through the palace gates as soon as reasonable."

"Understood." The elf gave me a nod. "Let's get buffed up."

My eyes rolled around my Inventory window at great speed. While I could draw most things from there with just a thought, I wanted to take stock of which potions I'd have to hold my nose and drink. The first consumable would

make that more bearable—a type of cheese that made everything taste like . . .
more cheese.

A pretty Gouda buff if you asked me.

Next up were all the ones that increased my magical Damage, Crit Chance,
and Mana regeneration. Followed by Intelligence boosting, a minor all-Stats boost,
and then something to give me a bit more defense and evasion. At that point, my
stomach felt pretty full, so I saved anything niche for later.

Switched to spell scrolls and buffed my illusion magic, Skill range, and Health
regeneration. A couple of Party-wide auras to further increase defenses and attack
power. Ren and Wolf finished off their preparations, both of them now shimmering through several different colors.

I felt calm now. Perhaps one of the side effects of a potion. One last final
push and . . .

"Ren." I turned my head to the elf. "You know what the worst part of this
whole venture has been?"

"There's . . . just so many things. I wouldn't know where to start."

"I've grown tired of the taste of sweet cakes."

Her brow furrowed slightly as a tear sprung from her right eye and traveled
down her face. "You're a fucking *bastard*, Max. You're lucky I love you."

I smiled, reveling in the rebellion. *Yes.* Somebody had to love me, and despite
everything we'd been through in hell, we still wore the rings exchanged. A bind-
ing vow that not even this cursed place could undo.

"Everybody look sharp. We only get one shot at this, and missing is not
an option."

At their murmurs of readiness, we surged forth.

The palace itself sat at the bottom of a valley, three or possibly four long path-
ways leading downward to an open area where the gathered demons were sitting
right in front of the building that housed the king. Gaps in the lowered ground
revealed small pits of lava, the air waving from the heat as the amber glow illuminated patches of deep-red rock.

Without a way to teleport the bear, we had to make most of the distance on
foot. Surprisingly, we got within a decent distance before bright eyes started to
turn our way, and the gathered horde murmured that we had arrived.

It was showtime.

With still a way for Wolf to go, Ren started proceedings with a shot into the
closest demons, entangling roots grabbing at a wide handful and preventing their
easy surge toward us.

"Kneel, pathetic maggots," she called out. "Bow your heads and worship your
future king."

As her buffing Skill washed over me, I switched with my demonic ace in
the air and activated <Demon Form> at the same time as my shadowed card cast

three held spells. Growth scroll increased my size by 20 percent. Antivenom-shell scroll made me shimmer a deep-purple color and was mostly for the aesthetics. Quake scroll did no Damage but vibrated the ground in a wide area. As horns burst from my head, two large wings cracked at the air as they snapped open behind me.

The sea of Dazzle icons washing through the demons was pure bliss.

A second blast rang from Ren's location as a radiant shot blew through two demons before bright-gold lightning flickered around a dozen more, her new Skill scouring and burning the blight before us.

Wolf collided with the front row of the pinned regiment, trampling several before his claws cleaved another group to shreds. Pulses of stunning and dazing effects washed through any close to him.

I looked up to see a cloud of arrows moving through the air toward me. My sharp teeth upturned into a grin as the projectiles burst through <Card Fan>, the shield provided by Ren, and all my other defenses. Arrows pierced my body, far too many to avoid fully. I continued to glide down toward the horde below. The grin remained on my face despite the eight arrows in me and countless cuts from other near misses.

<Demonic Regeneration> started to overcome the injuries, my bravado not even caring to use <Last Act> to avoid the piercing points of the lobbed arrows. One by one, they were pushed out of my body—ejected to fall inert to the ground below. As soon as I was free from them, I turned invisible.

Near silent, I dropped and landed on the warm, rocky ground. Righted myself and brought my wings in as my hand extended. Ice-spear scroll burned away from my gauntlet and a five-foot-long piercing beam burst from my palm, cutting through the head of the nearest demon. As my invisibility faded, purple cards bloomed and encircled my left hand. I had thirteen additional scrolls of the same spell, and I rotated them into the holster on my arm every time one was cast.

I whirled among the maelstrom. Spears of ice jutting out from me in intervals as I ducked and followed up any Damage I caused. Magic cards spiraled out around my left like a reactive shield, lashing around to cut through opponents like a whip. Mundane cards spun around me like an obscuring cloud, causing the demons to wince away from the fluttering cardboard.

A hiss emerged from deeper in the army, and I turned my head just as a fel green orb snaked through the horde and struck me. I slid backward across the ground getting slicker with the blood of those beneath me. They had magic casters, and reasonably proficient ones for a change. Decent Damage and some minor debuffs.

I didn't really have the range or line of sight on them, so I flashed my wings to buffer the demons away from me and reveal a chair. Hopped atop it and gave them all a bow. Weight pressed on my back as Ren appeared, switched with her dove—straight into a crouched position. As soon as her rifle blasted, she was gone, and I dropped back to the ground on my feet, chair put away.

To follow up on her picking the brains of the spellcaster, several explosions of green gas rocked the middle of the army as my ace spun through the regiments setting off noxious-blast scrolls. While the System had originally pinned me down to illusion and demonic magic, my new card made me a fully fledged arcanist, limited by only what scrolls I had in stock.

I heard Wolf's roar from behind; he was catching me up already, and the first third of the army was starting to collapse.

Perhaps it was time I helped them along. With a grin, I clicked my fingers and cast <Finale>.

The cheers of the crowd gave us the energy and drive to slaughter halfway through the middle third of the army. We were . . . an overwhelming force. They brought out larger brutes, and Ren's rainstorm Skill scoured them into melting piles of demonic flesh as the constant bolts of radiant light burned through to the rock below. War machines rumbled forth, and my ace spewed acid and rust spells before covering what remained in oil so that the elf could light them up with a flaming shot. Packs became enraged but were broken and mashed beneath the unstoppable presence of the bear. Roger helped a little too, I assumed.

I dropped <Demon Form> to save my humanity from tearing away and going on vacation. Body was soaked through with blood—some of it my own. Without the ability to stun any of us, they just couldn't put out enough Damage to win. Any cut or slash I received was quickly patched up with <Demonic Regeneration>. A spear that impaled me all the way through was healed over with a spike from Ren's Mana-manipulated burst heal.

There was . . . fear in the demons' eyes.

We had become something of a nightmare to them. Unrelenting. Constant slaughter through scores of their number. My brain was too far gone to care about the System or why these Monsters were capable of more emotion than the ones up in the real world. If that even existed anymore.

Maybe *this* was it. Just continuous carnage.

I *loved* it. Hoped there would be no end to the demons. Perhaps we could just wait out here and hope that some more would be along shortly—we hadn't completely scoured hell, of course.

A chain lashed out through the crowd, bursting through my shoulder and dragging me toward whoever had thrown it. I slid across the ground, blocking a handful of attacks from the onlookers while a couple more struck me. A large elite had been the one to grab me and now stood ready to hit me with a large axe once his chain had brought me into range.

Not a big deal. I'd just use <Last Act> when he . . .

Weapon flashed down as my brow furrowed at the new debuff icon over me.

A spellcaster off to the side had disabled all my Skills.

CHAPTER THIRTY-NINE

Showpiece of Work

Over the near two months of my time in this world, I had been somewhat accustomed to pain. A certain amount of near deaths and plenty of cuts and bruises. All physically survived, albeit with some lingering mental exhaustion—I was sure.

And so, as the large axe broke through my left clavicle and embedded halfway into my chest, the tall demon standing in front of me probably didn't expect me to smile.

"Quickest way to my heart *isn't* my stomach, it seems," I said, blood spluttering from my mouth.

His head exploded—probably from the sniper rifle rather than my terrible joke—and the weapon sank away from the wound with a terrible slurping sound.

Ren appeared beside me, hand against my back as my ace created a protective dome around us. Only lasted ten seconds, but without concentrated healing, I had less time than that to continue existing.

"You're not allowed to die until we've desecrated that throne, asshole." The elf pooled her Mana into her heal, the delayed burst causing my skin and bones to graft back together. Almost as painful as the split.

"I'll not die until this entire world stands and applauds me." I wavered, but my grin seemed to comfort her. She then vanished to be replaced by her dove as I brought a health potion up to my lips.

Disgusting but necessary.

Not only had I almost had my heart torn in two, but slightly farther in the other direction and I would have lost my left arm. Something I didn't think even Ren's healing would be able to fix. While there was plenty of magic I could weave single-handed, the amusing idea of having a rotating barrel prosthetic armed with twenty scrolls like some kind of shotgun arm wasn't a healthy thought to have right this second.

Barrier dropped and my purple magic cards circled around me as I healed. Slicing through the demons who thought I might be an easier target when injured. Incorrect. I turned my head to see the spellcaster readying up to disable my Skills once more.

I shook my head slowly.

His chest exploded, fire consuming him from within and setting his long robes alight. The demonic cannon dropped behind him by my ace card had fired off a lit lantern.

I tried to flex out my left arm as <Demonic Regeneration> patched up the last of the external wound. Ached like crazy, my muscles still bearing the brunt of the trauma.

If anything, the pain just made me . . . angry. I'd been able to ignore and quell it for most of the time that we'd been in hell, but that feral hatred for demonkind started burning back within me, as if placed there by the axe itself. Purple electricity sparked around me.

They *feared* me, and I'd let them. Become what they abhorred and ran from. Except they wouldn't be able to escape. An unknown voice echoed deep within me from somewhere else, assuring me I needed to kill all demons. So I would.

Demon ace below me as I jumped up into the air and activated <Demon Form>, the card activated a scroll of air gust followed by a second, pushing me high up in the air to hover above the battlefield.

What remained of the army were small dots now. Occasionally, a slim beam of golden light flashed through, bursting through several demons before a crackle of radiant lightning snapped between others like fireworks. Wolf became a comet snaking through the night sky as fire burned a trail behind his charge, trampling and impaling scores of the gathered Monsters. The white blob of Roger mopped up behind him and made sure the elf wasn't flanked.

There were patches of deep red. Some green and yellow from spells cast of bile thrown up. A sprinkling of white where bones had emerged from the melted fleshy parts of some demons. Reflective metal picked up some light. Two lines of purple darting around as I weaved through the remainder of the army. Not really much of a painting of anything other than war. One that they were losing.

I looked over at the palace. Some temptation within me wanting to zip over there right now and burst through the roof. How difficult could it be to kill one more demon?

It would only take getting caught out like with the spellcaster, and I'd have no backup plan. It had been a while since I was a solo showman, and for good reason. I half expected the king, princes, and remaining elites to come pouring out from the palace to assail us. Join the fray and fall in short order.

But they had some common sense in staying put and maintaining control of their battleground. If it were me, I'd put all sorts of traps and preparations around the doors leading into the throne room. Oh, it *would* soon be me.

All I needed to do was . . . get rid of the trash.

Switched positions with my demonic ace down on the ground and dropped my wings and horns away. I had gotten a good view of the battlefield and knew we were getting close to overrunning all that remained.

Just needed one last push.

I grinned and let the hate overtake me. Burst forward in flashes, as if my brain only cared to see the death blows. Cards blooming just in front of my hands as though they were punch blades, I ducked and weaved—slashing out and cutting through demons. Dropped <Finale> again as it had come off cooldown. Activated the enchantment on my Boots of Quickness to gain a boost of movement speed.

Cast a spell scroll of random element, which added 10 percent Damage of a random element to every attack that landed. A whistle passed my ears as one of Ren's shots scoured the air just beside me.

Despite the anger and ache vibrating through my body, I felt . . . calm and . . .

I stopped, my next card not having a target. Looking around, I spun on the spot to look for something standing upright and breathing. A handful of demons escaping into the palace but other than that . . . there was an uncomfortable silence to the area.

Hundreds of corpses littered the warm ground. Pulses of heat from the dotted lava pools making the air suddenly very stifling. It was a macabre sight that would have cracked and broken a Max from the past. These days, the only thing preventing me from writhing around among the shattered bones and disemboweled figures with the elf was the fact we had more corpses to create.

I checked myself for physical injury, but it was hard to tell since I was covered head to toe in blood and gore. My regeneration had patched up everything minor that had been inflicted on me—to the point that I barely registered the attacks. Left side of me still ached despite the wound suturing itself together—I'd need to give it a proper look after a wash.

Oh, to have a *bath*. A thing of distant memory. My body shed odd tears just thinking of clean and relaxing water. We never knew we had it so good.

"Need any more healing, trickster?"

I turned my head as the rest of the Party caught me up. The elf had a few more sprays of crimson across her but had kept at enough distance to avoid most of the more visceral parts of the combat. Wolf was almost as covered as I was—although his fur had been cleaned off, leaving only the thick armor slick with the red stuff. Roger's arms were bright scarlet, but other than looking exhausted, he was doing fine.

"System wise, I am feeling alright. I think just on an existential level I might be falling apart." I gave her a glum shrug, which caused a spike of pain down my left side.

"Well, you almost died again, so be more careful of that." She yawned and smeared blood across her face as she brought her forearm up to cover her tired expression. "There's a cooldown and shit."

I cycled back through my notifications to see if it had split my heart. There were a few low- and critical-Health alerts I had long silenced but nothing specifically telling me the organ was fucked. That was my *Ren-loving* heart, so it was a good thing she had saved it.

"I am maybe three hours from finally losing my sanity," Wolf stated rather plainly. "Either we win and escape very soon or I will become an untenable monster who will probably die in short order because I am old and suffering."

A scowl upon my brow, I stepped over and dropped to my knees before him, grabbing his head to hold it against my chest. "I forgot what I was going to say to you on the way down here. Sorry, Wolf."

"We're all suffering, brother," Ren assured him. "Together we will escape and live free again."

The bear grunted, a little too polite to push me away from holding his face—even despite the circumstances. "I'd suffer a lot less if there was more opportunity to sleep and if the two of you quit trying to breed for more than ten minutes."

She shrugged in return. "Believe me, there are worse ways we could try to maintain our sanity than our deviant acts. Between that, my Skill preventing certain mental afflictions, and Max's corruption resistance—well, we've just about survived."

"Good experience too," I added, finally letting go of the bear to stand back up. "We might hit eighteen after killing the king, just as Roger foretold."

We all turned our gazes to the rabbit, who was standing off to the side with his arms crossed. A rather awkward expression that turned into a grimace as our attention focused on him.

"I may be a demon, but you three are fucked up." He shook his head. "There needs to be a worse place than hell for shitheads like you all. No offense, boss."

"*Some* taken." I rolled my eyes. Our wavering sanity aside, we were just products of our environment. Excluding the fact that both Ren and I came into this world from the starter island as murderers and with the intent to carry on that tradition on all that stood against us.

A worse place for us? Othea itself was miserable. Behind all the springtime woodlands and quaint villages was a corrupt Player twisting anyone with some hate in their heart for the world into a killer ready and willing to tear the System down.

If we didn't stop the Lady and Crimson Shadow, she would eventually find a way past the barrier, and who knows how far she could go then. We didn't want regiments of level-twenty Players against us—or even the Crown. That said, perhaps regicide *could* become a new hobby.

I licked my lips, which just filled my mouth with the taste of demon blood. "Plan, Max?"

With a groan, I closed my eyes. Roof would have been nice, but we didn't really have a way of getting Wolf up there. Front or side doors were a nonstarter, as they'd be expecting that. Part of me wished I could throw out my Domain and bring about a giant card to just slice through the whole building like I had against the titan zombie.

Didn't have the strength for it—both in literal sense and my Power bar was still middling, despite all that I had done in that fight. While enacting such an exertion of my mana, it usually caused me lots of physical and mental damage to maintain it. I was already a ragged bag of loosely held-together parts.

We'd just have to do this a little simply.

"Circle the building and find somewhere that doesn't have an obvious entrance. I believe we have some scrolls that could create a hole in the wall without creating too much of a ruckus. Once we are in there, kill all the bastards." I grinned as I stared at the palace, wavering in place slightly. "Focus casters and anyone capable of debilitating me."

"Do *you* have to be the one that kills the king?" Ren's eyes narrowed.

Wasn't quite insane enough to think she'd want to betray me to steal the crown. Even though she wanted to become my Demon Queen, Roger wasn't convinced putting on a crown would change her in that way—so she'd settled on just being an elfin queen. Probably better that way, in the long term.

"You know it, moonflower. Unless it's a matter of life or death, I need to claim the power myself fair and square." Or at least as fair as I usually played.

"Fine. Let's circle the left side then, as it's closer."

I nodded, and we set off, just as I received a notification.

[Tanya: Max. We have news.]
[Tanya: Hope this isn't a bad time, but you'll want to know this, I'm sure.]
[Tanya: Lady in Red . . .]
[Tanya: Crimson Shadow has taken control of Candlekeep.]

CHAPTER FORTY

Stat Check

My jaw continued to work as we walked to the side of the palace.

The news that Candlekeep had fallen was . . . irritating. Even if we were in the normal world, it wasn't guaranteed that we would have been able to do anything about it anyway. But just knowing that the Crimson Shadow was succeeding was enough to ruin my mood.

And how? We had been reducing their numbers to the point that they were struggling to assault the city—it couldn't be that she had found another enclave of Players to wrap around her finger to bolster her power. Not knowing was figuratively killing me.

Ren placed a hand on my shoulder, bringing me out of my thoughts. "I know you're overthinking things, trickster. Let's deal with one problem at a time."

I nodded and gave her a smile. She was right, as always.

Tanya and the other two groups were close to where the Eternal Wardens used to be, just waiting for us before engaging. Not that they were incapable, but given that I was the expert on bullshit, they wanted us to catch them up before they walked into whatever nightmare had befallen the group. Hopefully something we could twist to our advantage.

Only then could I focus my ire and overwhelming abilities on erasing Lady in Red from this world. We were getting close to being more than anyone could handle. All we needed to do was get Wolf a Guardian's powers, and the three of us could trample any opposition to dust.

That said . . .

I ran my hand along the stone wall as we circled around. Warm, as expected. Not overtly evil in a demonic way—which was disappointing. Worst yet, I couldn't feel the draw of a Guardian within the walls.

"I can't feel it either," Ren confirmed, her bright blues seeing what I was doing.

"Perhaps a good thing." I shrugged and wrinkled up my face. We didn't exactly want to be pushed right to the edge in this fight. As long as I got the killing blow, then . . . Well, I was done with this place.

The bear sniffed at the air before pausing and turning around. I followed his gaze to see a couple of large groups of demons standing at the top of the valley. Not approaching, just watching to see what happened. Perhaps hoping to be on the winning side.

Ren brought her rifle up and looked down the scope at them. "Nothing much to note," she informed us. "I could give them a warning shot?"

I shook my head. "No. They know they are outclassed. Just the sight of the carnage we have caused is crippling enough for their spirits."

The elf licked her lips but lowered her gun. "Well, I hope they got their kneeling knees on today because we're about to be royalty."

"An upgrade from princess to queen." I grinned, even as she rolled her eyes.

We moved down the side of the palace until I stopped and looked at the plain wall beside us. Without saying anything, the rest understood my cue. Scroll appeared in my hand as Ren and Wolf flanked my sides. Roger was behind us all, and I could feel his nerves. This was the final battle, after all.

Scroll disintegrated to dust as I cast false entrance on the wall ahead of us. A spiral of runes etched into the brickwork before it twisted into a circular entrance, leading into the room beyond . . . which appeared to be a bathroom.

The confused look of an elite demon currently seated upon a rather evil-looking toilet was quickly erased by Ren's shot. We stepped through, not wanting to be split up when the spell ended.

I looted the demon, finding mostly useless garbage at this stage. Another container called sealed demonic stash. I had a lot of these, but as the name suggested, they couldn't be opened. After the first week of not finding a key, I just looted them without a thought. I was sure to find a way eventually, but given my luck with random chance boxes, I paled at what further debris they'd grant me. My Inventory was already overloaded.

Light dimmed as the circle closed behind us, the four of us now trapped inside the palace. One single exit from this room. I stretched out my arms and relaxed. Felt calm, considering—but it *had* all been leading to this. Three weeks, give or take, of hell.

Now it was do-or-die, and those were simple instructions I'd follow to the letter, with no complaints.

We burst out of the bathroom, emerging into what looked like servant quarters. Clusters of bunk beds, drawers, and basic furniture, all with a hint of evil to them. No demons present—which made sense considering the situation. All hands were up and ready to serve and protect the king.

For as good as that would do them.

Roger had been able to tell us that the king himself was a powerful magic user, as well as pretty formidable in melee. As we strode across the dorms to the exit, we downed the rest of our potions, reapplying buffs that had fallen off and using the more powerful things we had stockpiled. Increasing our Damage and defenses to a degree that would make us sickeningly overpowered in the above world.

"Wait." Ren put her hand on me, and I turned to see her eyes were swirls of green energy. "They have a barrier over this doorway and demons waiting on the other side."

"They know we're here?" My questions came out flat—as we hadn't been exactly covert in our approach, and the king must have some manner of tracking.

"Perhaps. I can see which one is putting up the barrier." Her tongue ran across her teeth.

I smiled. "Care to ask them to stop then?"

The elf nodded, her eyes still that odd color—some manner of magic detection, I imagined. Rifle went up, and she fired a shot that exploded through the wall, chunks of the stone dropping to the floor.

Without waiting for the confirmation, I burst through the doorway. They'd definitely know we were coming with a bullet making the first appearance, and I didn't want them to have a moment to reposition or prepare.

I emerged into a lobby. Wide and with a tall ceiling, decorated with engravings and reliefs depicting demons and hellish acts being done to naked humans. All rather grandiose, if not a little macabre.

Large demon to the immediate left was already toppling over, half of his head missing. A second towering Monster to the right swung down at me with a mace as thick as a tree. These were some of the elite royal guard—fifteen feet tall and overtly muscled. Even the spellcasters—of which there were three others in this room—weren't wearing the traditional robes you'd expect.

The weapon struck the floor where I had been standing, flattening my ace and cracking the square tiles. From beside him, the cannon I was standing upon fired a spear through the side of his leg. As the demon hunched over to grasp at the wound, my two magic cards spun in the air like saws to slash through his throat.

A gust of wind blew past me as Wolf tore down the chamber to reach the casters at the other end. We'd found three different speed-boosting consumables he could stack with his charge and other Skills. It turned him into a blur, if only for a few seconds. My hand raised to use the silence-area scroll to see how *they* liked being prevented from using their Skills.

Turned out, they didn't like it at all. Third one barely had a chance to switch to a melee weapon before Wolf was upon him—the first gored and the second Ren had erased.

There were wide doors to our left, up a handful of stairs. Ornate. Clearly led to the throne room itself. Before we could consider this option, the doorway at the end near Wolf swung open, and demons poured forth. Remnants of the army that had retreated or had been held in reserve.

Little did they know what they were in for.

Doors were terrible choke points. A radiant bullet slammed the first three through the opening before golden lightning crackled out through maybe a dozen more. Still standing atop my cannon, I sent my demonic ace over the heads of the fallen and into whatever room was beyond.

I activated three lightning storm scrolls in a row, the resulting static in the air tangible, as a wave of burned-flesh smell washed back through. I switched places and landed among the confused throng of dead and dying demons. First card I pulled was critical, which exploded most of the chest of one demon. Second card was also a critical.

Mundane cards circled me like a hurricane, magic power tapping into them just as they were about to touch demons. I became a tornado of violence, my sphere of influence expanding until the cards touched the walls.

I clapped my hands, and they all fell to dust, leaving no demon standing. Two panicked faces looked in from the door out of here, more in reserve losing their spirit.

"If you give me five minutes, I'll be the new king, and I won't kill you." I smiled and tilted my head. "Or step inside and join your brethren in oblivion."

Other than giving me grimaces, the two faces did little else other than sink away from view. As good an answer as any.

I stepped back into the lobby to find the others waiting for me. Roger had all but accepted he was mostly an observer at this point. Usually he would get stronger alongside me, but since I wasn't meant to be in hell, the System had been skipping on conventional norms for a while.

"Ready to entertain royalty?" Ren asked, giving me a soft smile as I joined them once more.

"Something something greatest show ever," I murmured, leaning forward to give her a brief kiss.

"I definitely miss normal bullshit." She sighed and rested her head on me. "Rather than hell bullshit. I honestly do hope that we can escape here and just be goofy magicians again."

Although *goofy* wasn't how I'd describe our dazzling feats, I was on the same page. For the most part, we had just been killers here. There wasn't much point trying to wow the demons with tricks, and after a few days we were just under constant exhaustion anyway. I wiped the saliva running down my mouth as I imagined a soft, clean bed.

"I miss the sunshine," Wolf said. His amber eyes were focused on the large doors before us. "Fresh running water. The rest of our friends."

We were now a group of fifteen once we returned. Not quite enough to retake a city, maybe—but I felt as though the three of us counted as a few extra bodies when it came to power levels. One quick detour to see what happened to the Eternal Wardens—and if they left behind any useful information about Guardians—and then we'd head toward Candlekeep.

Before going against the demon king, I had one last look at my Equipment and Stats. It had been a while as I had mostly tried to ignore the System bullshit down here, just as the System tried to ignore us.

**[Head—Headband of Woe: Magic Damage increases
5% per 5% Mana spent]**
[Shoulders—Hellborne Spaulders: +2 DEX, +8 INT]
[Back—Skinned Horror: +3 DEX, +5 INT, +3 Luck]
[Chest—Hellfire Wrappings: +7 INT, +10% magic Damage]
[Arms—Arcane Guards+: +5 INT, +5 WIS, +10% Mana (+3 INT)]
[Hands—Trickster's Gloves+: +5 DEX, +8 INT (+3 INT)]
[Belt—Compounding Arcane Belt: +10% INT]
[Legs—Brilliant Studded Leathers: +5 INT, +10% Mana, +5% defense]
[Feet—Dire Boots+: +6 DEX, +10% movement speed (+3 INT)]

My jewelry and other accessories gave another +20 Intelligence, +5 Luck, +25% magic Damage, and +30% Mana. Stats sheet didn't show the effects of potions or scrolls, but even the base numbers surprised me, after so long without checking.

[Stats]
[Strength—8]
[Constitution—9]
[Agility—8]
[Dexterity—38 (22 + 16)]
[Intelligence—106 (22 + 63 + 12)]
[Wisdom—13 (8 + 5)]
[Luck—24 (16 + 8)]

CHAPTER FORTY-ONE

Pact Up

I placed my hand against the large ornate doors and pushed.

They opened smoothly. Almost without resistance, as if they were weightless. No groan or creaks. Truly a set of doors that befitted a king. Soon to be *mine*, I hoped.

Perhaps more interesting than the smooth entryway by manner of several factors was the room that it led into. Wide and tall, with a domed ceiling decorated with black and gold. Spiraled patterns that might make sense if I had the time to stand and stare at them for a while, but at a brief glance they were just dizzying.

Centerpiece of the whole throne room was the throne itself, and its current occupant. The seat was made of a dark material—obsidian but a swirl of energy rolled around the surface almost like faint waves of dry ice. Spiked with various skulls on the ends of some of the longer protrusions. Many humanoid but others were various beasts or creatures I couldn't even imagine.

The Demon King himself was every bit a cliché as I could have imagined. A towering humanoid of dark red flesh, easily twenty feet tall if he stood. Hoofed feet, dark leathers covering little of his muscled form, yellow eyes, sharp fangs, and two large horns of a black almost as dark as the throne. He wore a tired but amused look on his face, his position in his seat casual and unbothered. On his right side, a tall flaming greatsword hung in the air—hovering in place as an eye in the hilt observed us.

To his left stood a cloaked figure. A long beak extended from the darkness of their wide hood, so they were probably some manner of bird demon. Hunched and rounded, two clawed hands clasped at a long staff. The magic weapon looked as though it was made from the twined sinews of many victims, like gnarled wood. Pale strands woven together rose up to encircle a large skull that constantly bled from the eye sockets.

The rest of the pristine marbled floor was covered by his elite guard in waiting. Two dozen, at least, heavily armored demons of various shades. None smaller than ten feet tall and each armed with a wicked-looking weapon that either glowed with insidious intent or dripped unknown poisons and toxins. Eyes glared at the three of us as we stood in the opening.

I was almost thankful that they hadn't immediately attacked so that I could take in the splendor and absolute weight of energy and power in this room. Even the titan zombie had nothing on the king and his retinue. We had been constantly punching above our level in this world, but this Monster wasn't meant to be assailed by Players—let alone so few.

As the star of the show, I took the first few steps forward. Tense and ready to burst into violence. If they had allowed us a brief second to fully drink down the sight before us, then there was a chance one of us could get a monologue off before heads started to roll. I almost craved it.

A quick glance to my two companions, and neither seemed to be shrinking away under the power before us. Ren looked stoic; perhaps her exhaustion just too great to care anymore. Wolf, on the other hand, was a lot more agitated than normal—eager to chew through this last hurdle. And I . . . was calm, considering.

"Mortals," the king's voice boomed out as he leaned forward. "I don't know how you've managed to survive down here, but your luck has run out."

"On the contrary." I smiled and continued forward slowly. "This is the first time we've had the chance to entertain royalty, so luck is truly on our side."

"If only for a few more seconds. You don't understand how outclassed you are."

I looked around the room at all the demons, just tense and ready to try to take us apart. Part of me missed the System giving us a little heads-up about levels and Monster names. Mostly, however, I had been enjoying the feeling that this was more akin to real life compared to our previous experiences with Monsters in Othea. Even if they were still constructs of the System, being able to hold a conversation was a novelty.

It made dazzling them all that more pleasant.

As I opened my mouth to speak, I found no words came out. Instead, my throat felt tight and constricted. The king's hand extended, and I felt weightless, my feet rising off the floor as the pressure on my neck increased. I extended my hand in an attempt to cast something, but my vision blurred as my eyes bulged out.

With a sickening crunch, my head exploded, sending brain matter and blood up into the air like a geyser.

The perfect firework to start off this soon-to-be massacre.

While my corpse dropped to the floor, the real me stepped out among the group of demons on the right side. A shot rang out as Ren fired for the spellcaster beside the king; a blazing shield of swirling orange light protected the birdlike demon from even the high-caliber rifle. Two cards of bright purple spun into my hands, and I jabbed them forward like daggers into the kidneys of the opponent in front of me, who hadn't turned.

And then all hell broke loose. *Heh.*

Wolf powered into the left side of the throne room, stunning and disemboweling the first demon he came across as my ace dropped area-effect scrolls. Reduced armor. Reduced speed. Weakness to debuffs. Oh, we were going to *debuff the shit out of them.*

I felt elated. Not a traditional show by any means but a culmination of all we had suffered through and overcome in our little jaunt through the hells. We were already overpowered by Player standards, and now the bloodshed had acted as a lubricant for us to force the dial even further.

<Last Act> was easy to reset now. A simple matter of dropping 20 percent of my own Health through <Bloodletting>, my <Demonic Regeneration> and passive recovery from items and Ren topping my Health up to full again within seconds. They needed to pin me down to put pressure on—but I was as slippery as anything. Perhaps also lubed from the bloodshed.

That brought distracting thoughts up that I didn't need right now. My glance went over to the elf as she skewered a demon with the jagged bayonet before blowing a hole straight through them into another opponent behind.

I felt the displacement of air before I saw the attack from behind me—but I swapped places with my ace, and the axe attack instead bounced off the rounded cylinder of my cannon left in my wake. Purple card went out and slashed through the back of the knee of a demon approaching Wolf. They stumbled and dropped in front of the bear, who leaped up and tore the face off of the demon with a quick bite.

Then I went invisible, my cannon firing a blast of confetti through the throng as I walked over to the center of the room once more. I could . . . feel something in the air. I glanced at the king, who was rising from his throne to take up his sword   but that wasn't it.

Instead, I looked back to the open doorway. Another smile widened across my face.

Before my invisibility wore off, I spun on my heels to face the throne once again, using a smoke-cloud scroll to create a cloud of obscuring mist around me. The wall of gray dispersed almost immediately as scores of hell birds rushed through the doorway and into the chamber, swirling the smoke away to reveal me now in my <Demon Form>.

But that wasn't all!

As my bird friends swooped past me, I allowed them to take spell scrolls from my outstretched hands. Although I couldn't interact with them directly, I sent my ace around the room. It passed through the hell doves without harming them, instead just acting as an activating wick to burst the spells from the claws of the small demons.

The Demon King stretched out his neck and twirled the sword in his hands, readying up. Crackles of energy from constant spells, blasts from the sniper rifle, and the roars or crunches over by Wolf filled the throne room.

"The rumors were true then." The king grimaced, glaring at my wings and horns. "Far beyond any other mortal that has dared step foot in my kingdom. I can see it in your eyes . . . You would never settle for less than the throne. There is no point asking for you to join my side."

"Correct." I grinned, birds still swooping around me to retrieve more scrolls to take into the battlefield.

My cannon fired off another blast of confetti, and the king didn't even flinch. I could feel the power in his sword, even from here—the weapon was a demon too. My mundane deck burst from my belt and swirled around me, the air now thick with cards and birds. As I stretched my fingers out to show the white gloves I now wore, I could sense the threads of magic that joined them all to me.

A network where I was the anchor, able to control and utilize everything to my benefit.

Before I could make the first move, a wave of heat buffeted me—a shock wave burst out from the king, tensing up to launch toward me. He would be much quicker than me, I was sure. I snapped my fingers as he burst forth, putting the advanced version of <Shuffle> on him.

Slowed—something that reduced both movement and attack speed. How fortuitous . . . Although a debuff that instantly killed him would have been preferable. I'd just have to wait for the refresh.

I switched position with a bird near the throne as the large sword cut through the air where I had been standing. A purple trail remained where it had swiped, as if he had scarred the atmosphere itself. Several of my hapless hell birds burst into fine mist from the strike.

Just to my left, the spellcaster was gathering up some crackling energy, ready to cast something at me. I raised an eyebrow at the shadowed demon as my <Card Fan> absorbed the strike. "Lightning, really? But it's only *just* started to rain."

The demon opened their mouth to squawk at me before looking up. A cloud had formed, suddenly ejecting bolts of radiance straight down upon them. The golden beams fizzled and burned as they struck the orange shield, but the spellcaster had to focus entirely on holding their spell up to not become scoured by Ren's Skill.

Wolf was protecting the elf as she stood with one hand extended, blood already running from her palm. Before I could lend the power of my cards to aid in the destruction of the defensive spell, I caught the glare of the king—he was switching focus to Ren.

Transposition was on cooldown, so I just powered up a card as quickly as I could. The bear stepped in the way, ready to intercept any strike—but the large demon didn't even lunge for a swing. Instead, he held out his hand.

Ren rose from the floor, a scowl on her reddening face as she glared at the Demon King. Yet she didn't drop her spell, despite her Health plummeting, as she was squeezed just as I had been. An intense anger surged through me like a lava burst, and my wings snapped back to launch me toward the king, my card spinning through the air toward his neck.

He shimmered a deep gray as my card passed straight through him, dissipating as it struck the wall over the door.

The king turned his wide grin to me to gloat. Intending on dragging this out to make us suffer. Then shock flashed across his smarmy expression, and his arm sagged slightly. He dropped the elf to the ground. She panted and gasped for air as her extended hand shook, Wolf almost sitting on her to keep her blocked from view.

Relief slowed my charge, my temperament cooling so that I didn't speed head-first into the sword.

Our eyes turned to what had waylaid the attack.

Beside the king, his eyes wide and panicked, stood Roger. His mace was bloodied from where he had struck the tall demon, but that looked to be as far as he had planned.

"*Worm*," the king sneered and clicked his fingers.

With one last glimpse toward me, Roger unraveled in a spiral pattern, as if reality was peeling him away. It dragged on for ages in my eyes, seeing the calm realization in his eyes torn apart, even though it happened in a near instant.

And then he was gone.

CHAPTER FORTY-TWO

Crowning Achievement

For the first time in weeks, I felt fear.

Roger had been erased. Aside from my eyes seeing him unravel to dust, it also struck me in my core. Not necessarily an emotional response to his demise, but he and I were linked. Did this mean I was about to become unraveled as well? Or lose some of my demonic powers?

It didn't really matter, for as soon as the flash of fear washed through me, it was replaced with fury almost as quickly.

I slammed into the Demon King, a dagger in each hand, only barely piercing his thick skin. For a System-created, he truly was powerful. Probably not meant to be assaulted by Players—especially not by just three. He growled and pushed me away, grabbing me instead of swatting me from the air.

Ren dropped to her knees, her arm hanging slack as she downed a potion with the other. She had finally overpowered the spellcaster's shield and scoured them with bolts. Wolf roared and leaped for the king, almost equally as angered at seeing the destruction of the rabbit demon.

A large wall of spikes burst from the marbled floor, blocking the bear off from landing any hits. I struggled and squirmed against the grip of the Demon King as he held me up, his large fist squeezing down on me.

"Such a wretched rat," he spat, eyes burning into me. "Not worthy of having *one* silver crown, let alone eight of them."

I didn't have the temperament for words at this stage. Instead, I drew my right arm back and lashed out toward his face. With no hesitation, he opened his large mouth and bit my hand clean off—halfway up to my forearm. With a crunch as he crushed my left shoulder, he then threw my body to the floor.

<Last Act> allowed me to step out of brief invisibility, still fully intact. A gamble but what was new for me? I gave my corpse a glance before looking up at the king.

He finished swallowing down the faux arm, licking his bloodied lips. The others were fighting more of the other elite demons, which was a shame—mostly because I wanted them to see what I was about to do.

I dropped <Demon Form> and rubbed at my head where the horns once were. "A short but worthy battle. It was nice knowing you, nameless king."

"Wretch! You act so *insolent*," he growled and brought down his sword from the air into his hand. "Acting as if you had won. You will revere the name . . ."

He paused, and I took one last deep breath.

In his eyes, I then vanished—to be replaced by my demonic ace. And *yes*, I had activated transposition to switch places with it. Only, I had been holding it in my hand. The one that he had eaten.

From my perspective, I didn't have a chance to see the look on his face or know if he had any last words, or even the realization that I had outplayed him. Instead, I just knew warmth and darkness. At least for a moment.

And then I unloaded every bulky item from my Inventory as quick as my broken Ability let me. The tangible space around me tried to deny me, the System unsure as to how the physics or practicality of my plot was meant to work out. After three confused seconds, where an improbable number of chairs cluttered around me—the king's physical form could abide it no longer.

With a visceral ripping sound that filled my ears, bright light flooded through the darkness as the demon tore in all directions. I dropped to the ground and rolled across warm entrails and gore. Gasped for air and tried to wipe the blood from my eyes.

I had not gone without my own Damage from the venture. Even watching my Health now tick up from my regeneration and bones click back into place, it had been a risky endeavor. I had become partially crushed myself before he gave out. A warm pulse of healing righted most of those wrongs, as I turned my blurry vision over to the elf.

The created wall had crumbled to ash, showing my two Party members equally bloodied but healed up. Any demon still living had paused in place, frozen in surprise or terror at seeing their king ruptured from the inside out.

I grinned, blood escaping from my mouth, as my aching legs took me over to my reward. The golden crown that had rolled away from the surprised head of the demon, now just inert. I shuffled one of the bloodied wooden chairs upright and sat on it. And just . . . looked down at the piece of headgear.

Relatively simple at first glance—only a few steps above the plain silver crowns. This golden one had faint engravings on it and a sinister red gem at the forefront. My eyes were drawn to the pile of ash where my former pact demon had been standing.

Ren stepped up behind me and put a bloody hand on my equally gore-slick shoulder. "He gave his life to save me, trickster. Roger wasn't such a bad egg after all."

I opened my hand and drew his card. Floating two inches above my hand, it was blank. Plain white. Not only was the rabbit gone, but the System hadn't replaced him. He was only meant to be summoned in the overworld, and any deaths would send him back here. Perhaps it didn't know what to do now that he was erased for good.

With the empty card still hovering there, I turned my tired eyes around the throne room. There were still a few living demons, including the two princes remaining—who had kept out of battle as much as possible to save their own skins. Nobody seemed keen to resume the fight after seeing what I had done to the king. Plenty of them had their glowing eyes focused on the crown lying on the floor.

Floating above the shredded corpse and soaked furniture was the demonic sword. The eye on the hilt was looking at me. I tilted my head and observed it. It didn't look angry at me. Impassive, maybe. But the stare was intense and unblinking.

"I just had a new position open up, if you're looking for regular work." My voice came out rough like I had caught a cold. I grasped at my plain card and held it up to the weapon.

It maintained eye contact with me for a few moments before it started to fade away. Similar to how Roger had been destroyed but calmer and more controlled. As it did so, lines started to draw on my magic card. Grooves of deep purple and black that were sharp and angular before circling around with a flourish.

The design was a simplified version of said demonic sword. I blinked a couple of times to make sure I wasn't just imagining it before I allowed the card to fade away.

"Does . . . the sword talk?" Ren asked, half hopeful and half apprehensive.

"We can test it." I furrowed my brow and looked down at the crown. The weight of it was . . . It had been what we had wanted. What *I* had wanted. Ever since we set off in hell. To not take it up would be pissing on Roger's sacrifice.

As Wolf went to sniff around the lumpy remains of the previous king, Ren put her arms around my neck from behind and leaned her face down close to mine.

"I'm with you. Whatever you decide and whatever happens."

I rested my head against hers for a moment before she relinquished her grasp so I could lean forward. I took up the crown into my hand and raised it to place upon my head.

It merged with the others.

With a sigh, I stood and stretched out my arms and then legs. Despite the tension in the room, I turned calmly and regarded the demons that hadn't been smart enough to run yet. My eyes fell on the two princes, and I gestured for them to come over.

They were apprehensive but did so, shuffling through the small crowd to stand before me. Each double my height. Muscled beyond normal means. One of them had a mouth wide enough to swallow me whole.

"Kneel," I commanded.

Each prince wavered before dropping to a knee, hanging their head low.

I was pretty sure I heard the elf briefly purr from behind me. "As your new king, I offer my first proclamation. No, wait . . . *before* that." I spun on my heels to face Ren, who had clearly been ogling me.

"What is it, your majesty?" she asked, biting her lip.

"I have the capacity to marry us under the System. You will become queen of hell, beside me. Till death do us part."

She stepped closer and put her hands on my cheeks so that her bright-blue eyes could dig into my muted purple ones. "I accept. There is nothing I want more."

"Then it is done." I leaned in, and we shared a slow kiss. As we parted, she was all smiles—and I realized that I was too. There was no tangible benefit to this . . . No, that was a lie. We were both now immune to the corrupting influences of hell. No slowly being ground down. No overheating. No madness.

I turned from her. "My next edict . . ."

The large demonic sword burst back into reality between the humbled princes, quickly rotating in a full circle to lop off both their heads with the same swipe.

"No princes or successors," I announced as their heads bounced across the marbled floor. "I will be the *last* king here, after which I will put together a council to have a democratically elected official lead hell in my absence."

That was assuming that we had a way of leaving here.

I took the two crowns and absorbed them too.

"Alright. Now everyone *fuck off* out of my palace." I crossed my arms as the sword hovered over to flank me.

After a couple of moments where the demons were still trying to process everything, they eventually got the nerve to leave. Cautious footsteps became something of a stampede, as they were all keen to get away from my glare.

Soon enough, it was just us three left.

I sighed and rubbed at my head, walking across the room. With little ceremony, I sat myself on the throne. It was warm and uncomfortable. Didn't even get much chance to survey my kingdom from this new precipice before the elf had climbed up with me, straddled across my lap.

"You might want to give us some space," she said, craning her head back to look at the displeased bear.

"Actually, Ren . . ." I placed my finger on her lips as she turned back to face me. "I was thinking we put a pause on this."

"But it was my *fantasy*." She pouted, something that easily wormed into my heart. A total break from her usual stoic and dour attitude.

My eyes were too focused on my menus. On the new Skills that I had gained now that I snapped hell in half and made it my own.

I now did double Damage to demons, which made sense with how easily I'd dispatched those princes. My kingship also granted several boons to my summoned demons and my demonic form. The third skill was perhaps more important and had totally been a handful of ice cubes on the passion Ren was trying to stoke up.

"We'll do it next time we're here, I promise." I smiled and struggled to run my bloody hand through her matted hair.

Her pout remained. "*Next* time?"

"Yes, my dear. I can now create a portal between hell and Othea, anytime I like."

CHAPTER FORTY-THREE

Death Forged

Ren's vibrant eyes continued to read my face as she sat atop me. "You're saying . . . we could go home at any time?"

"I believe so." I smiled, despite feeling like lukewarm garbage.

She clicked her tongue and slid down from my lap, standing up on the floor beside the throne instead. "I *really* want to be clean, Max."

Despite all that we had been through, there was a weight to her simple sentence that struck me straight in the heart. I yearned for it too. A waking moment where we weren't covered in sweat, grime, and gore. To see the blue sky again.

I lifted my left arm, noticing that my STAR was golden. Deposing the monarch and his army had been enough to edge us to eighteen, just as Roger had said. Although the rabbit demon and I were on contentious terms for most of our relationship, I did miss him. The fact that he had stepped in to protect Ren of all people had earned him redemption in my eyes. I'd get a gift basket sent to his family.

With a sigh, I stood from the throne and beckoned Wolf to join us. Now more certain that the intended intimacy had been called off, he sauntered over. He looked tired. We all were.

"Did you want some position on my court, Wolf?" I asked him, unsure what I could really do at this point.

"I will never come back to this horrid place," he replied, sneering at the dead bodies littering my palace.

"A fair answer."

Ren knelt down beside him and ruffled his chops. "We're leaving here soon. You get anything good from your eighteen level up?"

"Defensive Ability. Doubles my armor and healing received but I can't move or attack."

She nodded. "That pairs well with what I just got, which is an aura that constantly restores Health to the whole Party. How about you, Max?"

"Ah, I hadn't even checked yet." I held my arm out and activated the thing.

The usual stats and other boring information went across my vision, and I mostly ignored it. My eyes had grown tired of the intangible text during our time down in this world, and I had avoided the System as much as possible in hell—just as much as it had avoided us.

Two Passives gained, as usual. Nothing too spectacular. Critical hits regenerated my Mana for five seconds. Dexterity now gave a percentage as armor. Nice to have but I'd always been a bit of a glass cannon. Partially due to my own recklessness.

But the active Skill was . . . interesting. <Active Learner> allowed me to copy the last damaging Ability that struck me. A blank Ability where I could lock or replace the copied Skill at will but it reset to nothing overnight. For once, the System had eased back on the bullshit it allowed me. Otherwise, I'd find the most powerful attack I could survive and then keep that forever.

"Hey, Ren." I turned my eyes away from the menus to look at her. "Can you hit me with a <Smite Shot>?"

The elf didn't hesitate and, with the barest of movements, flicked out a throwing knife from her belt. Radiant light burst around it, right before it buried itself in my thigh.

"Ow. That hurts more because I'm a *demon*," I noted.

"I thought we swore off this manner of foreplay?" She stepped forward to pull the blade from me, a slight scowl on her face.

"No." I shook my head. "This wasn't . . . for that. I wasn't sure if this would work, but it looks like my cards count as magical projectiles, which is enough." Into my raised hand, a purple card appeared between my fingers. After a moment, it then burned into a golden glow.

Ren crossed her arms. "So I copied your Skills, and now you copied mine?"

"Only if damaged and only one at a time. <Smite Shot> is probably one of the most useful things I can steal for my card attacks at present." <Entangling Shot> would be good too. I started to wonder if Quinn could blow me up with his boomerang, and I could copy that even using <Last Act> to not die.

I turned my wavering attention to the other two, who looked only seconds from begging me to take them out of here. The demonic sword had vanished. It wouldn't be able to swap bodies like Roger used to, but I had a feeling that the blood of its victims was what kept it around longer. A very *specific* feeling that had to come from my innate demonic knowledge. Or I was making it up. Reality was mine for the bending.

"Alright, stand back." I stretched my neck out. "I haven't done this before, so . . . apologies if I fuck it up." With a grin at my expectant crowd, I quickly messaged Tanya for the coordinates of their current location. The portal didn't work quite that simply, but I made do with what I had.

My eyes closed as I stood and held my hands out. Took a deep breath. Focused.

There was a thrum of energy, and I opened my eyes again to see a doorway forming. It looked like the inside of my dressing room door—or at least a blurring of all the common ones throughout my touring life. A simple gray with a silver handle. Off-white frame that needed a dusting and a piece of paper taped to it. Words and lines on it illegible but I was willing to guess that it was supposed to be a set list for the evening.

And it just stood there, on the marbled and blood-slick floor.

"Ladies and bears first," I offered, giving them a bow.

Any apprehension we had on this working went away in a flash as Ren near darted for the door. It opened to reveal something dark beyond, not the rest of the throne room. Any clues I could glean from the sight were eclipsed by Wolf as he pushed in straight after her, taking up the majority of the doorway as he squeezed through.

I took one last glance around my palace before following on. More of a demon than ever. I was keen to get back to being a great magician once more. While it had been optimistic to think we would have found another Guardian down here, we had still changed the world in perhaps a worse way. A genocide against demons, where I had toppled the ruler to claim hell as my own. Surely nothing bad would come from that.

My feet passed over the threshold and onto soft grass. My heart melted as a cool breeze washed over me. Any thoughts that the darkness could have meant I had messed the portal up flashed away in realizing it was just nighttime. Almost as soon as I had fully traveled through the door, Ren's hand was in mine.

Tears of relief practically poured down her face—as they did on mine, I now realized. Even Wolf looked ready to burst.

"Max! Ren! Wolf!"

We turned to the side, now spotting the two campfires raging just behind us. My eyes ached from the change in temperature and lighting, and aside from the trees silhouetted against the night sky, I hadn't started picking out details of our surroundings.

Tanya and Quinn ran over, stopping a few feet away once they got a sight of us.

"Oh my god." The Fateweaver covered her mouth as her own eyes glistened. "You all look like living nightmares."

I smiled but couldn't find the words. It had been about four days for them, but close to a month for us. It was overwhelming and so detached at the same time. They had wanted to come in for hugs, but in seeing the sharp armor, torn clothing, blood and bile matting our hair, and soot-and-sweat-caked bodies—well, they changed their minds rather quickly.

"It *has* been a nightmare," Ren offered, seeing that I was briefly tongue-tied. Her eyes went off to the side where a small cluster of buildings sat. "Are there *baths* in there?"

"We were going to ask you to sit and eat with us," Quinn said, shuffling awkwardly. "So that everyone can get up to speed. In seeing you both, I think a bath would be a better start."

My brain softened, and I allowed autopilot to take over while I dissociated a little. "Thank you, friends. We have spent almost a month fucking and murdering our way through literal hell. But I'll say a word to the others."

The pair nodded at us and relented as Ren and Wolf followed me to the campfires. The other two groups were there, all eyes on us. A mixture of confusion, worry, and surprise. Familiar shapes of those we briefly knew a while ago.

"Thank you for all gathering and being so patient," I began. "Although I have returned, I am not *officially* here until the morning. I crave a wash and a sleep before I could even consider engaging in earnest conversation with you."

I took a deep breath, and my eyes narrowed at the people sitting here. Their faces illuminated by the flickering flames, casting them into an all-too-familiar light. My jaw clenched.

"None of you . . . are demons, right?" I could feel the muscles in my arm tense up, ready to bring a card out.

A hand on my shoulder made me relax instantly. "You'd feel it if they were, trickster. Come, bathe with your queen."

I turned and looked at the elf. She looked as terrible as I felt as our vacation caught up to us. Cracking at our psyches as we tried to fit back in the old box we were so comfortable with. I gave her a nod and left the camping adventurers to think I was crazy. *I was.*

Into my hand appeared a few scrolls that I handed over to Quinn as we passed. "You're in charge of Wolf," I told him. He could only nod.

It was hard to see the details of our journey beyond how much my eyes were watering. Before I knew it, Ren and I were in a hot-water bath together. We sobbed, both in joy and relief. Constantly, sometimes with emotion and other times it just happened like a tap was switched on. We needed to empty and refill the bath three times before we could settle in it without it getting immediately dark and cloudy.

After what felt like hours, we were clean again. I carried her to the bedroom, and we consummated our marriage. Soft and tender. Two souls completely shattered but together. She fell asleep immediately, about ten seconds before I did.

And then I awoke, as if I hadn't slept at all. A fresh breeze rolled in through the open window, net curtains waving alongside the soft gust. Sunlight illuminated half the bed, warming the parts of me not up against the elf. I turned to her to see that she was already awake, although probably not for long, given how she still looked a little groggy.

"How strange that today feels like heaven, in comparison," I said, leaning over to give her a kiss. I still ached too much to consider it a bad dream, but my brain was keen to move on.

"*Death forged*," she whispered. "We're unbreakable now. Check my name."

I raised an eyebrow and inspected her in the Party window. "Ren *Russet*? You took my last name?"

She nodded and smiled. "It's not conventional for me, but . . . I came to this world running away from my family. Then I spent time being a bitch, trying to organize us into the same roles I was trying to avoid. When the System offered me the name change, I took it because *this* is my new life. Being *your* family. Being strong together and making our own lives."

"Well then, moonflower." I ran my hand through her once-again-radiant hair and cupped the side of her face. "I believe we have an audience to dazzle awaiting our reemergence."

Ren bit her lip. "I have an idea for that. You'll love it."

"I'm all ears."

"I'll tell you once we're dressed and ready." She gave me a quick peck on the forehead before leaving the bed, not even bothering to obscure herself like we used to. "I'm going to run us another bath because we deserve it."

"And so much more," I murmured, watching her circle the bed to go to the bathroom. "I'll catch up on Inventory-management bullshit. It's been a while, and if I need to perform, then I need to be prepared."

The elf paused at the doorway and leaned against the frame. "I love you. I'll let you know when it's ready."

I tipped my lack of top hat. "Love you too."

She vanished into the other room, and I sat myself up with a groan. My Inventory had been a cluttered mess of whatever the demons had dropped, and I'd had little patience for organizing it while down in hell. Other than memorizing spell-scroll locations, I had given up on doing most of my usual tricks. Demons just deserved to die.

I shook my head, realizing the irony.

Tabbed through from messages to Map—we were close to the Eternal Wardens—to my Equipment, where we had gotten surprisingly few upgrades from the throne room battle. Wolf was the luckier one there with some nice boots from the former king. I skipped past my Inventory screen for now and pulled a face, jumping over to my Skills instead. It had become a very long list, with not only my actives, but two Passives per level and a handful of demonic Abilities.

Switched to my Quest tab and paused. My brow furrowed.

"Ren? Did you pick up any Quests in hell?"

"No?" she called from the other room. "Other than leveling, I didn't see any System pop-ups."

I rolled my tongue around in my mouth. "Check your tab."

A few moments of silence followed.

"Holy fucking shit."

CHAPTER FORTY-FOUR

Emerge on Top

We stepped out of the house in pristine suits, sparkling blue and purple that matched the vibrancy of our eyes. The two greatest magicians in the world who had survived hell and become stronger for it. Changed, in some ways more subtle than others, but greater for it.

Another reason for the spring in our step was we were now level twenty.

While the System saw fit to ignore us during our vacation, it was still working in the background. Hell *had* Quests, in fact, and we had been gaining them and completing them without knowing—the experience and rewards unclaimed until I'd clocked the overflowing tab. Other than copious amounts of useless gold, upgraded chance boxes to sit beside the ones found in hell, and a few decent spell scrolls and potions—the rewards themselves fell rather flat.

Level nineteen granted me an Ability called <Take a Bow>, which was another Dazzle-removing Skill like <Finale> and <Shatter>. This one allowed me to turn ten icons into another demon summon. Weaker and shorter lifespan than the usual ones I could bring forth, but given that I could quickly drum up hundreds of the Dazzle icons against a group of enemies . . . I'd get as many as I desired.

My level-twenty upgrade to my Class Keystone, <Demonic Magician>, just added a sharp edge to the rest of my Abilities. Those hostile to me would gain Dazzle icons just for being in my presence, increasing every ten seconds. It made monologues even more dangerous, just not for me.

Ren had gained another ranged attacking Skill, and her final Oathwarden Ability would keep me alive even better—she assured me. Despite everything we'd been through, she still refused to give me the exact details of what her Class Keystone did. I had a decent guess but also saw through her reasoning for not giving me the exact wording. If I knew for certain that it gave me one last chance at life before my health hit zero, then I'd exploit it consistently.

Beneath our clothing, we were toned. More muscled and athletic than before our jaunt into the depths. Further below that surface, our hearts had melded. It felt like we had lived a lifetime together, knew each other inside and out. A marriage after only two or so months of meeting seemed rushed, but given that death could come for us any day, it was the right thing to do.

And as the pair of us stepped over to the gathered others, I felt on top of the world. Ren had slid her plan softly through my wanting ears, and I could feel the anticipation radiating off her.

"You certainly look better," Tanya said with a wary smile. "Glowing, in fact. Are you guys okay?"

Wolf was over to the side, without armor or clothing. Lazed about asleep on his back with tongue lolled out. Several large empty plates lay around him, and he had been cleaned through. I'd left them with some scrolls of water spray to wash him off last night. He looked content and fulfilled.

"Better than ever," Ren answered. "We both have *abs* now. It's pretty wild."

"No . . . long-term effects?" The Fateweaver furrowed her brow. "It might be good for you to decompress and tell us what happened."

I shook my head. "I assure you, Tanya. We are fine, and in fact . . ." I paused and frowned, a pained expression darkening my face. "Oh . . . *Oh no* . . ."

"What's wrong, Max?" Ren took a step away, adding to the concern of Tanya and the approaching Quinn.

With a growl, I stumbled back and clutched at my face. "*Ah*, I think I'm . . . *No!* I was corrupted and can't control it."

All eyes on me. Panic had the Fateweaver frozen in place. Quinn wasn't sure whether to grab at a potion or his sword. As the rest of our small army clambered up in unease, it was too late.

My top hat fell to the floor as horns burst from my head. With my face shadowed, long fangs caught the light as two wings grew from my back and flicked out wide with a leathery crack.

"I'm finally free," I roared. "Now I can kill and consume you all!"

Ren's rifle was up, a swirl of radiant energy pulsing down the long barrel. "I'm so sorry, Max," she hissed, tears streaming down her face.

Before she—or any of the stunned audience—could act, a large demonic sword emerged from the ground with a hellish rumble, striking me between the legs and cutting up through my stomach and chest and finally cleaving my head in twain.

The two sides of my body shuffled before flopping over onto the grass, spraying blood and entrails all over the place. As my patron sword hung in the air, single eye looking rather peeved at being roped into this, Ren turned to the others.

Rifle held out, it was now replaced by a rolled-up cloth that she allowed to unfurl. As soon as it hit the ground, she swept it away to reveal me—back to normal.

Somebody at the back threw up. Tanya stood with her mouth agape—a mixture of shock and annoyance leveled our way. Quinn was still staring at my dead body with his one eye. Wolf slept through the whole thing.

"*Motherfuckers,*" the Fateweaver eventually said, while Ren bent over doubled, laughing—something almost as surprising to the rest of the Party as my faux death. "I see your trials didn't make you any less of an asshole, and now you're both as bad as each other."

"We have a lot to tell you." My face was an apologetic grin, but I secretly loved it. If only the elf had chosen to copy <Last Act> as well. I turned my gaze from the ire of our Party to see the goblin healer, Ruby, step over and prod my fake corpse.

"Trauma aside," she murmured, also shooting me a glare, "this is some interesting shit, Max. What happens to *this*?"

"Fades after a certain time. Blood and everything too—otherwise, it'd have some interesting uses, I'm sure."

The goblin nodded, thoughts distracting her from how annoyed at me she was. "Even temporarily . . ."

"Alright, assholes," the gruff voice of Fiona called from the side. The woman was clearly not impressed with our shenanigans, least of all because half of her Party had paled and gone off their breakfasts from the sight. "Sit still for five minutes and let's get up to date."

So we did so—and ate alongside our tales. Although we hadn't gone without food down in hell, there was something about eating under the blue sky, surrounded by the rich greens of the woodland that just settled my aching soul. I felt more at home here than I had even back on Earth. A strange thought.

We told them about all the demons we'd had to kill through from the moment they left until we reached the palace. The Domains we had to survive, the new powers the three of us gained, and finally my ascension to the throne as king of hell. Roger's death, my new patron, and then the System-officiated marriage between Ren and me.

I left out the frequency and degree of depravity that our more salaciously spent time encompassed. Somehow, I had kept a hold of a *shred* of dignity, and we had already gained a fair share of dirty looks just from our demonic entrance—which had now faded away.

At times, the others grimaced or raised their eyes in disbelief. Leyla's group especially was totally out of their element, yet none of them seemed to think I was lying. Especially when I revealed my demonic transformation was just something I could do and control easily. Quinn and Tanya knew full well what sort of bullshit I got into and had more stoic and concerned expressions—saddened to hear that Roger had passed and then equally mad that they hadn't been present for our wedding.

"We'll need to have a proper celebration," the Fateweaver insisted. "Maybe when this is all over."

I looked at Ren, and she nodded eagerly, her face radiant with happiness.

"And what of the elephant in the room?" Quinn asked. "We can see it in the Party window . . ."

"Ah. One of the other benefits of being stuck in hell was being unattached from the level cap. After almost a month of grinding through demons and unwittingly completing Quests, we are now level twenty."

Fiona rolled her eyes and sighed. "No doubt that means just you three are more powerful than the rest of us put together then."

"Maybe just me alone," I said *modestly*, "but that's not the point. A show has many moving parts. You can't rely on the star to carry the performance."

"*Stars*," Ren corrected.

"Stars. Apologies, my love." I put my hand on her leg, and she held it there. We were already sitting as close to each other as possible without merging. No doubt we were going to be one of those annoying couples—at least until the rest of the trauma washed away and we settled back into this normality.

"This puts us on great standing against Candlekeep," Quinn offered.

I shrugged. "Perhaps. We've long agreed that the Lady has either some bug or her Class Keystone allows her to gain power in ways that skip normal progression. With a whole city under her control . . . if she is able to draw from the System-created citizens or something, we don't know what we're up against."

Fiona nodded solemnly. "Unfortunately, Max may be right. Our two scouts are now feared dead, so we don't know what has happened in the city since it was taken. All we are able to tell is that it hasn't broken the barrier between this area and the third . . ."

That was the goal of the Crimson Shadow, as far as we understood it. Ironically, not unlike our trip through hell, the Lady sought to depose the current Othean royalty and take the apparent power for herself to try to find a way to escape this world. Without a care for how many corpses she left in her wake.

There was the temptation to think that we were now uncontested in power. We had rolled through everything in hell and emerged victorious, max level, and full of all sorts of bullshit. It was almost sad that I had no more Skills to earn. There was still Equipment growth, although we wouldn't find anything level appropriate in this second zone, so we could forget that. Tokens were the other thing. None of my newer Abilities had been upgraded yet, so that was about the only source of power we were lacking.

"No news from the Eternal Wardens?" I asked.

Some awkward glances between those gathered before Tanya shook her head. "Assumed dead. We took a brief look at the town yesterday, from a safe distance. It looks . . . weird there."

"We're rather accustomed to weird," Ren said. "How specifically?"

"It's quiet," Fiona offered. "In a very spooky fuckin' way. Zero life remains— even the System-created are absent."

"Blood or signs of a fight?" I asked.

Quinn looked out to the woods, as if trying to recall it more vividly. "No blood or bodies. There were deep scratches in all manner of things. Houses, the stone road, the temple in which the Wardens resided. Not . . . destroyed, oddly. It was as though a giant cat had just used the town as a scratching post."

I pulled a face and looked at Ren. "Recovered enough for fighting more eldritch abominations?"

"Fuck yeah." She grinned. "Let's tear the world in half, trickster."

"Your wish is my command." I stood from my chair and then stepped up atop it. The others winced, expecting me to explode and shower them with my split organs.

I had slightly something better planned—although it was tempting.

"First though . . ." I said, my eyes narrowing at the congregation. "Let's think of a name for our Guild."

CHAPTER FORTY-FIVE

Right Back at It

I knelt beside my Hellhound and gave him a pat. Both he and the Imp I had summoned had slightly changed. They both wore tabards now. Royal purple with silver-blue edging. My ascension to becoming king hadn't improved their Stats, but they certainly looked more the part.

"Good boy." I gave him another pat and stood up. We had settled on a Guild name.

For once, I hadn't pushed to the front to be center stage and the one who ultimately decided or guided the process. I felt . . . no need. There wasn't much else I wanted from this world, other than a break from the violence. I had enough fans in the deep and up here. Nearly uncontested in power. Satisfied with most things.

The Imp gave me a bow before I sent him away, but I let the dog linger so he could roll around on the ground with Ren, trying to lick at her face. While she giggled and pretended to fight him off, I turned to the others and smiled.

The Unbreakable.

Not the worst name for a Guild, and it certainly had a certain amount of . . . grounding, for what we were. Ren seemed to think it was inviting trouble our way being so brazen, but she had said it with an uncomfortable amount of excitement on her face. Naturally, I agreed and accepted the proposition of the name.

Perhaps if we invited the malady so openly, things could end sooner than us having to track it down. It would be inevitable, either way. We knew how this worked.

Quinn stepped up beside me, his eye looking at the elf cavorting with the pup. "You know, seeing her like this is almost as unsettling as when you returned."

I saw his point, to some degree. Ren had always been rather stoic and proper, for the most part. Now she was laughing and snorting as the demonic dog tried to give her kisses, her outfit getting dusty as she writhed around on the ground.

"We became broken in some ways, but reforged." I gave him a shrug. "There's a certain amount of elation within us, as we are back in this normal world."

He pulled a face in return but gestured to the bear. "Wolf doesn't seem that unusual."

"No?" I followed his gaze. On the outside, Wolf didn't appear any different. Now back into fur only aside from his bowler hat, he remained stoic as we had eaten and prepared to set off this morning. Apparently, after getting washed down last night, he passed out and didn't wake up until breakfast was cooking. "He is just tired, ready for all of this to be over."

"Aren't we all?" Quinn replied, giving me a grim smile.

More than ever.

If anything, our time in hell made us realize how nice the normal world was. How great it could be once the blight of Lady in Red had been erased. We were close now; I could feel it. Our misadventure, giving us such a power boost, just drew where we could rid this world of the Crimson Shadow forward. Perhaps even tomorrow or the day after. It burned within me.

"Let's get moving," I announced to them all, allowing the Hellhound to sink away back to my hell—much to the chagrin of Ren.

Thus, the gathered group packed up and got themselves prepared to go. My Party decided to go ahead at the front, with Fiona's group at the back. Leyla's five were the weaker out of all of us, so the middle seemed safest for them.

As we started walking toward the town where the Eternal Wardens had holed up, Tanya moved up beside me. Apparently they had been a little selfish with any tokens that they had found, not knowing when we would return and needing any power they could grasp onto for themselves. Given how things turned out, I didn't blame them for it. They did have three tokens for each of us, however.

In return, I gave them a bunch of spell scrolls and potion bottles. I could spend all day drinking them otherwise and still not run dry. As they juggled and looked through all that I had provided them, I decided which Skills to upgrade.

<Demon's Ace> seemed like the contender for the most important to see what it could do. The result, as the token vanished, was somewhat surprising. I could now dismiss the card, and it would explode in a short radius. It meant waiting a while to summon it back from hell, so it didn't seem super useful, but I knew better than to discount an additional trick.

Next up was another active Ability—<Take a Bow>. I hadn't even had a chance to use it yet, but upgrading it granted the demons summoned by it some additional time on this plane, along with a short burst of a defensive boost for when they appeared.

The third token I wasn't too sure. Active Abilities always had the best returns compared to the Passive Skills, so my hand was wavering between <Active Learner> and <Spotlight> . . . although, as I looked through my expanded list, perhaps <Shared Hand> would be nice as well.

With a shrug to myself, I settled for <Shared Hand>. Not only would my Party-shared cards protect a little more Damage for my allies, but they would now regenerate like an aura. Every ten seconds, a new card would appear around the party member with the least remaining. All things going well that would probably be Wolf or me, most likely.

"Isn't the sunshine nice, trickster?"

I turned my eyes away from the System windows to see the dazzling smile on the elf's face. Her hair was bright, radiating light under the glow of the sun upon it—hurting my eyes slightly. She was right though. What I wouldn't give to see some clear running water.

"Would you like to live out in the forest when this is all done?" I asked.

"More than anything." She looped her arm around mine. "Somewhere like the cottage would be a dream."

I tried to imagine a life without conflict or the need to grind. Just Ren and me out in the middle of nowhere, peaceful and with time to decompress from our adventures. Despite me believing the end was just around a corner or two, that kind of life felt miles away. Unrealistic, somehow.

"I'll do everything in my power to make it happen," I promised her. It was also a promise to myself. "I will also need some time to see what I actually have to do to run hell."

Quinn interjected from just outside our conversational bubble. "So you're actually the king then? Is it like a Guardian's power?"

While we were slightly outside the prying ears of the other two groups, I caught the other two members of our Party up fully. Everything to do with my apparent ascension and the new Abilities I had gained on our accidental jump to max level.

"So could you make a portal from hell to the city?" Tanya eventually asked.

I shook my head slowly. "No, I don't think . . . I am pretty sure that I could only come here because you two were already present. A Party thing."

"So if one of us got caught and imprisoned," Ren said, "you could teleport in and free us. Stage our rebellion from the jail cells."

"Yes." I tilted my head. "Although, it is unlikely they are interested in taking prisoners at this stage."

Their actual motivations were slightly murky, but the fact that Ren and I were still alive and breathing was probably the biggest sore spot the Lady had. If she had a way to try to kill us, she wouldn't hesitate. Every attempt so far had failed, and while they . . .

I paused, and Ren stopped beside me.

"Something wrong, trickster?"

"Hmm. Just a couple of my brain cells collided." I gestured forward, where we were approaching the town. "A little while ago—I forget how time works—we told the Lady we were going to meet the Eternal Wardens as a distraction."

She wrinkled up her nose. "And now they're all dead or disappeared."

Got it in one. The Wardens were the only other known Guild or group still standing against the Crimson Shadow. If they had been erased so simply because we had put the crosshairs on them, then . . . I didn't really know.

I didn't feel bad about it, which might partly be due to our recent vacation. Not that I wanted more corpses instead of allies, but the group had hardly been helpful to us. Instead of filling my head with useful information, they had tried to drag me along to no doubt run errand side quests to unlock the stupid fucking lore to understand this goddamned bullshit that—

Ren placed her hand on my arm, and her icy-blue eyes cooled my fever off immediately.

"Thank you, moonflower." I shook my head, and my usual show smile returned to my face.

"Residual corruption, right?" She gave me a gentle pull, and we set off to catch the others back up. "I feel it sometimes. It's like a wave of nausea but for mental breakdowns."

"Yeah. You've seemed normal, however?"

She raised her eyebrow and gave me a wink. "I've had to put up with you for weeks. Do you think some droll hellish energy is going to affect me?"

Her smirk gave it away, however. No doubt it was part of her holy side that allowed her to heal through or otherwise negate the mind-bending draw of corruption aftershocks. Despite being king of hell and having immunity to it, my soul had suffered enough prior to that. I had put on a brave face, but I had been nearing death in that last week. If only everything healed as quickly as my actual Health.

The other three members of our Party had stopped a little farther ahead, although it didn't look to be just because they were waiting for us to catch up. Ren and I exchanged a glance as we made our way over, the body language of the human pair enough to get our backs up.

Overhead, the tree cover started to peter out, showing us a decent number of clouds making their way through an otherwise sunny day. The reason for the dwindling cover was apparent as we joined the others at this brief apex of a hill. Down below us, the road then dipped and curved to the town.

And it looked deserted. The buildings—at least from this distance—seemed undamaged. There were certainly no smoldering wreckages or piles of debris to set the stage for whatever story had transpired here. Zero signs of life whatsoever. Not even an idle System-created civilian.

My scouring glance twisted away from this potential tomb of the Eternal Wardens, however, as I clocked that the group wasn't even looking down to the left. Instead, they were tense and gazing to the right. To the north.

And as I turned, I saw why.

From this vantage point, we could see across a great deal of the second area in that direction. Mostly trees, as expected—but the thing that had my heart racing was the odd hue painting the horizon and landscape far off. A deep-red glow marred the sky at that very specific location maybe a mile or so wide. It reminded me of hell.

That was Candlekeep, or whatever the Lady had done to it.

CHAPTER FORTY-SIX

Disjointed

The short distance down from the hill and to the town proper took much longer than expected. Mostly due to the other two Parties needing to stop at the crest to gawk at the red hue painting the northern sky and discuss among themselves what it could be.

I found myself tapping my foot impatiently at the bottom, where the rough path became more orderly brickwork. It wasn't their fault really. I just ached for progress and had never been good at herding the masses. We had a whole show's worth of extras, and as nice as that was, it shouldn't be *my* responsibility.

All it took was a glance at Tanya, and she gave me a nod. Adjusting her chest plate, she started striding her way back up the brief hill to figuratively grab the ears of our allies and drag them down.

My gaze then went up to the nearest house. Something of a guard station on the road before the town. I vanished, replacing my hell dove, and immediately bumped into Ren, who had done the same thing. We grabbed at each other to avoid tumbling off the roof, and I rolled my eyes.

"Looks like we share the same singular brain cell," I said as we stabilized.

She shot me a grin. "I was about to say the same thing."

I adjusted my feet on the red tiles of the roof and looked out at the town. There was a central building far larger than the rest, made of light-gray stone rather than the muddy tones of wood and tile that comprised the rest of the area. I was willing to bet that was the location the Eternal Wardens had been stationed.

Surrounding this main building were the smaller shacks and fabric-covered boxed areas that might be an open market. If there were any people to run or observe such a thing. Over on the right past the shops was an inn, which had an opposite on the left, which I couldn't tell its purpose—but it looked important. Two rows of residential houses then encircled these other locations, making the whole town almost a spiral in design.

"It's kind of eerie, isn't it?" Ren asked, although she looked rather nonplussed.

"I had hoped to see signs of a struggle, at least." I took my top hat down and rubbed at my hair. It still hadn't received a cut. "Unless they were teleported away or something?"

"The Shadow have had some connection to the eldritch," she said with a shrug. "There are all kinds of unknown bullshit that could have happened here. Might even be a trap for us."

My eyes went from her and back to the groups now moving down to where Wolf and Quinn were in discussion over something. I deflated, and the real horror sunk into my stomach.

"You know, moonflower, it's not really about *us* anymore."

The elf raised an eyebrow but nodded. "We're already at the peak."

"The true trial is keeping these poor lambs safe."

That might be bigheaded of me to say, but I often had an ego raring to be let loose. There was some dry truth in the statement, however. The original three of us had been powerful from the start, but after everything we had been through, we didn't have much left to fear. The Lady and Candlekeep was surely the pinnacle of our trials, but until we got there . . . any trap or Monster or assassins sent to erase us were probably going to be zero actual threat to us.

But to our allies, they could be deadly. We had sown so much chaos in trying to bring order to this world. Filled too many shallow graves. There were no awards for putting on a great show if the audience was just a pile of corpses. So this was it. We *all* needed to win.

"How do you propose we get down from here now?" Ren asked, drawing my thoughts away from our overarching goals.

We had missed the window for transposition to switch us back. Still, we had options.

"May I?" I gave her a smile, and at her nod, I lifted her up across my arms. Wings burst from my back, and I floated us down to the ground before putting them away again. I let her down from my arms, but her eyes lingered on me. Burning. A nudge from my side had Wolf there, my top hat in his mouth.

"Thanks, brother." I gave him a nod. My temporary horns had the downside of popping the headwear straight off of me. I'd have to be careful about that.

"See anything useful from up there?" he asked as I placed the hat back in its rightful position.

I shook my head. "Just as empty as it first seemed. No signs of a fight. You getting any sense of the place?"

The bear made the show of sniffing the air. "No, nothing out of the ordinary."

Worrying. We turned to see the two other groups make their way down. Fiona and Ruby broke away from the pack to follow Tanya over to us.

"This place is giving me the chills," the fighter complained. "Most places have been kinda dead, but this is . . . It's like it's always been empty."

I knew what she meant. Without any evidence that something had gone wrong here, it was believable enough if someone had said the System had just never populated this town. Created but abandoned. We knew better.

"Are we planning on splitting up?" the goblin asked.

I shook my head. "Although that would cover more ground, if this is a trap I don't want us to be separated. Something killed or transported the Eternal Wardens and potentially the whole town."

Ren agreed, our rooftop conversation having made clear how we both felt. "Do we have any idea how large their Guild was?"

Ruby and Fiona exchanged a look before the fighter pulled a face at the elf. "As far as we know, it could have been the full twenty members allowed."

So we might be dealing with a threat that could take on four whole groups of Players. Even assuming they weren't all level fifteen, it wasn't a good sign. Perhaps it would have been better if we hadn't told the others we'd returned from hell and went and saved the world ourselves. As much as that sounded like I wanted to protect them, it was closer to being a decision made via my ego. They had a part to play, and we'd keep them safe.

After the other groups finished murmuring among themselves, Tanya beat them into marching formation again, and the three Parties moved into the town, toward the temple. Wolf and I took the lead, while Ren was busy explaining something to Quinn. My attention was fully on the surroundings, so I didn't catch what.

It was fair to say I was on edge.

Wolf could feel it too, despite it still feeling ordinary, but most of his senses were better than mine. His mood had been pretty decent for most of the walk over, and it was easy to guess that he was glad to be back in familiar terrain. As soon as we had reached the town, he had settled into his usual dour self once again. Once more into danger. I felt terrible that we couldn't have a real rest.

I put my hand on his shoulder as we walked. "How are you feeling, brother?"

He grunted at first before shooting me a glance. "There is an empty joy within me. I have so much, and yet it doesn't feel . . . real."

"Because this is a created world?"

"No. I am just . . . more complex than I *should* be. The range of emotions I have experienced as of late is troubling. I feel sad and morose, even guilty over the death of the rabbit. In the before times, even the death of my siblings didn't produce the same depth of feeling."

I nodded but wasn't sure what to tell him. He was a bear somehow given sentience. "I'm pretty sure I'm not meant to teleport, turn invisible, or transform into a demon. Both things as strengths, friend, but in different ways."

"Perhaps." He raised an eyebrow and look back over to the nearest buildings. "I appreciate the attempt to console me. If it weren't for you two, I would probably have been hunted down. Thank you for treating me as an equal."

With a smile, I tipped my hat. "Leave the soppiness for after we save the world, brother."

He didn't reply, but the look that he gave me told me all that I needed to know. We were both aware he was getting on in age. His loyalty and effort were unwavering, but he could only go as far as his body could take him. If there was one thing I hoped that we could claw out of the System, it would be to . . .

Live forever? Even thinking that, it sounded untenable. Maybe Wolf was ready for eternal rest or would get bored with immortality. Would I?

My brain sidetracked into thinking how I would spend infinite life alongside Ren. Being king of hell didn't appear to make me a permanent fixture in the System, so our chances weren't too high. Once we had erased the Lady and could see the rest of Othea, perhaps life wouldn't be so dangerous.

Then I'd have to contend with the fact that I was stuck in this world for good.

My eyes went back to the buildings. Rustic, albeit pleasant houses. Windows and open doorways, dark but empty. I stepped over close to one to peer inside better, but it didn't hold any secrets. Simple open-plan kitchen and dining room. Modest and gloomy.

We had discussed skipping this side quest entirely. As much as I wanted to keep our little army safe, I didn't really care for the Wardens. They had information on the Guardians, but did we really need it? The true reason was if the Crimson Shadow had dropped something nasty here to wipe them out, we didn't want whatever spell or entity to then come up behind us while we marched on Candlekeep.

It was just pragmatic to stay safe and have this last bite of what the second area had to offer before we made our final stand.

So it made me feel slightly validated as I gradually felt more tense as we got deeper into the town. I turned to look behind me, and I could see the apprehension on the faces of most of our followers. Ren stepped away from the fixer, leaving him to walk beside Tanya.

"You can feel it, right?" She glared at the empty buildings as we fell into step. "Something very wrong."

I nodded as we breached the rows of residential buildings to break into the start of the market stalls and stacks of crates. The temple was now visible, just across an open stone square.

Worse than something very wrong, this area felt like something very *Guardian*.

CHAPTER FORTY-SEVEN

In Search of Answers

We had been aware of the other person with Guardian powers for a while now—or at least it had partially sat at the back of my mind while we dealt with more pressing matters. It had been roughly a month since we were attacked by the exploding individual, and after that, they had kept out of our way.

Perhaps because it would be too obvious now, with most of the area drained of real Players. Anyone turning up solo would be suspected immediately. Especially with the Crimson taking over Candlekeep. Could they be *here*? I couldn't be sure just yet, but something about the temple was off.

Our three groups had stopped just outside of the building, milling about in a loose formation so that we were keeping an eye on every direction. Even without my Guardian sense, the others could feel something was amiss. The market square didn't look intentionally abandoned. No debris or decay.

While the others had been out of earshot, my Party had agreed that we'd split our focus when looking after the wayward sheep under our care. Ren and Wolf would protect Fiona's group, and Tanya and Quinn would join me in making sure Leyla's group didn't come to an undue end.

It had been difficult to arrange who should be doing what. Putting Ren and me on the same detail was overkill, and the two in our Party who weren't overpowered needed an extra hand that Wolf wasn't able to provide. Something about opposable thumbs. Splitting into two roughly equally powerful teams felt a lot better than three lopsided groups along the current Party lines.

Lucky me, as the group I had been designated to help looked like the more nervous and easily murdered ones. Now that I paused and thought about it, my own life was a struggle to keep tied to the mortal plane, so I shouldn't judge too hastily.

"You mentioned deep scratches before, Quinn?" I turned and raised an eyebrow at the fixer.

He pulled a face and rubbed at his eye patch. "That has been bugging me too. Either they have gone or some of us need our eyes checked."

More likely the former, even if he only did have the one of them these days. It had been mentioned in passing that Fiona had witnessed the scratches too.

For all her faults, I trusted her to be levelheaded, even if short-tempered. Her time back in the first area to reflect looked to have done her some good, and she had been a better leader for her group. The Paladin gave me the occasional awkward glance but didn't seem to hold any grudges. Their new member was a male spellcaster, judging by the long staff he walked with. A wide-brimmed hat that shadowed his features and a large backpack loaded to bursting gave him an appearance that was a mix between plague doctor and globe-trotting adventurer.

"Are you thinking it might be a mimic situation?" Ren asked from beside me.

My thoughts about her group to protect faded away as I glanced at her. "Unlikely. If you wanted to shoot the temple to see, I don't mind."

With a nod, she whipped around, rifle up. Golden light spiraled down the barrel, and she blasted out a shot to the up and left of the doorway—the approximate location an eye would be if the building decided to come to life and eat us.

The crack of the impact echoed around the empty town, followed by the clatter of broken stone falling onto the long steps. Other than sporting a dent, the temple didn't budge.

"Shame," the elf murmured, casting her eyes around the surroundings before she stood and relaxed.

"Alright then." I clapped my hands together, drawing everyone's attention. Briefly, I noted how shocked some of those present were at seeing Ren's weapon in action. Those from versions of Othea wouldn't have seen anything like it. I almost got annoyed at it stealing some of my thunder, but a smile was enough to feel like I was in charge. "We're going to go into the temple and search for clues about what happened to the Wardens."

"But no *being weird* about it," Ren added. "Stay together within sight of others. Don't touch, loot, or taste anything. Report anything *weird*, especially if there's a little voice in your head telling you to keep it a secret."

I nodded and concluded on her warning. "Keep things nice and simple. Safety is paramount. It might just be empty in there, but something erased their entire Guild from this area, as well as the System-created. I do not want to add to that number. Am I understood?"

A group of nodding, murmuring Players stood before me. They agreed, even if they were unsure. Even if they didn't entirely trust the man who could turn into a demon. After all, what choice did they really have? Better to be safe around me than put some distance and escape my protection. I was a powerful ally, and they knew it. But I was only worth that acceptance if I could actually keep them away from death's door.

I made a gesture to the elf, and she and Wolf led Fiona's group first. As much as it pained me to be at the back, in truth, I was only a split second from being beside her. She knew it, and the fact that my demonic ace was floating in the air made it clear to everyone else. Between her entangling roots, her shielding Abilities, and the walking destructive quagmire that the bear had become, they were an effective frontline force.

Quinn looked a little more nervous as we let Leyla's group go in front of the three of us, while Tanya handed me over a small idol.

"Speed and dodge increase," she said, denying me the chance to interact with the System and find out. "I figure you don't really need the Damage one anymore."

"Thanks." I gave her a genuine smile and tucked it into my belt. "I remember there was a time I worried about my magic cards being able to cut skin. Now I could slice this whole building to ribbons if I desired."

"Have *any* of your desires changed?" the Fateweaver asked, tilting her head as we walked over to the steps.

"Hmm." My quest hadn't really wavered since the starter island. Stop Lady in Red. "When I was on the island with Ren, I rather foolishly told her I wanted to become a hero. While my aspirations lead to the same point, I feel rather abstracted from the title. I want to do right by this world and to carve a space for Ren and you all."

"At any cost?"

I exhaled and shook my head. "Too far gone for that manner of question. How about you though?"

Tanya smiled and glanced towards the fixer. "I think these last few days have given me the space I needed to decide. Don't get me wrong, Max. You, Ren, and Wolf, you're amazing. But going from my Party, to under the Lady's thumb, to managing you three . . . I needed a break."

"But you're ready for what's to come?"

"Too far gone for that manner of question," she reflected at me with a grin. "I'm no longer fighting to escape, but fighting for the right to exist, if that answers your question."

"It does." I gave her a nod. She had accepted that she was going to live for this existence and not let the ghosts of her past haunt her. It couldn't have been easy, but she seemed a lot happier in spite of our circumstances. "And I'm sure you're just waiting for an excuse to die in my stead, Quinn?"

He grunted before turning his eye from the surroundings to me. "No offense, my friend. I still owe you my life, but I have a reason to stay alive that is stronger than my duty to repay you."

"If you say it's because of love," I grimaced, "I may just throw up." Although, I hadn't quite mastered the art of vomiting on command—something Ren had gained mastery over in hell, which had seemed amusing at the time. Now it felt . . . as strange as it should, in the cold light of day.

Tanya stifled a laugh and beamed. "That's rich coming from *you*. Let's focus on the task now."

Ren and the others were already at the top of the steps at the doorway. If there was anything immediately untoward, we were about to find out. My shoes stepped lightly on the wide stone stairs, raising us above the level of most of the smaller market stalls. Not a terrible place to have to defend, if it came down to it. Assuming the enemy had no way to deal with stone walls, of course.

Most of them would have.

The Parties had gathered at the entrance to wait for us to catch up, which only briefly stressed me out due to us being all clumped up. The reverberating waves of corruption deep within me were eager for paranoia to take over, but I resisted it.

I shook off the preshow nerves and narrowed my eyes at the temple interior.

The large building was mostly one big hall. An arched roof surprisingly devoid of any engravings, paintings, or other symbolism that you might expect. The floor was dotted with stone benches in seemingly no proper order at all. Like they had been moved? Perhaps, but they looked heavy, and there were no signs on the floor that they had been dragged about.

At the far end was a raised platform and podium for someone to speak to the congregation. Two tables that were mostly devoid of anything but empty candle holders and pale-gray coverings. A pair of doors, one at the back left and one at the back right. Closer to us, the right had an indented groove in the wall, with wooden shelving built in. A shallow dip on the floor had a small hole at the center.

"Ritual foot washing," Ruby explained, "and a place to put your stinky footwear once your little potato mashers are sparklin'."

"You know anything about which deity might have been worshipped here?" I asked her, having been as distant from the world's lore as possible.

The goblin pulled a face and waved her staff to the end of the room, causing the bell on the top to jingle. "Short answer: no fuckin' idea. Actual answer: I've been pondering it for days, and I reckon it's a Guardian."

I exchanged a look with the elf. Her expression didn't change, but I could read it like a book. Unlike all the books we hadn't read since arriving here. "If the Eternal Wardens have been shaking up at the site of a Guardian, then it sounds like they caught its attention and it made them leave. Permanently."

"If I may," Fiona's new spellcaster interrupted. His name was Percivus, I was half certain. "I can smell a trove of books from a mile away, and at least one of these back rooms has a library of merit."

"Good." I tipped my hat to him in thanks. That meant we wouldn't have to work our way through the empty town trying to find where they had stored the information about the Guardians that they were so adamant about denying me. "Join my group for a moment? Swap with Quinn and then Ren can take your Party to search the other rooms."

Neither man looked particularly pleased to be split from their usual companions, but I wanted to go to the library, and I'd rather have the potential bookworm with me than Quinn. Despite his other qualities, I was sure he would be more bored in a library than even Wolf. Ren, however, was keen and understanding of the split duties.

While she gave her group some stern words, I stood in silence, completely enamored with her. Leading as equals, just as we had always envisioned. After getting them up to speed with her expectations, she caught me gawking at her and shot me a sly grin I was all too familiar with.

I turned to see the group under my charge, who had been waiting patiently for my instructions.

Leyla's group of five looked more tense than if we were in immediate danger. All from the atmosphere of the empty temple. Perhaps I should take them all on day trips to hell to acclimatize them to danger a little better. Although . . . it was potentially a bad thing that I was so desensitized to violence.

"Right," I began, finally taking hold of my slippery thoughts. "Let's go wrangle some mysterious books."

CHAPTER FORTY-EIGHT

A Page or Two

My fleeting desire to court the impressive tomes fizzled out almost as soon as we entered the library. Something that was clearly visible on my face, as Tanya grinned at my expression.

I had never imagined it to be anything elaborate, but what the room had to offer was somewhat lacking. If anything, I was glad at least that it meant we wouldn't be searching around here for too long. The chamber was small, the back three walls holding bookshelves of polished wood, yet there weren't that many books upon them.

"Alright." I gestured Tanya and the spellcaster over. "Keep the others busy on guard duty while us two search the library."

"As you wish." The Fateweaver gave me a nod and stepped away to arrange the awkward adventurers.

"Percius, was it?" I asked the man as we stepped onto the slightly raised platform where all the books were. Behind us now was a raised stone area, not quite a table or lectern, but the wooden chairs there suggested that was where the reading had been done.

"That's right, Max. Are we just looking for clues about their disappearance and anything to do with Guardians?" He tilted the brim of his hat up, allowing some light to illuminate his usually shadowed features.

Younger than I had anticipated but plenty of wisdom hidden away in his eyes. For a moment, I wondered how he had found his way to this world before the present situation caught up to me.

"Correct. How the Eternal Wardens vanished is the most important thing, if not at least so we can avoid the same fate. Anything on Guardians is useful, but I could go without the lore as long as the power stays with me." In saying that, there was a slight residual hum in my right arm.

"Understood. I'll start on this right side and you on the left. Then we'll meet in the middle?" He gestured with his head, causing several bottles and random objects to clink together on the outside of his large backpack.

I gave him a nod of approval, and we did just that. Immediately, I realized I wasn't exactly sure how in-depth the check should be. Did I need to take them all down and rifle through a few pages to gather up the context of the contents? Most of these didn't look like they had useful blurbs on the backs or titles that fully summarized the internal subject matter.

The first I plucked into my grasp was titled *Grass and More*. A quick spray through a selection of pages determined the *more* was just grass-adjacent vegetation. Why this was necessary or interesting was beyond me. The prospect of digging through a dozen or two similarly drab books had me . . .

I paused as my eyes caught sight of something unexpected.

A familiar spine that couldn't possibly exist on a book in this world. Yet still, my hand reached for it, ignoring all others. Pulling it from the shelf and taking the heavy tome into my hands, I turned it to see what lay on the cover.

Demonic Rites and Foul Magicks, it read.

The very book that was the cause of my transposition to Othea. I held it for a few moments in disbelief before I gathered my senses up. After all, I had been holding it when I went through the portal. If it somehow got transferred but taken away from me, the System could have made this copy. Did that make *sense*, however?

For someone so used to suspending disbelief to the limits, I was frankly tongue-tied.

I turned, stepping over to the stone table, and placed the book down.

"Something useful?" Tanya asked, eyeing between me and any potential doom ready to pounce from the shadows.

"Hmm. Oh? I don't know. Something *interesting*, at least." I shook my head and opened it up to the first page. *Yes.* It was exactly the same. The comforting familiarity mixed in with the apprehension, knowing that this had a hand in . . . I didn't know what. It couldn't just be a coincidence, however.

I continued to flip through pages, each known to me, until I got to the page showing the portal. Pink light against the gray stone in the illustration. I ran my finger down it, as if tracing the memories of that evening. Interesting. Most of the book was just folktales and other such fairy-tale mulch. Even being a Demonic Magician, nothing in this old tome really held much importance to me, aside from this page about the portal.

In an act that probably earned me a few valid scowls, I gripped at the book and tore the page out slowly. Folded it and put it in my pocket. That might come in use in the future, and part of me didn't trust the System to hold on to it in my

Inventory. After a few moments of idly staring at nothing, I cleared my head and snapped the book shut.

Percius was giving me a dull look, probably having a dim view of me mutilating a book. "Found what you were looking for?"

"Yes and no." I shrugged and returned to my side of the library. Part of me felt as though I had ticked a box off, but I wasn't sure what I'd really accomplished there. Maybe just some minor joy in the fact that I had something to remind me of home, for all the good that did. Home now was anywhere with Ren. The showman had long died, no matter the way I'd ended up here.

Much like Tanya, I had come to accept that what we had at present was very real and in many ways better than our prior lives. We had a lot to fight for here. I would ensure we won and that nobody else had to sacrifice their life to make that a reality. A troublesome thought that half distracted me from taking down books from the shelves and glancing through them.

In fact, my awkward mood helped the whole process breeze by, even if it took longer than I expected. Ren's group reported nothing interesting found and were now standing guard back in the main hall. Between the spellcaster and me, we had procured three books on the Guardians of the world but nothing else overtly hinting at where the Wardens had gone.

"Either it was the Crimson Shadow, or they dabbled in something with a Guardian here and paid the price," I surmised before we had even opened one of the books.

"I had assumed you would have been more of the studious type," Percius said, glancing me over. "Not that kind of magician, eh."

With a shrug, I put my hand on top of the pile of books, each one vanishing as soon as I touched it, until my hand rested on the table. "I'm much more of a practical learner, I'm afraid. Seeing is believing *and learning*."

I'd never used this function before, or needed to, but if the System held a written item within it then you could get it to produce a summary. Not only that, but search through the produced text for key words. Any irony that I, of all people, would have been able to ingest the world's lore quicker than most was completely lost on me as I chose to ignore those thoughts entirely.

Instead, I swept through each of the books in turn, picking up some key phrases as I went. What I learned was . . . not entirely interesting but might have the clue we were looking for.

"The Eternal Wardens were trying to summon one of the Guardians here," I explained, the ears of everyone in the room piqued to listen in. "There isn't meant to be any more in this area that we have discovered. This is only my assumption, but I can imagine they wanted to bring one here, kill it, and use the power to go against Lady in Red."

"But it backfired?" Tanya asked. "Something went wrong and possibly teleported them to where the Guardian is?"

"Possibly." I gave her a shrug. That was just speculation, as we hadn't found any proof at present. "There's something about what each Guardian power represents, but I'll vomit out that information once we are back with the rest of the Guild."

"Are you going to keep a hold on those books?" Percius asked.

I raised an eyebrow. "What books?" With a small flourish, I swept my hand over the plain table to reveal the stack of tomes once more. "I have a copy of all the pertinent information in my STAR. Did you know it could do that?"

"Yes . . ." he replied, pulling a face before lowering the brim of his hat once more.

Well, *I didn't*. Not that I could really recall a time where that would have been useful. Skipping through the world had clearly left more than a few gaps in our knowledge of the System, not just the lore.

We left the room to join the others in the main hall, everyone looking a little calmer now that we'd been here a while and nothing bad had happened. Ren looked pretty bored but practically slid across the floor to join me once she saw we were making our way over.

"What did you find out, trickster?" she began. "Is my Guardian cooler than yours?"

"You have the best Guardian, as it is what you deserve."

"Bullshit." She rolled her eyes. "We all know you're the System's favorite."

I smiled and looked around the gathered congregation. Is that how they all felt? There was a certain amount of power that I had accumulated over my journey that put me on another level compared to most. Not just literally but in every sense. It would take maybe ten seconds for me to kill all the other Players in this room, aside from my own Party of course.

"Actually, the truth is more mundane, I'm afraid." I gave her a glum smile as thoughts of murder sank away. "Although flavored certain ways, Guardians don't really represent differing core values or certain aspects of the System as we first assumed. There are shallow hints at thematic differences, but that just allows people to read into what they want to believe. When you get down to how they empower us, they are essentially wish fulfillment, in a way."

The elf crossed her arms, but her slightly grumpy expression didn't change. "It's more that the Guardian chooses how to bring that wish into reality that is the crux of it. I wanted to be your equal, and so I got to copy some of your Skills. A little too basic an interpretation, if you ask me."

I nodded. "I suppose mine was to just ascend beyond my capabilities, unshackle myself from the overworked magician roots. In a way, my demonic powers culminated in unseating the king of hell."

Tanya furrowed her brow and looked over at the exit. Toward the north. "So what does that mean for the two others who have Guardian powers? The Lady sounds like she has something like yours, Max. Except instead of hell it's up here, taking over the normal Othea."

Although I had some thoughts on the matter, I let them roll around my skull a little longer and gave her a shrug. Lady in Red clearly wanted to gather up an army strong enough to take over the world to try to change and escape it, and her Class seemed to rope in others like some manner of pyramid scheme. The unknown Player who could clone bodies we knew even less about, but I was willing to bet their wish had been something about avoiding injury in this world. Now they could do everything by proxy. Still an assumption.

"There *was* something we found out," Ren said, some of her ire waning. "The Eternal Wardens were customers of the black market assholes."

I shook my head and sighed. It meant in part they were to blame for the kidnapping of Quinn and me. Part of me detested them for it but only because it made them sound weak. Having to buy their power at the expense of random innocents. Perhaps they got what they deserved.

"Anything lootable?" I asked.

"A few bits for the others that might be useful, but you know we aren't likely to get much anymore, trickster."

Such a shame to peak in my career so soon. All downhill from here.

While I was about to gripe even more about how overpowered we both were, I paused and pulled a face. The information we had found had been reasonable at best. It ticked off the long-held questions in the most half-hearted way it could. The System had created these Guardians of power, and any Player foolish or lucky enough to manage to kill one had their wish granted—if only in a way that the System itself wanted to.

But the Eternal Wardens had vanished. They had sought out this power and hadn't been enough to earn it. Or perhaps they had, and it wasn't a terrible end that had met them.

Things were never that easy.

As I gave the temple another narrowed glare, my arm tingled with the very real potential we were about to find out *exactly* what had happened to them.

CHAPTER FORTY-NINE

Remain Blank

The fifteen of us were now standing back outside the temple in the open space between the market stalls. Despite the apprehension, nothing bad had happened to us in there. Not that I was disappointed—but maybe underwhelmed. Leyla's group had picked out a few items from the side room; the dwarf in her Party who was more beard than person now had a tall hat upon his head. It would have looked ridiculous had I not burned the part of my brain that dealt with that sort of thing to ashes.

"Hey, trickster?"

I turned my attention to Ren. "Yes, dear?"

"I shot the temple up there, did I not?"

My brows knitting together, I looked up at the front of the building where she had indeed fired a bullet into it not that long ago. Any evidence of this act was no longer present. As if it had never happened.

"Just like the claw marks," Quinn murmured, the rest of my Party paying attention to our conversation. They knew to stay alert—especially if I was out of sorts.

The first conclusion I jumped to froze the blood in my veins. The System was resetting this area back to a default state. If that was so, were the Eternal Wardens just vanished as they weren't part of this original setting? Such a conclusion made me feel ill, as that could mean we could be wiped from existence at any moment. Just for standing in the wrong place at the wrong time.

I edged my mental state away from this cliff's edge. That explanation—while completely valid and possible—didn't sit quite right with me. The building had regenerated, but we had been here longer than that time. We were fine, so it was unlikely to be the reason. It also didn't explain the claw marks.

There had been no spell books or other mysterious tomes in the library but plenty of empty shelf space. I wondered if . . . No, I shouldn't speculate.

"Alright, Detective Demon Ass, what are you thinking?" The elf scowled at me, but there was no true ire in her question.

"Well . . ." I rolled my eyes. Despite playing off that I could see through any trick, I didn't feel qualified for this situation. "If I were to make a very large assumption, I would say that the Eternal Wardens caused this themselves."

"No shit," Fiona interjected from the side, her group now listening in. "They got too big for their boots and fucked themselves into oblivion."

"*Sounds like my teen years,*" someone murmured at the back to a chorus of light chuckles.

"Rather, I mean intentionally," I clarified. Shit, I really hated hecklers. My right hand twitched before I calmed myself. Smile never wavered. "Accidentally summoning something they couldn't handle was step one. Step two was something cast a spell that saved the area, somewhat literally."

Ren nodded along, ever my supportive equal. "Rather than set their hubris made real on the world, they set up something that reset the town to a prior state. Probably only works on the structures?"

So the System-created had just vanished, maybe dead or cleaned up by the refresh. The Players equally as dead and any evidence of the bloodbath had been erased.

Wolf looked up at me, not looking too enamored with standing around doing nothing. "Are you able to sense and destroy the spell, brother?"

"Hmm. I can make an attempt? I'll probably need to hold Ren's hand to do it, however."

The elf rolled her eyes but complied. She was fully aware I *did not* need to do such a thing but played along because a little romance greased the squeaky wheels of our turmoil-laden existence in this world.

I calmed my breathing and closed my eyes. It had felt so simple in hell, but up here was so . . . noisy?

Rather than the gray notepad filled with white outlines detailing the dummies following me along—the elf having pointed ears and a little more shading drawn in—with a couple of lines of magical power, it was instead a mess. Spaghetti gone wild. Everyone was wearing magical items or had a buff or aura around them, complicating my detection.

It was like trying to pick out a thread of white yarn in a blizzard. Couldn't see the overarching energy of the town with all the busyness clouding my immediate vision.

"Sorry," I eventually said, deflating and shaking my head. "It turns out three groups of Players is rather radioactive. I'll need more space to see with clarity." Either that or someone was intentionally obscuring my view.

A quick glance at those gathered didn't pick out any obvious suspect. I trusted most of them anyway. We had saved Leyla's companions, so I didn't think they'd betray us. Fiona and her group were fine, other than the Paladin and spellcaster who were partial unknowns. Even the lion man, Magnus, had held a softer expression toward us since meeting back up.

They had grown to accept us, seeing the necessity of us being rather cutthroat.

"Perhaps we can just move on?" Tanya suggested, still staring at the spot Ren had shot. "If this area is inert, we have nothing to gain here."

She had a point, but I wavered in agreeing with her outright. I still felt like there was something threatening here. There had been a constant hum in my arm that signaled the proximity of Guardian powers. Some hint as to what the Eternal Wardens had done would have been nice. What if they had been successful, and this was the result of their new strength? No, that didn't make sense.

So what if it was the Guardian here, maintaining control of the town after having slaughtered everything in it?

I ran my tongue across my lips. That tasted more like reality. Something similar to a Domain. The question wasn't whether we should leave this place, but were we allowed to?

While my eyes switched between all the vacant buildings in the area, I started to feel like a fly trapped in a spider's web. Just because I was a fly armed with a flamethrower and a handful of grenades, it didn't mean I was in any less danger.

"No," I eventually said.

"May . . . I ask why?" Tanya asked.

"Yes."

She exchanged a glance with the elf, and Ren gave my hand a squeeze. "Focus, trickster. Use your social skills."

"Get into formation," I murmured. "We've just about worn out our welcome."

She nodded, her expression immediately becoming stern. After letting go of my hand, she joined Tanya in getting everyone arranged and prepared. For what? I wasn't entirely sure just yet.

Wolf remained by me, his eyes narrowing at the market stalls. "Are you sure, brother? I cannot sense anything."

"Have you ever heard of the expression *can't see the forest for the trees?*" I was fully aware that he was a bear and probably hadn't, but the System often worked miracles with translations.

"I've seen a lot of both in my time," he grumbled.

"Same, brother." I flexed out the fingers on my hands.

If anything, my failed magic sense had been a clue in the making—if not the breadcrumbs to lead me to this conclusion. We couldn't see the monster because it was exuding normality. The town was proof of this. It had the power to return things to how they should be. In some ways, it *was* the town, but unlike the mimic buildings in hell, it was both subtler and more overt at the same time.

My demonic ace hovered beside me, and I loaded it with three spells scrolls.

"Remember," I told the bear. "Keeping everyone safe is priority. Let me be me and focus on that."

He grunted but gave me a nod. It wasn't that he didn't want to keep people safe; he just liked to be at the forefront of any fight. I was being strict. *I wanted a perfect show.* Flawless, with no injuries. A high bar that would break me when I inevitably failed, but I had a lot of pressure to perform.

Something that a nod from the elf helped release, the steam powering me forward to the steps of the temple. I stopped only four up—just enough to be set apart and higher than all my peers. Such a comfortable position for me.

"Oh great Chameleon," I called out, my stage voice taking the words through the open space with clarity. "Won't you grace us with your presence?"

My open-armed invitation was met with silence for several seconds. Just before any of my cohorts could murmur a question as to my intention, a loose spray of dust came off the edge of the temple.

All eyes rose up as the air above us flickered, the shape of something emerging perched on the building above us.

The books had at least given me the names of the Guardians. They didn't mean much in a vacuum, but now, with the context clues, I was partially certain this was the *Chameleon*. Mine had been the Siren.

Rather than some manner of giant reptilian creature, the body shimmering back into visibility was something slightly different. The shape of the body and the way it gripped at the edges of the temple certainly had familiar tones of such a lizard, but it had dense, coarse fur of muddied brown rather than scales. Their head was something more like that of a lion, although slightly flatter in appearance. Bulbous eyes of swirling green light looked over our groups, moving independently. The wide jaw full of foot-long fangs opened and closed slightly as it breathed.

"More morsels come to destroy and ruin?" the Chameleon asked, long fingers cracking at the stone as its grip tightened.

"Would you rather we left you in peace?" I responded.

Both eyes swiveled down to stare at me. "Were you not Guardian killers, I may have shown you leniency. Some of you anyway. *So destructive, so destructive.*"

They were clearly agitated, seemingly a being that craved order. I wouldn't be surprised if the place they had been summoned from *was* ordered and the current chaos here was maddening for them. So they had decided to maintain the town to a certain state. Then we had come along and put our dirty mitts on everything. Moved books. Brought chaos.

The problem now was . . . I wanted one of my Party members to have Guardian powers. Wolf would be preferable, but I'd accept it being either of the other two. Strength meant survivability. A few steps closer to our overall success.

While the creature looming above us was looking at us like we were a freshly prepared hot meal, I was glaring at them with the exact same desire. I could even feel Ren eager to put a few new breathing holes through the Monster, even as she was standing a good two dozen feet away from me.

"I offer you a compromise then. A deal we can make—to leave this place in order." I could feel my eyes glowing brighter, my true nature so eager to burst out from this false act of pleasantry.

The Chameleon looked repulsed at the notion, literally recoiling away from me as if I was a bad smell. "What could you even offer me that I couldn't take for myself?"

"Lay down your life and give over your power and we'll make it quick and painless." A burning sensation ran through my right arm. It wasn't as visceral a reaction as against a Player who had Guardian powers, but it was close—if only because it was now fueled by cold hatred.

The Chameleon paused, just staring at me blankly. I wondered if he could sense it. No—he certainly could. While he had made mincemeat of more Players than this before, it was different now. The king and queen of hell, empowered by Guardians ourselves. He was outnumbered, and the System was whispering in his ear.

"You must have caught me on a good day, mortal," the creature spat before running his long tongue across his sharp teeth. "I will allow you to leave if you never return here."

The relief spreading through the others was almost tangible.

[Max: Take the others and run. Wolf, protect their escape.]
[Tanya: Understood.]
[Wolf: ppps]

I flexed my hands out and grinned up at the chameleon. "Sorry, pal. I will have to decline."

"Foolish! Your hubris will crush you before I tear you to shreds." He snarled.

I clicked my fingers, and the others turned to run. Ren remained in place, and the bear physically stood between the row of our companions and the threat of the Guardian.

"You are under the mistaken belief that we are in your lair," I said, my expression cooling off. As horns started to sprout from my head, my hat fell off, bouncing down the stairs behind me.

"Unfortunately . . ." I continued as my wings snapped out. *"You're in mine."*

CHAPTER FIFTY

Moving House

I could see the tension in the Chameleon.

He wanted to dive forth and chew on the escaping Party members. Perhaps his plan all along, even after pretending to make a deal with us. But now he knew as soon as he moved we would be fighting, and some of his confidence had washed away. I could almost hear the cracks forming in his ego. A powerful Guardian of the System who was meant to be almost unparalleled in power.

Now hesitating due to a couple of small humans in sparkly outfits.

Against better judgment, Tanya and Quinn were hanging back nearby. Their loyalty to our group stronger than the desire for guaranteed safety. It wasn't ideal, but I couldn't fault them for it. I could protect two better than twelve, so I ran with the change of plan.

"The Siren was a lot surer of themselves when they attacked me," I said, my unblinking glare burning into the Chameleon still perched atop the temple. "Are you just the weakest of the Guardians?"

He growled and snuffed his nose in disgust, the dense mane around his head waving back and forth. "Goading me with your insolence won't save you from your fate, even if you let the weaker ones flee."

"*You* let them flee," I corrected him. "Or . . . did you know you had no chance of stopping me? Is that why you are frozen with fear and unable to strike?"

The powers of this Guardian were odd, or at least what we knew of them. Some sort of self-correcting aura that repaired the base System layer around them but couldn't re-create the townspeople. The Siren had drawn me into a pocket dimension of her own that was filled with fingeresque people intending me harm. The Chameleon didn't feel that much more dangerous than any other Monster we had faced.

He was tiring of the back-and-forth, so we were about to find out.

"Luck has a filthy habit of running out just as you need it most, little one. You clearly are an irresponsible gambler." Energy hummed around his body, causing my arm to burn. "Time to stop being a blight on this world."

It would be unfair to say that I was foolish for underestimating him. Mostly because I'd given up on calling myself bad names. But I felt his movement before my eyes saw him—more than likely he had just teleported.

His claws lashed out, the large creature now beside me on the steps. Both <Card Fan> and Ren's shield were up as soon as he moved, and his attack didn't slash through me. The force still knocked me back, and I stumbled down the steps and . . .

Stabilized myself, now in a building. The living room of one of the houses. The floor above me groaned from the weight of something as I tried to understand what had just happened.

A forced teleport? It didn't feel like one.

The wooden planks of the floor above burst down, and the Chameleon fell to crush my hell dove. I spun on my feet back outside on the street, the side of the temple off to the left. Expecting everyone else to still be standing by the front, I couldn't see them.

[Max: Teleported too?]
[Tanya: Inside the inn? With Quinn.]
[Wolf: oooos]
[Ren: Not teleported. The town moved.]

Ah, ten points for my protégé. It wasn't just the ability to reset the town to a default state, but the Chameleon could manipulate all the building blocks within it. Shift them around like some manner of puzzle. That seemed pretty fun.

I turned my gaze back to the house as the long claws of the Guardian tore the front of the building off, pulling his face through to glare at me with his bulbous eyes.

"Nice trick," I told him as I brought up magic card. It was red, crackling critical energy. "I bet I could kill you with a single strike."

He growled, and then I wobbled and felt disoriented. It was like the whole world had just shifted around on a dial beneath my feet. My view swished around to the right down the street before I gathered my senses and turned back.

The house was now back to how it was before, the Guardian no longer there.

Even the power in my arm that warned me of problems such as him seemed to calm. He was moving away, perhaps to one of my allies.

I cursed under my breath. This wasn't ideal, and I would not have some upstart ruining the show at this stage.

[Max: T&Q tele NOW]
[Tanya: Done. Stay safe.]

If the Guardian appeared by those two, I wasn't confident they could survive. That sounded unfair of me, but without our support they were on the same level as most Players—and the Chameleon had killed twenty such people recently. I would never forgive myself if something happened to them.

I turned my head back to see that said Monster was just down the street from me, appearing in complete silence. Hunched down, ready to pounce like a house cat staring at a bird.

"Almost had a little snack before they vanished. Will you run away scared as well?"

"Oh, no." I smiled. "With them out of the way, now I can really go all out."

He went to respond, but my critical card struck him on the top of the head, having dropped from the sky where my demonic ace floated. Didn't burst him open—he *was* hardy. As he growled and opened his eyes again, I was standing right in front of him.

"It must feel strange being on the other side of a boss fight, huh?"

The Chameleon opened up his mouth, but instead of trying to bite me, they sprayed a burst of liquid over my body. By the way that it melted straight through my clothing and burned at my skin, some high-powered acid sounded correct. As my organs ruptured through my thinned skin and my right arm split off to land on the ground, the Guardian gnashed his teeth—pleased with himself.

I stepped out of invisibility beside him, using <Grand Acid Breath> myself. Thankfully, the System knew well enough to keep my own body safe from the attack that I had copied with <Active Learner>. My own vomit spray covered his left eye, burning through the orb until it burst.

He screamed, and the world shunted violently. Darkness washed over me— my eyes adjusting to find that I was now in a basement.

[Max: Be wary. He is coming for one of you two.]
[Max: Left eye blinded, enraged.]
[Ren: Copy.]
[Wolf: pp p]

After I had first snubbed him, he went for the weakest of us. Once they had vanished, he came back for revenge. Humbled again, he just wanted to shift me

out of the way. The appetite for further lessons rubbed away. Now he just wanted
to kill.

I could be wrong, of course, and as I looked around at all the muted wood
and rough stone in this darkened area, I almost hoped he would come for me again.
Resilient or not, I could feel his confidence waver by the second. An egg cracking,
my desire to slurp down the yolk almost a disgusting perversion. All that power
for our group just dangling in front of us.

Hanging around down here wouldn't get me what I wanted. I went for the
stairs, pushing up through a trapdoor that took me into a kitchen. In the background, I could hear the tearing of wood and collapsing stone structures. A roar
of the bear.

I took a step and then wavered, as I was now in a different house.

This was getting exhausting. Hopefully, he would go for Ren next, and she
could finish him off. I was only slightly ashamed that I hadn't killed him in one
hit like I had said. A bet lost, which was unlike me. Maybe he had magical resistance or something that muted the effects of my cards. I should really stop playing with my food.

The town shifted again, and now I was outside. Down the road to my left
was the Chameleon facing down the road to his right. He had been bloodied
and was breathing heavily. Wolf hadn't died so must have won their scuffle. The
Guardian was clearly not having a good time picking targets. At what point
would he try to flee?

I had a feeling he wasn't able to. Tied to the town in some way. I frowned as
I tried to locate where my demonic ace had gotten to. The shifting seemed to work
in chunks, so despite everything I had been putting out, we were going separate
directions, if not within a certain distance of each other.

The Chameleon spun in place to face me as my cannon appeared beside him.
Three quick blasts of confetti before he darted away—not wanting to shift the
town again.

I ran my open palm around myself in a circle, expecting him to show up beside
me again. He did not, but instead I heard the crack of Ren's rifle from the other
side of town.

[Ren: Sent him running.]
[Ren: Likely to get desperate.]

There wasn't another shift in the terrain. He had run from the elf in a more
mundane way, but it appeared he had either extreme bursts of speed or minor
teleportation, like when he had first attacked me. When I had won out against
the Siren and enacted my Domain for the first time, she had shown her true form.
I was willing to bet that the Chameleon had one last trick up his sleeve.

A thought that was punctuated almost as quickly as a spike ran through my arm. I twisted away from the pain, the pointed piece of . . . brickwork slowly sank back into the wall across the street. If I didn't know any better, that building had a green light glowing in the upstairs windows, making them look like eyes.

I narrowed my eyes, able to spot the Dazzle icons hovering over the roof. That almost felt like cheating.

A light illuminated me, causing my purple suit to sparkle. I took my hat down from my head and bowed, <Spotlight> forcing all attention on me. No more running. Twin magic cards burst into being and swirled around me as I twisted away from another jutting spike. It was as if the fabric of the house was being stretched out beyond what the normal material was capable of.

I twirled my attacks in through the upper windows, and the glow faded.

Fingers clicked, and two new cards came out. Two fire Imps. As I switched to the next house eyeing us up, I turned invisible and ran from my summonses. A spike lashed out and impaled the forehead of the first before he could get his spell off, but the second leveled a fireball straight into the side of the building.

I switched places with my demonic ace up on the roof of the temple, dismissing my Imp just as another spike went out to kill him. It just ran across the stone street instead, creating sparks. I stretched out my wings and sighed.

A dove landed beside me before it was replaced with Ren in a flash. Her left side was bloodied, her suit torn, but she didn't appear to be injured.

"Such a shame you're not equipped well for property damage, my dear," I said, a wry smile across my face.

"You'd be surprised, trickster." She lifted her nose up and flared her nostrils, some faux disdain leveled my way.

I brought out a critical card. "*Would I?*"

She brought her rifle up, putting her foot on a box summoned from her Inventory, as she narrowed her eye down her scope. A pulse of heat bloomed from her rifle, charging up as the end of her barrel started to glow from the intense temperature.

"I never told you what my newest attack Skill was."

CHAPTER FIFTY-ONE

Rise Again

I wasn't too sure at what point of my new existence I grew accustomed to violence. Even less sure of when I grew to adore it. Well, I didn't love it, as much as I saw the benefit and admired the strength we had gained.

So it was now, with Ren standing there, her rifle practically radiating danger, that I held my breath in excited anticipation. There was a tension there. Twice as much I'd normally be interested in one of her Skills because I knew she had <Mana Manipulation> now. Whatever the System had given her wasn't supposed to be pushed as far as she was pushing this next shot.

I almost knew exactly what was going to happen when she pushed that trigger—as if the effect made such an impression on me that it resonated back through time a few seconds before my living body actually experienced it.

And then, as she aimed for the Chameleon-infused building down below us, she shot, and I learned in real time.

A blast of hot air washed over us with the blowback as a ball of white-hot energy burst out from her rifle at great speed. Far too big to fit in the barrel of the weapon, it looked more like a bowling ball—a miniature sun—than anything like a traditional bullet. As it lobbed through the window, it did not disappoint.

The ground vibrated as a flash of bright light briefly blinded us. An explosion rocked my ears as wood and brickwork blew out of the building, collapsing all the internal structure. As my eyes adjusted, the edges of the exposed brickwork had bright-red blood lining it.

"You think that did it?" she asked.

"I think something else exploded," I murmured. "Ah, my heart, I mean. Do you feel like you have any further Guardian powers?"

She pulled a face, still looking down at the destroyed house. "I feel like . . . I will never reach the high of that first shot again. My life now is a dull shade, forever shadowed in the desperate search for a larger and more impressive explosion."

"Gross," I said, looking around the town. "You're even starting to sound like me."

The town shifted, and I found myself inside the temple. A quick spin and Ren wasn't here with me. Neither was the Chameleon. I smiled and summoned my patron sword. It didn't look too happy to see me, but it was hard to read the single eye.

"Fancy some sightseeing?" I asked. "We have a Guardian giving us a guided tour of this quaint town." The sword did not respond.

But the town switched again, and I was on the road near the . . . east? I scowled at the streets, my patron no longer here. Just as planned. I dropped two Hellhound cards and then activated <Take a Bow>, bringing out another eight demons.

"Hold tight, pals. Things are about to get bumpy." My cannon appeared by my side, and I stretched out my hands. A rifle shot cracked from the other side of the town.

And then we switched again. Top floor of a residential building. No demons with me anymore.

Just as soon as my eyes had focused, I moved again. Outside the front of the temple. Then again, I moved and was in the storeroom of a shop. Swapped again and I became dizzy, just closing my eyes and focusing on staying standing.

Once more and then a pause. I opened my eyes and wavered in place. My stomach settled, and I looked around. Present location seemed to be . . . Oh, I was in an alleyway just outside the main marketplace area.

[Ren: Front of the temple. Now.]

I didn't take a step but switched with my demonic ace that zipped there in a second. I spun to see quite the sight.

Wolf was lying there on the stone road, soaked through with blood. In his mouth was the torn throat of a very battered-looking and unmoving Chameleon.

"He kept trying to escape," Ren explained. "I saw the Guardian switch away from one of your demons twice, not wanting to risk getting attacked more. There were too many, and eventually he landed too close to Wolf by accident."

The bear had his eyes closed, but I could see him breathing.

"Everything okay, brother?" I knelt down beside him and put my hand on his bloodied head.

"No," he stated, barely moving his mouth.

"I'm so sorry. Now you bear our curse." I removed my hand and wiped the blood on my slacks. "Pun not intended."

He managed to expel a long, groaning sigh before one of his amber eyes opened and looked up at me. "If you're expecting me to perform tricks now, you will be sorely disappointed."

I was already. While it was a big stretch to assume he would become more like me just as Ren had, there was still part of me trying to arrange the show pieces.

"Do you know what you can do now?" the elf asked.

"I don't care," Wolf replied and closed his eyes again.

A glum smile on my face, I stood and turned to my equal. Her expression was a reflection of mine, although she had a lot more of her own blood across it. "Could you let the others know what has happened?" I asked, feeling just as exhausted as the bear now.

She gave me a nod, and her eyes went off to the side to look at her windows.

I sighed and sat myself down on the ground, leaning my back against the bear's side. As much as he wanted to be left alone, I knew my way to his heart. Even as the Chameleon's blood soaked from his fur into the back of my suit jacket, I could feel the tension in him melt away.

"Could we stay like this for a while?" his deep voice rumbled through into my head.

"We have time," I agreed.

It wasn't long before Ren joined us, and I put my arm around her as we sank into the comfort of the bear. The three of us had endured so much, and it never seemed to end. Nothing quite grounded us like mirroring those early days where we huddled up together for safety. A simple action on the surface.

We managed to stay like this, in silence, for a good fifteen minutes. Although the other groups hadn't gone quite that far, they had waited to meet up with Tanya and Quinn, who had teleported reasonably nearby. Once they spotted us, the pair ran over ahead of the others.

"Everyone fine?" Tanya asked, concern across her face. "You look like shit."

"It's mostly the Chameleon's blood," I offered, giving them a tired smile.

"Mine is mostly mine," Ren disagreed.

Wolf just grunted.

The other two Parties stopped and gawked at the destruction. Bullet holes, ruined buildings still smoldering, and the bloodied mess we currently sat just beside. For most, this was a disturbing scene. We barely registered it, still too dissociated from reality after hell. Although, perhaps this amount of filth and gore was slightly uncomfortable.

"I reckon the town is saved now," I said, moving away from my companions to stand back up. "To some degree. As keen as I am for us to plow forth into further malady, I ache to get washed down. Maybe eat something. A stew?"

Tanya nodded and turned to Quinn. "Get a fire and pot started up, babe." She caught herself, blushing slightly before glaring at the others. "Set up a camp for lunch. I want a lookout and rotating patrols, understood?"

I held my hand down to help the elf up, giving her a knowing grin. We both thought the other two were a good couple, and I could see the giddiness in Ren's eyes at the Fateweaver using a pet name for the fixer.

"Thanks, Tanya." I gave her a short bow. "I appreciate you organizing everyone."

She gave me a wry grin, waiting for the two groups to start moving away before turning to reply. "When we first joined up, Fiona wanted to take the lead position and I had to fight to lead in your stead. I had to bust a few balls to keep them under control, but they do as they are told, for the most part."

"You know I don't see myself as the leader."

"If your view on reality was the accurate one, we'd all be in the shit," she said, her smile remaining. "I kept them together, but we're all following your ambition and bullshit. Go get cleaned up and we'll take care of Wolf."

With another nod of thanks, we were away. Over to the nearest house and up to where they had an all-too-familiar bath setup. We got in together and helped each other wash off, something natural that we didn't even need to agree to. Our hunger for some hot food was even so great we managed to escape the comforting water with only a couple of shared kisses, nothing heavier than the empty weight in our stomachs.

By the time we were sparkling and fresh, the fabled stew was ready.

It didn't appear that Wolf had moved at all, but he was now clean, at least. The corpse of the Chameleon had been moved somewhere out of sight and the streets washed of any blood and gore. I remembered now most people were put off by eating around dead bodies. Some uncomfortable scenes from our time in hell flashed through my mind, now seeming slightly more insane than they had felt when there.

"I've missed stew," Ren whined, making a beeline to the campfire, Quinn holding an empty bowl ready for her arrival.

I walked over to the bear instead. "Don't tell me you are still sulking, brother."

He grunted, almost sounding like a growl. "I'm not sulking. I am just overwhelmed."

"What can I do?"

Amber eyes opened up to glare at me. "There is nothing you can do. Let me just process for a while longer. That is all I ask."

"Fine." I gave him a soft smile. "I'm here for you." As he grunted, I turned and almost walked straight into the goblin. "Oh, sorry, Ruby."

"I rubbed some goop on him," she said, gesturing to the bear.

"Yeah? Did you find out anything?"

"I found out that he doesn't like goop being rubbed on him." She grinned, and we walked over to the stew pot. "Nothing overtly fucked with him, as far as I can tell. Poor old man is exhausted though."

Maybe his Guardian powers would give him some way of energizing or allow him to live longer. Wishful thinking, I knew. We all had an expiry date, but for his to be so much sooner than ours seemed . . . unfair. There was no real option available to us just yet.

"If it was up to me," she continued, "I would have him retire. Or at least rest for a month or two. When I suggested it, he told me to fuck off."

"Wolf said that?" I raised an eyebrow and looked back at the motionless bear. "That's unlike him."

"Eh, I was being annoying as shit. I deserved it." The goblin grinned at me. "He's a stubborn one, but you know him best, Max. You feelin' alright?"

"Yeah." I nodded, my mind elsewhere, before I repeated, "Yeah. I'd let you goop me, but I have just bathed, and it's nice being clean for a change."

"Understandable. Eat well then. That'll do you better than any of my gross stuff." She nodded and left to go back to her Party.

I turned as Ren placed a warm bowl in my hands, vegetables and meat piled high within it.

"Looks like Quinn learned from the best," she said, grinning. "Not only that, but we found out what happened to the bastard Wardens and have erased the Guardian causing problems here. I'd say that was a successful day, huh?"

My eyes went over to the bear, who was still lying with his eyes closed, slightly away from everyone else.

"Sure," I replied. "Everything is great."

CHAPTER FIFTY-TWO

Spinning the Dial

It was times like these that I was glad that I wasn't like the old Max anymore. The workaholic version of myself would have burned out and been beneath the boots of one of our many enemies by now. Things were touch and go for a while, before I had accepted that both Ren and I could take a step back occasionally and enjoy what we had earned over our journey here.

Now, instead of rushing ourselves straight to Candlekeep, we were laughing and exchanging stories with the other groups we had become attached to. I still wouldn't describe myself as a social butterfly, but I echoed the relaxed atmosphere now that everyone had warm food and a couple of drinks in them. I still had my *humanity*.

Perhaps that sounded like something odd when I could turn into a demon, but we had killed and ground ourselves into dust for so long that sometimes I wasn't sure if I could be anything close to normal again. But we were. Even Ren was all smiles, only scowling as I regaled them all with the tale of how I made it out of the black market cave.

The only thorn in this otherwise amazing experience was the fact that Wolf wouldn't tell us what his Guardian powers did. His mood took a while to improve, but he looked more of himself now that he had been filled with plenty of food. Normally, I wouldn't be such a stickler for prying, but I had only been partially truthful about the different Guardians having the same power.

Well, they granted strength based on the wishes of the recipient—that was true, and in fairness I wasn't entirely sure . . . but it was possible that the theme of the Guardian also influenced how the powers were given out. The Siren was about desire. Part of me screamed out to break away from my old life, the restraints of being a magician haunted by being unable to put on that last great show for his mother. I had been granted my demonic powers, fully merging all the parts of my existence here. Now I could rise above my prior struggles.

I wasn't sure which one Ren had. She had wanted to be equal to me, share the slice of bullshit pie that the *System* granted me. It had been something she had said long ago, on the beach—a memory still as clear as day to me. The Chameleon was about *change*. Given that Wolf hadn't seemed any different, perhaps it could also be about a lack of change.

Not to say a *lack of change* sounded like a power.

"You alright, trickster?"

I turned my unfocused eyes back to the elf. She really was dazzling, even back when she'd had the permanent grumpy expression, but now she was almost angelic. I wasn't sure how we had ended up married, but if this was still some manner of coma dream, my brain had good taste.

"I'm considering a brief holiday in hell," I said, watching her blue eyes for a reaction.

"You're thinking that time dilation would give you a few extra days of training before we reach Candlekeep." Her poker face didn't budge by a hair.

She could always read me as if she was writing the script herself. "Perhaps. I know there are no more levels to be gained, and our time might be better spent getting power tokens on the way to the Crimson Shadow . . . but you know I'm a workaholic."

"No." She leaned back and put her legs up over my lap. "Pretty sure I beat that out of you."

"You can take the credit if you like." I smiled and glanced over at Wolf. "Actually, I think most of us don't have the appetite for hell, and I don't intend to vanish from the group again."

"I have the appetite for *one* thing in hell." She smiled and closed her eyes. "When this is all over though. Now that we're back in the real world, I'd like to save it before getting into all the many, many fun things I have planned for you."

I stared at her, hoping she'd open her eyes so I could read into that more. She kept them closed. Perhaps I could rush in and kill the Lady as soon as possible. Maybe before sundown if I was quick.

There was a time when our unseen antagonist had tried to win me over once I had received my Guardian powers. She must be shaking in her boots now that we had three of them on our side. She had two at most. Our efforts on cutting out the strongholds of her power had surely weakened her overall control on Candlekeep.

I was prepared for war.

"I'll just pop into hell to make sure things haven't fallen to shit already," I eventually decided. "Probably a good idea for me to check in once a day, given that it's a handful down there."

"Go on then, my king." She opened one eye as she removed her legs from me. "Just don't have too much fun without me."

"I shall hate every second we are apart."

She rolled her eyes, and I stood up, stepping away from the gathered camp-fires everyone was gathered around. Almost seemed a shame to leave them really. Most weren't even interested in why I had moved away from the group. Which was okay. I didn't need to be the focal point of every situation.

I cleared my throat for no reason.

Hand waved through the air and the same doorway appeared. Part of me worried that I'd come back to find the camp in disarray, bodies strewn around the place as something had taken advantage of my absence. Another ego thing, as Ren and Wolf could protect everyone, even without me.

I opened the door and stepped through into hell.

Warmth washed over me as the crimson tone of the foul place filled my eyes. I turned to see a small demon sitting on my throne.

With wide eyes, he gradually slid from it, back onto the floor. "J-just keeping it warm for you, your m-majesty."

"I am well within my right to tear you in half, slowly." I ran my tongue across my lips. "But you should just leave instead. Do not mistake my mercy for weakness."

"Y-yes, your majesty." The small demon grasped at his head dramatically as he ran down the steps and toward the large doors of the throne room.

I watched him leave, his small feet padding against the stone floor. About ten feet away from the exit, my patron burst up from the floor, the long sword blade slicing the escapee in half cleanly.

My head tilted to the side at the group of similarly impish demons sitting around a table playing cards. Ever since my entrance, they had remained frozen in place, as if I could only sense movement.

"Have I really been gone long enough for the throne to have *squatters*?" I asked rhetorically.

They were smart enough to remain still and quiet.

"May I make a suggestion, master?"

I turned my eyes to see that the speaker was none other than my sword. Their voice was muted—hollow and sinister. "Oh, so you *are* able to talk."

"Only in hell, master. The demons are not used to democratic reason. If you assign me as the voice of your will, I will command them in your absence." He floated closer to me.

As much as that sounded like a blasé excuse for him to hold sway over hell, it took the matter out of my hands and gave my patron something to keep him busy.

"What is your name?"

"Hori the Unquenchable, master."

"Hori, you are now the voice of my will. You are going to gather the six strongest demons and the six most cunning demons in hell. They will form the council that determines the politics of hell. If one of the strongest kills one of the weaker, then execute all twelve. If one of the cunning ones tries to betray another on the council, execute all twelve."

The eye on the hilt stared at me. "It is likely we will go through many council members, master."

"As it has to be. Eventually we will get a workable group. The first edict is to replenish and rebuild. The war to usurp the previous king weakened and destroyed a lot of hell, so the first thing to do is work toward prosperity and power as a whole."

"As you command, master."

"Also, kill these dumbasses." I pointed a finger at the panicked gamblers. As my patron whipped through them in short order, I shook my head. "I need to be respected, despite my absence. I'm giving the denizens a chance to have some self-reliance. If I have to rule with an iron fist, then I might as well give the crown to someone more bloodthirsty."

"Unfortunately, master, only your death would allow the crown to part from your head."

I exhaled through my nose as I regarded my patron. We hadn't had the time to bond or really get to know each other. I didn't think he wanted to lop off my head to take the crown for himself, but it was an option on the table. Certainly not as affable as Roger but likewise not as insolent. So far.

"If I have detractors, then set up a tournament system. Strongest three challengers will get to face me when I make my visits to hell."

"As you command, master."

I had no intentions of losing, but giving them a goal would focus their strength, and a tournament would weed out all but three of my potential enemies. Gave me an outlet to show off my power to the masses and burn some calories at the same time.

"That will be all, Hori. Thank you."

The floating sword dipped as if it was giving me a bow. "Welcome, master. The prior king did not have your foresight or shrewd intellect. Serving you will be much more fulfilling."

I gave him a nod as I waved a return portal into being. "I will call on you when your services are needed."

Then I was through it, back into the much cooler market square of the town by the temple. Ren was up beside me before my eyes had even adjusted.

"I missed you *so* much," she whined. "We've never been so far apart, even though it was barely a handful of minutes. Tell me *everything*."

Blinking away the dazzle in my eyes, I smiled and put my arm around her. "First, I killed some dissidents, then I appointed my patron as my official spokesperson. After that, I arranged for more controlled, constructive violence to take place. Maybe some blood sports on occasion."

"Ugh." She put her arm around my waist in return. "Sounds hot. Wish I had gone to fawn over you."

"Plenty of time for that in the future, moonflower." I glanced over at the groups. "How's the mood here?"

"Mostly trying to ignore the fact that we are about to go to war. Tanya was showing me the Map, and there are a few stops along the route that can help get us some extra power before we get to Candlekeep."

That sounded good. I gave her a nod. We were almost at the limits as to what strength the System would really allow us. No more Skills, decent gear was unlikely, our Stats may be static now with no further levels. Our Inventories were already full of potions and scrolls. The last thing we could do with were more power tokens to advance our Skills.

I had no doubt that was exactly the sort of detour Tanya had arranged. I fully intended on getting anyone lower than level fifteen up to that as well. For as little as we knew what would be awaiting us in the city, I wanted to take no chances.

It was unlikely we'd get a second chance.

The group started packing up while I went over to my Party. It was time to find out the first stop on our dazzling tour toward the city.

CHAPTER FIFTY-THREE

Disenchanted

First stop on the way to Candlekeep wasn't too far from where the Eternal Wardens had met their end. A Monster field for the lower level among us to catch up.

Unfortunately, Guilds didn't share experience. Twice as disappointing was that Ren, Wolf, and I were too high level to kill things for the others to receive credit even if we did rearrange the Parties so that one of us was in each.

I watched the dinosaur-like creatures fall in the battle with a rather sour expression on my face. While the bear could act as a physical blockade, even if not attacking, and Ren could heal and shield the other groups, I was at a slight loss.

We'd never had to contend with experience share outside of the normal Party dynamics, but even if I just hobbled the System-created, it put a huge dent in the experience the killing group would receive.

Quinn stood beside me, perhaps content enough that he didn't need to put himself in danger for once. "Isn't it funny how life works out?" he asked.

"Very true." I nodded slowly, not knowing exactly what he meant but fully on board either way. It would only take a glance at my current situation to know that life had dealt me a rather strange hand.

"I never thought I'd fall for a woman like Tanya," he continued, "but there's an *edge* to her. I can only thank you for bringing us together, friend."

I blinked away the remnants of confusion over his initial statement. "Oh. Well, she brought herself in. I only chose not to kill her. Your charm did all the rest."

He chuckled and shook his head. "You give me too much credit, Max. What drew us together was not my unquenchable spirit or any notion that love was in the cards. Just two people desperate for normality and safety. It just so happened we had the right ingredients between us for a blooming passion to germinate."

I pulled a face, totally ill at ease with the phrasing he used. "I'm genuinely glad, Quinn. Doubly so, as now you have a reason *not* to sacrifice yourself in my stead. You can live on."

"Don't death flag me, friend." He turned his one eye to me and smiled. "It's not my convictions or love that prevents me paying back the blood debt, but I have truly given up knowing if you are dead or not when you use that Skill."

"True enough. I *am* tiresome." I gave him a wide grin. "If you want to repay the debt, just protect her and keep her safe. Nothing would make me happier than you two surviving and finding a place of contentment once this is all over."

He seemed fulfilled enough with this change of plan. "Consider it done. That also means you and Ren have to make it through. Wolf too. We have all been through too much to lose each other."

I gave him a nod but couldn't find the words to respond at first. With all the magical scrolls we had found, none had been for resurrecting allies. How likely was death once we got to the city? While part of me liked to think that us powerful three would be taking on the bulk of danger, there was surely plenty to go around. Maybe I had some karma coming my way.

"As much as I would like to hope that all fifteen of us will make it through . . ." I said slowly. "It seems hypocritical of someone who has killed so many people to care to such a degree to make the narrative care for my thoughts on who should be protected."

Quinn looked me over, his single eye reading my expression, before he gave me a tired shrug. "Just *think*, Max. Any of these poor souls you save would be your fan for life."

I had to admit; I did like the taste of that phrasing.

My mind was elsewhere now, however. As Tanya called him over for something, my brain was focused on the area around us. If I couldn't kill Monsters, then I would run protective measures over everyone here. Things were never as simple as moving from one place to another, and we had suffered enough ambushes in our time here to know better.

Not that we were exactly a soft target anymore. While one dinosaur screeched and fell over dead, another burst into flame. It wasn't going to be quick experience, but Tanya had a plan. We'd grind here until dusk and then to a nearby town that had a couple of easy Quests to complete. Sleep the night away and then start fresh in the morning.

Logistics and morale were important for an army, she had told me. As much as the enemy literally lit the sky ahead of us, we needed proper rest and full stomachs. Any glimmer of confidence we could gather to tell us that this wasn't going to be a big deal. Deadly.

But was it? I didn't even know, to be fair. There was a chance we would just roll over Candlekeep and usurp the Lady even easier than we'd turned hell upside down. It wasn't a . . . *realistic* possibility, however.

In fact, I fully expected to be attacked tonight, if not before.

It would be disappointing if we weren't. Our enemy would benefit from it to the point that it would be negligence if they didn't try to needle us on the route to Candlekeep. I didn't know Lady in Red's past, but I was sure she had some cold cunning in her for her to get this far. A cruelty to her that hated a threat just lingering beyond the borders of her control.

I watched as Wolf walked away from the front lines, his expertise not really needed while they waited for Monster respawns. He came up near me and then flopped over onto his side.

"Everything fine, brother?" I asked.

"Yeah. Just making use of the fine weather." He rolled so that he could look up at me while we talked.

I nodded. It *was* a good day, all things told. Compared to hell, this was heaven. A mild warmth that lingered if you stayed out in the sunshine. It brought me back to the cottage, and I imagined the three of us hanging out by the swing. The flowers. Such peace. Something to fight for.

My focus returned to him. "Still keeping that large maw closed about your Abilities?"

The bear grunted but maintained his gaze. "You will know when it is time, no sooner. Some things only work that way."

I rolled that statement around in my mouth before giving him a bow. "I accept and will pester you no further." He had a trick up his sleeve, and it would be rude of me to force it to appear when it wasn't time—ruining the whole performance. It was clearly something important to him.

"Thank you." Wolf closed his eyes, soaking up the rays.

Would be nice if he could give at least *one* clue though. I pulled a face and looked over at the fighting groups. Fiona's Party was still engaged with two dinosaurs. The feathered creatures fell back as she swiped at one with her mace, and the spellcaster froze the other in place, allowing Magnus to nearly decapitate it.

Ren looked relaxed, not really straining to heal their frontline fighters or put shields on them. Bored, possibly. The babysitting was part of the process, unfortunately. We had leapfrogged everyone in these first areas of the world thanks to our vacation to hell. Dragging weaker Players into the coming battle seemed unfair. The least we could do was to prepare them for . . .

Whatever was coming.

My eyes went to the many chance boxes I had accumulated lately, including the demon-flavored ones. I suppose it wouldn't be the worst thing in the world to eventually open them.

Frowning at the ground around me, I chose several spots to drop useless gear. A pile for each Stat. Then, I went and opened ten boxes at a time. Gold, potions, scrolls, and the occasional miscellaneous item I kept, but any gear I couldn't wear I dropped to one of these piles.

A little garage sale in the making, people started to accumulate as they took a rest from their fighting. I continued, opening and dropping. Nothing was as good as my hell gear. I stopped, not because I was running out of chance boxes, but because the surrounding ground was too cluttered.

"I can disenchant gear," Percius offered, some slight hesitation to the statement. "With enough shards from magical items, I can craft power tokens."

"Holy shit." My eyebrows raised quickly enough that my hat almost fell from my head. "*Where* have you been all my life? Ren, did you hear this motherfucker?"

"I have, like, a *billion* shit boxes too!" the elf said, practically running over.

"Party members get first dibs if they can use the gear," I said, waving my hand impatiently yet diplomatically. "Otherwise funnel everything into this man here."

"There's a cost—" he begun.

"I'll pay it," Ren and I interrupted at the same time.

And thus began what I could only describe as the least efficient power-token factory ever to exist. I couldn't believe he hadn't told us sooner—although, judging by the surprise on Fiona's face, he hadn't told them either. A secret Skill that made him incredibly valuable and important.

Now we became uncontested. Ren and I opened and spat out magical items to the floor in front of us. We had four runners who would take the gear to Tanya. With everyone's Equipment screen shared with her, she went through and designated gear to a Guild member—or handed it to another runner who brought it over to the spellcaster, who melted the item down into token shards.

Wolf sat beside him, paying off the cost. We'd finally found a gold sink that wasn't sweet cakes.

And we had an *obscene* amount of extra gear. I kept two rings, as we had now unlocked the third and fourth slots by becoming level twenty.

[Ring of Hope: +5 INT, +25% Mana, +10% Mana regeneration]
[Scryer's Hoop: +3 INT, +3 WIS, +6 Luck]

The rest wasn't useful for us main trio, but once we switched to the hell gear from the demonic boxes, they were soon vacuumed up by the others—their old gear going into the pile to be broken down instead.

I felt rather pleased that our hoarding and distrust of these random loot crates had eventually worked out in our favor. I was sure that we weren't about to get a ton of tokens from this whole effort—but it would be better than just keeping things around in our Inventories.

The one downside was the amount of time it was taking. Sure, the other two groups—and even Quinn and Tanya—were getting a power boost, but the feathered dinosaur-like Monsters were now just walking around idly instead of being crushed to death for their experience. I could see the ire on Tanya's face—that we were ruining her plan.

She was in charge of our schedule, after all. I shouldn't be interrupting the production.

"We'll do part two of this later," I announced, ceasing spewing the useless items onto the grass.

"Good," Ren agreed. "It was doing my eyes in."

I swept my hand in front of me and picked up everything still by my feet, straight into my Inventory. The grid boxes were cluttered to the point of breaking, but it would have to survive for now. "Go and grind experience. We have little time before dusk, and then we're moving, whether you have leveled or not."

It was enough convincing to get them to change track. Now, with a few pieces of improved gear each, the process of slaying Monsters took even less time. I could tangibly see the benefit of our little gear explosion.

Percius stayed behind, still getting caught up on disenchanting the last pieces of gear moved to him. The process of creating tokens probably took a while as well, but he could at least leach experience while the rest of his Party acted. With Ren backing them up, they wouldn't miss his offensive Skills.

"How was that?" I asked him, a wide smile on my face.

"Expensive. For you," he shot me a brief grin before looking back at his work. "I'm not sure there will be much to take back from Wolf once all is done."

"Oh." I raised my eyebrows down at the tired looking bear. "I didn't give him any. That's all his own gold."

"*I hate looting,*" Wolf grumbled.

Percius hesitated before glancing between us. "The second phase—combining the shards into power tokens—doesn't take gold but instead uses a lot of Mana."

"You need potions?" I went through my Inventory. "I don't really use them . . . so I have a large stockpile. Greater mana potions would probably get you to full, right?" He was nodding in my peripheral as I looked through the windows. "I'll split the stack, so . . . I'll trade you three hundred and fifty."

"What?" he asked. "You have . . ."

"Just of the greater version, yes. I'm keeping the masterwork and max ones for myself, the latter just for the amusement. So, how many tokens are we getting out of this process so far?"

He shook the disbelief from his head as he went into his own Inventory. Beneath his wide hat, I could see his eyes widen farther the longer he looked.

"*Oh shit,*" he murmured.

CHAPTER FIFTY-FOUR

Heart Taker

In terms of power tokens, we had a lot of power tokens.

Sixty before Percius grew sick of the taste of mana potions. There would be more to come, but with the stash of loot still waiting to be sharded and the process not being an exact science, we didn't know how many we'd even end up with in total.

Now that we had found a source of power, the question then became one of how we intended to distribute it.

I had suggested four each—something Ren had scowled at me for. While she wasn't going to say out loud that we two should get thirty each, I could read that intention from her. We were already powerful though. After a little bickering back and forth, I grew tired of the discussion and made an executive decision.

Twenty tokens per group to distribute among themselves as they saw fit.

Everyone either thought this was a great idea or could see that I'd be annoyed with any further arguing over the matter. Not that I had been anything but affable . . . but they had seen me fight, even if only briefly. With plenty of magical items still to unbox, I intended to get Percius alone later and take all the tokens for myself. Well, for my Party, at the least.

Thus, with dusk taking us away from the Monster grinding and toward a small town, I walked with our group to decide who would get the current load of tokens. Four each was my suggestion still.

"We have already decided," Tanya was quick to inform me. "You and Ren are getting ten each. No complaints or debate to be had."

I opened my mouth *to* complain and debate, but she had me there. Sixty had felt like a lot at first, but now distilled down, it only meant one Skill upgrade for me and Ren. Or I could dabble with pumping up ten of my Passives . . . but I knew the real money ticket was improving my core rotation.

Humming to myself, I divided up the tokens as we walked. My mind was already elsewhere, imagining ways in which we could get magical items in bulk to fabricate into further power tokens. If only we had met the spellcaster weeks ago, we would have burned the candle to the end to drown in the upgrading stones. Every second was precious now.

"I didn't even know there was enchanting," Ren said idly.

Tanya raised an eyebrow but didn't look all that shocked. "Really? There was a tutorial back in the first area, but it doesn't surprise me you missed it."

"It's one of the five key gear-advancement mechanics," Quinn informed us. "Enchanting, gemming, proficiency, reinforcement, and preference."

I exchanged a glance with Ren, and she picked up the slack to allow me to avoid looking silly. *Sillier than normal.*

"We've seen gems before." The elf nodded sagely. "Fuck knows about the rest."

Not quite the save I had been hoping for.

Tanya pulled a face. "You did *none* of those? Perhaps this is on me for assuming . . . but you've gone this far without at least proficiency and preference?"

"Perhaps it would be best," I said, nodding slowly, "if you told us what they were so that we could pretend we've had them all along."

"Preference is just something that lets you get gear upgrades more often. It tailors your drops—even from boxes—to be more likely to be your Stat choice, even if not always an upgrade." Her face continued to contort into a grimace. "I thought the gear mix we've had was just because of the Party dynamics . . . but you've been on *full random loot* all this time?"

"What's proficiency?" Ren asked, allowing me to ignore the pointed question leveled at me.

"Simply put," Quinn replied, "you gain benefits based on certain gear designations. For example, my proficiency is in medium armor, and I get a bonus to evasion-based defenses and Damage using Dexterity-based weapons."

"I can turn into the Demon King," I murmured.

The Fateweaver just shook her head and sighed. "It's no wonder you're so malady stricken, Max. Even if you've gotten decent Equipment through brute forcing the drops, you're missing out on a decent chunk of Damage mitigation at the least."

"Ah." I grinned. "I just deal with that nowadays by avoiding getting hit at all."

"How well is that working out?" she asked, a tired expression replacing the disdain.

"I'm still in one piece. So I'd say—*Ow.*" I flinched away as Ren hit me in the side of the head.

"Shit, sorry, trickster." The elf pulled me in closer to inspect the damage. "I thought you would use <Last Act>. *Oh no.* We aren't on the same page anymore." She squeezed me tighter. "I'm too young to get divorced. Tell me it's not over, Max."

Tanya sighed. "I think hell clearly affected your sanity. Keep moving now, children."

Wolf looked up at her, almost as tired of our shenanigans. "I'm normal," he stated.

While the Fateweaver didn't deny that, she gave him a silent pet on his shoulder before moving on. Our group had accepted it, but for us humans from contemporary Earth, having a talking bear on our side didn't really come *close* to normal. It was just something we couldn't really question, even after learning that we came from different worlds.

This was home for us now, for better or for worse.

Not that we even knew this world properly. I held Ren's violent hand as we walked to catch the others up. Woodlands around us, a stone road leading us to the next town. We were in quarantine here. Left to struggle and squirm in a feature-absent sandbox while others hid behind a protective wall waiting for the Lady or whatever bug had infected the System to die off.

Part of me was mad that we hadn't been contacted. Surely someone would know what we had been getting up to. The cure that they didn't care to lend a helping hand toward. Never mind dazzling them once all was said and done, I had a few stern words to pry their heads open with.

In truth, the hope was just that there would be a place for us all when this had settled. No need to bounce between high-stakes violent events. Just Ren and me and a cottage in the woods. Probably Wolf too, for as long as he could. Time to relax or pick up hobbies that weren't about turning people into corpses.

I blinked away these thoughts and concentrated on our surroundings. Now, with the sun lowering in the sky, a lot of this path was shaded. Open fields would appear, dotted with farms or similar housing, or groups of Monsters. It reminded me of a theme park ride I had gone on once. Thankfully, there was no singing.

"Getting closer to ambush o'clock, trickster." She gave my hand a squeeze before letting go.

"I'm not so sure." We had a knack for this by now, and I trusted her intuition completely, but it was too soon. "If they are near, then they'll be waiting for when we are weaker to pounce."

There had been plenty of people who had thought they could just run up and sucker punch us with only the element of surprise on their side. We'd even come close to losing such engagements. With our current standing, that wouldn't be enough to best us. Some of the other Parties, sure, but ours was nigh unflappable.

My eyes went across the canopy. Of course, that didn't stop people from trying to flap us.

"Dungeon tomorrow," Tanya interrupted, unable to sense our foresight at work. "The lockout time works via unique Party compositions, so we'll send in all three at once, then swap a person for the second go through. Rinse and repeat."

"There will be enough combinations?"

"Yeah. I doubt we'll be doing it hundreds of times, so it'll be fine. To try to stabilize the time to complete, we'll probably have you three as the leaders, and people will rotate between you."

Splitting up. I raised an eyebrow at the elf, who was doing the same already at me. I wondered which of the three groups our imagined stalker would deem the weakest. Then, could I fake a weaker Party and be a part of it to reverse the jump on them?

In fact, the process was so clear and rote in my mind it went past premonition and landed in the murky pool of fiction. I had erased it from possibility by living it out too realistically in my mind, and the System didn't like repeating punch lines.

That or my short return had mushed my brains up just that little more.

"Sounds good," I eventually decided, realizing I had just been silently thinking for a while. "Chances of decent loot?"

"Middling," she replied. "But with a disenchanter, everything works toward new tokens now. Have you spent yours yet?"

I shook my head, as that seemed better than telling her I was distracted with fighting imaginary ambushers in my mind. They'd avoid my group, surely. Perhaps a quick area-of-effect nuke or assassination of one of the softer targets from afar. Nothing so overt as . . . *Oh*, I was doing it again.

My eyes flicked through my screens, and I spent all ten tokens on my demonic ace. Now it could hold five items and even loot items into itself. It wasn't the most dangerous or destructive power-up, but it made the possibilities that more endless.

"Did you pick, Ren?" I asked her.

"Of course. Tell me yours first."

I raised an eyebrow and shook my head slightly. "No, *you* first."

Her bright-blue eyes rolled. "I'm pretty sure you believe that our choices will be aligned in some manner, further proving we are soulmates or some other sap. Correct?"

"That's right. But that's what *you* think as well."

The elf shot me a grin. "Naturally. My chained shot can also be certain debuffs now instead of just elemental damage."

"And let me guess . . ." I grinned. "One of those effects is an attempted disarming shot?"

"That means you have something that can pluck the weapons out of the air?"

"My demonic ace can now." I beamed at her, and she beamed right back at me.

The familiar gruff tone of Fiona grunted from a little way back. *"You two are truly insufferable."*

"Insurmountable," I corrected.

"Irreplaceable," Ren cooed.

"Irritating," Wolf grunted, shaking his head.

All of that and more. We were still riding the high of . . . everything really. Living. Flourishing. It was only natural for us to be a little too much before we became grounded again.

Her Skill really was useful though. The System once again smoothing the process of us becoming the multi-tool required to dismantle every facet of the Crimson Shadow. I opened up my hand, and the ace was there in it, hovering over my palm.

I swung it out, watching it curve in a wide arc through the field beside us. Energy flowed down my arm as I manipulated my Mana, empowering the demon. Our Guild watched as the dark rectangle burst through the bodies of five of the Monsters in the field—bipedal creatures with fur and long beaks.

As they dropped over dead, my card spun back over to my hand, and I caught it.

I held it out at arm's length, and the rest of the groups watched in awe as four clumps of bloody meat dropped out of the held card onto the road in a series of splats.

"Monster hearts," I announced.

I received a single, pensive round of applause from someone at the back.

Some days, that was enough.

"Only four, trickster?" Ren tilted her head. "Did you forget how to count?"

"Oh." I made the faux show of patting around my suit as if I had mislaid the last organ. "Ah, here it is. The first heart that I stole."

I pointed right at her with my finger.

"Dickbag," she said but was unable to hide her smile. "I hope our ambushers target you first."

Oops. She might not have realized she had just cursed me.

No . . . I cracked a wide smile. It was a blessing.

CHAPTER FIFTY-FIVE

Inn Patience

In what was possibly the first time in my life, the unthinkable had happened.

I had been *wrong* about something.

Although, I didn't really feel like vocalizing this point and inviting everyone's comments on that. While I had expected danger to be looming around the next corner, the rest of the day went by without incident. It was almost disappointing, if it wasn't for the fact that I adored spending time with those around me.

Standing above the corpses of my enemies was a close second but also something I wasn't about to tell Ren.

Instead, we had arrived at the town. Content enough to see that there were normal System-created people going about their business. Still awkwardly robotic and simple, but it was good enough for us to buy supplies and find lodging for the night. The three of us chose to sit out on doing the Quests, seeing as we were max level already, but found enough humor in sitting and watching the others running back and forth doing the mundane tasks.

We were keeping guard, of course. It was just peaceful. Unfortunately.

It didn't take long for everyone to be done, and after grumbling about terrible rewards for a while, the Guild settled into having a few campfires set up while we ate and talked among ourselves.

Conversation turned to the worlds we had all originated from. I told them about what I had learned, and people tried to work out the differences between their home worlds. Most seemed to come from a version of Othea. It took a lot of back-and-forth for them to decide on the three versions of that world.

From my understanding, the one that Ren came from was what came to mind when a fantasy world was imagined. It had magic and various types of ancestries, like something out of common pop-culture knowledge back on Earth. Mentally, I named this Fantasy Othea.

Quinn and a couple of others came from a version that had no gods—or at least their powers were much weaker. Magic was scarcer, and life was much harder. At first I was willing to brush that off as him being from a different area of the same world, but there were major geographical differences others brought up, and his view was echoed by the Paladin in Fiona's Party. I named this one Grimdark Othea.

To my surprise, Percius was from the third unknown Othea. After he let slip that he knew what Ren's sniper rifle was, I immediately needled him with questions. Not from Earth, as he was well acquainted with orcs and goblins—something that was a factor in him joining the Party with Ruby. I had long suspected the man who'd attacked me with dual chainswords wasn't from Earth either.

A world of technology *and* magic, the spellcaster told me. Although—he assured me—he was a bit of a luddite in those matters. He had been running a delivery through some wastelands to deliver arcane crystals—some manner of magical battery—when a portal had gobbled him up. Sci-Fi Othea was close enough a descriptor for me.

The three Earths were harder to differentiate, but I knew two of them already. Contemporary Earth and Supernatural Earth. Normal Max from the first, and demon hunter Max from the latter. It was the easiest way to explain the presence of hell and actual demons. The third Earth was either too similar to one of those two, or we didn't have anyone from there.

It was a long conversation that led us through into the early night.

Was there a point to it?

People liked to reminisce about where they had come from. Each of us was a whole story before arriving in this System world. Going back probably wasn't possible, but I didn't see anyone who looked as though that was their goal. Most importantly, it was something to distract us from what was ahead.

It worked so well that I totally blanked on what Ren was telling me as we settled into our room at the inn.

"Hmm? Sorry, I was miles away." I gave her a sheepish smile, but the scowl I had expected wasn't present.

"Tell me what's on your mind, trickster. You know it's dangerous for your skull's well-being for it to be too full up."

I nodded and lay next to her, pulling the covers up. "Just thinking about the future, I guess."

She smiled and put her face closer to mine. "Quiet days at the cottage?"

"Sure, at first. I'm not sure . . . that will be enough. Talking about the worlds this evening, there are just so many questions I need answers to."

Ren narrowed her eyes but nodded gently. "The *adventuring bug*. We will never be satisfied sitting idle for too long."

"Dangerous," I murmured.

"Unavoidable. You and I have the strength and willpower to create change wherever we go, fix the problems that others can't. I bet you that Lady in Red is just the first stepping stone."

"Here I was thinking everything would be rather pedestrian after." I leaned forward to give her a kiss. "Although, I'm sure there is a good reason why you are still fully dressed in bed."

"As are you, trickster." She ran a hand down the side of my face. "Are we *addicted* to danger?"

"Yeah."

There was no denying it at this point. I had seen her eyes after we had defeated the Guardian. The drab expression when standing around being the healer while the others got experience from the Monster fields. We had been built around overcoming odds to the point that if we weren't being challenged for our right to exist, we were bored.

So it was how we came to be lying in bed together, in our full outfits, waiting for the ambush.

It *was* coming, and we knew. Not just foresight this time, but as soon as we had arrived in our room, there was the feeling. The Guardian power of the person who could make clones or puppets. They had waited for everyone to retire for the night, so they couldn't have good intentions.

Running through the potential scenarios had been why I had been too distracted to listen to Ren. An attempt on our lives was fifty-fifty. Prime targets but the hardest to kill. They'd know that, especially after last time. If they were smart, then they wouldn't be coming alone. A fight in the dark wasn't ideal, but we had ways of lighting up an area.

"How long do you think we have?" Ren asked. "I wouldn't mind a bit of sleep."

I closed my eyes. The feeling in my arm signaling a Guardian's power was close was faint. Somehow I knew to filter out the two in my Party. "If it were me, I'd wait until . . . three in the morning or something. When people are most settled and down for the count. I don't mind staying up to keep watch if you want a nap."

She didn't seem too pleased with the idea at first but eventually gave me a sigh. "Fine. Crack the window a little so that I can put my bird out as soon as I'm up. The rooftop is the best place for me to be if we are attacked."

"My demonic card is already in the tavern across the road." We had to split the Guild across two lodgings. "I was hoping to sneak some more tokens from Percius, but he is really sick from all the mana potions. I told him the next batch is all mine, however. Sharing is fine, but I'm a little power hungry."

"You won't even share with me?" she asked, putting on a pout as her bright-blue eyes twinkled.

I leaned closer to give her another soft kiss on her forehead. "*No chance,*" I whispered.

The elf groaned and turned to face away from me, only partially annoyed at my greed. I took this as a sign to exit the bed, an act that received a second groan.

"You know that if I stay in bed to hold you, one of two things would happen. Neither is likely to be a beneficial for our defenses." I stepped over to the window and pushed it open slightly, a wave of cool air coming into the room as Ren muttered something under her breath.

The times we spent apart were few and far between these days, the month spent in hell acting as a time multiplier for our relationship to the point that we felt like it had been years together. Out of everyone in this world, she was both the last person that needed my protection, yet the one I would have to protect most.

I pulled out a wooden chair from my Inventory and sat beside the window. Just out of range of the cold breeze coming in. What was I really waiting for? A gut feeling to come to fruition. An ache in my arm knowing that we had gone uncontested for too long. Slaying a Guardian would have let the other two know. Our strength multiplying would not have gone unnoticed.

Yet still, there was something that gnawed at me. Like a bad smell I'd only get slight whiffs of but couldn't place. Danger was just outside of my sight, creeping at the edges of my peripheral. This opportunity, where we were all in one place and supposedly sleeping, would be too good to pass up. One of the few times before our attack on Candlekeep where we were weak and unprepared.

So, why did I feel like something wasn't quite right?

I looked over at Ren. She was still facing away from me, bundled up under the covers. I couldn't tell if she was asleep or not. Chances were she could tell that things were tense here, given that she had similar powers to me. She was also tired, and soft beds were a luxury after the rough existence in the other plane. The rest of the Guild shouldn't have much trouble getting to sleep. Tiring days all around.

At the heart of it, that was what was giving me pause for concern. I worked my jaw before bringing up my chat messages.

> **[Max: Are you awake, brother?]**
> **[Wolf: sssd]**
> **[Max: Stay alert if you can.]**
> **[Max: I have a bad feeling.]**
> **[Wolf: ssop]**

One day we would teach him how to use the Chat function correctly. At least for simple messages. Having him awake made me feel a little more at ease. We couldn't stay up all night if we wanted to be functional tomorrow, but I also knew as soon as I drifted off, things would go wrong.

Not that it was my role to ensure everything went smoothly. I mean, I *was* the star of the show . . . The performance of the whole team ultimately reflected on me. My reputation was at stake. The show must go on, and I must . . .

This was terrible timing for a wave of corruption to flow through my mind. I took a deep breath and cooled myself. There was an odd desire to return to hell, but it slowly petered out as my sensibilities took control again.

The elf shifted in the bed, turning over to scowl at me—very clearly still awake. "You know, I can tell when you're acting corrupted."

"I haven't moved."

"Those little cogs in your head whir a little faster. An off-kilter clicking that sets me on edge. *Therefore*, I cannot sleep." She continued to glare, but I could tell that she was secretly thankful for an excuse to talk more.

"I'm sorry to trouble you, moonflower. I may need your full attention while I stand guard, lest I fall to crazed thoughts."

"I reluctantly accept that I'll need to watch over you. You'll owe me one, trickster." While her eyes were narrowed, a smile illuminated her face.

With a tip of my hat, I thanked her.

Together, we waited for the impending doom, content enough that we would be ready for anything.

CHAPTER FIFTY-SIX

Unrested Development

As it so happened, *doom* didn't actually come for us. I would have perhaps felt foolish if I could feel anything other than the dull throb of lack of sleep clouding up my head.

My aching eyes looked between the window, where the first rays of daylight were seeping through, and then to the elf in bed. Despite taking the view that we were way off the mark about an ambush, she had been unable to sleep. The both of us had remained quietly in position, on edge like we were in a trance.

The feeling that the other Guardian user was nearby had faded in the very early morning, but I still felt *something* was wrong. Not knowing was aggravating me. It didn't seem reasonable that they would have gotten cold feet over making an attack on us. There was too much at stake and . . .

It was just a single word through my chat messages that filled me with life once more.

[Ruby: MAX]

I vanished from the room, appearing in the lobby of the tavern across the street. Both Ruby and Wolf were there. Both seemed exhausted.

"Max," the goblin repeated, worry on her face. "I can't wake Fiona."

We said nothing further, partly because I didn't have the brain space for anything lucid, and she led me toward the room. Wolf stayed put, mostly because the staircase wasn't built for someone as wide as him.

Up to the next floor and then around into her open room. The fighter was still bundled up in the blankets. Still breathing. After only knowing her in the armor she usually wore, seeing her in basic nightwear was odd. Took away all that bluster, made her seem human. Vulnerable. The scars did indeed run down from her face, past her collarbone, and under her sleepwear.

More important than that, however, was the icon I could see over her head.

My eyes switched to the goblin, who had circled around to the other side of the bed. "Did you sleep last night?"

She shook her head, looking equally as odd in a nightgown. "Stayed up late to work on my alchemy and then couldn't drift off."

I nodded and went to the Guild chat.

[Max: Report in.]
[Ren: Here.]
[Wolf: swww]
[Ruby: Here.]
[Quinn: awake^]
[Tanya: Here.]

I waited for five more seconds, but no further replies came in. Sure, it was early in the morning. Far earlier than people would usually be up. I was beginning to put some of the puzzle pieces together and didn't expect to see anybody else reply in the near future.

"I think it's a curse," Ruby complained, "but I can't figure out what."

"It is. I can tell you exactly what." I gave her a grim smile as I explained.

[Soul-Linked Curse: Unbroken Slumber—Target remains in a permanent state of sleep until the caster cancels the spell. Caster cannot cast any other spells while Unbroken Slumber is active. Targets become immune to sleep if they are currently awake when the spell is cast.]

A trap.

I worked the taste of reality through my mouth. Something that was meant to incapacitate all of us. I was sure that whoever cast the spell wasn't going to just let things go and couldn't attack us without breaking the spell. That meant they wouldn't be working alone . . . and either went for backup once they realized they had missed a few people or felt they had all the time in the world to bring a proper assault down on us.

"So we'll have to find and kill the caster to get rid of it?" Ruby asked. She looked half tempted to go and find some goop to smear on the sleeping fighter.

I removed a scroll of dispel curse from my Inventory and held it out. It turned to ash, but the icon remained over Fiona. "Short answer: yes."

This was a problem, as it meant that most of the Guild was now out of service. Vulnerable to attack. I found my eyes drifting around the room as I tried to piece together something that made sense. A plan? The exact nature of how the curse caught us up? My gaze eventually fell back onto the pensive goblin. It was time to lead.

"Stay put. We'll communicate over Chat," I told her. Before she had the chance to nod, I was away. Now atop the roof with the sunrise painting me a warm reddish tone.

A dove landed beside me before Ren replaced it in a flash. "What's happened, trickster?"

"A sleeping curse. I believe it affects the area of this town. Possibly some manner of runic or arcane trap that had been set. Those who were sleeping will forever sleep. Those who weren't cannot." I put my arm around her as we looked out to the shifting hues of the sun illuminating the sky.

She grunted and leaned her head on my shoulder. "We have to kill the caster, I take it?"

"Got it in one, moonflower."

Ren took a deep breath and sighed. "Then next you'll say we have to go find them, but we can't leave the sleepers undefended. Wolf would need to stay behind, but I would say that he doesn't have a way to protect people from ranged attacks. You'll tell me that I should stay and you'll hunt the caster down, and I'd object, telling you that I am a better tracker and have a sniper rifle. You'll insist that you go anyway, out of some dumb duty to keep me safe. I'll resent you for it but ultimately accept your plan. Then, I'll kiss you like this."

She pulled me in tighter, gripping the back of my neck as she kissed me deeply. She moved away and scowled.

"I'll call you a dickbag and tell you I love you. You'd better come back to me in one piece, asshole."

I opened and closed my mouth a few times. "Oh. I'm always impressed with how much we are on the same page. Here." I held out a scroll, which shimmered as I pressed it against her. "This teleport is bound to wherever you are. If I get into any trouble, I'll be back in your arms in no time."

"Hmm." Ren held my face between her hands. "You aren't going to say it, but there's a chance the caster is retreating to Candlekeep. As big as your ego is, you still want the whole Guild to go against the Crimson Shadow."

"I'll leave as soon as the caster is dead. I know my limits." While I smiled, her eyes tried to read more pages of my mental diary.

"So full of bullshit," she murmured. "Come on then, Max. Get this show on the road."

I swung my eyes away from her and into my Guild Chat.

[Max: Everyone who didn't report in is likely in a coma state.]
[Max: We need to move everyone into the tavern.]

Consolidating all our soft targets made them both easier to protect as well as putting them at greater risk of being deleted by an explosion or similar. It was less trouble than having everyone split around, especially as I needed to get everyone on the same page.

After nearly an hour of hoisting the Guild members around, the six of us who were still awake—and now even more exhausted—were gathered in the bar area of the tavern. Devoid of any System-created other than a rather perplexed barkeep who was ignoring our conversation entirely.

I rolled out my aching neck, half wondering if I'd just drop to the ground asleep as soon as I stepped out of this town. No, I could endure. I turned my eyes to the Fateweaver.

"Tanya, I want the proximity-detection idols up. All of you need to focus on the defense of the sleepers, while Ren will scout from the rooftops. At this stage, *anything* that approaches will be killed on sight."

I didn't need to ask Quinn and Tanya what they had been up to that they had missed the cutoff point for staying awake. The notion of it being one of her idols held no weight once I saw their disheveled appearances and the sheepish way they had answered my sole probing question.

Not that I didn't trust them, but I was still antsy about leaving everyone here. Between Ren and Wolf, there was little I felt they couldn't handle. Plus, even if they got out of their depth, one message and I would be three seconds away from appearing back here. Not perfect, but it's what we had.

That said, there wasn't a face in the crowd that wanted me to leave. While they each carried heavy bags under their eyes, it was I alone who held the weight of the group's fate. Some ego involved, sure. But I was certain one of them was about to crack and relent to the fact that I was the . . .

"*Fine.*" Tanya sighed and rubbed her eyes. "If there's any one of us who can bullshit out of any dire situation, it's you. That doesn't give you the right to be reckless with your life. Understand?"

I looked among the gathered group for a glance of sympathy, but it was a hard sell. The toughest crowds just meant I'd need to try harder to win them over. I gave the Fateweaver a bow.

"Trust me," I replied, "I have no intention of meeting my end just yet." Thankfully, I managed to reel myself away from filling that sentence with a few stage-show references.

"A lot of people depend on you right now," Ren added. She had her arms crossed and had been simmering away behind a very valid scowl. To my benefit, I had also managed to withhold the statement that I thought she looked cute when mad.

The exhaustion was making my brain and tongue a little loose and frayed, however. The reason for her renewed ire wasn't due to my vanishing act, unfortunately. We'd already made the decision on the roof, and that deal was settled. The trouble had climbed back out of the grave once she realized that I wouldn't have the protection of her aura.

An aura that protected me from trauma, alongside some other important Status effects.

Now she was certain I was going to return a bloodied pulp.

A little pessimistic if you asked me, which she most certainly didn't. Her glare remained the second most effective, as Wolf wasn't happy about my solo adventure either.

But what was I to do? We were fortunate so many of us were night owls. A version of me from a little while ago might have left Ruby with the others and taken my Party to defeat Lady in Red. Even if something bad would happen to the sleepers. Now I was a little more audience centric and hated the idea of further needless loss of life.

At least for those allied to me. Candlekeep would soon be snuffed out by my hand.

We said our goodbyes, my time up. I needed to try to cut the caster off before they got too far away. Candlekeep seemed like a valid route of escape, but they might have holed up somewhere else.

I stepped out into the daylight, and Ren appeared in front of me. Before I could say anything, she put her arms around me and pulled me into a hug.

"You'll be without my Oathwarden protection when you're gone," she said softly. "Don't forget you promised not to break my heart again."

I held her. Who would have thought the grumpy foil to my suave charm back on the starting island would become such a natural part of my everyday life? I had spent most of the time moving the catatonic Guild members trying to think of a way that we could go together, but it was too risky. We were putting the others before our own selfish desire to never part, and I hoped that the System respected that.

"Do not fret. The show cannot run without the full cast. I will go to any length to return to your side."

She leaned back and gave me a peck on the nose. "No need for melodrama, trickster. Kill any fucker in your way and then do the opposite when you get back."

By the time I returned, it would be our turn for sleep while the others watched over us. Best-case scenario, our plans had been delayed by a day. Worst-case scenario . . . Well, I wouldn't think about that.

Ren moved away, and I gave her what I hoped was a convincing smile.

Although some part of my heart ached, I jumped up into the air, landing atop my summoned patron sword as if it was a hover board.

With a tip of my hat, I flew away from all my friends and safety. It was time to hunt.

CHAPTER FIFTY-SEVEN

Solo Tricks

While I had no doubt earned a few cool points by flying off on my sword, it turned out that it wasn't really made for such a purpose. It wasn't *just* because the eye on the hilt was constantly glaring at me throughout the journey. As soon as we were well out of sight of the town, I dropped down on the grass and sent the sword back to hell.

Not only did that wave of being sensible wash over me but so did a heavy amount of exhaustion. Outside the area of the spell that had been cast, I could now sleep. It was almost tempting too. *Just a quick nap and I'd be on my way.*

I shook my head and straightened my back out. *No.* The show was more important. Even as I felt the grains of my sanity drop through like an hourglass in my mind, I wouldn't rest until I had completed my mission.

With an unnecessary snap of my fingers, I switched places with my demonic ace high in the sky and turned into a demon. My wings caught me, allowing me to briefly hover in the air before slowly gliding forward. They weren't really good for anything more than short-term flight, but for gathering my bearings, it was very helpful.

My eyes scoured the northern scenery for three quick seconds before I switched places back to the ground.

There was a group heading this way. I'd need to get closer to learn if the caster was among them, but I hadn't a feeling they wouldn't be. Why risk losing the advantage?

More worrying than that was that farther north there were more groups of Monsters. I didn't have enough time to see if they were all heading this way, but the fires and the way the area near the city glowed with crimson light . . .

I'd never really had the time for video games back on Earth, but the situation reminded me of one I had seen once. A real-time strategy game where you had to build bases against an opponent, and then you would send out units of certain troops to capture locations or hunt for resources.

Not content with taking over the city, the Crimson Shadow was now expanding out and conquering the rest of the area. Unfortunately, we didn't have the time to fight fires. Cutting off the head of the beast should be enough to stop the progress of the blight seeping into the world. Something that I was partially tempted to go and attempt right now.

I drummed my fingers against my side. Actually, I was pretty sure I could feel the cold stare of Ren burning into the back of my head even as far away as I was now. I'd stick to the task at hand—the first port of call being intercepting these Monsters heading for the town. While I trusted the few Guild members still awake to handle themselves, I might be able to dig out some clues from the corpses I was about to make.

My demonic form dropped away, and I picked my top hat back up from the ground.

A good twenty minutes of walking later and . . .

Well, no. It wasn't really *good*. I ached and felt sleepy. We sorely lacked a way to travel faster than plodding along on foot. Even in the masses of scrolls and potions I had under my belt—figuratively speaking—there wasn't anything that was good for more than short bursts of speed.

And I wouldn't be caught running. Not headlong into danger. That would be a good way for me to crack open my skull, which I was *specifically* supposed to avoid. I didn't want to get into any trouble with the others.

Maybe they wouldn't find out though . . .

I was well aware I was slightly losing it. That didn't make it any easier to keep my mind out of control, but the lack of third-party accountability was troublesome. No protection from mental maladies, the threat of corruption still lingering at the edges of my mind, and a lack of sleep. Adding that to my desire to be completely uncontestable, I was likely to smudge the line soon enough.

What line that actually was I wasn't sure.

I paused and looked up at the trees. In a reversal of my usual luck, I could be the one to drop an ambush for a change. I hadn't gotten a good look at the approaching group, but I was sure they weren't Players. Too tall and uniform. If the Shadow had access to sending smarter Monsters at us, they'd do that rather than risk what few actual members they had left. We'd already cut down all the weaker parts of the group; the part that was able to fail upward remained.

With a few deft hops, I was up in the tree. Maybe overkill when I could turn invisible and teleport, but with enemies on their way to attack my friends, I wanted to go the extra mile.

My eyes switched through my Inventory, arranging everything. Demonic ace filled with five items. A hell bird already summoned a bit farther back into the woods. I could hear the growing applause of the audience . . . No, that was footsteps. Clamoring for the door, the crowd had to find their seats before the show started.

I hummed with potential, eager for the taste of Dazzle icons as if they were the only thing that could satiate me. Partially true.

Six figures stepped into view. Tall, bipedal, covered in dense black fur. Jackal-like heads and golden eyes that matched their sporadic armor. Each with a long weapon of similar metal. Powerful, I was sure, even if the System remained silent on what they were.

I dropped from the tree and landed in an empty space in front of them, causing their march to halt. "*Ta-da!*" I said, giving them a bow as I took down my hat. Not the most overt entrance, but my impatience had run roughshod over my need to impress.

"That's one of the forsaken," one of the Monsters said, his voice low and gravely.

"Man in Purple," the first agreed, baring his teeth at me. "The *prime* target that we must kill."

At first, I was most impressed at their range of vocabulary. Much like the demons in hell, it seemed these Monsters were capable of more thought and free will than most of the other System-created we had come across. Almost made it a shame that they had been sent to assassinate me.

"How about this," I countered. "Join my side and I will allow you true freedom."

The leader of the group didn't even spend a second to deliberate it. "No. Her will commands us, and we will not be swayed."

Rather than parley further, the group of six brought up their weapons. Surely they wouldn't be simple melee beaters. I raised an eyebrow, clasping my hands behind my back.

"Well, I at least gave you the choice." As I smiled, purple electricity cracked around my body, arcing back and forth. The first of them tensed to leap forward, right as my demonic ace dropped from the invisibility I had cast upon it. It was directly in the middle of them and burst out with a cold wave of magic as it cast frost burst from a scroll.

Three of the Monsters became rooted to the ground, ice shackling their feet. The leader hadn't been affected and lashed out at me with a long halberd. Quite a nice weapon, all things considered. Almost ornamental—which meant it had enough flare to make it quite fitting to be a prop in my shows.

I sidestepped the strike, which paused right before it hit the ground. White light trailed the bladed edge as the inertia took it at a sharp angle back toward me. It found my neck wanting and promptly lopped my head clean from my shoulders.

"Pitiful human," the leader spat.

<Active Learner> had picked up the Skill he had used, which was <Redirected Strike>. Once active, a dodged attack would turn into a critical hit instead. A respectable cooldown that prevented it from being too abusable, but all the same—it was something fun to play with.

I emerged from invisibility as the Monster gloated over my faux corpse. "Boo," I announced, flinging a magic card at him rather lazily.

He twisted and dove from the attack by instinct, my slower card rather easy to avoid. The purple switched to a bright red as it became critical, and I controlled it back into him with a flick. Not terribly accurate but, in striking the back of his shoulder, it burst and rendered that limb inoperable.

One of the frozen creatures had a bow. An arrow burst out toward me as soon as I had come back into sight. I summoned a shield into the air, the long projectile bursting through and shattering my <Card Fan> as well. My eye turned to the side as they drew a second arrow up, while another cast a spell at me.

Quite the interesting fight. They were like a full Party of varied classes—once I had taken a moment to clock their weapon choices. Even as a ball of fire rushed toward me, I could see another Monster casting some manner of healing spell on the leader I had wounded.

I switched position with my dove, the bird immediately immolated in the burst of fire. My feet shuffled for a comfortable position atop my cannon as it fired out the first bloom of confetti. Demonic ace pulsed with energy as it activated a second frost burst. Their ranger had already spotted me off at my new position in the trees—even before the colorful paper washed through the terrain—but the others were a couple of seconds slower.

Ranger. Healer. Spellcaster. Leader. Fighter . . . And the fact that I couldn't see the sixth meant there was some kind of rogue. The fighter didn't look too pleased, being one of the ones stuck by the ice both times, leaving him unable to come and hit me with his mace.

As a second arrow whistled through the air toward me, the leader also threw his halberd—gaining a Hellhound latched to his empty hands as a reward. I was already out of defensive options and took the arrow to the right thigh. The thrown weapon hit my cannon and then went into my Inventory—as did the arrow, my <Demonic Regeneration> starting to patch up the wound. Not quite enough Damage to refresh the cooldown on <Last Act>, so I'd force it.

While the leader wrestled with my Hellhound, a lightning Imp unleashed his spell through the group of Monsters. I had a card in my hand that I pooled all my Mana into before drawing through my Health as well. Just enough to drop below 80 percent. Then I flung it.

Right wrist held by left hand, I controlled it through the air, zipping around those gathered.

To their credit, their defenses were considerably better than most I had faced. The fighter used a shield to deflect the card before the spellcaster put up a magical barrier to protect himself and the healer. A slight cut across the ranger, who couldn't roll away due to the ice, and then the card dissipated against a plate of armor.

Cannon blasted a bag of flour out in an arc, causing a cloud of fine particles to quickly fill the space in front of me—silhouetting the shape of the rogue trying to sneak up on me. Follow-up shot was a lit lantern.

I switched places with my Hellhound, bringing the stolen halberd down on the flat-footed leader.

He went to catch it by instinct, his fingers flopping off as I drove it into his clavicle.

Fire reflected in his eyes as the flour ignited, exploding and setting the rogue on fire. "Just what are you?" he growled as the blade inched deeper into him. Screams echoed around the woodlands as their healer tried to help the burning creature out.

"Oh." I smiled, purple lightning still arcing around my body. "More of a monster than you'll ever be."

CHAPTER FIFTY-EIGHT

Special Guest

I took a deep breath in and then released it. Repeated this motion, as I tried to quieten down the show tune blaring in my ears. A little ditty for yours truly alone. Blood dripped from my hands, warmth clinging to me in patches all over my suit. My aching eyes looked away from the 30 percent Health warning that was slowly ticking up to my demonic patron.

The sword was equally running with crimson, droplets falling to the grass as though he was self-cleaning. Perhaps he was. His single eye regarded me with its usual impassiveness, focused on the star of the show rather than the faceless audience who had faded into obscurity.

Or at least an early grave. Plus, I had only removed the face of *one* of the Monsters.

"You can go now," I told him, shattering both the music rolling around my skull and any postbattle mania threatening to turn me to mush.

It was hard to gauge the difficulty of the fight, all things considered. After all, the times where I fought on my own had become few and far between. Survival was almost guaranteed, although it had been touch and go without Ren's usual healing and shields that I took for granted. Not to mention Wolf taking part attention of a group. I didn't think it would be too out-there to suggest that these six creatures fought better and more cohesively than a lot of Players we had met in our time here.

In fairness, they had been designed that way. Real people were . . . unpredictable. Flawed. Most Crimson Shadow probably hadn't been working together for very long, and it was hard to get that unit effectiveness put in place without time and respect.

I shook my hands off as my patron returned to hell and surveyed the destruction. Extensive. I would be willing to admit I had gone a little over the top. Two purple cards still danced around me in orbit, only controlled by my subconscious still. After letting them fade away, I pulled my foot from a sticky mess of Monster guts.

No trauma.

Not entirely unexpected, given the things I'd seen and done lately. These being thinking and talking creatures felt odd. As if it put them closer to Wolf . . . or me, I supposed. Created by the System but with some manner of free will. To think the whole world should be filled with such Monsters, but instead we had been left with this empty and unfulfilling existence.

[Max: No sign of spellcaster.]
[Max: Intercepted a group of Monsters coming toward you.]
[Ren: ARE YOU OKAY]
[Max: Not until I am back in your arms, moonflower.]
[Ren: I miss you~]
[Quinn: Could you at least do this in private^]
[Ren: never]
[Max: I'll keep you updated.]

The group hadn't given up any information when pressed for either the location of the spellcaster or what was actually going on in Candlekeep. Not surprising but still disappointing.

I looked over to a shaded area under the trees, wondering if I could steal a nap. *A very well-deserved nap.* The last time I had tried that, I had been kidnapped and nearly tortured to death. That said . . . I *was* very tired. Instead of submitting to rest, I dug through my Inventory.

Into my hand, a fire-resistance potion. While I didn't need the actual effect of the magical liquid, it had the side effect of tasting . . . spicy. A little like aniseed and pepper that stayed warm in your throat like a rough whiskey. Based on the one time I'd mistakenly tried that alcohol. Tasted horrible but might perk me up.

I downed it while holding my nose. Coughed as the empty bottle went back into the stack in my intangible space. I blinked away the watering eyes and felt slightly more alert. Less likely to be burned.

Looting through the bodies gave me little of value. I took the remaining weapons as they looked nice, but other than some gold and basic items I'd funnel to Percius, it wasn't worth the effort. Other than saving the team back at the town a headache anyway. Ren and Wolf wouldn't have had too much issue with that group, but I was happy to take that burden away from them.

I stretched out and considered my options. There had been a lot of activity closer to the city, but it didn't tell me much about what the best plan now was.

The longer we went without waking up the others, the worse things would get. Our plan of grinding out the Dungeon for most of the day had been shattered, but we couldn't exactly march on the Lady immediately.

Not without a nap first, at least.

Like before, I switched into the sky to get the lay of the land. Eyes scoured for any sort of hint of whom to impress to death next. I returned to the ground with such a target.

Over to the west and slightly north, there was another stone tower, much like the one where we'd assisted Leyla's Party in getting their kidnapped friends back. There was another group of System-created around it, as if they were guarding it. It was also a reasonable distance away for a spellcaster to run off and get some sleep for themselves after ruining our night.

Sure, I was filling in some of the narrative gaps there to suit my tired expectations, but I had long learned to trust my gut. Never mind the System fudging things to my benefit. I was more than capable of having a decent idea of what was ahead. A lot more bloodshed, for certain. Some answers and resolution to the current problem . . . I was willing to say *yes*.

With that decided mentally, my feet took me off in that direction. A good hour or so walk, where I would no doubt start to become further frayed at the edges. Such a shame that the only places I could teleport to were behind me.

I snapped my fingers. That just reminded me of my other responsibilities.

With a grin on my face, I stepped forward into the warmth of hell. The familiar throne room now had a wide table in it with a dozen chairs in various states of being knocked over or being occupied by bloody corpses.

As a group of Imps dragged one of the large bodies out through the doorway, I turned a raised eyebrow to the floating sword.

"This is the fourth set of council members, my king." His impassive eye turned from me to the mostly decapitated group bleeding out everywhere.

"Excellent. Any challengers impatiently awaiting my return?" The more time the demons in hell spent bickering and being killed off by my very clear and mostly fair rules, the less time they'd have to gather up against me.

"Just the one. Buk'la Apku. She *has* been told that you wanted three top challengers, but she keeps killing the others who rank that high."

I nodded diplomatically. Quite a strong demon then. Killing her would be a good idea, but it sounded like she was doing a great job of getting rid of any upstarts that might threaten my crown.

"Do me a favor," I asked my patron. "Tell her that I offer her the position of King's Champion and War General. She'll have to continue testing any potential challengers, but if she still wants to try for my crown, that is fine—I just can't right now."

"As you wish, my king." The sword bobbed in the air. "It is likely she will want to challenge you. If you have to subjugate her, it is fifty-fifty on whether she would prefer death rather than serve in that position . . . but I believe the offer is fair to you both."

"Glad to hear it." I eyed my throne. Given that there was time dilation between here and the real world, I could probably get some sleep here and it would be much less time out there. Even abandoning my Guild for a couple of hours was untenable, however. Anything could happen, and I had to push forward until they were safe.

I waved my hand to produce the return portal back to the area I had come from. "Oh, and great work in the fight. I appreciate it."

"It is my pleasure to serve . . . although I question why you do not wield me and are more than happy for me to act independently."

"I wouldn't want to do you a disservice." I shot him a smile. "You are competent alone, and I am more comfortable using spells . . . but we'll see what the future brings."

Cool air washed over me, somehow making me feel more tired than the warmth of hell. Back in the forest, the clearing filled with the blood and corpses of my last act. I walked toward the tower I had seen, my outfit vanishing as I told the System to repair it—leaving me to travel in my underwear.

Something that was sure to earn the scorn of Ren were she here, all the while as she ogled me like she hadn't seen it before. There was a danger in being without my armor, sure. That was the end of that thought. The only benefit was arriving to my next fight looking as dazzling as I deserved to be.

My demonic ace hovered up beside me as I filled it with new items. Assaulting a regiment and tower was a big ask, in some ways. Especially alone. Luckily, I had more than one trick up my sleeve—in fact, I was known for them.

I hummed to myself, climbing over fallen logs and trying to avoid nettles as I wandered toward my target in my lack of clothing.

With my tired eyes flicking through my tabs, I somehow managed to cancel the cleaning process on my gear and had to restart it, adding another five minutes of exhibitionism to the total. While I grumbled to myself for the action, I only had myself to blame.

Something that echoed around my skull as I stepped on a rock, hopping from the pain to then step awkwardly on some angled terrain, twisting my ankle. I rolled across the grass and slid to my side. I groaned. The only thing making this a terrible place to have an impromptu nap was more stone hidden among the soft grass—something the side of my head had found the painful way.

Time rhymes or something like that.

Still, there were some pretty flowers here. I should take a couple for Ren. Pushing myself up to my feet, I withdrew a regeneration potion, if only to make me feel better about . . .

I paused, the glass at my lips, as my eyes looked slowly to the side at the figure now standing a dozen feet away.

"Oh," I said. "Lady in Red, I presume."

CHAPTER FIFTY-NINE

Unknown Shades

Part of me was sick with disappointment. Lady in Red had been such a mysterious figure out of our reach for so long that the eventual reveal felt . . . premature. I had wondered if, in finally seeing her, there would be a twist where I'd recognize her from somewhere.

But no. Before me stood a woman in a thick red dress, a similarly colored wide-brimmed hat on her head. Conventionally attractive, although she looked almost as tired as I felt. Slightly off too. If she told me she was a vampire, I would believe that wholeheartedly. Black hair down just past her shoulders, pale skin, and a wry smile full of confidence. A lady in red.

"Correct, that is the name I go by," she said, even if my question was more rhetorical. "Before you try to attack me, this is a just a Visage of me. I am not here." Her dark eyes ran me up and down like I was a piece of meat ready to be diced up. "I must say, Max. You are full of surprises."

I drank down the potion, hoping the System would hurry up and put my clothes back on. Once the gross tang of the drink left my mouth, I gave her a sour expression and shrugged. "To what do I owe the displeasure? Here to beg for your life?"

It was a miracle that I had my temper in check. I wasn't sure whether it was learning that the mythical woman was just a flesh and blood idiot like the rest of us or her presence commanded something else that had me calm . . . but I was a hair trigger away from testing if the Visage thing was just a ruse.

The wry grin left her face. "You are an impudent toddler messing in things you don't understand. Ready to burn the world to ashes so that you can rule over whatever debris remains."

I practically spluttered with indignation. "That is what *you* are doing. How many people have you killed or corrupted so you can rule on high?"

"I'm doing what is *best* for the System," she snapped back. Her body was tense, but she hadn't budged an inch aside from her face.

Crossing my arms, I turned to face her properly. "Only by your own metrics and worldviews. Flawed and murderous ones."

The Lady worked her jaw, clearly holding back a rebuttal. Eventually, she exhaled through her nose. "Max. You are smart and competent. I'd much rather a strong ally than a foolish enemy. You have undone my work through the last two areas, but I promise you, if you or any of your hapless Guild steps into Candlekeep, then I will kill you all."

"Threats don't really work on me." I shook my head. "I don't know how or what you've been doing, but we will not stand down when our lives are at stake either way."

"Those strong and loyal to me have a place. You've seen the fully realized System-created now, have you not? My team can fix the System and set things right. You can help with that."

I had to admit that I was interested in and impressed with the Monsters that I had just dismembered. Not quite enough to betray my friends, those I loved, and the people we had lost along the way. Even the assholes I had murdered to get here deserved some closure and not to just be a stepping stone for me to jump into the Lady's arms at the first attempt at coercion.

My hand went up. "I'm done talking with you." I snapped my fingers, and my outfit appeared back on me. "Peddle your silver words somewhere else."

Her expression twisted into disgust, as if my dismissal was something foul to gobble up. While she sneered, I wondered if she was about to reveal that this was a ruse and she really *was* here. Something told me she wasn't that shortsighted.

"As you wish, Max." She shook her head, the sour look falling away to be replaced with a confident smirk once more. "I have given you enough chances to be a part of the winning team. The people who not only want to but *can* save Othea. When you lose everyone you love and have nothing but death to comfort you in this failed existence, don't come crying to me."

Not allowing me to get the last word in, the figure started to dissipate, as if she was made of dense smoke. The fact that she had an icon over her head telling me she was nothing more than a Visage created by someone was a spoiler I had been trying to ignore, but I didn't want to take any chances.

Twin purple cards spun out around me, spiraling in a tight orbit as I drained my Mana to empower them. With an increasing tempo, I twisted them around in an expanding circle. Grass and flowers were lopped and shredded before my attack dissipated about twenty feet out.

I regained my breath, fresh blood running from my hands as a few trees slowly collapsed in the background. I had scoured the area near me, everything in that radius torn to pieces. *Safe* wasn't really the right word, but I was alone.

Stretching out my shoulders, I sighed and decided how to break the bad news to Ren.

[Max: Hey . . . moonflower.]
[Ren: Did you DIE? I'll be so pissed. What's with that guilty message?]
[Max: Still living, I promise you.]
[Max: I had a run in with Lady in Red. Sort of.]
[Ren: Did she DIE? I'm so pissed. What do you mean *sort of*?]
[Max: Some manner of projection of her real self.]
[Max: She just wanted to try to entice me onto her side once again.]
[Max: Gave vague allusions to something bad I've already half forgotten.]
[Ren: How annoying. I thought up all those new bad words
to call her in hell.]
[Ren: I hope I'm there next time.]
[Max: Me too. Anyway, be alert as she is likely to try something untoward.]
[Max: Now that I've turned her down again.]
[Ren: Last ditch of desperation yada yada. We're safe.
You stay safe, handsome.]

I smiled as I closed the windows down. It didn't really matter what the Lady was up to or if the Crimson Shadow had been working for some greater good all along. I knew those were just words to try to sway me, but even if true . . . I just fought on the side of *Ren and me being on top*. Stars of the show, happy and peaceful. Or at least with as much peace as we could stand.

Truth was, I didn't mind being the bad guy if it meant being beside her. We'd taken our fair share of lives trying to do what was right. *The road to hell is paved with good intentions.* Fuck that. We had been to hell. Traveled that road out the other side and continued committing sin ever since.

As my feet took me in the direction of the tower once again, I remembered I was also losing it slightly. Not the best time of day to be ruminating over moral quandaries.

I pulled out a sandwich from my Inventory. Prepared earlier . . . or maybe yesterday. The System didn't care to tell me, and it tasted as good as if I had only just created it. Normally, I didn't like to eat while on the job. In fact, I wasn't even hungry. I placed it back into my Inventory half eaten.

Instead, I spun out a card over my palm. Just to get a feel of it and keep my hand busy as I walked.

Just how could the Lady create System-created that actually acted and thought as if they were real? While one part of me would love to see the world fully fleshed out and filled with active towns and a thriving population, I doubted that she had used a normal and safe way to do it.

The fact that the first example I had seen from her was a group that was sent to track me down and kill me painted my expectations for what the future might bring. Perhaps she should have led with the negotiations before putting a hit out on me.

I kicked a small rock through the grass as I walked absentmindedly. Not that it would have changed my answer. Even if we all swore fealty, it wouldn't be long before our power was too much of a threat. We were just two forces opposed to each other. Nothing would ever change that.

But could I really change *anything*? After all that I had been through . . . was there even a realistic end goal to my attempts? I felt drained, my energy completely leaking from my body like a colander. It wasn't even fear but . . . a worry that I wouldn't amount to anything. Why should I?

Demonic Magician but what did that really mean? I was the king of hell but didn't feel competent enough to decide on whether I wanted to eat a sandwich or not. I'd been getting by on luck and the System holding my hand . . . so what would my life be like beyond that? Even if I could win—whatever that meant— the prospect of being content with my lot seemed just as fantastical as . . . all this other bullshit.

I sighed, and my body shivered as a cool wave of . . . maybe just a fresh breeze? The cool air washed over me, despite being properly dressed now. I stopped for a moment and frowned out at the empty woodland in front of me.

"You look like you have a lot on your mind, Max."

I turned an eyebrow to the side. "I certainly do, Ren."

There she was, my faithful companion and other half. Bright-red hair flowing in curls over her freckled and scarred face, deep-green eyes burning into me. In her hands she held her signature battle-ax, the sharp and hungry edge glinting as it caught the sunlight.

"I'm surprised you didn't try to attack the Lady. I guess that's what you keep replaying in your head." She smiled softly—but there was a desire, just the smallest spark, hinting that she wanted to find out the contents of my skull firsthand. One of the few places Ren hadn't been. Unless after the horse attack . . .

"Oh, you know me." I grinned. "I am a master of seeing through illusions, so I knew she was just a weird cloud version of herself. That's not what I'm thinking about, however."

"No?" Her expression dulled a little. "How about getting to this tower so we can save our friends then?"

I nodded eagerly. Close enough. "Got it in one, moonflower. However, a much more important thought has just crossed my mind."

"Right . . ." Ren brushed some copper curls behind her ear before grasping at the hefty melee weapon once more. "Like what?"

My facial muscles ached as I smiled wider. "I was just thinking, my dear . . . The day is young, and I have just killed off the threat to our sleeping Guild. Why don't we make the best of it and have a bit of a date together?"

She shook her head slowly. "Keep your head in the game, Max. Just turn around and let's get to the tower."

Maybe she was right. Even if I was crazy—*and I was crazy*—I shouldn't be putting my own desires over the priorities of the Guild. Friends needed saving. Something that had become my responsibility.

"You . . ." I ran my tongue across my dry lips. "You don't think we could just run away from all of this? We deserve a vacation, do we not?"

"Max." Ren's hands tightened on the axe, her knuckles whitening. "You are clearly tired. Let's sort this tower out and then we can rest."

Ever the fountain of wise words, Ren was right. There was plenty of time for being selfish after the day was won. The next few days needed a lot of winning, at least. I should be trying to work beside my elfin wife, not arguing with her. After all, I had traveled all this way for the sole purpose of destroying the tower. Would be rude to be late for my appointment.

I gave her a bow, and she shuffled slightly. My head swam slightly with vertigo as I stood back up straight, and she looked tense. Things had been difficult for us all lately. "I apologize, Ren. You, of all people, know how I get when I am tired and stressed."

She nodded her agreement with that statement but had little to add.

With a smile, I turned to lead her toward the tower. Today was going to be *one of those days*—I could feel it.

Right before I felt the displacement of air as Ren's axe whistled through the air toward the back of my skull.

CHAPTER SIXTY

Disillusioned

The thing about using <Last Act> was that it had to be a conscious decision for the most part. Usually, the split second of pain or flash of immediate danger was enough for my lucid brain to trigger the reaction even when attacked by surprise. Exhausted, manic, and beside the one I loved, I wasn't exactly physically on high alert.

I doubted that the woman standing over my corpse knew the nuance of this Skill, yet she looked just as surprised when I appeared from invisibility with a smile on my face.

"How?" she asked through clenched teeth, stepping away from my faux corpse to brandishing her axe at the ready. "I *knew* I had you charmed."

"Even though my Skill removes most maladies, part of me still believes that you are Ren. *Are you?*" I raised an eyebrow and my right hand. "No, that's a silly question. To answer it, I have three points." The woman who might not be Ren bared her teeth, a red sheen blooming around the head of her axe—something that matched the red handprint on her forehead. An odd fashion accessory that didn't really suit her, or perhaps that was my own personal preference.

"First off," I began, "you cannot see this, but I have a very specific debuff on me right now." I pointed my hand in the air where it would be if she could see it.

[Mild trauma]

"You see, faux Ren, it is only fitting that the greatest showman in the world would also have the most powerful impostor syndrome. *So* much so that I could traumatize myself with it. It makes sense, don't you agree?"

"*No.*" She should probably attack me now if she wasn't Ren. Clearly tense, she had expected her potential ruse to work, and now her options were limited. I knew this.

The real Ren would protect me from trauma—a known fact. My brief panic about being successful or competent wasn't particularly damning, but in my current state, it had affected me in a very real sense—even if current events had washed away my self-doubt.

"Second, as I told you, I am a master of illusion. You really didn't think I would notice you weren't Ren?" She *might* still be Ren, and I'd feel about silly about the rest of this conversation. "So before you decide whether to attack or teleport away— your only real options—let me present you my third and final point."

Teleportation was probably her safest bet. They'd tried this thing before and knew of the success rate. Perhaps knowing my lack of sleep would have me exhausted, and that I was alone, I could be taken advantage of. Normally I'd allow that from Ren, although I couldn't remember the bite of an axe being part of that. The puzzle pieces were misaligned.

Still, it didn't really matter anymore.

Every spear, sword, and sharp object dropped from my Inventory at once, agony flooding my eyes as my tired brain ran roughshod over my current limits. Almost immediately after, my demonic ace used a scroll of air gust at the exact same time as my wrist-mounted holder fired off *exactly* the same spell.

Even with the flicker of her defensive Abilities, the faux Ren couldn't fight back against it. The double gust blew the collection of weaponry like a dandelion losing its seeds. A few were dodged or blocked, but the sheer number made it an inevitability. As most of the items thudded and slid along the grass behind her, the woman slumped over, pierced like a pincushion.

She *wasn't* Ren.

I knew that for certain now. Even with her Skill no longer affecting my mind, I was also sure my heart wouldn't have survived me killing the real Ren. For this Crimson Shadow assassin, I felt . . . nothing. Not even anger or disgust. Disappointed, maybe. Another life thrown away, their souls spent like currency to try to buy me out. I was consistently outside the scope of the Lady's budget, but that didn't stop her from trying to haggle for my demise.

Just something that left me with blood on my hands and a sore need for a sandwich.

Now I only had half of one. Doomed to only being partially satiated.

I sighed and rolled out my neck.

If there was a lesson to be learned here, it was that the Crimson Shadow were incapable of learning lessons. Maybe the Lady was a little more lax with letting her Players get murdered now that she was able to create functioning System-created.

Neither was truly a threat to me . . . and yet she now had more pawns to waste. As long as she stayed out of reach, she would be safe. Her minions would only need to get lucky once to be rid of me. It would almost be negligent for her to not constantly send minor threats our way. Even if we flattened them time and time again, our resources were being drained. We *would* tire.

The chance of us catching up on a good sleep was now slim. Maybe if we set up watches throughout the night . . . but even then I'd be paranoid. As much as we felt as though we were backing our prey into a corner she couldn't escape from, the Lady was also playing to the tune of something sly. Drawing us into her lair and flipping to showing her strongest hand while we were still recovering.

I stooped down beside the impaled woman as I idly recovered all my weapons strewn about. Double casting a scroll alongside my demonic ace was probably not intended. Then again, I was sure the System had long given up trying to put me in a reasonable box.

The gear on the woman was boring at best, but I took everything magical for Percius to destroy later. Four power tokens, which I assumed she must have found along the way, as the Crimson Shadow seemed to pool important resources rather than leave them on the soon-to-be corpses sent my way.

I huffed to myself as I stood, taking the last of my exploded Inventory with me. The thought of the first time I used <Last Act> circled around my mind. How pleased I had been that it had erased my trauma until Ren shattered that illusion by telling me it was her new aura. Not that I should complain . . . but since that day, we had barely spent any time apart. I had grown used to my sanity being shackled together, even with corruption pulling on the chains.

Now I had trauma. Sleep would fix it, but I couldn't sleep. Instead, I just pulled a grim smile and started back off toward the tower. My tired brain ran through the checklist of things I'd need to do.

Kill the spellcaster. Teleport back to Ren. Sleep in hell.

Whatever came after that wasn't as important. Sticking with three simple steps would keep me from stumbling before I could accomplish anything worthwhile. My skull was already on a collision course with a hard object. All I had to do was delay the inevitable until I was back around people who could put me back together after the fact.

My eyes cycled through my Inventory as I walked, trying to put things back in order. The elephant in the room was that this spellcaster might be the puppet master with Guardian powers. It was the reason we had been unable to sleep even before the spell went off. It was partially likely that they were also just escorting the person who cast the magic. I would find out when I got closer to the tower.

The thought of becoming even more powerful was . . . sickening to some degree. What could a second Guardian ability even grant me? If it was wish based, would it just decide on what was second best? I didn't even know what my other wish would be, aside from saving this world . . . I had pretty much all that I could ask for.

Everything else would come naturally, surely.

I paused at a stream running through the woodlands, briefly enamored with the sound of it. Calming. My eyes drifted back and forth over how the flow of the clear water picked up the morning sunlight. It relaxed me in the worst way. Reminded me of the cottage and Ren. Drew me closer to taking a fateful nap. I blinked slowly before switching positions with my demonic ace on the other side of the embankment.

It felt . . . sad to leave it behind. Even as I stepped away, toward my goal, part of me wanted to stay and rest.

To keep my mind sharp, I spun out a card of purple energy and swirled it around my hand. I wasn't too happy to have gotten myself into this situation. Bravado had convinced me I could just go off on my lonesome to solve this problem.

With clearer minds, we could have arranged something a little safer. I had tipped the balance too close to the rest of the Guild being the priority—the truth being I would not forgive myself if anything happened to any of them. Even if the three of us—Ren, Wolf, and I—went off to do this mission with enough teleportation to come back to Ruby should anything dangerous arise . . . it still left too much potential for things to go wrong.

It still could. For as powerful as we three had become, we worked best together. Our bluff had been called, and the Lady now knew I was still awake and on my way to break the curse. The Crimson Shadow didn't know who else had avoided the sleeping spell but would find out as soon as they got within sniper-rifle range.

I hummed to myself as the magic card danced in the air in front of me. Maintaining a basic one had become something that barely dented my Mana these days. The only reason I didn't have two of the things circling around me constantly was it took a little too much of my concentration, even if minimal.

It was much different to summoning one of my demons when . . .

I paused as my card vanished away. How strange. I hadn't allowed it to dissipate. Perhaps my tired mind wasn't focused enough to keep it in check—that seemed a reasonable deduction. My hand raised, and I attempted to bring out a new one.

Nothing happened.

Confused, I looked around, half expecting to find someone else sent by the Lady to mess with me. However, unless they had excellent stealth capabilities, I was still alone. Working my jaw, I tried to bring out one of my faithful Hellhounds to the floor beside me.

Nothing happened.

The part of my mind that was suffering the most started to wonder if the System had finally caught up with the paperwork I had been creating and decided to cut me off from all the undue power. With slight panic in my eyes, I brought up my STAR menus and went to my Skill page. Everything was still there.

I frowned at my hands, glaring at my outstretched palms as if they could be the cause of this new malady. No. Despite everything I had been through, they looked the same as the day I had arrived here. Just . . . now sporting the ring that signaled I was married to Ren.

She wasn't the likely culprit, however. Nor did I feel there was anything specifically wrong with *me*. As I continued to walk and fail at summoning cards, I looked over at where my demonic ace should be. It had vanished as well.

With a raised eyebrow, I opened my Map.

Exhaustion made the travel take no time at all. Without realizing it, I was very close to the tower now. Even without knowing the exact details, the puzzle picture was clear enough.

They had some manner of antimagic field over the area.

I smiled and flexed my fingers out. This would be a difficult show to perform.

Time to do some magic the old-fashioned way.

CHAPTER SIXTY-ONE

Twirl and Bow

My thighs burned as I sat crouched just behind a thick bush. While the month spent grinding through hell had done wonders for my natural fitness, I wasn't superhuman. Some days I felt barely human at all.

I blinked away my roving thoughts to glare at the tower ahead of me. It was similar in design and construction to the one we had fought through nearer the center of this area. Probably—if my vague recollection of the lore was correct—it was an outpost for the Crown, or whatever the King and Queen's royal guard called themselves. A stone wall surrounded a courtyard area, a wide-open gate sporting three figures dressed in plate and holding spears.

The red accents to their armor and sloppy crimson handprints on their breastplates gave me little pause over whose side they were on. From where I was positioned, I could see maybe a dozen of these guards positioned or patrolling around the inside of this compound. The tower itself was three stories high, and although the thin windows were darkened and offered no hint of who might be inhabiting the structure, the two guards with crossbows up in the battlements signaled that there were likely to be more inside.

Something of a hindrance for someone who could no longer cast spells or use any magic—demonic in nature or not. No shielding, feigning death, teleportation, invisibility, demons, or a cannon to assist me. A smarter and more put-together Max might call this a wash and head back home. Perhaps suggest that Ren should have been the one to carry out this assassination after all.

Unfortunately, that Max wasn't home right now.

All I saw were audience members that needed dazzling.

I had spent ten minutes observing the tower, and little had changed. No odd noises or lights. Other than the set patrols that repeated every one minute and thirteen seconds, there was no other movement here. The System-created guards were level fourteen, which wouldn't be an issue for me normally . . . but without the use of most of my repertoire—and the sheer number of opponents—I was in for quite the show.

In saying that, I doubted I would be able to bring out my Domain either. How droll. My eyes left the tower, my sluggish mind content enough I knew what lay before me. I spent a few minutes rearranging my Inventory for the new acts I needed to pull off. Despite Percius disenchanting a lot of gear, I had still kept a few decent weapons that had worthwhile effects.

Not to mention all the potions and consumables were fair game, even if the scrolls wouldn't work. With how quickly I could cycle through my menus and manipulate items, perhaps this would even be a fair fight for a change.

I ran my tongue across my teeth and considered my entrance.

Most acts on my regular playlist were out of the picture. No easy Dazzles, appearing on the roof, or flashy showmanship. They were likely to attack on sight, which ruled out the charisma approach. I only slightly regretted using up all the disguise potions with Ren. Still, where there was a will . . .

Much like the first tower, I chose to approach it from backstage. It was the most common way a magician arrived, of course. With the dense tree cover, I approached the back corner of the perimeter wall without those at the top of the tower spotting me. Not that it made the next part of the plan any easier.

From my Inventory I created a ladder made of stacked chairs and small tables. Barely stable, but it only needed to be utilized once. Hopefully, in addition to fixing the curse, I would be able to find whatever—or whoever—was causing this magical interference and put a stop to that. If so, then my escape was guaranteed.

Before committing to stepping out on stage, I decided sending a message over to the others would be a good idea. I was no longer able to teleport to Ren to assist them—plus I needed someone to tell me to break a leg. If only to save my skull from the effort.

[Max: About to assault the tower.]
[Max: There is an antimagic field, so I'm working around that.]
[Ren: . . .]
[Tanya: Isn't that most of what you do?]
[Quinn: What about demons^]
[Ren: He can do a lot more than that, but that doesn't sound safe.]
[Max: I am fine. More than fine. Finest.]
[Ren: You have trauma, don't you, you motherfucker?]
[Max: Oh no, Chat is now magical, and I can't—]

I left the message there, sure that even if I survived the tower, then the others would break me in half on my return. Unfair of me, perhaps. If it were Ren in this situation, then I'd be worried sick. I was sure she could read between the lines and knew that I couldn't return.

With one last dust down, my suit looked in near-pristine condition. Hat fit comfortably on my hair that still needed a cut. I was smiling and wasn't sure for how long that had been the case. Everything was in order.

I hopped on the first chair, my makeshift heap of furniture groaning and rattling as I stepped between the various layers. Just as the whole thing threatened to collapse, I reached the pinnacle and leaped over the wall. As soon as I landed, I dropped to a crouch, obscured by the shadows of some large crates.

Without the ability to scout or otherwise glance into the courtyard proper, I instead held my breath and waited to see if any of the guards had spotted me. To my benefit, it seemed as though System-created were even more blind to Players that were much higher level than them. I had first noticed when the Guild was leveling yesterday, when Wolf had to be almost upon the Monsters before they cared to attack him.

That didn't mean I could get away with murder, especially when the guards here were already set to look out for intruders. With one of said guards just around the other side of these crates, I had expected to at least alert one of them. Yet, silence followed my entrance—something usually soul shattering for a prominent magician such as myself—aside from the sound of the patrols going at their regular pace.

I was pretty sure that at some point I had acknowledged that I was not built for stealth missions. It was almost the opposite of how I preferred to do things. I wanted to be seen. I wanted to impress. I wanted to eat the other half of that sandwich.

My hunger could only be quelled by the bedazzlement of my foes. A tale as old as time.

From my Inventory, I pulled out a gold coin, shifting myself slightly to fling it over against the back wall behind me. There was a sharp clink of the metal hitting the stone wall before the flat circle bounced across the short grass.

As if acting to the script I had written out, I heard the guard nearby grunt and shuffle in his armor. Into my right hand I withdrew a slim blade, whereas my left held a thick cloth. I listened intently as the guard walked around the crate, his metal armor scraping slightly against the brickwork as he moved through the gap toward the sound.

Through the shadows of the nearby canopy and crates here, he stepped out from the gap, his eyes looking at the back wall where the coin had struck. Before he had the chance to look to his right where I had been hiding, I was there upon him.

Slim blade cut through the small space between his armor, just above his clavicle and into his neck, as my left hand wrapped around him and covered his mouth with the cloth. His muffled surprise was drowned out with his own blood as I pulled him to the ground. Not quite silent but it didn't take him long to be out of the picture.

I went to loot him, pulling out some low-tier magical gloves, as well as two flasks of water and a handful of gold coins. Pretty much as expected, although that gave me something else to consider.

Most of my Equipment was magical in nature—providing Stats and other such benefits. Did the aura affecting this area also prevent those from being used?

A quick check of my Stats screen showed that I was still receiving the benefit of everything I was wearing, so thankfully, whatever spell had been cast here did not mess with gear. Silver linings.

It was unlikely that I'd be able to repeat the same process with the rest of the guards. Other than one of the patrols, nobody else really came close enough to get distracted by something so simple. Not only that, but as soon as I ran out of space for corpses, it would only take one of them getting spotted for the alarm to be raised.

Even exhausted and slightly insane, I still had an ego about me. This was still an easily winnable situation. As much as the sensible part of me still clinging on to the edges of whatever wits I had left knew that getting inside the tower would be difficult once I had been found out, I still felt there was a way as long as I was still breathing.

I held my breath and drew out a crossbow into each hand. There were three more loaded ones in my Inventory, and the majority of the guards didn't look to have ranged capabilities. My favorite kind. Aside from the ones on the roof and perhaps a few others. Without my usual defensive Skills, I'd need to be careful about taking too much Damage.

Exhaling, I stepped into the gap where the guard had come from. Sunlight illuminated the courtyard ahead, the silver-and-red System-created standing around a stark contrast to the dull grass and shadows provided by the tower.

My hand went up, and I fired the first bolt. The guard ahead of me reacted by instinct, twisting to the side to dodge the attack. Unfortunately for them, the Skill I had stolen earlier from the doglike troupe wasn't a spell. The dodged bolt bloomed with critical energy as it struck my actual target slightly downrange from the closer one, the extra power enough to drive the sharp projectile through their helmet.

Second crossbow had already been fired as soon as the man had spun to the side, this bolt striking him in the inner elbow where it was less protected. Clutching at the wound, he dropped his spear as his arm became limp.

Enter stage right. Before he had the chance to recover and yell out, I was upon him, my Knife of the Trickster finding an eye socket with ease. Of course, this amount of open violence caught the attention of the rest of the crowd. Three bows were drawn on me as the rest of the outside guard turned and started to make a beeline toward my position.

I ran my tongue across my teeth, a wide grin cracking through with electric mania.

This was what I lived for. What I killed for. That and sandwiches.

With a quick flourish, I swooped a cape around me, obscuring me from my detractors. Their arrows found a place within the thick velvet with a series of hard thunks. I spun away from the wooden door I had withdrawn to protect myself, almost stumbling straight into the first guard with his spear held at the ready.

I rolled backward across the soft soil, the sharp end of the guard's weapon piercing the air above me. As he approached for the follow-up, he paused and yelped in pain as a bear trap snapped shut on his leg, denting the metal greaves into his skin.

Wolf had been pretty annoyed at me for looting the trap considering its name, but I had then snuck it away when he wasn't looking. *System-Created Crimson Shadow–Corrupted Guard Trap* didn't have the same ring to it. Just as effective, however.

The guard crouched to grab at the trap, and I swung around with a sledge-hammer, striking him in the top of the helmet with a dull clang. As he clattered to the ground, I brought out a shield into my left hand, swapping the heavy hammer for a flail in my right.

Dazzle icons were few, but for once in my life, I didn't care.

As the next arrows were drawn at the ready and another ten guards consolidated on my position, I held back a wild laugh.

The fans were eager for my autograph, and I was desperate to oblige.

CHAPTER SIXTY-TWO

Down Step

Sweat ran down my brow. Blood warmed through patches of my suit where blades had shredded the fabric. My muscles ached, and even the pulse of adrenaline keeping me in the fight was barely enough to erase the exhaustion constantly weighing me down.

Still, the smile hadn't left my face.

Eight guards were dead. Seven still remained. Six seconds of silence had passed as five circled me warily. For their efforts, three were maimed yet held steadfast. Two were at range still, bows tense and ready to fire once they had a clear shot at their target.

That being *me*. Number one.

They had surprised me, briefly. Back at the other tower, the guards there had been as simple as we had expected of the System-created. Here, they had more intelligence. Not quite enough to make them believably living, but they actually had some manner of tactics and self-preservation.

I had half expected more to emerge from the tower, or perhaps the spellcaster would stand atop the battlements to do something to me—not *cast magic*, I hoped—but whoever or whatever was inside was keen to allow the current guards to finish me off. Unfortunately, I wasn't that easy to steamroll.

One made a move.

After the skirmish so far, I failed to gather the strength to bring the shield up. I had switched my main-hand melee weapon about six or so times during the fight. A few of them littered the blood-flecked grass surrounding me. I didn't have the Stats for such a prolonged scuffle.

I jumped into the air, landing atop a summoned chair. The spear that had been thrust toward me went between my legs, hitting the backrest of the wooden seat. It shuffled and tipped from the force of the strike, sending me off-balance. I hit the ground at an awkward angle, rolling away from the furniture plucked back up into my Inventory. A terrible escape that left me open to two of the group.

As they loomed over me, spears angled downward like I was some fish in a barrel, I gave them that reality. Both weapons jabbed down at me, the first getting stuck in a summoned wooden barrel, while the second struck flesh.

Oh, what I wouldn't give to be able to teleport at this stage. It was like I'd had my wings clipped.

I rolled across the grass and back up to my feet, narrowly avoiding getting pierced through by an arrow that whizzed past my head. While the first guard that had attacked was trying to pull his weapon from the barrel, the second looked at the large fish he had impaled instead of me with a quizzical expression on his face.

The shield went back into my Inventory as I withdrew the last loaded crossbow into my hand. <Redirected Strike> was back up, and I used the same trick I'd started this fight with. The critical bolt blazed past the first guard dodging out of the way and buried halfway through the chest of one of the bow-wielding System-created.

I summoned a greatsword beside me to deflect the attack from my right. To my left, a cloak swirled through the air, obscuring my side. Some old classics but they worked. My eyes felt dry and cracked. Doing all of this on a good day was a struggle. In my present state, it was only by how overpowered <Sleight of Hand> was that I could survive.

While I didn't have the time or brainpower to really consider what the System considered magic when it came down to the spell around this area, it at least allowed me the bare minimum to perform. Potions were fine. I had healed that way, despite disliking the taste still. The stolen Skill was okay and effective. There was only so much dodging and blocking I could do, however.

I had tricks to get out of situations, but I wasn't an extended-battle sort of guy, I repeated internally. My magic often cut short any fights, usually right around the neckline. It was my own fault, of course. Knowing that I would have no magical capacity yet still needed to kill my way through a guarded tower. Did I like a challenge?

Part of me was willing to accept that I liked being opposed. Or perhaps opposing a greater evil force. Fighting against the odds just came part and parcel of those sorts of heroics. I didn't want to struggle. It was just acceptable.

There was an end we were aiming for. Everything had a purpose, despite whatever trappings you could labor it with. Even what the Lady had planned, she had a goal. We were opposed, and whoever was left standing after our long-overdue showdown would determine the fate of this world.

That all seemed very highbrow while I currently stood, drenched in sweat, muddied, and soaked through with blood. My goal was *to live*, and these remaining guards stood opposed to that.

Before they could ready themselves once more, I took the initiative. A renewed burst of energy filled my limbs as my brain gripped tight on the purpose briefly brought to the front of my mind.

As the closest guard on my left kicked back the barrel he had withdrawn his spear from, I hopped atop it and jumped down on him. Out of my hand I threw a bag of powder, which caught on his spear lifting toward me. It burst, spraying out the contents across his face. Something I had scooped up from hell itself. The System called it Darkfire's Agony, but for me it worked well enough to blind my opponent.

I collided with him—his spear now slightly offset piercing through my jacket and missing my side—knocking him over and bruising me. Not much for wrestling, I turned and rolled from him, leaving behind a few chairs from my Inventory to prevent him from lashing out. Not particularly needed, as he seemed occupied with trying to clear his eyes of the hellish dust.

Another arrow whipped past me as I wobbled back up to my feet, the long shaft embedding into the ground just behind where I stood. There was still a good distance between the melee and the one remaining bowman, and I briefly cursed—for probably the dozenth time—the fact I couldn't use my magic here.

What was surprising, however, was the expressions on those who remained.

For the most part, the System-created we had met in our travels had been rather impassive and simplistic. As if they had been made with the sole instruction to stand around and just fight whoever gets close enough until either they or their attacker were dead.

But the guards here now looked worried. As if their morale was wavering and the possibility that they could flee was just waiting in the wings. Despite being allied with or corrupted by the Crimson Shadow, they did not seem as mindless as most under the control of the Lady. If I could just twist the screws, there was a chance I could scare the rest of them off.

A renewed smile crossed my face. I had been stupidly hesitant to try it out, just in case it failed and I had a further identity crisis. But now was as good a time as any.

"Feast your eyes on your imminent demise," I said, cringing internally at the unintentional rhyme of my threat.

<Demon Form>

Two large wings broke from the back of my suit and cracked outward, snapping a gust of air toward my opponents. Horns grew from my skull, knocking my top hat off. My grin grew wider as my canines extended into fangs.

Part of me expected the guards to just shrug off my transformation. Few non-Players had shown fear in all my time here, aside from those paying fealty down in hell.

But this broke them.

"Tactical retreat," the one with the bow called.

The few System-created who had the capacity to backed up into a small squad, their spears held out toward me as if to ward off any potential attack. As a group, they started to head toward the opening in the wall.

That was pretty handy, as I was growing tired of fighting them. However, I couldn't risk them regrouping and causing an issue later—especially if they decided to find backup. No doubt the Lady had other plans or assets in the area and wouldn't want to give up the spellcaster too easily.

That's if he was even here. More fool me if this was a wild-goose chase and I was getting beaten up for no real gain. It would be a decent trap actually. Lure me somewhere where I was at a disadvantage and then . . . perhaps fill the tower with some powerful melee fighter after I get worn out with the guards.

Almost felt too good an opportunity. I would be disappointed if that wasn't the case.

I leaped from my position, my wings taking me into the air and extending the distance so that I would come down on the retreating guards. It would be a mistake to let them leave. I made my entrance to the second act with a heavy swing of the sledgehammer. My target crumpled into a mess of bent metal and shattered bones as my wings knocked another back.

With their morale broken, they were less of a threat. It wasn't that my demonic form made me that much stronger—although it *did* improve my physical capabilities—the pendulum just swung extra hard in my favor.

I withdrew the obsidian sword from the last of them, each cut down in a matter of seconds. Wiped the blood from my mouth after having bitten the throat out of another. Looted them for all that was worth. I turned my head to the side to regard the tower once more.

It stood, static and unyielding. No hint as to what might lie inside. A glance upward revealed that the two guards posted up on the roof were no longer there. Perhaps a good thing, as it meant less chance of me taking a crossbow bolt through the skull. I was half tempted to try to get up to the roof with my wings, but they weren't the best for flying, and putting myself high enough into the air to break my legs without any of my usual bullshit to save me sounded pretty dire.

For now, I let my demonic form fade away. The wings shriveled up as the horns fell from my head. I covered my messy hair with my hat, retrieved from my Inventory. All the wounds received during the fight were slowly healing—not quite at my usual regeneration speed—and I was keen to press on before either my adrenaline wore off or I took some hits that I couldn't so easily recover from.

I stepped up to the front door of the tower. Reinforced wood and sturdy as they came. Usually they appeared without the large handprint painted red across the dark wood, but the Crimson Shadow seemed to leave their mark wherever they went in some manner. Even without trying the handle, I could tell it would be locked.

Just a hunch, based on experience.

Usually not a big deal, as I had a hundred and one ways in which to circumvent a locked door. Without my magic, I had fewer options, but as always—preparedness was the key.

Well, so was the skeleton key I had in my Inventory. Another useful tool looted from hell, I had a handful of the single-use items. Not much need of them, until now. That was, of course, how most of the items in my storage lived.

I spun one of the keys out on my index finger before grasping it. To my eyes, it looked just like any other iron key, although I wasn't really an expert. As long as the door knew what game we were playing, everything would be fine.

Readying myself for the inevitable ambush as soon as I entered the door, I placed the key in the lock and turned. A satisfying click came from the mechanism, notifying me the plan had been successful. Everything was going my way.

Oh, and I had also picked up a curse from the interaction.

CHAPTER SIXTY-THREE

Darkness Unyielding

I paused and waited for something terrible to happen to me.

My left hand held on to the door handle, not yet willing to push it open until I knew how much trouble I was in. When I wasn't immediately wracked with pain and managed to maintain control of both my body and mind, I then turned my eyes up to my debuff icons to see exactly what kind of malady I had been cursed with.

[Curse: System Mute—You are unable to access your STAR temporarily]

Despite being able to read this message clearly, every word of the description understandable, I did not *accept* it. For ten slow seconds, I remained in place, hoping the curse would just disappear before I had the chance to test it.

No such luck.

I tried to bring up my menus, but nothing happened. No Inventory, nor Map, Stats, or even the Chat. I couldn't believe this was something even possible. But now I was . . . normal.

For some definitions of *normal* anyway. Now without magic, a way to contact those in my Guild, or even my overpowered ability to manipulate my Inventory items . . . I felt more out of place than even when I had first arrived here. Standing at the precipice of whatever was waiting for me inside this tower, I wondered now how much of a mistake it would be to even enter.

I let go of the handle and took a full two steps backward.

Not a retreat, I convinced myself. I just needed a moment to regroup and consider my options. It had been a while since I had such a lack of variety of tricks in my act, and I wouldn't want to disappoint the critics just behind the curtain.

Fully aware the mania was taking me toward an early grave, I still couldn't shake it. I flexed my right hand by instinct, trying to draw out one of my magical cards. Still no dice. I tried to summon some dice from my Inventory. Even with my eyes making the same micromovements I had practiced hundreds of times, my palm remained empty.

I turned back to the pile of mangled guards and walked over to retrieve one of their spears. A little improvisation was required. While they didn't have the manpower to secure the spellcaster in this tower against *everything*, they had done pretty well to make it unpalatable to attack. No spells, no STAR, no outside help.

Anyone who wasn't a fool would turn away and not risk it. I was certain that if it was just the STAR that was inert, I could still use my magical spells innately. Similarly, I had full confidence that I could take the tower with just my <Sleight of Hand> even without my magic to back that up. Without either, I just had to use the tools around me.

Starting with equipping myself with whatever I had available. Set pieces were only as drab as you allowed them to be.

With a smile on my face, I approached the door once more. Not really confident that I was about to sell this change of pace from the norm . . . but what choice did I really have?

I pushed on the door handle and swung it open. Two crossbow bolts greeted me, bouncing from the metal plate covering my suit. Dented and uncomfortable but saved. The lower room beyond was circular in shape, the stairs at the back leading up to the next floor. Two guards with crossbows crouched behind overturned tables, one now trying to reload as the second discarded his ranged weapon to draw out a sword.

With a lunge forward, I threw the spear like a javelin. It collided with the guard emerging from cover, returning a dent to his own breastplate. Not enough to damage him but he paused, briefly winded. I used the opportunity to grab a chair off from the side and spun, launching it at the crossbow-wielding guard. Continued my movement to leap over the closest table and barrel into the staggered man with his sword up.

His blade scraped along my stolen armor, and I turned him so that he couldn't get a good follow-up on me. I avoided a kick from his metal boot aimed at my shin before ducking his punch. We spun away from each other, and I twirled a dagger around in my hand.

The guard looked perplexed, glancing down at the empty sheath on his waist, right before his unclasped belt dropped to the floor. The other guard had managed to reload his crossbow and was waiting for an opportunity to fire on me. I couldn't allow it. Stepping back, I circled my opponent so that he was in the line of sight. Two sidesteps back and forth to avoid the swings of his sword.

I darted in, bringing my dagger down to slash at his neck. He blocked it, just as I knew he would. While he was intent on not letting my blade land, my left hand came in and unclipped the buckles on his breastplate. Even as he shoved me away, the reflective metal slumped to the side of his torso at an angle.

It was enough to make his next blow awkward and ineffective. I took the swing of it into my right shoulder, the sword barely piercing through my suit to my skin. With the dagger swapped to my left hand, I brought it up into his exposed flank. Just under his ribs. He staggered away to clutch at the wound, and I disarmed him along the way, turning myself to the other guard.

By pure luck, my crossed weapons deflected the bolt fired at me, a long cut down my arm much better than taking the projectile to the chest again. I growled and flung the dagger out at the man as swapped to his own sword—too slow. By the time he had recovered from blocking the smaller blade, I was on him, driving the tip of my sword into his clavicle.

I finished them both off, dagger through the throat.

My left arm burned from where it had been cut by the crossbow bolt. On inspection, it hadn't been the glancing blow that I had expected. Down into the muscle, for the length of most of my forearm. My suit shredded and soaked through with blood. Limb currently still operational even with the damage, so I wouldn't complain.

I picked up the belt and put it on. Sheathed the dagger. Took a helmet, my spear, and the sword with me. Would have loved to have looted the two men, but the System wasn't granting me the option.

In fairness, I had been expecting a lot worse than just the two guards. They probably weren't the two from the roof, however—but the floor with the spell-caster on it would be the most well defended. Given all that they had thrown at me so far, I couldn't imagine what could be worse. Thankfully, the current aura around the area probably affected the enemies just as much as me. I wouldn't have to worry about . . .

I paused my inner monologue to listen.

It was reasonably quiet, as expected. But there was something else . . . just the gradual, occasional hum of something. Not really magic, whatever sense I had for that wasn't picking up on the Guardian's powers or anything more malign. Machinery, maybe? Technology had been few and far between in this world, but I wouldn't put it past the Crimson Shadow to have put together something to make these spells so powerful. No normal caster should be able to maintain an antimagic field this strong for so long.

I glanced over at the stairs. They hadn't sent anyone down against me, so they must be in a decent position already. If Ren were here, she would probably brow-beat me into looking for traps. I palmed at the air, trying to withdraw my half-eaten sandwich. Nothing. What a cruel world.

With one last look around the chamber for anything else that might be use-ful, I shrugged to myself and stepped over to the stairs. Immediately as I got to the base of them, a terrible smell hit my nose. Something I was unfortunately familiar with, due to my time spent in hell. Burning flesh.

That all but erased any appetite I had left. I placed my fist, as I was still holding the spear, against the wall as a moment of vertigo ran through my head. I was way too tired for this. Way too traumatized and manic. Unfortunately, I was also self-aware enough to see the irony of my situation.

I had come to this world overworked and far too focused on trying to be the best magician to function as a regular person. I had learned to temper that. Enjoy life and take it easy when I needed to. Now I was standing before a gauntlet of ever-increasing pressure, and I strived—single-mindedly—toward coming out on top. All the power and strengths I had fought for now erased.

Maybe that was the point.

I was being fractured and brought down to my base components. No . . . I needed to stay out of my head. Thinking would get me killed.

Pushing away from the wall, I hit the stairs with my feet. Beat them in short order to arrive at another locked door. There was the possibility that this was cursed as well. I also couldn't dig out a skeleton key to find out. Luckily for me, this doorway wasn't as sturdy as the outside one.

I shuffled to the side and wedged the tip of the spear into the slim gap by the hinges. Leaning into it like a lever, I put as much force as I could into the wedged weapon. It started to bow, threatening to snap—before there was a loud crack. With a groan and waft of displaced air, the door buckled from the hinged side, masonry falling down as the inside was revealed to me.

Just as a crossbow bolt flew out, almost blinding me. I swore under my breath as I pressed myself against the wall, partially obscured by the wrecked door. Warmth ran down the side of my face. A centimeter to the left and it would have gone straight into the socket.

Perhaps worse than even that was the smell. While the door hadn't been great at preventing my entry, it had done a stellar job of restricting most of the odor. Whatever was burning was on this floor and had been doing so for hours at least.

If anything, the Crimson Shadow had missed the mark by not putting a tougher Monster on this floor. The guards were deadly, sure, and maybe they expected anyone sensible to have given up before this point. It was also likely that they didn't know some of us would avoid the sleeping curse, and more reinforcements were on the way. There was no use speculating—the Lady and her ilk often did things ineffectively, only gaining ground by their underhanded methods.

Throwing things at people seemed to put them off guard enough for me to close in, so I wasn't about to stop that tactic until it stopped working. I adjusted my grip on the spear, finally energizing myself enough to move before they had a chance to reload their crossbow. I wasn't keen on getting any closer to that machine giving off that smell, but everything was an obstacle to getting to the spellcaster.

I launched the spear in the general direction of my assailant, hopping over the shattered remnants of the door. The smell was almost overpowering—my eyes darted immediately to the right side of the room where a large machine of deep browns and dark metal hummed away. Box shaped, something that was more like a furnace.

To my surprise, I had managed to hit the guard straight in the face with the spear—my lucky streak clearly gathering up speed.

Of course, that was something immediately dashed, as the machine had distracted me from the powerful Monster hiding on the left side of the doorway. Another axe whipped through the air toward my head. A repeat of earlier in the day.

This time, there was no illusion.

CHAPTER SIXTY-FOUR

What's Cooking?

For a long while, I had become numb to pain. To a certain degree, at least. Had taken my share of injury—more than most, I was willing to bet—but the part of me that was quite attached to my mortality wasn't keen on taking any more punishment than I deserved.

As I struck the floor with a thud, my vision spotty, I reckoned I had reached that point. My arms felt sluggish. The sword already escaped from my grasp. I pawed at the ground to push myself up but was unable to gain purchase. My nose burned with the thick fog of the humming machine, causing my eyes to water. All in all, not exactly the way I planned to go out.

I heard the footsteps of my opponent behind me. Heavy. With singular purpose. My teeth clenched in anger, knowing how many were relying on me not fading away. *I was the star of the show.*

Wings burst from my back, immediately severing off as my opponent slashed down. I had saved my own skin through my demonic form blunting the strike. Although my demonic strength was weaker, it gave me enough of a boost to roll over to my front.

Standing over me was a female Minotaur. I didn't need the System to tell me that, for several reasons. Short brown fur, eyes full of fury, and a harness made of thick leather straps. The bloodied axe she held looked eager for more of me. I just really wanted a sandwich. Her follow-up slash came down, and I grasped at the spear on the floor, bringing it around just in time to block the downward slash. The axe split halfway through the weapon's shaft, and it buckled toward me.

I didn't even have anything to say. No STAR screens to come through and tell me how injured I was. The throbbing at the back of my head, and how slick my hair was back there, gave some hints. As the Minotaur withdrew her weapon, I lashed out with my shoe, catching her in the shin.

She grunted as she stepped back. "Stay still, human."

"No," I managed, although the effort exerted made it feel more like an extended monologue. With whatever strength I could muster, I tossed the split spear at her as I rolled away. Getting to my feet was a lot more difficult than I could remember, despite having the same amount of them. I wobbled and wavered as if I were surfing, riding the shifting brickwork and avoiding the shark snaking toward me.

I shifted, mostly inadvertently, as her next strike flashed past me and struck the wall. I winced from the sound and shot a glare at the machine across the room that was clouding my mind and distracting me. My left hand refused to go for the knife on my belt, so my right stepped in. I back slashed wildly, only catching some light purchase on my assailant due to how unpredictable my movements were.

She growled and grabbed at my neck with one hand. I stabbed her forearm to convince her to let me go. It took three strikes before she saw my point of view and relented. As she released me, she pushed me back with the blunt end of the axe. I stumbled and hit the back of my head against the wall, sparks flooding through my vision again. Something wasn't quite right.

I slumped down as her sharp blade once again slashed against the stonework. Powdered granules of gray rained down on my bloody hair as my eyes finally caught up to reality. I was rather tired of this charade. What I wouldn't give for Ren or Wolf to be here assisting me.

The Minotaur spun the double-headed axe around in her hand; the wall doing more damage to one side of her weapon than I had to her. Rather than strike me down where I sat—miserable—she took a couple of steps back and held her axe at the ready.

"Lots of fight left in you." She grinned, which was uncomfortably sinister. "Stand and make your death worthy."

I wasn't a fan of that plan.

She wasn't going to let me get out of it by remaining in place; that loophole was soon to be patched up as she would put a hoof through my skull at the mere suggestion. I wasn't quite immune to that sort of attack yet.

I flexed my toes in my shoes. They were numb, as was my left hand. It had been so long since I had been humbled that I was almost *happy*—or perhaps that was just due to the blood loss.

Still, I smiled as I struggled back up to my feet. System-created who could taunt and grant temporary mercy—that was the real tasty morsel here. For all the bad Lady in Red had done to get to this point, I was almost envious that she had managed such a feat. If it *was* even her and not something she was just taking credit for.

"I warn you," I said, slurring slightly as I shook in place. "I'm rather famous for winning things like this."

"You are a rat looking for cheese where you do not belong." Her tongue ran across her large but rather flat teeth. "Soon your head will be decorating my horns."

I wasn't about to say it out loud, but her horns were a lot stubbier than I had expected. Barely had the space for my skull. My right hand came up, and the dagger slipped from my loose grip. I pulled a face as it clattered to the floor.

"Oh, may I pick that back up?" My grimace was hopefully convincing.

Although her dark eyes narrowed at me, she gave a brief nod.

Much more impressive than the Crimson Shadow bringing these smarter Monsters to life was giving them the same flaws the gang had. I could even laugh if my head didn't feel like it was about to explode.

I shuffled my legs into a sturdier stance and leaned down to reach for my blade. Blood drops pattered to the gray bricks, along with some sweat. Making a right mess of the place. To think, this was all due to a sandwich. My right eye twitched in time with the occasional hum coming from the infernal machine. Fingers wrapped around the handle of the dagger.

Slowly and deliberately.

All eyes on that process.

I stood back up straight, vertigo almost tipping me over backward. "May the best magician win then." My mouth all smiles. My eyes burning purple. My plan clicking into place.

The Minotaur had enough word games and intended to make this a short duel. My left hand lashed out, splattering her face with blood. The cut on my arm had been bleeding all this time, and by cupping it and leaning over, I had managed to gather up almost a handful of my precious red liquid.

That didn't stop her from slashing out, however, but when she had cleared her eyes, I was gone. Dagger in her side told her I had moved to her blind spot, but as she turned and punched out with her fist, I wasn't there either.

"Quit hiding, worm," she hissed, turning in place as she held her axe ready.

I made my appearance, jumping up behind her and putting the belt around her neck. I fell back with my body weight, more due to exhaustion than intent, and pulled the loop tighter. Stealth and evasion weren't really natural traits I possessed, but distraction and obfuscation were. I had made minor noises as she turned to keep her eyes in the opposite direction to my actual location.

Or at least that's what I told myself. I took an elbow to my left arm as she tried to push me off, almost breaking the numb limb. She didn't have the range of motion to hit me with the axe as I kept my body as close to hers as possible. After three failed strikes, she dropped the weapon in favor of grasping at the belt to pull it away. I knew that she was much stronger than me.

As I braced my foot against her back, I let go of the belt with my right hand and pulled the dagger from her side. The Minotaur tried to buck and shift away from the inevitable, but all that did was tighten the grip of the belt around her throat. She wavered before dropping to her knees. Before she tried to roll on the floor to escape the pressure, I brought the blade into the side of her head.

First stab was blocked by her hand; the second was clear. It was over by then. The rest that followed were just insurance.

I dropped the dagger as the Monster slumped over, my ragged breathing agony for my lungs. Part of me knew I had taken more Damage than I had registered, but adrenaline had me ignoring it. At least until I could win.

For a moment I just stared, dumbfounded, at my own survival and the gall of my enemy to be overconfident again. *Why couldn't they learn?* Eventually, when it felt like I wasn't about to spontaneously combust or turn into a puddle, I scowled at the machine.

It was difficult to take in, not half because of my wavy vision. I had no doubt it had something to do with either the sleeping spell or the STAR-removing curse. I stepped over to it, the taste of ashen flesh in my mouth. Whatever it was, it was foul.

There were no dials or moving parts. No switches or buttons to press. Perhaps this wasn't the whole of it, and it was controlled from the floor above. There was a handle on the chunkier left side. I wasn't looking to get another curse, but I sought answers.

I gripped at the warm metal handle with my right hand, my left returning to being useless. As the muscles in my arm screamed in resignation, I pulled it up.

A large section of the metallic contraption opened up on a back hinge, like I was opening up a barbecue grill. An apt comparison once I saw what was inside. Even without my System, I knew who and what this was.

On top of sheets of vented metal a figure lay, burned beyond comprehension. The heat washing over me was sweltering. Yet they still lived.

Eyes of glowing light turned slowly to me, a strange amount of panic in them at seeing their trance interrupted. This was the spellcaster. I wasn't exactly sure how I knew, but all the puzzle pieces fit the narrative I was eager to believe. This machine was using up his life to maintain the spell on the town where my Guild was being kept captive. Like a blood ritual, just more incendiary.

I slammed the lid shut before he could move.

No. I was done with this place. Stepping back, I extended my palm toward him. Paused it in place and forced my left to come up and hold my right wrist. I couldn't fight against a spellcaster like this. It took enough of my willpower to keep my brain from leaking out of the back of my skull.

But I was uncontestable. This was all connected. I just had to trace the lines until I drew the picture I wanted. My teeth clenched together as I forced my willpower through my hands.

At first, nothing happened. Rules were enforced.

Then I started getting my own way. My extremities burned as if I had stuck them inside the infernal machine myself. I shook and vibrated with agony. The blood leaking from my injuries felt warmer against my cooling skin.

With a reality-ripping burst, my patron demon shattered his way out of hell, plunging directly into the machine.

I dropped to my knees as I watched him carve his way through the metal like butter, shredding the trapped caster with little difficulty. If only I could have done that at the start.

Such thoughts fell from my mind as messages pinged through my Chat. I skipped through them to the last one, something that gave me more energy than fighting for my own life. It was sent a little while ago.

[Ren: We are under attack.]

CHAPTER SIXTY-FIVE

Clearing the Schedule

It seemed obvious that the ideal time for the Crimson Shadow to strike out at the sleeping Guild members would be when I was fully out of the picture. The message from Ren had been sent several minutes ago, probably just before my fight with the Minotaur.

The teleportation scroll was already in my right hand, without really thinking about it. Left hand brought up a health potion to my lips, but my eyes went over to the doorway that led to the next floor. Part of me wanted to explore and find out if there was anything else malign hiding up here in this tower. The rest of me screamed to return to the others and help defend.

After a few moments of hesitation, it was another Chat message that swayed my eventual decision.

[Ruby: People are starting to wake up.]

That was enough for me. I had removed both the STAR and magic restrictions on myself, as well as ended the sleeping curse on the Guild. I activated the scroll and vanished from the tower.

With a flash of blue light, I emerged into clear air. A fresh breeze cleared my lungs of the foul smoke from the burning machine as I took a deep breath. I was on the roof of the tavern.

"*Motherfucker,*" Ren said, shooting me a glare intense enough to almost make me fall to the ground. "Get back to killing."

The fact that my trauma status had vanished as soon as I had arrived beside her had been briefly distracting. *I felt good.* Slightly more alive, as my regeneration paired with a heal from the elf to patch up the wounds I had accumulated in my solo jaunt. Now, allowing the temporary elation to erase my exhaustion, I looked out to the woodlands to see who was attacking us.

From the looks of things, it was . . . originally two full regiments of some manner of Monster. To her credit, Ren had kept them from getting too close to the town. Several bodies lay strewn back through the forest, where trees had fallen from the battle. Now, those who remained were hiding behind pavises arranged like short walls.

"They're using some kind of Skill," she continued, glaring daggers at the gathered troupe. "Even my best shots can't pierce their shields."

The scarred crater around the point where most of the trees had fallen was probably where she had used her explosive shot, but most of her others did direct Damage. Without a clear bearing on the targets, they were both at an impasse. Crossbows and shortbows had been utilized in opposition, but they didn't really have the range to fight back against her.

It was terrible, but I smiled. After having all my Abilities taken away, I felt like a god once more with them returning to the grand stage. There was no need to flourish for this performance, however.

Those who stood against the Guild would fall.

I used <Demonic Transposition> to switch places with my demonic ace, who had been hovering out behind the gathered walls of shields. As soon as I arrived, twin cards of bright purple slashed out from me. Three of these Monsters fell, cut to ribbons, before the rest even clocked my arrival.

But as soon as they were in disarray, we had the advantage. While they broke rank to fight against me, it gave Ren openings to shoot. Her rifle echoed through the area as she blasted a head open, lightning then crackling from her target to the ones beside them, causing them to drop their shields. Several ran at me, hooked blades raised in the air.

I saw now that they looked like humanoid rats with a distinctly Roman flair. Perhaps not historically accurate but it was close enough for my muddied mind. It didn't matter at this point; they were all about to be dead.

In truth, I had expected worse. I could only assume that the intention was to catch us all asleep, and having Ren and I awake threw a wrench in their plans. The pair of cards slew through the majority of the rat men before the doors of the tavern burst open and the rest of the Guild—now hastily dressed back in their battle gear—yelled and poured forth toward the Monsters.

That was enough to cause them to rout. They didn't make it far before the pair of us cut any remaining down. I turned my attention to the rather grumpy-looking bear, but the appearance of a white dove beside me interrupted anything I was about to say.

Ren switched places with the bird, immediately grabbing me by the shredded and bloody suit. She pulled me in for a brief kiss before pushing me slightly away, glaring at me as if she was considering tearing my head off.

"I'm considering tearing your head off," she began. "You almost died, didn't you? Asshole."

"Just a little trauma and a few cuts," I lied brazenly. My eyes went into my STAR to dig out the logs from the fighting. Nothing good. "It was no sweat at all."

"Well . . . you got it done, at least." The elf glanced over to the side at the others. "I wish I could have been there though."

While the Guild picked through the Monsters for loot, I filled her in on everything that had happened. It didn't improve her mood any, but she deserved to know the full picture.

Eventually, once I was done talking and had started on my half-eaten sandwich again, she sighed and shook her head.

"I can't believe those kinds of curses could even exist, trickster. I thought we were overpowered and outside the scope of the System, but the Lady seems to have more tricks up her sleeve the closer we get."

As much as I wanted to point out that *I* was the magician and thus had the most trick-laden sleeves around, I managed to hold my tongue. She had a point anyway. No doubt Lady in Red had picked up those with the greatest power along the way and kept them safest near her, rather than leaving them guarding one of the towns like the others we had slain along the way.

Even able to create Monsters now, her numbers were slowly dwindling.

I put my arm around Ren, partially to keep my exhausted legs from collapsing me to the ground. "You might not like this suggestion, but I think we should catch up on sleep in hell."

She wrinkled up her nose and looked up at me, her bright-blue eyes not filled with so much ire now. The promise of any kind of sleep was irresistible. "Fine, but we need to discuss this so that the group is still protected, even if it's just for a few hours."

Six of us needed sleep. Ren and I could do so in hell, and the time dilation meant we could get a full night in only a couple of hours in the real world. Wolf needed sleep too but wouldn't want to come with us. It would also put him in the position of being the strongest one out here, having to protect the others—even Tanya and Quinn needed rest.

It wasn't that I didn't trust the rest of the Guild to keep us safe, but I didn't want to take unnecessary risks. We were at the stage where everything had to be all out. No holding back, just in case we got left behind. Or dead.

There was one other option. I looked over as Tanya, Quinn, Fiona, and Leyla approached us. Ruby was in the background talking to Wolf.

"Ruby filled me in on what happened," Fiona said, still looking a little groggy. She rubbed at her head as she glanced at the bodies of the rat men. "I guess thank fuck you all didn't fall asleep as well."

Leyla nodded. "We would surely be dead, so thank you."

I waved them away. It was just a necessary procedure, not done for thanks or accolades. Plus, nobody had been there to witness me. A fate almost worse than death. "Of course, I'm sure you all would have done the same in my position," I said diplomatically. "Right now, we should leave this area. I have . . . a plan."

The fighter rolled her eyes. "Is it to get sleep? We can't siege a city when our best are exhausted."

"Correct." I brought up my Map. "We had planned to go to the Dungeon for farming anyway, so why don't we do that—and allow those who are tired to sleep inside it?"

They weren't convinced at first but could see my reasoning. Assuming we could clear the starting areas of the Dungeon, nobody would be able to attack us from outside. Each Party would be safe in the little pocket dimension for as long as needed. We'd need to change things around so that those needing sleep could be protected, but it was better than leaving people out in the open world.

Under the weighty stares of me and Ren, they eventually agreed to the plan. Without further ado, we left the town for the Dungeon.

With the sunlight beating down on my tired body, the travel itself was arduous but thankfully short.

We swapped Quinn and Tanya for Percius and Magnus. The pair would be able to watch over Wolf while the caster disenchanted the rest of my useless magical gear. Once we were rested, we'd return from hell and complete the Dungeon with them.

Upon reaching the Dungeon itself, it appeared to be some manner of old monastery or chapel. The door was a swirling vortex of color, indicating that it led to an instanced area. Not something that I had really questioned previously, but now, with my experience of traveling to hell, it made slightly more sense.

In our groups, we arranged ourselves before stepping in. I didn't have the energy to give them much of a pep talk or speech before we went ahead, but they didn't need it. Or at least I hoped they didn't.

The first room once entering was the main chapel itself. Something modest and gloomy. A few stone pews, stained glass windows, and a staircase leading down into the floor where the stone statue at the front had been toppled. Green light emanated from the descent.

"Should be safe enough," I determined, looking down the spiraled stairs with my nostrils flared. "I'll block this doorway just in case, so you have enough time to call us if something happens."

Wolf huffed and looked up at me. "I'm sure I can handle a few Monsters, brother."

"Be that as it may, you call us, and we'll be here." I smiled and gave him a pat on the shoulder. "I'm going to eject every item I need disenchanted onto the floor, and then we'll be off."

Percius gave me a pensive nod. I could see why he had kept his Skill secret for a while. Unfortunately, it was the easiest and best source of power for me before we set forward toward the city.

Ren sighed and sat down on one of the pews, knowing that this wasn't going to be a quick thing. In fairness, had I the normal aptitude for Inventory management like others, it would take forever. My eyes skimmed through the boxes, barely registering the actual inputs normally required—the items just popping out into reality with a thought.

There were many of them. I had to keep walking about the chapel to find new areas to pile up all the trash items I had accumulated. While I had long thought that any item could be useful eventually, in truth, I often used the same handful of things. The usefulness of all the random shoes, swords, and hats was now in becoming shards to make power tokens.

So I had been right all along.

While the caster looked terribly overwhelmed, I traded him some gold and mana potions.

My hand went out, and the doorway to hell bloomed into existence. Ren and I stepped through with barely a goodbye, the prospect of rest more important than social graces.

Back into the warmth and the familiar throne room. I wondered if I could go other places rather than here every time. Over to the right, my patron demon was hovering over the meeting table where the current council had been in mid-argument.

The sword hovered over, as the demons paused, frozen in place as if they were scared I might execute them just for doing their job a little too loudly. An amusing thought but not the right way to run a kingdom.

"Bedroom?" I blurted out before my patron could engage with the normal formalities.

In perhaps sensing my urgency, he just turned in the air, pointing off to the side with the tip of his blade.

We left, allowing the council to continue their—probably short-lived— meeting about something or other. I should probably learn how to govern properly, eventually. A side door opened up into a rather impressive chamber, a wide four-poster bed on one side, all the furniture within an odd black wood. All accents red and gold. Somewhat cliché, and I was almost disappointed at the lack of skulls.

Not the safest place in existence, but for us now . . . this was home.

My exhausted brain barely registered lying on the bed, any thoughts completely evaporating as soon as I hit the soft pillow.

Perhaps the last sleep I'd ever have. I had earned it.

CHAPTER SIXTY-SIX

Night Day

My eyes opened up, and for a brief moment, I forgot that I was in hell.

"You were right," Ren said, pushing herself up into my blurred vision. "I would get used to it."

It took my brain a couple of seconds to catch what she was even alluding to before my blinking eyes cleared. We had both fallen asleep in our magician outfits, way too tired to even undress beforehand. It wasn't the first time, but she had remembered way back near the coast when she had first decided to take up the mantle of being my protégé.

"Of all the things we have gotten used to," I said, pushing myself up into a seated position. "That is probably the least worrying."

The elf gave me a peck on the side of the head before slipping off onto the floor to stand and stretch out. "How's your Health Report today? Any complications from your head injury?"

I brought the screen up, and it was blank. "Full recovery." I tried not to think about what it had said yesterday. The axe blow to the back of my head had almost done me in—I had been running on pure fumes and willpower for way longer than what was healthy. Standard at this point.

"Do you have any business to deal with in hell, or can we just leave?" The way she was looking at me hinted that she was insinuating we should definitely do the latter.

"There's someone who wants to challenge me for the throne, but I made them a job offer instead. Best that I should see where that's at first." I gave her an apologetic grin, which she begrudgingly accepted.

I understood it. We were on the precipice of our final battle. Any distraction was just delaying the inevitable. Still, with there being a time dilation, a few minutes here wouldn't affect our time back up top by much. Plus, you never knew when a side quest could give you something usable against the final boss.

My suit could do with a fix as well. I hit the button to tell the System to do just that, dropping myself down to my underwear.

"Come on," I encouraged her, "we'll be done before my suit is ready, I promise."

Ren rolled her eyes but followed along as I left the bed to head to the throne room. Once we emerged, I was partially surprised to see that the long meeting table was empty. Over beside my throne, my patron demon hovered. The sword turned to face us as I walked over.

"Had to dispose of another council group?" I asked.

He made the approximation of a shaken head, turning briefly from side to side. "No, my king. This one has actually survived three meetings without breaking the rules. Too early to celebrate but we are gradually weeding through those too power hungry or sinister."

I nodded. "And of my challenger?"

"She has been killing through the others intending to step against the throne but insisted that she would only talk to you." The eye on the hilt stared impassively. "So she has neither accepted nor declined your offer."

"Rats." I pulled a face and looked at Ren, who was now standing with her arms crossed.

"*Before* the suit comes back, you said." Her glare had no anger in it, but I had a feeling she'd hold it against me if I broke that promise.

"I'll go see her now," I told my patron. "Are you . . . able to teleport us or at least guide me to do it?"

"Yes, my king." A purple sheen of energy washed over him, and then we were transported.

Straight into what looked like a fighting pit. Sharp metal poles encircled a crater that had been dug into the stone. Dried blood and aged bones littered the perimeter. Right in the middle was my challenger.

A large demon, easily . . . eighteen feet tall. At first I thought she was hiding behind part of the fighting arena before I realized it was a tower shield of immense proportion. It looked like some manner of eldritch monolith, eight feet wide and just over twenty tall. Runes danced with foul light up and down it. I imagined she could only work with the weight of it due to her size and having six arms.

Her three left hands held this giant shield, while her three right each had a long whip. I wasn't sure how she was able to utilize three whips at the same time and wasn't keen on finding out. At the end of each weapon was a barbed metal shape.

"Hello," I said.

She turned her head down to gaze at me, her red eyes a stark contrast to the dull gray of her skin. "My king," she said, her voice low and rumbling. "What an honor to finally meet you . . . in my fighting pit, of all places."

I eyed up the edges of the arena, now seeing a crowd of yellow eyes peering down through the shadows above. Part of me wondered if showing up here in just my underwear was a good idea. That said, I was almost wearing more than the demon, so I was in good company.

"You have received my job offer. In exchange for your fealty, I will spare your life," I said and smiled.

"Sounds like king is scared," she growled, her own grin crossing her face.

"I come to you without my regalia or battle dress, arriving in your home turf. Unfortunately, I have *nothing* to fear from you." She was tensing her hands on the handles of her whips. I was clearly close to being tested.

"You are a tiny human. I think I have a chance." Her tongue ran across her sharp teeth.

As much as I liked getting rid of threats, she was actually useful down here for filtering out all the other dregs trying to vie for my crown. More importantly, I didn't have the minutes to spare before my outfit came back on.

"Any hand that opposes me, I will cut off. If you think you have a chance, I will take that head as well." I held my hand out and frowned. "Do you have an umbrella though? Feels like rain."

The demon furrowed her brow, unsure if I was pulling her leg. "No rain in hell," she snorted.

But then it started. A patter that increased in severity in a moment. It was blood, and the screams that started up from the crowd watching us signaled whom it had come from. A simple card thrown out while nobody was looking, to swirl around and cut at any throat it could find.

"Not threatening." The demon shrugged.

"Then strike me."

I didn't even have the chance to roll my eyes alongside that statement before she lashed out with the trio of whips. Faster than expected but by now I *should* be expecting that. The barbed metal tips cracked against my body in an instant, completely severing me into several fragments.

Interesting. She had used a Skill called <Fear of Flaying>, which I had now stolen.

I stepped out of invisibility as she gloated over the piles of what remained of my body. "The crown stays with me, I'm afraid."

She turned her head and lashed out with her whips again. I switched place with a hell dove, the bird bursting into a cloud of feathers. "Stand still!" she yelled.

"As you wish." I smiled and held out my hand, waiting for her to turn around. This time, she didn't get the chance to attack.

Ren and I stepped out from hell back into the dungeon just as my outfit popped back on.

"Dickbag," she murmured, her arms still crossed. More than my perfect timing, she was annoyed at getting sprayed with blood—leaving her suit looking worse than mine had been. Almost.

Percius stood, blinking away the screens that had lingered in his eyes for too long. "Ah, back already."

Wolf was still asleep, and Magnus looked bored out of his skull. The caster had managed to disenchant perhaps a quarter of the large hoard.

"If only you had my Inventory Skill," I said, "you'd be done in minutes." By my rough approximation, we had gotten a solid twelve hours of sleep in hell. Out here . . . maybe four had passed? Not even that.

"Or if they made mana potions not taste terrible," he countered. "The other teams are doing well. They don't have the luxury of getting that sort of rest."

We could have safely slept out here like them, but the more time we spent active and alert in the real world, the better we could watch over the others. A bit much to put all that responsibility on our shoulders but given that we were so powerful it felt only right.

"No rush to complete the Dungeon then?" I looked over at the green light seeping through the cracks in the pile of loot I had left there.

Buk'la had accepted the offer to be my champion. Whatever that meant. While having a right hand that killed any of my detractors would eventually give rise to rebellion, that was a can I was kicking farther down the road. Did I need to worry about that just yet? No.

Percius shrugged. "If we are aiming to exit at the same time as the others, then we don't need to do it if they are still sleeping."

That meant we needed to do something else to pass the time. I watched as Ren walked across the room before sitting and leaning against the sleeping bear. Perhaps a few minutes of not putting ourselves in danger would be nice.

I joined her, and although Wolf grunted, he didn't stir. Ren leaned her head on my shoulder, and we remained at peace.

It took another couple of hours before Wolf stirred and Percius made some headway with the pile of magical items. After ten minutes where he kept gagging after taking a mana potion, I allowed him to stop.

While he transmuted the shards into power tokens, I went around and vacuumed up the remaining loot.

"How did you get covered in Max's blood?" the bear asked Ren, sniffing at her outfit.

"It wasn't by choice."

I rolled my eyes as I returned to them. "It wasn't mine either. For a change."

With the others ready and eager to stretch their legs, we went to descend into the Dungeon.

It was a wholly underwhelming experience. Perhaps it was because we were overleveled or just overpowered. Undead themed. A necromancer and skeletal soldiers. Any one of our main trio could have soloed it, so having all three of us here was overkill.

We cleared every side path and bonus Monster and even let some of the events run over time to kill more rather than do the intended mechanics. We played rock, paper, scissors for who got to kill the final boss—the necromancer himself—even though Wolf didn't really understand the concept of the game.

Ren won and put a bullet straight through the Monster's skull before we even got into range for him to start a monologue. It was pretty terrible experience and loot even for Percius and Magnus.

The plan had been to farm this all of today. The sleeping curse had put a big dent in that plan, and now I was unsure if I could even stomach running this even one more time.

[Max: Anyone else run the dungeon yet?]
[Fiona: Halfway.]
[Max: Decent experience/loot?]
[Fiona: Not fantastic. Simple and safe.]
[Tanya: We've done the first couple of rooms.]
[Quinn: And it's pretty bad^]

I drummed my fingers on my belt. There was an executive decision to be made here. Our options were either to grind this for whatever it was worth . . . or head to the city tomorrow. Every hour wasted was time the Lady and the Crimson Shadow grew in power.

Ren stepped up beside me, clearly able to hear the thoughts echoing around in my skull.

"What do you think we should do, moonflower?"

"I think tomorrow we save the world."

With a smile, I nodded my head. Sounded like a show for the ages.

CHAPTER SIXTY-SEVEN

Sweet Cake

In the grand scheme of things, it wasn't a long time before we were standing not too far off from Candlekeep. The Dungeon was run over and over again throughout what daylight we had left. We had slept, running watches for the night, and were now rested. Percius had managed to get us forty power tokens with only throwing up from the mana potions twice.

I gave ten to Ren, ten to Wolf, and then used the two upgrades for myself to allow me to summon three demons at a time and conjure three magical cards at once.

It wasn't the flashiest of upgrades, especially so late in the game . . . but I saw it as a roughly 50 percent increase to both routes of attack. With no true path to tread to raise my Stats or gain further Abilities since leaving hell, we were pretty much done. Once we started with the potions and scroll buffs, we'd be all over the place numerically but still the strongest in the world.

While Ren cuddled with a trio of Hellhounds, I took Fiona over to the side.

"A city siege," I said, looking over at Candlekeep itself. It was bathed in red light—something I felt was even more hellish than my kingdom below. The towers and structures within seemed normal enough. It hadn't been taken destructively. "Can't say I'm too well-versed in them."

"Typically, the defender has the advantage." Fiona sighed and rubbed at her short hair. "Thankfully, other than the keep at the back, the city isn't a castle or designed to hold off a large-scale invasion."

I nodded but didn't consider our Guild of fifteen to class as large-scale. We had managed to get this close without running into any of the packs of roving Monsters aligned with the Crimson Shadow, but I was partly worried that meant we could get surrounded once we dug in. That said, we couldn't exactly chase down these lower threats—no doubt they were bait to delay us.

Candlekeep was nothing like the cities back on Earth. Much larger than any of the towns we had been to so far in our journey but not beyond the scope of us attacking it. We could see three entrances from here, and although the city was surrounded by a wall, it was relatively low. Lady in Red had made some effort to clog up the few wide roads with debris, for all the good that might do.

While most of the buildings we had seen had been traditional fantasy fare and predominantly wooden, Candlekeep was mostly stone. There were still plenty of wooden beams and structures half wooden, but the expanse of gray brickwork before us was the perfect canvas for the red light bathing the area.

"Three sources of light," I thought out loud. "No doubt those are what are maintaining the corruption over the city."

One to the left side of Candlekeep, and one to the right. The third was at the back, at the top of the keep itself. A tall, square building that was built to defend against traditional warfare and the most likely place the Lady and her closest would be holed up.

"You're thinking we should destroy those as our first priority then?" The fighter tilted her head to the side, but her gaze remained on the sources of crimson light.

I grunted. "No doubt they are protected from ranged and magical attacks and have powerful fighters standing by them. We are expected, so if they are important, then they won't be easy to bring down. That said, I think we should send a Party to each."

She turned to me and stared at me for a moment. "You're putting a lot of faith in us."

With a smile, I gave her a brief nod. The stage would get too crowded with all of us vying for attention. Splitting up made us weaker, but also spreading out a little farther would stop us from being such an easy target. No point strolling up to the gates in a clump and getting nuked by everything the Shadow had ready and waiting.

"I would like to pretend I could do it all myself," I said. "My ego has me thinking I'll be the star of the show, and if the Lady believes it, then their biggest hitters will be aimed at me."

"So you're being soft and don't want us getting caught in the crossfire?" Fiona shook her head and turned to look at the gathered Guild. "I understand though. Destroying the towers might switch the control of Candlekeep from her to the System once more. Then we'll have the guards come to our aid."

"I'll be giving everyone teleportation scrolls and the best health potions I have." I joined her in looking back at the others. "If we can avoid death, that would be *nice.*"

"We should be so lucky." Fiona gave me a grim smile. "I'll go inform the troops of the plan."

With a nod, she then left. More fool me for pretending that I knew what I was doing. All part of the illusion. Cutting down the Crimson's Monsters shouldn't be too difficult for a full group—it was the Players that might be there that had me on edge. Something I couldn't shake, even after Ren stepped up to me near silent, the hell dogs now gone.

Rather than say anything, she just held my hand. The two of us looked at the city ready to be sieged. We'd come so far from humble and grumpy roots, and this was the finish line, in a way.

"It's strange," she eventually said, her voice quiet. "I expected there to be more weight . . . some gravity to this day after so long. It feels like any other really. In no time, it will be *tomorrow*, and this will be the past, as if all the worry and struggle were worthless."

"We're never beating out time, my dear. What we fight for is to have a tomorrow with less stress and violence." The Max who endured the present wasn't too happy about being put through the grinder once more, but perhaps this would be the last time. "What do you think of my plan?"

"Leyla's group is quite green. While Fiona and her Party have learned to kill Players, I don't think the other five are that ruthless or efficient about it." Ren paused to exhale through her nose. "That said, I trust them to pull their weight. We're all fighting for the future here."

In truth, I was willing to go into the city with just our Party. Hell, even the three of us . . . if not solo. I wasn't about to tell the others to stay home or even give them the choice. The teleportation scrolls were the only out that they could use to save face—and their lives—and I'd hold no grudge against anyone who used one. Even for the most just cause, most mortals didn't want to give up their existences.

I let go of her hand to pull her in for a hug. "I'm going to go and divide some consumables among the others. We'll march as soon as we have the stomach for it."

The elf leaned back a little so that she could glare at me. "I don't know how many chances we'll have to say this, but I love you, Max. Don't die before me."

"And you don't die ever." I gave her a kiss. "I love you too."

As the corrupting effects of hell had worn off, we'd settled into a more normal stage of our relationship again. It was still unbelievable to me that we were married, but without the mania mashing our brains together, it was nice to feel so comfortable still after everything. As much as I wanted to keep her the safest out of everyone here, there was nobody else I needed by my side through thick and thin.

I stepped away and filled the Guild with Stat- and defense-boosting potions. Scrolls with beneficial auras and extra healing. It wasn't foolproof or enough to swing the battle in our favor easily, but every chance reduced the risk of failure.

We'd be attacked on approach, I was sure.

After that, who knew what the Lady had in store for us? She was likely to be desperate, sending all available pawns our way to save her own skin. Whatever Players still remained alive and aligned with her. These new Monsters she was somehow able to create. Spells and traps beyond my current knowledge.

It would be foolish to say I wasn't worried. Fights against other Players tended to be very short and visceral. While a siege sounded like a long, protracted affair, I was sure once we came face-to-face, the battle against Lady in Red would be something high stakes and decided in little time at all. One of us would become undone.

I looked over at Wolf, the bear still eating the last of his fill. Mortality was a fickle thing. Whether Ren popped the Lady from half a mile away with her rifle or I dueled the woman to death over protracted one-on-one combat, it all ended the same. Each of us was destined to fall away to dust in the end.

With a long sigh, I shook the malaise from my head and finished off a sweet cake.

A fitting final meal.

CHAPTER SIXTY-EIGHT

At the Gates

The Guild burst out from the woodlands and rushed across the fields before Candlekeep itself. What was once a pleasant collection of square farmland had been burned or withered to nothing but dry dirt.

Wolf led our Party, the bear blazing hot amber as his charge Skill provided us with additional defenses.

Leyla's group took the left flank a little way behind. Their rogue had a Skill to conceal their movements, making them harder to pinpoint.

To our right were Fiona and her Party. Percius had covered them with a moving magic-resist dome while the fighter and Magnus buffed their movement speed and Damage absorption.

My heart was in my throat, already sick of running. We were out in the open, even if somewhat protected. Ahead of us, my demonic ace pulsed with the occasional detect-trap scroll. I only had three of those, but they should at least stop us from running directly into something.

One minute before we were in range.

Our two other groups arced away from us slightly, intending to get to the other entrances. We forged straight ahead. The entrance along the main road—although barricaded—was the clearest route to getting inside the city. From the looks of it, this road led all the way through Candlekeep in a straight line. That made things simple enough.

I had given the others the plain advice to kill without hesitation and to go all out from the get-go. There was no point holding back at this stage with everything on the line. Aside from the minor chance of possession or falling under Lady in Red's sway, I trusted the Guild to do what was necessary.

My demonic ace reached the barricade, at the limits of how far I could send it. Two barrels of oil ejected out of it right before Ren whispered the Elfin word for fire. Her rifle cracked out a blazing bullet even as we ran, striking through the payload. A flash of amber blew away the wooden debris, setting everything alight.

Three cards of purple light flickered around me, ready to be flung forward. Our approach now fully telegraphed, the first action of the defenders bloomed into the sky.

Large bolts, pointed like arrows, flew high into the sky from the middle of the city. Bright green and made of fire, they arced over like mortars to dive down into our three groups. Magical, as they looked to be tracking us slightly.

The first of which came down toward Fiona's group. Percius held up something in his hand as they ran, and his dome-like shield over the Party shimmered between blue and gold. The magical mortar struck them on the side, deflecting back into the air at an odd angle and dipping down into the ground behind them. It exploded in a plume of dark-green gas, vibrating the earth.

Second one was coming straight for us, but it exploded high in the air—my hell bird blocking it from coming any farther. Third was for Leyla's group but had overshot by a great deal as their movement speed increased with a short burst. The next volley flew up into the sky, and it looked as though we'd get to the city before there was time for a third.

We had already solved this puzzle, however. Ren and I sent three birds out to intercept the giant arrows. As they exploded high over the city like fireworks, our first set of opponents appeared at the gates.

They looked like wingless gargoyles. Eight feet tall hunched over, with long jagged faces and gray skin. A handful of them, perhaps. Before I had the chance to ready up my cards to attack, Wolf surged forward even faster, his paws leaving bright-hot prints across the stone road where he ran.

Like a runaway train, he burst straight into the group of enemies. I was deafened briefly before a shock wave of sound woke my ears back up, bringing with it a flash of warmth. Dust billowed out from where the clash had taken place, and my eyebrows raised at the aftermath.

The gargoyles had been incinerated—reduced to a fine mist of blood and ash. Wolf himself stood in one of his defensive stances, light running over his fur as he glared into the city. I didn't have the time to wonder if that was part of his Guardian powers or not, as the rest of us caught up to him.

We were now in Candlekeep. Everything steeped in crimson light, it was hard to pick out much detail at first. Over to the left, farther into the west of the city, was one of the towers. To the east was the second light. Straight ahead, at the end of this long main road, was the keep itself with the third corrupting beacon.

The road had been barricaded as well. Almost wall to wall across the street, furniture, stone-and-metal debris, and overturned carts, all had been arranged into lines to make it difficult for anyone to waltz straight to the end. It was also sparsely defended with groups of random Monsters. Some of them with ranged weapons but others just looked ready and willing to pounce with their claws once we got close enough.

Rather ineffective when two of us could travel by the rooftops. No doubt trying to get ahead by dipping into the side streets would just waste time and have us getting tangled up in disadvantageous situations. I deserved to be in the limelight. Center stage.

In saying that, Ren vanished to appear on the closest building to our left, immediately firing out a chained lightning shot at the first group of enemies.

"If things go to shit, stick by Wolf and keep each other alive," I told the pair behind me. They were capable but too fragile to dance to the sort of danger Ren and I craved. After they returned nods, I drew three more cards into my left hand.

Hellhound up beside Ren. He would be able to help detect anything sneaking up on her. To the right, two fire Imps on top of the house there. A wry grin peeked at the corner of my mouth as I flicked out my magical cards.

The first hundred or so feet of the road were a piece of cake to grind through. Wolf thrashed and burst through any terrain blocking our way. Between Ren and my Imps, any opponent hiding away was either severely weakened or dead by the time we could get to them. My cards finished off the stragglers—and even an ambush from a side street that Ren couldn't get eyes on was quickly humbled.

If anything, it made me anxious about when we'd see actual Players. Any Monster just didn't have the power to do anything to us.

[Percius: Within the walls, getting through the resistance.]
[Percius: Monsters only.]
[Urist: Same for us.]
[Max: We are forging ahead. Keep me up to date.]
[Max: Divert comms.]

We had much farther to travel, by about double, I reckoned. As the others were slower at getting things done, the hope was that they'd be able to disable their towers just as we arrived at the keep. If that wasn't an important part of the puzzle . . . well, at least it kept everyone busy.

"Can charge again," Wolf grunted, planting his legs apart as bright light bloomed beneath his paws.

"When ready," I replied. At this rate, we'd get there in no time at all.

Wolf didn't need telling twice. As soon as I had given him the go-ahead, he burst forward. Debris and Monsters alike were reduced to cinders, the blast wave blowing back both dust and warmth our way. The System was keen to tell me that some of the shredded defenders were City Guards, level twenty. Clearly corrupted and, were we not overwhelmingly powerful, they'd be a worthy enough challenge. Or at least give us a slight reason to pause.

As this brief thought crossed my mind, Wolf stopped in the air mid-bound. Frozen in time. From a side alleyway, a large barbarian-looking man burst out toward the bear, a greatsword held over his helmeted head that had a singular horn jutting from the top.

Finally, some Players attempting to stop us.

I switched places with my demonic ace beside Wolf, landing atop a chair to fire a drawn crossbow near point-blank into the target. He blurred, dodging the bolt, but it was enough to delay the swing of his weapon. My mundane cards burst out from my belt, swirling around in front of me like a cloud of smoke. As my brain idly switched which ones were the purple magic kind, I closed my eyes.

A line of magic drew away from the frozen bear. With a smile on my face, I opened my eyes again and sent three of my normal cards up to the rooftop where Ren was positioned. A little message she would understand. Not two short seconds later and her rifle went off, echoing across the city. A house several down on the left exploded, raining wood and stone across the main road.

Wolf landed back on his feet, and I turned invisible.

Before the barbarian could adjust, the bear lashed forward through my fading cloud of cards to strike at him. The first claw he blocked with the flat of his blade, but the second cut through his bare torso. Just as Wolf leaped forward to bite at the man, he vanished away with a teleport.

One Player dead, and one injured.

"Unfair," Wolf complained, sniffing at the air where his opponent had just been standing.

I faded back into view, just in time to see the house that the elf was perched upon explode. She was flung through the air, twisting and switching with her dove, but the bird hadn't been in place to land her safely on the ground—just soften her fall. Instead, I caught her in my arms, something surely only possible due to the Stat-increasing potions.

We turned back to face the building as the brickwork started to dissolve away as if it was covered in acid. Ren held her rifle up as a Monster unfurled from within the wreckage. Another eldritch abomination like we had faced previously. Hardened skin that seemed to be leaking whatever substance was melting the house away. An extended, beak-like face, thirty feet up in the air. Long limbs that ended with tentacles instead of fingers. Standard fare.

"Contact behind," Quinn said from a little way back.

I turned my gaze away from the towering creature to see that the gate was now swarming with Monsters brought in from afar. My prior guess about the potential ambush had been correct. Orcs and goblins, for the most part, each of them streaked with red to show their allegiance to the Crimson Shadow.

"We'll hold them back," Tanya confirmed, her face stoic. "You focus the Monster."

"Trouble ahead, brother," Wolf grunted.

My gaze swiveled the other direction, as a large object had been positioned much farther down the main road. The green light blooming within it was enough of a hint that this was the arrow launcher that had tried to get us before.

I smiled and put the elf back down to her feet.

A little faster paced than I was used to, but the show was in full swing.

CHAPTER SIXTY-NINE

Cut After Cut

Through the chaos, I remained calm.

Something thanks to our entrapment in hell and every time we had been ambushed by the Crimson Shadow. Live under the constant stress of imminent violence and you eventually become numb to it. Even with five times the current odds, it would just make us more resolute rather than spook us.

Tanya had set off a couple of her idols left near the gate entrance, slowing and poisoning the horde trying to assault us from the back. While Quinn was eager to bloody his rapier to defend his better half, my trio of Hellhounds dropping straight into the middle of the attacking force had caused enough disarray to bog their approach down to a crawl.

Wolf had protected us from two of the arrow-shaped mortar rounds. His fur was singed, and the terrain around him smoldered from the superheated explosions. He could endure one or two more, but his defensive skills could only last so long.

The abomination looming over us now sported a few extra holes courtesy of Ren's sniper rifle. Unfortunately, a shot to the head and then the heart didn't seem to be killing blows on the hulking creature. Instead, fresh goo spilled forth from the wounds, the acrid smell of burning wood and stone following in its wake.

As for my contribution? I'd handily admit I was giving current proceedings only a small slice of my attention.

I was waiting for the coup de grâce. Assailed from three angles, they had left one side of the street clear. This was the first very real attempt to snuff us out, and they wouldn't be leaving an opening like that when the stakes were so high. Perhaps the barbarian and spellcaster who had frozen Wolf were meant to be part of it. Wolf's sudden burst of speed might have caused them to show their hand early. It was pointless to speculate, but my mind was open and alert to the possibility that we had another attack coming our way.

No, what we needed to do was rotate acts.

"My cards can't reach the cannon. Do you think you could shoot it?"

"Sure, if you keep this big bastard at bay."

"I'll clear the gate, brother."

We circled around, and Tanya and Quinn fell back to support our new roles. The occasional arrow, bolt, or low-level spell came our way from the Monsters farther into the city, but we had the defenses to dodge or weather them constantly. With the other two focused on keeping us alive, we buckled in for the next stage of our performance.

Wolf ran back down the cleared street, the fear in the eyes of the greenskins evident as they struggled to distance themselves from the hounds nipping and chewing on any who fell due to the poison aura. Ren hopped up to her own summoned chairs, crouching and looking down her scope. Three magic cards spun around my hand as I readied to strike out at the abomination.

[Fiona: East team down to 4, have pushed Players back into tower.]
[Fiona: West team making slow progress, suppressed.]

My eye twitched, but there was no Guild message to say that someone had died—so they'd probably teleported. Making Fiona my second-in-command for this venture was mostly to prevent too much clutter over communications. Leyla's team would relay things to the fighter in a separate Chat, and I'd be sent the important details only.

[Max: Almost halfway to the keep. They are trying to slow us.]

Due to the nature of how the city was built up, there was no way my cards could assist either of the groups from here. Even if Ren had the range, she wouldn't have the angle to hit things on street level with so many buildings in the way.

My magic cards spiraled off, powering up as I sank my Mana reserves into them. As the creature swung their large arm down at us, I severed their hand off just below where the wrist would be. The giant tentacled appendage crashed down on the roof beside them, breaking through into the upper floor. While the abomination screeched, viscous liquid gushed from the created wound, splashing over the main road near us. The stonework bubbled and steamed as the corrosive substance ate away at it.

Ren fired at the same time as Wolf collided with the orcs and goblins.

One end of the road bloomed with bright-green light as the mortar overloaded and the magic ruptured, destroying the machine along with anyone within forty feet of it. The other road flashed with flickering amber as the bear tore the unprepared Monsters to shreds. Above us, the air hummed with light purple as my cards zigzagged through the injured creature until its head was severed clean off.

I shook the blood from my hand as it collapsed. Senses burned from the overload of magical explosions, scoured debris, and fresh gore.

"Looks like their scheduling is fucked," Ren murmured, her attention moving to the sky.

I turned to see what she was looking at. A cloud of light blue made its way toward us before I made out what it was. Some manner of flying Imps, similar to those in hell, but these looked like frost variants. Each held a shortbow and was readying to fire down on us.

Ren's rifle cracked and burst one of the small Monsters, a dark energy bouncing between a dozen others. Each of them dropped their weapon, just as my demonic ace used a slow-movement scroll among them. A rather weak speed debuff, but against Monsters that relied on wings for flight, it caused them to struggle to stay aloft.

I was about to send off a few cards to cut them down as they dropped, but I paused. There was a new debuff icon over me.

[Duel of Honor: You have been challenged to a martial duel to the death. Mano a mano.]

My eyes left the Status message to see a Player standing out down the road, a few barricades in. If there was a prize for looking like the generic pop-culture version of a samurai, this figure would take it handily. The weapon on their side that they were waiting to draw was probably a katana. The mask on their face obscured their features, but naturally it had a crimson handprint over it. They looked to be waiting for me to get in position.

Ren clacked the bolt of her rifle back and forth and raised it toward them. "I . . . can't fire on them?" Her brow furrowed.

"Some kind of forced duel," I murmured. "Clear everything else while I sort this."

She nodded and twisted around to the others. I stepped forward, a grim smile on my face and hands in my pockets. My opponent remained unflinching.

"You know, it's rude to ask for a private show without booking in advance," I told him. It took a few moments to walk around the next two barricades, but he saw no need to fill that silence with a response.

I raised an eyebrow as I stopped. Now a good fifteen or so feet away from him. It wasn't often a Player let me get this close to them without verbal or physical—

Any chance to finish that thought was cut short as the samurai clicked his sword up an inch from its scabbard. Then he was behind me, the rush of air from his movements hitting a second after he visually moved. The top of my body slid and slopped down onto the road, his blade having sliced me straight through the midsection.

I stepped out of <Last Act> invisibility and yawned. "Imagine using your ultimate from the get-go and failing. I'm in a hurry, so—"

To my partial surprise, the man twisted on one foot to face me and then did the exact same move again. Perhaps he was always this fast, and it wasn't a powerful long-cooldown Skill. Even with all the Abilities and boosts I had under my belt, I was still unable to see him move—which was rather impressive.

Instead of cutting me through again, there was a burst of sparks as he twirled away.

My patron demon hung in the air in front of me, having deflected the blow.

"A martial duel, you say?" I smiled, and the floating sword twisted in the air so that I could grip at the handle. "Go easy on me. This is outside my comfort zone."

It was hard to tell if my opponent was angry or not with his face covered, but I considered the way in which his black ponytail bobbed about to signal some frustration. He moved, and so did I.

His speed had slowed, but he was still remarkably quick. Able to block any of my attacks—but my patron was able to deflect and parry most of the strikes of my opponent. I didn't know if it was a limitation of the odd duel—or just my ego—but I felt I couldn't use my magic against him. That didn't mean this had to be *honorable*.

The samurai twisted, adjusting his footing as he slipped on some marbles. My patron guided me, breaking through the attempted parry and cutting into the shoulder of the man. He grunted and stepped back to bring his guard back up.

"Let's make this quick," I said, my smile widening. "Shouldn't keep a Lady waiting."

I let go of my patron and withdrew a shortsword into each of my hands, kicking forward a footstool summoned on the ground. He slashed it in half with ease and was only just able to bring up his guard to deflect the dash from my patron. I was in there too, flailing recklessly with both blades. Twirled away from his thrust. Crossed the blades to block. Flourished them around, turning them into daggers.

We had both taken a fair share of cuts. While I had been damaged more, I was also healing up from my <Demonic Regeneration>. My demon had a time limit on him that we were getting close to, and I wasn't keen on trying my luck on my own again.

"Take a seat," I said. "It's going to be a long show."

I then ejected a chair from my Inventory toward him. Again, easily slashed in half—but then he had to block my patron before turning to another chair coming his way. I sent several at him, each severed in turn as he blocked my patron. In the midst of the chairs, I sent a small bag his way.

He cut through it, only realizing his mistake halfway into the act. As he braced himself for flash powder or some manner of blind, instead gold coins clattered against the stone road. The brief confusion was enough to set him off guard. As he clashed with my patron, the sword forcing him into a test of strength, I spun toward him like a cyclone.

Far out of effective range with the daggers I held, I switched to Jokkar's mace right as it was too late for the samurai to do anything. The studded end of the weapon snapped his arm and sent him rolling across the ground. Cinders and smoke from the rest of the battle washed over him as my shadow darkened his mask.

"This one's for Roger," I spat, bringing the heavy mace down onto the man's head, crushing it like rotten fruit. The debuff on me vanished.

I looked around to see that everyone was gathered and ready. The gate was clear, if not pasted in bloody body parts. Ren had been picking off any City Guard or Monster foolish enough to stand around out of cover.

**[Fiona: East team inside the tower. Heavily injured
but disabling the beacon now.]**
**[Fiona: West team has broken the stalemate, pushing
enemy back to this tower.]**

I nodded to myself, turning my eyes to the keep.
My harshest critic was waiting for me.

CHAPTER SEVENTY

Finders Keepers

The rest of the city cracked and buckled beneath our advance. Paltry groups of Monsters were flung our way, but even as desperation settled in for the Crimson Shadow, our Party was just unstoppable once the ball was rolling.

It was clear to me that they were just buying time now. After fumbling with the ambush meant to stop us, the Lady would pool all her important resources into protecting the keep. With a Party at each of the beacons, she couldn't afford to lose any more powerful pawns throwing them at us one by one.

An almost tangible reality, as no sooner had I thought this, I paused. A pain and warmth ran down my right arm.

"Shit," Ren swore, able to feel it too, while the bear just grunted.

"What is it?" Tanya asked, looking around for looming danger.

I didn't know for certain, but this puzzle had so few pieces that it was easy to see the picture even without knowing how to fit them together.

"The Lady has just killed the clone-making individual," I responded, my own eyes trying to make out any clues from the keep ahead. "That means she has the power of two Guardians."

"Let's hope it's too much for her and her head pops off," Ren murmured.

Downplaying my ego aside, splitting the powers among the three of us wasn't just through generosity and happenstance. Without knowing enough about the Guardians and their powers, it was equally reasonable to assume that they wouldn't like being squished into one mortal form. Lady in Red must be biting her nails to think that taking that risk was worth more than having another ally on her side.

I tried to ignore what it might mean if I killed her.

The sky flickered, some of the crimson bathing the city growing duller. As we looked over to the side, one of the beacons went inert.

[Fiona: East beacon disabled. East team heading home due to injury.]
[Fiona: Hold for western updates.]
[Max: We are almost at the keep.]

No deaths but down to ten of us left in the city. I couldn't fault Leyla's group for taking a bow and exiting stage right. Depending on how grievous their injuries were, they might not be much use to us anyway. Better they live than fall so close to the end.

Wolf sniffed at the air. "Something lies in wait ahead."

"A trap?" I narrowed my eyes at the set of wide steps leading up to the keep's large doorway. There was a suspicious lack of anything at all defending it, aside from the scorch marks from where the mortar had exploded.

Ren fired a shot into the air and then held her hand out, the bullet bursting high up and turning into a cloud. Jagged bolts of lightning fell down from it, stopping a good forty feet in the air, as the whole area around the keep was protected by a magical field.

"No choice but to find out firsthand," I said with a shrug. Even as my demonic ace passed through the invisible barrier and swirled around the area by the door, I was unable to get it to cast any spell scrolls while I remained outside the bubble.

The potential ambush aside, it was strange to have come all this way and *this* was the end. After having survived the gritty ruthlessness of her gang, we had gone from strength to strength chasing down the Lady. Defeated titans and great beasts, gained Guardian powers for the three of us, and made a few allies. There were new Players in the first area that had no clue about what was going on right now, nor what the world was really like before we had come along and carved through it all.

As a Party of five, we stepped along the last part of the main road, entering the protective bubble. Nothing immediately happened, but I could see Wolf was still on edge. We all were.

"They're probably expecting us to knock," Quinn said. "Why don't we make an entrance worthy of our spirit?" His hand went down to where his explosive boomerang was stored.

I smiled and stepped to the side. "Be my guest." An ambush just inside the doorway was tactically reasonable. Blowing the door inward would put the advantage of surprise in our court.

He withdrew it and took a deep breath. As we all watched him draw the item back, winding up for the throw—that's when the trap was sprung on us.

A crocodilian beast appeared to our right, both Ren and I turning on a dime to fire on it. The System told me it was some form of Basilisk just as its brains blew out of its severed head near instantly. A second had appeared on the other side of us. Wolf roared, but our focus had been drawn away by the other.

The second Basilisk breathed a cone of yellow gas over the group of us. Ren and I switched with our birds back to the road just as the Monster blinked away with a teleport. Wolf was dazed, shaking a dizziness from his head after one of his Abilities had burned up.

Quinn stood in front of Tanya, arms wide to protect her. He was also now completely stone. A one-eyed statue, boomerang still in one hand.

"Quinn? *Quinn?*" Tanya took a moment to fully process what had just happened, the shock slowly registering.

"Hold on," I said, stepping aside as two stone birds fell down to the road, shattering. "Let me read the icon."

[Basilisk Petrification: Target remains stone. Victims of the Basilisk can be cured should the Monster be slain.]

"He isn't dead," I confirmed. "We just need to kill the Monster." The one that had conveniently teleported away and could remain stealthed.

The Fateweaver looked distraught. "He's such a foolish asshole. I am already *immune* to petrification. It should have been me protecting him."

Ren slowly circled the statue of Quinn, scowling at it. "You saw how those birds shattered though. Without a way of us finding that Monster near instantly, Quinn is vulnerable."

Tanya's face went through a series of emotions, looking between me and the elf. A conversation that needn't be vocalized and the conclusion begrudgingly accepted. "*Motherfuckers,*" she eventually sighed. "I hate this, but the alternative is unpalatable."

She stepped away from Quinn to give us each a quick hug, slipping us as many idols as she could make. With tears in her eyes, she returned to the petrified man and gave me a glum smile. "Fucking . . . don't fail us. Don't die, you assholes."

"You have my word." I smiled and took down my hat, stepping forward to place it on Quinn's head. Funny how things end how they started, but at least I didn't crack my head on this rock first. I slipped a card into the ribbon and stepped away. "This will let you teleport with him. If we can free him, then you're welcome to return, but I won't put you in any danger."

After she nodded her understanding, they both went in a flash of blue.

"At least he didn't die in your stead," Ren said, her bright eyes scouring the surroundings for where the Basilisk might have gone. "*And then there were three.*"

One of the differences between the Lady and us was that I didn't see my allies as dispensable assets. Their safety was paramount, even if that meant I had to personally struggle and suffer that little more. We could stand and defend Quinn, maybe spend time trying to hunt the Monster down, but that just gave the Crimson Shadow more of an advantage.

I adjusted my suit, ignoring the bloodied cuts through several parts from my duel with the samurai. The idol she had left me with was the one that increased the Damage dealt as well as the Damage I'd take. Some classic self-destruction that suited me. Sending my companions away had just cooled my temperament, however.

Into my right hand—which now sported a white glove—I drew a singular purple card. Dropped all my Mana and then dipped into my Health to empower it. Barely registered the healing Ren was providing me as I stared at the bright-white rectangle. Dazzled by my own power. Strong enough to cut through metal and stone.

As well as every other motherfucker in the way.

It left my hand at speed, and I held my right wrist with my left hand to control it. Straight through the wall of the keep, I angled it back and forth in a zigzag pattern. There were shouts from inside. The sounds of something shattering, followed by a short and sharp explosion. My ears hummed from the exertion, and then I let it go.

"You can sense her here, can't you?" Ren asked, her face like thunderous clouds.

I could. The second reason for my dulled mood. That and being without my hat.

"My charge is ready when you are," Wolf agreed.

It didn't quite make up for being blue balled over Quinn's boomerang, but after we put additional defensive buffs on the bear, he flashed forward and obliterated the large wooden door. Up close, the keep looked like the sturdiest structure we had come across. Much like the towers we had fought through but sized up to fit several regiments rather than just a small group.

As the cloud of dust and debris cleared, we switched positions with our birds to land inside beside Wolf. Ren's rifle went off, blowing the skull of a wounded Player open as the bear continued his stampede into a group of Monsters. There was a dead Player who had taken my card through the neck and three others who had been burned to death—to the bone—in short order by whatever had exploded among them. Inside this once banquet hall, a stairway at the back led up to the next floor.

A long table and dozens of chairs had been stacked up against the side wall to make room for the ambush and fight, and tapestries painted over by large red handprints decorated the walls. At least on the inside of the building, the glow of the beacons wasn't present.

[Fiona: West team disabling beacon. Two returned home.]

I shot her a quick message to ask who had gone back to the cottage. She told me the Paladin had almost died stopping a Player dealing the death blow to Percius, and they had both gone back straight after—her orders. Magnus was being patched up by Ruby and would be fine to continue soon.

Part of me wanted to tell them to head home after the beacon was shut off. I still had one ace up my sleeve that we had only briefly discussed. Guild recall gave everyone the opportunity to accept or decline a teleport to my location. But nobody had a second get-out-of-jail-free card. Me bringing them here couldn't guarantee their safety.

I shook my head. All of that meant nothing right now. The Lady was above us, and the beacon was even higher than that.

The sky rumbled, a dry storm shaking the atmosphere.

Wolf grunted, turning his keen nose toward the shattered doorway.

"We have a slight issue," he said as voices started to echo from the city.

CHAPTER SEVENTY-ONE

All and Nothing

Time was always a bit of a conundrum. I thought back to earlier today when Ren had said this day would go by in a blaze and then tomorrow would make it feel like a decade ago. We hadn't finished living in the present yet, and there was so much to do to make sure there was a day after this that we could all breathe easily.

Now we were being pushed to our limits, a strain between what needed to be done *right now* and all the other issues vying for attention.

"We need to split up," Ren said.

"No." I shook my head.

"Sister is correct," Wolf said, kicking some debris away from his paws to get a better footing. "Trust in us as we trust in you."

I had always been the one to put the weight of the world on my own shoulders and feel like I could solo anything, but having them go along with that delusion was almost sickening. We had three targets and no time to sit around dealing with them.

Whatever new abilities the Lady had gained from her second Guardian power seemed to include increasing her Monster-summoning capabilities tenfold. An army of creatures of various shapes and sizes had started crowding the city and was pouring down the street toward us.

Wolf wanted to stand and hold the bottom of the keep.

The beacons were surely a source of the Lady's power and control over the denizens of the city itself, perhaps even boosting what she was capable of. That was at the top of the keep, past where the Lady was hiding out.

Ren wanted to skirt around the outside and land up there to disable it, taking out anything guarding it.

I wanted them to stay safe while I twisted the head off of the woman who had started off all this madness. As much as I had wanted for them to stand by my side, they seemed keen to do what was most efficient.

"Fuck. *Fine*." I shook my head, interrupted as Ren grabbed me and pulled me close for a kiss.

"Just don't die," she whispered. "It'll be okay."

I didn't have the energy to roll my eyes. "That goes double for the both of you. Wolf, I'll leave you with some demons, but they won't last forever."

"As you wish, brother." He huffed and gave a brief nod, his eyes focused on the door.

While the elf adjusted my suit collar so that I would look half decent for my main appearance, my demonic ace was ejecting caltrops, marbles, and grease onto the steps of the keep. It made two more quick passes to drop off any other trap or malady I could scrounge from my Inventory to make it as difficult for the attackers as possible. Lastly, I summoned my cannon lengthwise across the door to block it before three Hellhounds emerged from spell circles beside it.

"Get going already," the bear encouraged.

Ren ran her hand over the side of my face, smiling, before vanishing. The summoned dove fluttered in front of me before fading away.

I shook my head, weight heavy in my stomach, as I took to the stairs. The army of Monsters was just reaching my gathered traps now, their squawks and yelps echoing through the downstairs chamber. Wolf looked resolute, his singular purpose ready to be performed without hesitation.

For me, nerves rolled around my core. Something unlike me but it took me back to my beginner days. Before having an agent or a name for myself. As I stood on the small landing, my arm burning because of what existed on the other side of the wooden door in front of me, it felt like I was going in for a career-defining interview. Make or break.

My head swimming, I grabbed hold of the handle and pushed.

Tense and ready for an ambush, I was almost confused when nothing immediately came for me. The thick rug of dark gray that led from this door all the way to the other end of the room had a patch of darkness to it, blood seeping around the lighter stonework. The corpse of the prior Guardian killer lay there. Opposite me was a row of thrones, the center of which was occupied by none other than the devil plaguing this world herself.

Lady in Red.

Almost exactly like her Visage that had met me, her long, flowing red dress was darkened in patches from the spray of blood. There was a certain presence to her, her dark eyes almost glowing beneath the brim of her hat while she grinned at me.

"Max," she spoke, her silky voice devoid of malice. "What a *surprise*. Before you immediately attack me, there is something I want to ask you."

My right eye twitched as my right hand curled into a tight fist. I could see it now. Her unnatural ability to sway people. The subtle ways in which she was trying to control me.

"What could you possibly ask that could mean anything at this stage?" I asked through clenched teeth. Purple energy started to arc around my body as I fought her desire to placate me.

"Only to ask what you know about the world beyond this area. Is it not a fool who makes a decision without knowing the full picture?" Her smile twisted into a wry grin.

"We are in quarantine here until you are erased. Then the System will allow us access to the rest of the world." Blood seeped through my white gloves as I tried to bring forth a magical card.

The smile left her face, and she tutted, shaking her head. "Shame you are so misguided. It is only fair that I enlighten you, since you're so interested in saving this . . . world."

"What do you—" I began before we both vanished.

I blinked away the transition to find myself standing on grass and dirt. Swirling in place, the Lady was but ten feet away from me, her expression neutral. I was about to launch an attack before I noticed the icon affixed to us both.

We were both Visages.

"My goal here is to amend what the gods could not. Perhaps once you are aware, you'll see things my way." Her expression didn't change, but I couldn't keep my eyes off of her.

"Where are we?" I asked, my jaw aching from how much I was clenching it.

This time, she did give me a slight smile. "The barrier to the third area."

I blinked, my gaze now turning to the side. After a dozen feet of grass, there was the sheen of a wall. Impossibly high and . . .

Although I was sure I didn't need to breathe as an illusion of myself, my lungs were frozen as I stepped closer to the wall. Now only two feet from the edge, I fought the urge to empty my stomach.

"Frightening, isn't it?" the Lady said from off at the side. "Some of the Eternal Wardens *knew* about this but swore it to secrecy. Well, until they switched sides, at least."

There was no third area. No—that was really underselling the point—there was, in fact . . . *nothing at all* after the wall. Just an empty expanse like the world was flat. Infinite, overwhelming space.

"This can't be right," I said. "Maybe this is just how it looks while it's blocked?"

"Try to rationalize it all you want, Max. The truth is you don't live in a world going through a bumpy period. This is a *failed state*. An abandoned slice of existence where the creators have long left us to our own devices. We are a ship lost in an unwavering sea, and I intend to be the captain."

My mouth felt dry despite being intangible. "*You?* After what you've done?"

"Yes! Why, a god needs followers to ascend, surely." She stepped up beside me by the edge and gestured toward the oblivion. "There is some irony in you getting more powerful via people disbelieving in you, whereas I am the opposite. With your vanity title, we could rule from above and below. Biblical, in a way."

"Didn't you start this as a way to return to your home world?"

She was silent for a moment. "Part of me still lives with the hope that, in taking control of the System, I could find a way to save us all."

I narrowed my eyes, some of the warmth finding a place inside me again. "But what of those that you killed along the way?"

The Lady rolled her eyes. "I could ask you the same thing. You're thinking too much like a hero, Max. I'm looking at the greater world, how it continues beyond our petty squabble. We both know there are still new people arriving in Othea . . . Don't you want that stopped?"

"I . . . want people to be safe and happy." I glanced off to my right, pretty sure I was able to see the red of Candlekeep in the distance beyond the woodland.

"So do I, just on a broader scale. I was getting *so* close to reaching high enough power before . . ." Her face dropped, and she gave me a dull glare. "Before you and your misguided friends decided to disable two of my beacons."

That must mean Fiona's group was finally successful.

"Say . . ." My eyes looked between her and the now slightly dimmer red shade of the city. "This isn't just a ploy to have me killed off while you talk to my projection, right?"

She shook her head. "Unfortunately, if the spell was that powerful I'd have killed you much sooner. If your real body detects threatening behavior, then you return."

I wasn't entirely convinced, but I didn't have the option to <Shuffle> the condition away to return to my actual body. "I see. Oh, I wouldn't say I get more powerful due to disbelief anyway. I'm more of an entertainer than a cult leader." I leaned forward to look down into the space below the world.

"*It's not a cult.*" The Lady adjusted her hat and sighed. "The System granted me the opportunity to ascend beyond the normal leveling conventions, so it is my destiny. It would be rude to look a gift horse in the mouth."

"A horse almost killed me once," I said idly. It was interesting how she had a similar view of how the System treated her, thinking she was the chosen one due to being powerful. Both of us were just as deluded as each other, at the end of the day.

Both willing to kill or die for what they believed in.

"I'm not asking you to take the blood or become a follower, Max. Just stop hamstringing my progress. You've seen the Monsters I've been able to create? Some with actual intelligence."

All I could think of was my friends back at the cottage, nursing their injuries. My found family fighting on their own to buy me time to end this charade. Then, finally, the image of Hannah pinned up on that cross flashed into my mind, cementing what I knew.

I didn't care how bland or abandoned the System or this world was, as long as those I cared about could be safe. Lady in Red would never allow us that peace, whether she was a god or not.

"You really think you could be a god?" I asked, my face neutral. "What level are you even?"

"Now that two of my beacons have been switched off, I have an effective level of thirty-five. The Monsters I have created don't give as much favor as Players do . . . and you've been killing those off as well."

I shrugged. "Don't worry. I appreciate the chat, but you'll be joining them soon."

"Oh, *Max*," she replied. "You don't think I always knew that would be your answer?"

Before I had the chance to respond, I switched back to my real body—the feeling of disorientation immediately replaced by intense pain.

I bounced away from the barbarian and rolled across the floor, his horned helmet dripping with my blood and my chest screaming in agony.

As the Lady laughed in the background, I fought the urge to pass out.

CHAPTER SEVENTY-TWO

Clash of Ego

If there was one thing that was worse than having your ribs shattered and your internal organs pierced with a unicorn horn, it was *fucking nothing* because this was agony. Blood filled my lungs as I twitched from the shock. My spotty vision was still able to see the barbarian loom over me, his sword raised.

"Dead or alive?" he grunted.

"He is too much of a danger to our cause. *Dead*," the Lady replied.

The greatsword whipped around and lopped off my head—quite impressive considering the angle and me lying on the ground.

From across the room, snapping the healing charm Ren had left me took me out of invisibility. While I hadn't had the time to use <Last Act> on the initial strike, he had been slow enough with the follow-up. With how much pain I had been in, I was desperate to use it, so I hated him that much more for the delay.

"Rude awakening," I murmured, putting a health potion up to my lips. My magic cards bloomed up around my head, circling me as the man got into a fighting position.

The Lady stood up from her throne and clenched her teeth. "Idiot. You'd make your queen dirty her own hands?"

"No, my lady!" he bellowed, preparing to run at me again.

Personally speaking, it wasn't as cool a charge as Wolf's was. It made me wonder how the bear was doing. My demons hadn't vanished yet, and I reckoned I could get some out through the door down to him. Oddly, I couldn't hear any sound of fighting either. Something about this room must be soundproofed.

"*Whipped*," I murmured. "Oh, that gives me an idea." I clicked my fingers and grinned. From my Inventory I drew out a sheet of dark cloth to hold it beside me, enticing the man to charge me like a bull.

"I'll make you regret mocking me," he growled.

I wouldn't. He charged, and I saw how he had managed to get his attack off before I had the chance to come back to my body. Not quite as fast as Wolf but pretty decent. Naturally, I stepped to the side and swept the curtain away.

Revealing the doorway beside me.

He didn't have the chance to react, running himself straight through to hell and landing inside the fighting arena. I waved the door away, the curtain vanishing as I dusted my hands off. If my champion didn't kill him, the corruption of hell would.

"Always one step ahead, aren't you?" the Lady said, disgust all over her face. "I'll assume the elf is up top with the rest of the Crimson Shadow, as they aren't rushing to my aid. Such a shame I'll have to kill you myself."

"That's your first mistake," I replied. "I don't *believe* that you can."

She winced, more of a visceral reaction to the statement than I had expected. "If I needed your acceptance, I'd torture it out of you."

"See, that's where you and I differ." I smiled as I walked back over to the center of the room. "I also have people who believe in me, but they also trust me. No coercion or threats needed for them to follow me to the death."

The Lady snarled at me. "Where do *you* get off giving me a heroic monologue? The *gall* of it."

"See, I'm willing to bet that you don't have any powers of your own really. They're all for manipulating and using others. You're just stalling for time in hopes some of your minions make it here."

"You'd stake your life on that assumption?" She raised an eyebrow and drew a dagger from her belt. A jagged thing of dark metal that glowed red slightly. "Your first mistake was to come here being so misguided."

I smiled and shrugged. "*Yours* was installing this neat soundproofing."

Her eyebrow raised. "What do you—"

The thirty-odd magic circles blooming around the room cut her sentence off short. Her actual mistake was sending an army against Wolf. More than just a blockade, even if we couldn't hear my cannon, I had fired it off three times. That number of Dazzle icons was unprecedented.

Hellhounds popped from the walls and floor in droves, all eager to take a bite of the woman.

To her credit, she was fast with the dagger. Being more than ten levels over the hounds put her at an advantage, but for each of them she stabbed, she received a bite herself. I could see that she was healing, however. While only looking vampire-esque, I had a hunch that her dagger had health steal or a similar enchantment on it.

While I powered up a card in one hand, I sent ten of the dogs out of the room to assist Wolf. I had stolen the cannon blocking the way, so it was only fair I assisted him a little more.

I whipped the card toward the distracted Lady, and she deflected it from the air with her blade, turning to cut through one of the hounds. More than just being quick, she seemed to be increasing in power the more she killed. I wasn't likely to win a war of attrition.

She swiped down at a dog and struck a barrel instead, confusion on her brow as it shattered into parts. The next hound just completely vanished, allowing others to tear at her dress.

Up until this point, she had been my harshest critic. For the first time, I saw Dazzle icons appear over her head. Oh, right next to the one tallying up the Strength boosts from killing. I should be paying more attention. Her next attack struck a chair and then a large rock—her blade sparking as it connected. Some of her stacks of . . . Bloodlusted were now fading away as the hungry dagger found no purchase.

"Fool!" she yelled, pausing in place briefly before a pulse of crimson energy pulsed away from her, bursting apart my poor demons. The rest cowered and growled at her as this bloody aura persisted along the floor. "You truly seek to test me?"

Rudely, she didn't give me the opportunity to respond, as two giant crimson hands burst from the wall on either side of me. Rather than get squished between them, I swapped positions with one of my hounds, sending out a trio of cards at the Lady.

First was deflected, the second took a slice from the brim of her hat, and the third barely missed her neck. She growled and took the hat off, throwing it to the floor.

"Only fair as I don't have mine," I said. She didn't see the humor in it.

In fact, she lunged at me—an impressive distance covered, all things considered. A cloud of smoke burst up around me as I also turned invisible. My hounds jumped into the fray again. The inability to see me didn't seem to dissuade her as she lashed back and forth, the red glow illuminating the dense fog.

"Quit hiding!" she yelled, cutting down another Hellhound.

Then she paused as a vibration shook through the keep.

Ren had destroyed or disabled the last of the beacons. That was my cue to step in. She reacted by instinct, lashing out and cutting me across the chest. I ducked and rolled beneath her follow-up before I hopped up and activated <Demon Form>. The crack of my wings blew away the smoke, and the Lady stepped back with her arms crossed to deflect my next attack.

But I didn't attack.

Her intense glare fell from my new form down to her wrist. The nullification cuff sat there.

"What is . . . What have you done?" Any remaining color drained from her face, even as pale as she already was.

"What's the matter?" I cooed. "Don't even believe in yourself anymore?"

"Bastard!" Her eyes blazed wildly. "I don't need my Abilities to cut you to shreds."

Perhaps she was right. My Dazzle icons on her had faded already, barely lasting any time at all. Possibly something to do with willpower? I stepped away as she swung, the dagger slicing through the air. She was trying to exert her presence over me again. I could feel the hesitation in my brain like an illness. I dodged her next strike before realizing this was not the play.

I stepped into the next attack, taking the dagger through my left forearm. I swung around with my right holding a purple card, mentally unable to bring out an actual weapon. She caught my wrist and held me at bay, a sinister grin on her face.

"Thanks, asshole."

The pain of the stab wound radiated down my arm. I could feel my bones split and crack, the muscle fibers separating under the vibrating thrum of the dagger's power. Before I could jerk away, my left arm exploded, covering the area in droplets of gore. Unlike the time in the Dungeon, I wasn't left with a bony appendage to show for it. Nor was there magical smoke to fix me anew.

It was now just a stump, ending a few inches above my elbow.

Before the Lady had time to continue to gloat, her own face twisted with shock and pain, as my patron demon ran her through from behind. A burst of energy sent us flying apart from one another, and as I regained my composure, I could see a bubble of red light shimmered around her.

While darkness spread from the wound, soaking through her dress, she glared at me. A magical shield coming from one of her equipped pieces of gear, no doubt. Powerful enough to prevent her death.

I smiled and shook my stump, bemused by the lack of limb. "Just when I was thinking of joining you, you went and *left* me feeling *disarmed*."

"Idiot," she repeated, spitting blood on the floor. "I don't believe you."

Of course, it was entirely a fib, based on wanting to make a dumb pun. The amount of conviction used to admonish me was staggering, however. She *didn't believe me* so hard that she actually forced the System to give her a Dazzle icon, solely because that's how she thought my powers worked. I would have loved to investigate that notion more, but that singular Dazzle was all I needed.

I snapped my fingers and cast Domain: <The Grand Stage>.

Gone was the stonework of the keep's second floor. Now varnished wooden planks sat beneath my feet. Rich velvet curtains labored the sidelines as bright stage lights illuminated me from above. An audience of empty chairs lay in wait, while the Lady stood, still clutching at her wound. The area around her remained unchanged as the stone flooring of the keep, as if her willpower had bored a hole through my Domain.

"What is this?" she spat. "Trying to woo me with parlor tricks now?"

I held up the bright-red critical card in my hand. "Oh no," I said. "You don't deserve a performance anymore."

With all the Mana and Health I could afford to pool into the card, it snapped away from me like a gunshot. I dropped to my knees as it exploded—her shield overloaded and bursting itself. My Domain washed away as if the power expended had created a vacuum to suck it elsewhere. It was never going to be enough to hold her captive, but I just needed to keep the Lady frozen to one spot long enough to break her shield.

She stepped over to me, blood running from the side of her face.

"That doesn't solve *anything*, Max. My shield is gone, but so is your strength. What good are you now?"

"You're already dead," I replied. My smile was genuine. "Time for you to leave this world you detest so much."

Confusion and anger furrowed her brow. "What are you . . ."

A classic case of misdirection. While I wasn't looking to pull a coin from behind her ear, I did something a little better given her attention had been solely on taking my arm.

My patron wasn't meant to be the killing blow, but my demonic ace that was flat against the blade as it pierced through her was.

I grinned and snapped my fingers again.

CHAPTER SEVENTY-THREE

Standing Ovation

It wasn't really the gentlemanly way of killing someone. Often murder didn't really care about that kind of thing, however—and for *me*, just doing the deed was as good a result as any.

While confusion continued to wrack her face, the Lady had no clue what was about to happen. Somewhere in her torso, my demonic ace released five different concoctions of various poisons.

Maybe cruelty had been the point, and at the end of the day, I was no better than her ilk. I could have easily put a spell scroll or even a chair in there that might have killed her quicker. Instead, I watched as dozens of new debuff icons appeared over her head.

She also dropped to her knees and immediately threw up. Her hands shook as she tried to withdraw something from her Inventory to counteract some of the Damage. I didn't have the strength to stop her—at least, not physically. I blinked slowly as I hit her with the upgraded <Shuffle>.

"How could you do this?" she asked between dry heaves.

I didn't really have any words for her. My demonic ace and patron sword came and hovered on either side of me. Wings and horns fell away as I dropped <Demon Form>.

Her hand slipped, and the bottle she had taken out shattered against the floor. She was suffering, and it would only get worse.

I sighed and found the strength to push myself up to my feet. Wavered slightly, feeling lightheaded from the loss of blood. "I'll not gloat over your death, as you did for those you killed. This is revenge, but I take no joy in it. Violence begets violence." I shook my head and sighed again. "Any last words?"

"You'll *regret* this," she croaked, tears streaming. "I don't know how you can *live* in a world like this."

I withdrew my Knife of the Trickster and stepped over to her. "I guess seeing is believing." Using what little strength I could muster, I stabbed down toward her, intending on piercing through her eye. The punch line missed, as she managed to gather the willpower to dodge slightly, my knife cutting along the side of her cheek instead. Her eyes widened in seeing my final trick.

In losing my arm, I had stolen the Skill used by her dagger. The red glow faded from my weapon, but it was too late for her. The side of Lady in Red's head exploded outward, and she flopped onto the floor. I dropped my knife, and it vanished before hitting the ground. No elation. Just emptiness. Relief? No, now there was . . .

Pain wracked within my skull, my heartbeat thundering through my brain. The deed was done.

I felt the pulse of her Guardian powers circle around me like two marbles spiraling down toward a bottomless hole. *Three* was too much for one person to handle—I could tell. Painfully. Something else itched about the process though. With all my magic knowledge, I could sense the whole greater than its parts. This close to coming undone, the picture started to clear. There was . . . another purpose for these powers. I closed my eyes and forced them away toward these lines of magic. Guided even my own power to follow these routes. I blinked my eyes back open after a short period as a chill ran through, the process not destroying me.

The Lady was dead. I left my demonic ace full of enough spells to incinerate her corpse once I left the room. Now that my wits were returning, delayed messages pinged through my chat.

[Fiona: West beacon down.]
[Fiona: We are heading toward keep now.]
[Fiona: City Guards are now on our side and assisting.]
[Fiona: Killed several groups of Monsters plus a Basilisk.]
[Fiona: Keep beacon down. Ren is injured. Safe.]
[Fiona: Regrouped to assist Wolf.]

I practically ran from the room as my ace let it rip. It was no wonder neither of the others had joined me in the fight—and that last message was recent. I hit the staircase, my whole body complaining about every step.

The scene below was a massacre. Piles of dismembered Monsters lay scattered in piles, the whole floor below covered in blood and gore. In the center was Wolf lying down, soaked through in crimson as Ruby tended to his wounds. Lying up against him was Ren, while Fiona and Magnus kept watch over them.

"Holy shit, Max," the fighter said, clocking me coming down in a hurry. "Did you . . . I mean, are you alright?"

I nodded, but my focus was entirely on the elf. At the risk of sliding over spilled innards and slick blood, I ran up to her. The left side of her face was bruised heavily, her golden hair matted with gore. Eyes closed, but as I stood in front of her in panic, they opened slightly.

"Your arm's off," she murmured.

"It'll grow back, promise." I gave her a glum smile. "What happened to you?"

"Fell off the fucking roof and broke my leg." She nodded painfully at it. "*Same fucking leg.*"

"Hey, at least I didn't split my head open on something," I said, to which she raised a sluggish arm to prod at a surprisingly sensitive part of my skull.

Her finger withdrew to show me fresh blood. "Dickbag," she managed before pushing herself up and into my arms. Arm. "*It was great,*" she whispered. "Killed five Players using all sorts of bullshit magic and then disabled the beacon . . . which sent me falling off with transposition on cooldown."

"I wish I could have seen it." The magical side of it, at least. Wolf's actions were definitely more overt and visceral. It was hard to tell how many he had killed here . . . but it was *a lot.*

"Brother," the bear grumbled.

I let go of the elf to kneel down beside him. He was quite the state, and despite Ruby giving me eyes about my stump of an arm, she seemed worried about him.

"You did well," I told him, patting him on the shoulder. "I am proud, and we couldn't have done this without you. What can I do for you?"

He grunted, and his eyes lazily turned to me. "You can accept my apology."

"For what?"

The bear let out a long sigh. "My time has come. I have felt it in my bones for days, but I needed to hold out for this."

My mouth opened and closed, unable to find the words. "Perhaps you just need rest. This probably took a lot out of you." The slowly shaken head of Ruby told me otherwise.

Ren knelt down beside me, her eyes already wet. "What apology do we need to accept from you when you have given us your everything?"

His eyes went from me to her. "You accepted me as family. As an equal. When given the power to . . . have a wish granted . . . I went for something . . . selfish." Wolf closed his eyes. "I never . . . did like . . . that . . . hat."

The whole room fell into a deep silence. Ren pulled me closer and pressed her face against my shoulder. I looked at the useless floor and placed my hand up against him. With all the danger he put himself in for us all the time, who cared if he wished for something selfish? I didn't even understand what that . . .

I blinked away the blur from my eyes to look at my hand. It felt warmer up against his unmoving form. At first, just more than normal body heat but then I had to move away before I got burned. Ren looked at me with confusion, wiping away her tears as we stood.

Like a bonfire, Wolf's body burst into flames from the intense heat, fire licking around his body. We were all too dumbfounded to do anything except step away, dazzled by the bright flames. The fire ate his body away, reducing it down to nothing.

And almost as quickly as it started, the flames flickered and snuffed out. Wispy smoke hovered over the remains, which were surprisingly bright and brown. This shape of untouched fur unfurled out, and Ren gasped.

"Again, my apologies, brother and sister," the younger voice of Wolf said.

"Like a phoenix," I said, still unbelieving, as Ren launched herself down onto him. He had died and been reborn as a younger version of himself. His wish had been to stay with us, have more years we could spend together. I stooped down to hug him as well.

"As much as I hate to break up a reunion," Fiona called from the doorway. "Two things. Firstly, something has changed with the beacons. They're bright like daylight now. Secondly, there were a few Crimson Shit Shows still alive, and they've banded whatever Monsters were still around and are coming this way."

I stood, trying to brush myself down with my absent hand. "To the first thing, I filled the beacons with the Guardian powers. Don't ask me how or why. I'm *very* lightheaded." With a more confident smile, I continued. "For the second, perhaps we should bring everyone out for an encore?"

I hit the Guild-recall request, and nobody declined. We were *Unbreakable*.

Mopping up the remnants of the Crimson Shadow went by in no time at all. With the full force of the Guild joined by the returning City Guards, we had little issue at all. The fact that the remaining gang stayed loyal to the Lady even past her death wasn't as comforting as I had hoped. Perhaps better than the alternative but I was so far gone once the warmth of battle wore off that I barely registered much. Didn't really have the energy to celebrate.

I looked out at the woodlands, my feet wet from the fresh morning dew on the grass outside the cottage. It was a new morning, and things felt . . . surreal. After itching at my arm stump a little, I just continued to stare off at the horizon, the sun slowly rising. Off to the right, soft snoring came from Wolf's abode—which was little more than a large doghouse.

It wasn't long before the sound of the door behind me snapped me out of my trance, a few soft footsteps before Ren appeared by my side. She wrapped her arm around my right and held my hand, leaning her head on my shoulder.

"You feel out of place because we no longer have the pressure of conflict casting a shadow over our lives."

I nodded. "We are safe. The first day of the rest of our lives. What do we even do?"

"Well . . ." The elf stepped away from me and tilted her head. "Now that we have more time, perhaps you can teach me some real magic?" With a smile, she held out her hand to reveal a gold coin. "First though, how about a bath?"

Day 3 NE: I have decided to start curating a journal again. This time, instead of filling it with drab introspection, I am pasting my brighter outlook within. As the System is reluctant to give me a proper calendar, I deem the day we slew Lady in Red as Day 1 of the New Era.

Much to my surprise, the Lady wasn't the only one who could fix the System-created in the world. Far from it—and we have learned in the last few days that putting the Guardian powers in the beacons has done just this. Now smarter and more realistic people roam the land and fill the towns, and I was able to convince Ren and Wolf to give up their powers to put in two other beacons in the first area and starter zone.

Thankfully, it didn't take away our already given powers, which Ren is especially glad of.

Day 4 NE: My arm grew back.

Day 8 NE: The three of us have started putting on shows! While the audience of System-created is sometimes a little wooden, there is nothing that compares to sharing the warmth of the stage with those two. It feels good to use our Skills for something other than violence for a change.

Day 11 NE: Wolf seems to be growing at the rate of one year per two days. Already well into adolescence and eating a barn full of food on the regular. Still his usually grumbling self but it seems he'll plateau in adulthood again before his lifespan goes back to normal speed.

Day 12 NE: Hell has frozen over! Or, rather, they have finally managed to build up a sustainable and fair government system to run things down there—so I have become something more of a figurehead. I'd like to take credit for it, but it was really all their doing. One of Roger's many sons is actually on the council now.

Day 14 NE: Part of me had worried that without the constant need to strive to survive, things would fall apart with Ren. A needless worry really. Things are certainly more domestic now, but we are no less inseparable and in tune with each other.

Day 23 NE: I found out today how rusty the easy life had made us today. Ren and I had been relaxing in the swing outside our cottage when a figure approached us from the woods.

Not a Player that we had seen before but he didn't seem threatening. In fact, he came to us with an offer. Apparently he came from a different world, and there are a lot like our Othea out there suffering similar issues.

His offer was something simple on the surface. Safety. Not just for us but everyone in Othea. A literal joining of our world with his—a place of broken communities becoming something greater. There we could live a life without conflict, or there were options for adventure and even some striving against the odds. Ren and I shared a knowing glance at this.

I had to admit I liked the way his fangs caught the light in what seemed like a practiced technique. I respected the craftsmanship. The traveler asked if we had any knowledge of the way we got into Othea. As Ren described the portals, I dug around in my jacket and produced the folded page from that old book. After reading it, he pocketed it himself to give to someone more in the know and thanked me—assuring me it would be useful. We told him that—even if we believed him—it wasn't something we could decide on the spot. While we took a few days to consider his offer, I had to my mind was already busy with the potential of my future.

The greatest showman on *all worlds*. At least, that's what the flyers would say.

About the Author

Kleggt is the author of the Death of the Party and Demonic Magician series, originally released on Royal Road. Upon clawing his way out of the depths of Scheduling Hell as a Forever DM, he began writing web novels, channeling his love of world-building and oddball characters into his own LitRPG and progression fantasy stories.

RESPAWN YOUR CURIOSITY

follow us on our socials

 podiumentertainment.com

 @podiumentertainment

 /podiumentertainment

 @podium_ent

 @podiumentertainment